TONATIUH'S PEOPLE

TONATIUH'S PEOPLE

A Novel of the Mexican Cataclysm

John Ross

CINCO PUNTOS PRESS   EL PASO, TEXAS

FIRST EDITION
10 9 8 7 6 5 4 3 2 1

Library of Congress Cataloging-in-Publication Data

Ross, John, 1938 Mar. 11-
   Tonatiuh's people : a novel of the Mexican cataclysm / by John Ross. – 1st ed.
   p. cm.
   ISBN 0-938317-41-5 (pbk.)
   I. Title.
   PS3568.08434879T66 1998
   813'.54--dc21

                                        98-26237
                                        CIP

Cover image and interior photo by Nacho López
Copyright © Fototeca del INAH-México. Fondo Nacho López
Photo of John Ross by Marcia Perskie

Cover design by Vicki Trego Hill of El Paso, Texas
Book design and layout by John Byrd
Thanks—again!—to Suzan Kern for her good eye

To my parents

the first writers I ran into on Planet Earth

I WROTE *TONATIUH'S PEOPLE* mostly as revenge. Justice demanded it. The first draft was completed in 1990 after many months on the road with Cuauhtemoc Cárdenas as he campaigned for the presidency, an office he won at the ballot box and lost to electoral fraud. At the time, the Salinas gang was the focus of my vitriol. Today, on the brink of the millennium, the revenge motive is more structural. History has taught me true contempt for the rulers of Mexico and deepened my faith in the people's ability to make a real revolution.

Tonatiuh's People has been rewritten several times to accommodate political events. The text has demonstrated an uncanny aptitude for coming true—each draft seemed to prophesy what later would be confirmed as fact. To stay ahead of the curve, I had to project into a dim future.

Now, that future has arrived, and some facts here aren't going to jibe with the fictions we read in the dailies. My apologies for not getting it absolutely right—but it's more fun this way.

—John Ross
Mexico City / 1998

THE EYES OF THE GENERAL

IN THE YELLOWING PORTRAITS nailed to the walls of public offices, the eyes of the General are keen obsidian blades that swipe to the heart and seize it like a surgeon's laser. It is said they never closed, his eyes, not in sleep, and, certainly, not in death—despite all the professional skills of the nation's most distinguished undertakers. This phenomenon was much remembered at the funeral of his son, whose own incandescent black eyes, as fiercely incisive as his father's had ever been, would not close either, exasperating a whole new generation of funeral directors and their NAFTA-trained staffs, who injected relaxing liquids to melt the lids without success and sutured them shut with micro-thin surgical wire more than once only to have them fly open again and again. Ultimately, the mortuary scientists had resorted to the old ways and weighted Tonatiuh's bright, onyx pupils down with the increasingly heavy and worthless coinage of the country. But no artifice sufficed and the prissy little chief of protocol had finally conceded victory to rigor mortis, and now the smoldering orbs of Doctor Tonatiuh

Galván Sharatanga, the freshly butchered leader of the nation's most recent and wrenching revolutionary drama, cut right through the obligatory bullshit of a state funeral.

The line of mourners had formed a great humble river of humanity that stretched for at least 25 kilometers into and through the damaged, teeming capital—a two-day wait just to say good-bye. One by one, hat in hand, every seven seconds, the common citizens took turns standing guardia before the minimal bier of their jefe.

Hunched under the great cracked dome of the Monument of the Revolution, Raus digested this sad pageantry, counting heads and registering faces and the memories that went with them. He was startled to find himself still moved by the solemn, measured passion of the procession: the Indians, summoned by this long-anticipated assassination from the distant sierras, their huaraches slapping across the cold concrete floor in eerie cadences—gnarled old men in yellowing tunics who once had received from the Father a little wedge of land and saw in the Son their last hope of ever getting it back; shriveled old women, all-mothering eyes under dark shawls, strewing cempaxuchtl in their wake and whispering down into Tonatiuh's frozen face in the language of the Nahuas—as if he were their own lost son—their blessings for safe passage through the narrow place.

Monteks and Chamuls and Ziptotecs and Kichis and Yunques had come from their blackened mountains and bone-dry deserts to say good-bye to their adopted child—a delegation from each of the 56 Indian nations. The Purés had streamed in from Ma and Tzimah, Taneen, Yoom, Quim, and Zapicho to stand by the bier of their maximum leader. They hovered there briefly, with frightened, averted eyes, as if they thought themselves guilty of this new killing. Then, abruptly, old Tacho began turning wheelies before the coffin, waving to the TeleVida cameramen with an inappropriate grin of wisdom or extreme senility—you could not tell which—sweeping the old farmer's rubbery lips. A little man in a tall cone sombrero with a what-me-worry grin pasted to his mouth frantically pushed him out of camera range. The spectacle stirred a twinge of pain deep in Mickey Raus's bowels.

"¡Ayyyyyyyyyaiiiiiiiii...!"

A hoarse scream of grief punctuated the Tatas' grotesque pantomime. Cristóbal Cantú Cabañas clutched at his breast and plummeted to the cold stone floor. Tonatiuh's beloved old mentor—whose rich baritone rendition of the new national hymn, the one in which the Yanquis are called dogs, always closed the Doctor's meetings—thrashed about like a beached mackerel. Epauletted officers applied mouth-to-mouth resuscitation but were soon forced to roll the silver-haired orator out from under the splayed, swampy feet of onrushing ambulantes from La Bondad market. An unstaunchable army of smelly, pushing, grasping, aproned, potbellied street vendors surged into the rotunda, emitting low-pitched, dangerous rumbles.

"¡HOOOOOSTIIIIICIAAAA! ¡TONATIIIIAAAA!"

The mob pushed each syllable up from the bottom of its great scarred collective guts, and—in the soaring expanse of the earthquake-damaged Monumento—the roar was like thunder puking. Raus worried that what was left of the dome would collapse in the unruly din.

When the news nets had enough tape, the street vendors were ushered on by Citizen General Felipe Roque's sad-faced soldiers.

Jane Ann Arbus grabbed Raus's arm suddenly, dug her nails into his pale flesh, and kissed him wetly on his stubbly cheek. It was not her usual hello-good-bye-ex-lover-now-what-are-you-doing-here peck on the mandibles.

Raus tried to shrug her off. He knew what she was angling for. "Forget it—the guy was already flat on his back," he whispered hoarsely. "You saw the pictures..."

"You are going to win the Pulitzer with this one, Mickey. I'm going to tell them I knew you when you were one more barfly, mooching on the press club's phones and sloshing down their free booze." She chattered on in that slightly nasal, outdoor-girl WASP way that always reduced his Jewish knees to jello. Raus was immediately and profoundly suspicious of the attention Jane Ann Arbus was lavishing upon him. She looked fine, really, filled out, her bottom all round again. The night the morgue drivers had taken her to the airport, this country had her looking like one of its famous calaveras.

"Do you just fly in for state funerals these days?"

"Mickey, tell me the truth. The truth, Mickey," she hissed into his ear.

Raus put his finger to his lips and directed her gaze towards the bier. The First Family approached their murdered husband and father—Paloma, her slender, vulnerable shoulders wrapped only in a frayed black wool rebozo, high Inca cheekbones tensed in stabbing grief, and the three tall sons, each named for a Purepecha prince, woven around her into one dark suit of protection and support. The dignity of the tableau silenced the rowdy press pack. The family stood guard, motionless for minutes before the coffin. Then, as one, they bent into Tonatiuh, their eyes locked in his still-smoking mirrors, offering no clue at all to who those closest to the President accused of this utterly predictable act.

The film was rolling inside Raus' head now. It had been running ever since the assassination, unspooling frame by frame, the blue flame licking out from behind the Preacher, the surprised shimmy of the Doctor's shoulders as the three slugs perforated his shirt front, Paloma falling over him like a suddenly featherless swan.

Jane Ann touched him on the arm and he shivered. A stunning, stately matron stood stiffly down the waiting line, her thick heels clicking impatiently against the concrete floor. Tonatiuh's family stirred from the plain pine box, their eyes nailed dead ahead, stepping down the line of mourners with all the calculated dignity of bereaved royalty.

Behind thick veils, La India, María Cristina Terrazas Tamal Menchú viuda de Ahumada, the ageless directress of the National Anthropology Museum, walked stiff-legged through the gauntlet of soldiers and camarógrafos, knelt down and kissed the starkly staring dead president right on his blue lips. "Uggg," Jane Ann gurgled and Raus dug an elbow into her fattened ribs. Mickey Raus was hardly a native of this benighted country, but long years on the ground had taught him decorum when death came knocking. Soldiers assisted the still-beautiful old woman to her feet and La India passed on with one last tender touch of the dead man's dark cheek. Miners from far-off Jaquemate followed her to stand guardia before the long brown body of the Man They Called the Hope. La India's sole son and survivor, Reggio Ahumada Tamal, the nation's new president, had not yet put in an appearance.

The films kept unspooling behind Raus' shaded eyes, frame by frame, forwards, backwards, endlessly reeling like the Zapruder projections, looking for a sign, a new clue, the blue flame licking out from the crowd, just to the right of the Preacher, the President's immaculate white shirt front slowly blooming into a crimson orchid, Paloma falling over him like a plucked swan.

Who had really killed the Man They Called the Hope? *Not I, said the sparrow, with my little bow and arrow...*

Raus was tired and losing his famous nose for news and needed a drink bad. Almost instinctively, he found himself locked into the unblinking eyes of the Doctor, "through which shine the General" according to the corrido that once rang the length and breadth of the nation. The steady, polished obsidian chips, distrustful as ever, even in death, of today's news and tomorrow's next world orders, were always eager to challenge you to step back into the past and suck up a long, thoughtful draught from history's oasis.

I

A COINCIDENCE OF TRANSIT

October 12 – December 15, 1999

FROM THE BEGINNING, Michael "Mickey" Raus's connection to Tonatiuh Galván had been a coincidence of transit. Until that sweltering October day—how many years ago now?—before they both found themselves entrapped in the same terrific traffic jam at the teeming intersection of Insurgentes and the Paseo de Reforma, the Doctor and Mickey had traveled wildly separate, if curiously parallel, paths.

Taxi Andy rode the horn grimly although it was abundantly obvious that smashing mercilessly down upon the klaxon would never free them from the stinking, steaming traffic snarl in which they were embroiled. All around the bashed green Volkswagen Bug, the decibel level swelled. But Taxi Andy, wired to a Walkperson that endlessly reiterated John Coltrane's "Love Supreme," was hearing little more than the tenor man's swoops and scrapes. Raus reached over and delicately removed Andy's grubby fingers from the horn. "Th-Th-anks, b-b-boss" stuttered his driver, happy to be snapped from his Trane-induced trance.

Raus and Taxi Andy were mired in the midst of a mammoth 50-block jam-up, occasioned by one of those swirling demonstrations that daily enliven the misery of 5,000,000 capitalinos who, at any given moment, are trying to ram their automobiles through the megalopolis's clotted thoroughfares. Raus saw right away that this demonstration didn't feature the usual bedraggled peasant men and women in soiled white cottons who marched day and night through the littered streets of the city to call attention to the theft of their village lands. Nor was it the same old moiling mob scene cooked up by battalions of ragged damnificados, listlessly chanting "The People United Will Never Be Defeated" and dunning their government for the redress of some very real and acute grievance, like cholera-laced drinking water—sometimes in their underwear.

A short man in a makeshift loincloth, antlers sticking from his head, had just leapt across the windshield. All around the impacted autos swarmed figures in skins, beating drums. ¿Qué puta madre? "L-l-ooks l-l-like th-they're g-going f-for C-Colon a-again," stammered the sweating cabbie, taking deep glugs from a Mason jar of milky-white pulque that was always in his reach.

It happened like this every October 12, when the nation's Indian peoples marked the day they were found out by trying to dislodge the statue of Christopher Columbus from its perch in the middle of Reforma Boulevard.

Through the marred windows, Mickey caught a glimpse of a lanky, raw-boned man bailing out of a shiny black Shadow wedged next to the idling cab. It was the eyes that first pulled him in. They were very black, approaching incandescence, set close to a nose that penetrated straight ahead like the flat, chiseled blade of an ax, imparting the illusion that the man in charge of these features was absolutely certain of what would happen next. Raus had seen the pronounced nose before, the smoldering black eyes. He remembered them staring down the cameras, framed in a wool ski mask in the center of a jungle clearing. You could hear the chatter of macaws in the trees. Flashbulbs popped. Of course: Subcomandante Caralampio aka Doctor Tonatiuh Galván, the General's son. The ex-governor of Malinchico and the legendary hero of the struggle in the Lacandón. Raus had once cooled his heels for two weeks while being devoured in cold blood by determined red ants in a jungle village ironically called La Sur Realidad, waiting for an interview with the Subcomandante that was ultimately canceled because of a renewed Army offensive. Then came the negotiations and the amnesty, and now it was being nosed around that Galván planned to challenge the long-ruling Party of the Organic Revolution in the presidential election seven months down the road.

Mickey found himself shouldering his way through traffic vendors hawking little squares of chewing gum and giant bouncing balloons and disposable syringes. One ambulante threatened to impale Raus upon an eight-foot hat rack. An itinerant fire-eater breathed a ribbon of flame that singed his stubbly beard. Raus vaulted a rusty fender and nearly fell into a quintet of unkempt street urchins, trying to build their pathetic pyramids for pennies amidst the stalled, fuming cars and half-naked Indians who were pounding skin drums and wailing incessantly on shinbone flutes.

Raus finally caught up with Doctor Galván near the monument to the Emperor Cuauhtemoc. The mob was already starting down Reforma towards where Columbus stood. An aide-de-camp, nicknamed the Bishop, was at the Doctor's side. So was a thin Trotsky-faced comrade Raus would later know as Doctor Huipi. So was the cherubic, back-slapping Reggio Ahumada Tamal, El "RAT" by reason of his initials. RAT had recently abandoned the PRO, having, it was whispered, been passed over as the ruling party's presidential choice. Tonatiuh's old tutor, Cristóbal Cantú Cabañas puffed along behind, his hand clasped to his heart.

Raus thrust his hand at the tall brown man with the ski-mask eyes. Tonatiuh had traded in his jungle camou for an impeccably tailored tan Italian suit. "Mickey Raus, *Los Angeles Times*," he lied. Actually, Raus was then stringing for a doomed alternative weekly in Ukiah, California.

"Doctor, what are you doing at today's march? Does your

appearance here have anything to do with your possible presidential candidacy? Are you a presidential candidate, Doctor?"

"It appears that we were both caught up in the same traffic jam," Tonatiuh responded coolly, in perfect English—one of the few instances Mickey was ever to hear him speak in "the language of the oppressor." Raus realized his hand was still extended, dangling unattended in space. The Doctor's eyes bit into his, observing his embarrassment. The mellifluous blast of a conch-shell trumpet six inches from Mickey's ear broke the spell.

The demonstration immersed them. Here, at the hub of the busiest boulevards in the largest urban enclave on the entire planet, where dozens of gleaming skyscrapers and the splendid esplanades of international banks met the sleek malled commercial center of the futuristic Zona Rosa Plus, Indígenas were pounding drums while dancers in deerskins hopped among the spewing vehicles. An old man in bone anklets shook rattles and waved eagle feathers at the venomous noon, chanting short guttural phrases that sounded ominously like a declaration of war. Three bare-breasted bronze maidens, trundling braziers of pungent copal—the scent said to be at the center of the universe—skittered up the Paseo de Reforma. Many more women, all of them carrying large baskets of blood-red carnations on their heads, followed. At the head of the procession, the man with antlers cavorted with a thickly built warrior who was crowned by a magnificent headdress inset with iridescent quetzal feathers. A young girl, flying a white dove on a golden string, walked impassively between them.

"¡MIXICA TE'AUHUI!" the Indians shouted into the shit-brown midday smog that draped the air of the capital like a filmy curtain of disease, air so murderous that—according to a closely held government study that unsavory sources had recently put into Raus's hands—it killed 150,000 newborns each year. Of late, the atmosphere had turned so lethal that dead birds often plummeted from the sky by the tens of thousands, smashing into pedestrians, some of whom had taken to wearing hard hats and gas masks 24 hours a day for protection against the elements and those it disabled.

"¡MIXICA TE'AUHUI!" the multitudes howled in Nahuatl, the country's real national language. The old shaman shook his feathers now at the tall, graceful spire and blinding glass bubble of the DisneyMex Global Stock Exchange. Under the gigantic cranes topping off Floor 104 of the PRO's showplace "Tower of Vertical Modernization," Indians trundled six-foot cornstalks up the Paseo de Reforma.

The marchers moved within striking distance of Columbus. The statue of the Old Navigator had been installed a hundred years ago by Don Porfirio himself in an effort to convince foreign investors that after 400 years the animosities of the Conquest had sufficiently cooled to construct bronze replicas of the Europeans who had once despoiled these savage lands.

In the century that Columbus had loomed ponderously above the traffic circle—one hand to his pigeon-turd-stained, metallic brow, peering out for dry land in this vale of killer smogs and homicidal gases—he had been regularly assaulted by the more indignant indigenous people of this country, who, each October on the day set aside to mark the "discovery" of the New World, would try and tear the Captain of the Ocean Sea from his pedestal. This annual mayhem, always joined head-on by the riot police, had grown uglier each year since the 500th anniversary of Columbus's mischief. Last year's siege had been repulsed by a combined force of 10,000 secretos, preventivos, and granaderos. Hundreds had been arrested and only tens released. Militant Indian leaders were still lying in comas from the beatings they had received. Columbus, too, had taken his lumps; government welders had spent the year soldering his weakened stumps back to the pedestal.

Raus noted a number of burly men in RayBans and high-fashion leather jackets fondling their walkie-talkies on the fringe of the march, and scouted out a safe niche behind a bust of a long-defunct Admiral. Phalanxes of Grenadiers—as the SWAT squad was then elegantly christened—stood shoulder to shoulder in two squat circles, surrounding the nervous Columbus.

"¡MIXICA TE'AUHUI!" howled the mob, drums pounding, short flutes slashing to fever pitch. Then the women began to toss carnations at the visored Granaderos who immediately brandished fat billy clubs and swatted forcefully at the flying petals. Swat! Swat! Klonk! The clubs soon made contact with skull bone.

Just as the yearly melee was about to explode, the Doctor moved confidently through the seething mob. "¡Mixica Te'Auhui!" Tonatiuh intoned, flexing a skinny brown fist. With his back dangerously exposed to the riot squad, Tonatiuh launched into a long and serious discourse in Nahuatl that silenced the Indians' fury. Even the Police relaxed, reholstered their batons, and tilted back their visors to reveal physiognomies no less Indian than those who had come to tear their Discoverer down.

Doctor Huipi summed up Tonatiuh's words to Raus, who was illiterate in Nahuatl. His active white goatee kept poking Mickey in the ear. "He is telling them that if they succeed in tearing this idol down, the PRO government will only put up another one tomorrow, and that only when we unite our voices and take the government back will we be strong enough to destroy their gods and install our own..."

"¡MIXICA TE'AUHUI!" Tonatiuh concluded, much more forcefully than he had started out, his fist fatter, Raus thought, as if it had swelled with the accumulation of attentions focused upon him as he spoke. Every Indian within a mile radius of the demonstration roared back: "¡MIIIIIXIIICCCAAAAAA TEEE'AUUUUUHUIII!" The chanting came in waves, drowning out the angry, squalling auto horns and the amalgamated pounding of heavy construction. "¡MIIIIIXIIIIICAAAAA TEEEEE'AUUUUUUHUIIIII!"

Suddenly, an industrial-sized snap hushed the chanting Indians. Columbus seemed to totter under the weight of their voices. Then he did a brief, heavy-footed pirouette atop his pedestal and keeled forward with a great metallic twang, headfirst into the traffic circle below, like a monumental chunk of intergalactic shrapnel plunging from the heavens, narrowly missing a brace of startled Grenadiers.

"¡MIXICA TE'AUHUI!" The cry rose again like an urban tsunami, thundering up and down Reforma. "¡TONATIUH

PRESIDENTE!" The demonstrators swarmed through the dissolving police lines and, in one coordinated clean jerk, lifted Columbus to their shoulders like so many pallbearers and carried him off. "¡MIXICA TE'AUHUI! !TONATIUH PRESIDENTE!"

The annual riot had ended as abruptly as it began, the Indians moving off up the boulevard, merrily whooping as they labored under the statue's dead weight, the Doctor being hustled off by his cronies, the cops climbing back into their armored school buses, the monstrous traffic jam uncongealing in 17 different directions. Raus trudged back to track down Taxi Andy. He was utterly (and correctly) convinced that the startling vision he had just experienced confirmed Subcomandante Caralampio aka Doctor Tonatiuh Galván Sharatanga's decision to run for the presidency of this blighted land—an illusion that had extinguished lesser lights in other campaigns, and a story that he broke in a floundering northern California weekly eight days later, long before any reputable reporter on the other side of the NAFTA Line had looked seriously at so bizarre a scenario.

"THEY HATE US," he snorted at the gaunt figure who hunched just inside the fly-specked bar mirror. Veiled by cracked, smoky glasses, the Yassir Arafat stubble ripe upon his sunken cheeks, the other Mickey Raus appeared to agree.

So did Horace Pease who, after all, had initiated this round of recrimination. Pease—a pear-shaped gentleman in a once-debonair seersucker suit and Panama chapeau, a caballero paid a handsome stipend by one of the world's most prestigious dailies to flit around Latin America hobnobbing with mendacious chiefs of state—now straddled his bar stool, balanced only by a bulbous schnoz, which was flush to the mescal-stained zinc counter of the Illusions cantina, a downtown watering hole where the fourth estate was known to drink deeply.

"Don't concern yourself with me, laddie. I'm meditating on molecular phenomena."

"Barman!" gasped Raus. He had been a denizen of this dimly

lit saloon since he first arrived in country 28 years ago, in what now was about to be another century.

Poncho was already swamping out the hermetic little room. The bar gutters were running a gunky brown. Now the rubber-aproned fat man cast aside his mop in obvious disgust and hauled the Gusano Verde over to Mickey's side of the bar.

"Mickey, amigo, please, why don't you just go home? I have to open at 6 a.m. and there's no morning man."

"You hate us," hiccuped Raus.

"You have been telling me this same story for 30, 25 years, maybe. Right around now, you always start. It's like clockwork. 'You hate us. You hate us.' Who hates you? Who are us? Who cares? This is the last one. And that goes for your compadre, too."

The two reporters had been huddled in Las Ilusiones for hours. Jane Ann Arbus had been here, too, sometime in this long tunnel of the night. Other newshounds had been crowded around the table—sullen Sasha Vigo from *Protesto* magazine and her urchin lover, the colombiana, what's her name? Tatiana? Raus fuzzily recalled a high-octane screaming match in which he had insisted, with a great deal of fist-slamming-of-the-table-top, that Tonatiuh Galván was the "Incandescent Incarnation of the New Glorious Revolution!" Pease and Arbus warned that he was doomed to die a romantic death if he kept ranting on like this in public. "You know something, Michael, you are definitely drinking too much," Jane Ann admonished him like Mother Teresa amongst the drowning lepers. When he placed his hand upon her tumescent thigh to assure her that it was "not the end of history," Jane Ann jumped a foot off her stool and fled with her compañeras into the lurid night.

They hate us. All of them. They really hate us.

What was he still doing here?

Mickey Raus first stepped into the ghastly, voluminous terminal of the capital's old international airport very early on the morning of December 7, 1972, seven months after the late Richard Nixon had mined the harbors of Haiphong in the north of Vietnam, occasioning the last cathartic outburst of anti-war exuberance on the streets of San Francisco, California.

Raus recalled that he was hauling a steamer trunk containing all his earthly possessions, most of them made out of paper. Deep inside an unobtrusive black shoulder pack was buried a dog-eared copy of old John Reed's *Insurgent Mexico* and a half ounce of the first Humboldt County sinsemilla crop ever grown. Also nestled comfortably amidst Raus' baggage were his then unquenchable illusions.

Clutched in the traveler's right hand had been a vintage 1948 Royal portable, just like foreign correspondents whacked away on in old *LIFE* spreads. The typewriter, like his money later that same day, was immediately stripped from him by nimble chilango fingers, even before he emerged from the airport into the nauseating air of the winter's first thermal inversion.

Las Ilusiones had been Raus's first port of call that swampy Pearl Harbor of a dawn. The irony of the tavern's title seemed appropriate. Poncho had fixed him up with a Cadillac-mouthed whore who'd left him alone with the bedbugs in a semen-sheeted hotel room, bereft of all his paper money, definitely a sobering experience. It was Ponchito himself who later admonished the greenhorn reporter to watch his ass with a little more diligence. "My people hate you pinches gringos putos," he had spat in response to Mickey's sniveling. "It's just something in our blood."

At his elbow, Horace Pease snoozed fitfully, a fine strand of golden drool extending from his chubby lips to the dead boutonniere decorating his vomit-encrusted lapels. Raus reached over and downed the poor wretch's tumbler of mescal. He would have to sober up the *Times* man for the drive to Malinchico and Galván's campaign opener. Raus did not own—or even dare to drive—an automobile himself.

There had already been ugliness at the press conference that afternoon on Carlos Quinto street. With his family clustered around him and the Bishop and RAT and Doctor Huipi directing traffic, Tonatiuh Galván had confirmed that the tiny, geriatric Authentic Revolutionary Party (PAR) had registered his name as its candidate for the presidency of the Republic in the July 2, 2000 A.D. elections. Mickey Raus, Jane Ann, Horace Pease, Sasha Vigo, Tatiana (Tania?) and 12 other reporters all raised their right hand with the same question. Only Pease had the audacity to ask it.

"Doctor Galván, do you seriously think you will live until election day?" the *Times* man had purred insidiously.

"Señor Pease," Tonatiuh had shot back, incinerating the veteran correspondent with his dangerous eyes. "You—and your pals at the PRO—had better get out of the way. We are history happening."

Horace Pease was a perverse role model for the foreign press corps. He had not come south to find a revolution or make his bones exposing narco-políticos. Pease was native, born in the Mayatan, the scion of British planters with once-vast hennequen concessions granted them by Don Porfirio himself. He was still resentful of the revolution for having revoked them.

Although Pease traveled extensively throughout the continent, he reserved his most vitriolic commentaries for his accidental Patria. He hated the "greasers" that ran the country with typical racist venom—"And I assure you, my dear colleagues, that they loath us far more." Pease loathed them back with a dry, manic glee, moistened only by the immense quantity of poisonous liquids he inhaled.

Horace Pease had many skeletons in his closet. For years, he had allowed the PRO to pick up his bar tabs while at the same time mining the rich loam of ruling party compost. For the party leaders, the quid pro quo was that Pease never revealed more than they allowed him to know. Nonetheless, what he knew about the inner workings of the PRO mafias, he knew better than any other living gringo, with an emphasis on the qualifier.

The Galván candidacy intrigued him, he proclaimed, if only because he was "eager to know how the PRO will violate the corpse."

Ponchito was drumming in irritation on the cash register. Raus pleaded for just one more shot and the fat man waddled over, slamming the bottle down on the zinc counter so forcefully that the little green worm inside shot up to the top in helpless alarm. Pease stirred, saw that he was at least three shots behind, and thanked his colleague for arousing him from deep molecular studies. Then he began to gag ominously and staggered off to the stinking urinals. "For god's sake, get yourself together, man. We're off to Malinchico in a few brief hours."

Mickey was perilously exhilarated by the prospect of the Galván campaign. Here was a chance to strike back at the PRO and even revive his old John Reed ambitions...

¡Que se muera el PRO!

He toasted the shabby barfly face in the nicotine-smeared mirror and then, reflexively, cased the Illusions to see who might be listening in. Jane Ann was right. He definitely was talking too loud in public taverns these days. His caged eyes swept the narrow, fluorescent barroom. There were no other guests on the premises. He banged on the zinc counter with a lead coin. No one sprang to attend to him.

Raus never forgot that the secretos had come for him once, swiping him off just such a bar stool, sucking him into their subterranean charnel house somewhere out there past Tlanepantla. Probably because he was a stringer in a strange land, the agents had only beaten him to a pulp for a few days, smashing down his remaining teeth, forcing furiously bubbling Tehuacanes spiced with chile pequín up his already seriously deviated septum until he all but choked to death on his own screaming vomit. The Committee To Protect Journalists and Human Rights Watch had issued urgent action alerts and he was finally released near the airport. Nonetheless, the agony had bruised Raus's spirit as much as his thorax. There were those who whispered that the beating had taken the starch out of Mickey Raus, who'd always been known for his quick, independent pen. His drinking now was, by his own confession, often out of control, and he spoke out against the PRO government a lot more in his cups these days than in his erratic dispatches. The long slide had begun and Raus was terrified by the proximity of the bottom. He knew he was in free fall and Tonatiuh Galván was his last chance to land softly.

The guy in the gucky mirror seemed to concur. Both of them had few illusions anymore.

"Okay, Mickey. That's it, you're history." Poncho had few illusions either, but one of them was this cantina and he had to open up in a fucking hour and he couldn't open if he didn't close so for chrissakes, why didn't Mickey just go home? "And take your puke-stained friend with you—he's out cold in the pinche baño..."

"You hate us."

"Maybe we got reasons."

Raus slowly poured out the dregs of the bottle and gulped, the little worm sliding balefully down his gullet to join a quarter century worth of ancestors that now masticated upon his liver.

"They hate us, they really do," he was still muttering as he dragged Pease out of the toilets and into the dawn, breaking like a blood-red curse over the eternally damned city.

LONG AFTER LA BONDAD had begun to bump and clatter, Raus rolled the wholly clothed Horace Pease through the wreckage of his rooms and into the shower. Once the *Times* man had drip-dried, he guided him across Artículo 33 Street into the maw of the market. Doña Metiche ladled scalding hot menudo and ice-cold Negras at the two crudo newsmongers. The Flea dropped off *El Machetazo, Mejor Nada,* and the not very organic *El Orgánico.* The headlines screamed about the sale of the capital's dwindling water supply to a Japanese-U.S. consortium, International Water. Tonatiuh's campaign opener out in Malinchico ran deep inside. Raus and Pease slurped up cow intestine broth and cold dark beers and oozed oily beads of escaping mescal.

By his fourth beer, Horace Pease, ghastly white in a damp seersucker suit, remembered where he'd parked the car they'd rented for the excursion into the west. "It's all coming back to me now," he lisped through the thick film of cow tripe that furred his tongue.

THE TWO WERE OUT of the gaseous, infected city by noon. Pease gunned the rattling Nippon four-door through the misery belts that press hard upon the capital and across the industrial valley towards the distant foothills. Not an hour later, the *Times* man sailed across the state line into eastern Malinchico and the two were suddenly in pine-flecked mountains. Raus, his head to his chest, nodded fitfully. The mountain air—and a jigger of gin—motored his colleague's tongue.

"I suppose I'm partial to lynchings. That's why I'm heading for the scene of the crime, mate. This is not going to have a happy ending, oh no. Tonatiuh might as well have thrown his head into the ring along with his hat. Ha! The PRO hasn't given up a presidential election in 71 years. Why on earth would they start now?"

The Party of the Organic Revolution was born from the rubble of the great social upheaval that tore shreds in the nation's viscera between 1910 and 1920. Millions had died and only half a dozen generals had emerged from the bloodletting with any real power, among them Francisco Galván, the candidate's father.

"They will crucify Tonatiuh. Remember what they did to Colosio and Zedillo? Only this is going to be much worse. They'll overdose him with strychnine or shove amanita muscara enemas up his arse. They'll become frigging Shiites and order a fatwa. They'll cut off his head in the Zócalo and insert his genitals between his teeth!" the *Times* man rhapsodized.

"¡Aguas!" belted Raus, jolted awake to stare down a thousand-foot drop into a mountain ravine. Pease was sweeping suicide-style around hairpin turns that skirted the denuded Malinchico river canyons, into which angry swarms of Monarch butterflies—searching for certain missing pine trees to which they'd migrated each year for unnumbered millennia—sometimes drove inattentive drivers, their passengers, and their vehicles. Crosses and shrines to the Holy Virgin lined the twisting roadway.

"Ahh, this is the real movie, my son! Cowboys and Indians! Crazed butterflies! The bloody Wild Waste! Just look at that lovely clear-cut!" Pease narrowly avoided slashing into a bristling swarm of butterflies. He was swigging counterfeit Bombay gin from a paper sack.

"Tell me about Barcelona." Raus thought highway safety

might be better served if Pease was more focused. Dishing the PRO usually did the trick.

Licenciado Filemón Barcelona had just been forcibly selected by outgoing president Arturo Lomelí as his successor. After Zedillo mysteriously hung himself in a closet at Los Primos on the eve of the party congress, Lomelí had sworn before the nation that never again would the president be exclusively chosen by his predecessor. Nonetheless, Barcelona's anointing had been all destape and dedazo, the classic unveiling and big finger-point the PRO always employed to select its candidate—who, by virtue of representing the ruling party, always won by pre-arranged margins. Filemón Barcelona was an obscure, prematurely balding accountant who barely stood five feet tall in his platform Gucchis. His selection had surprised many in the foreign press corps.

"Barcelona's dead meat. The PRO is just chumming the waters with him, seeing what sharks will attack. They need to find out from what direction the bullets are coming—the Brontos, the Narcos, the Hanks…"

"That's how you see it, Horace? They will kill Barcelona like all the rest?"

The nation had been plagued by six years of political assassinations, all of them unsolved. Each year, new killings occurred and fresh layers of conspiracy callused over investigations of the old ones, until not even computer models could separate out the strands in the web anymore. You needed many more hands than two just to point fingers at the guilty parties.

"Barcelona senses that he's already dead and stinking. When Lomelí whirled around in his big swivel chair and leveled his finger at him, the little squirt ducked like he'd been shot. The Palace Guard had to call a chiropractor to unbend him from the fetal position! Watch Barcelona closely in public. When he's upset, he sucks his thumb. The PRO's been using a hypnotist to break him of the habit, but he still jerks his thumb towards his mouth when he's stressed. Choop, choop, choop."

Pease guzzled deeply.

Why had the PRO's provisional candidate agreed to so foretold a demise?

"Lomelí is like his surrogate father—Fili's father and Don Arturo were compadres; they founded TeleVida in the '40s. Filemón Senior blew his brains out when Junior was only three. There are those who say that it was young Filemón himself who pulled the trigger during a childhood game of Russian Roulette."

Pease viewed the upcoming contest as one between two dead men. "Tonatiuh is an even more willing candidate for martyrdom. He knows how much they hate him because of his papa."

General Francisco Galván came riding out of the steep ravines of Malinchico almost a century ago, right into the jaws of that massive, roiling mob scene of landless peasants that stormed back and forth across the nation for a bloody decade, riding old steam trains and wet, exhausted steeds to their doom in grainy old photographs, etching their insistence on justice and bread, land and liberty, into popular memory from Texas to Tierra del Fuego.

The savagery of this revolution of the landless can never be underestimated. A million were murdered, a million fled, and another million were never born—brothers gouged out their brothers' eyes, and fathers and sons stabbed each other in the back with machetes and axes. The national palace was bombarded, the capital ransacked by one army after another, and the Patria left in ruinous shambles. Those who claimed to have won assassinated each other with gusto. In the end, Francisco Galván climbed to the top of the corpse heap.

Today, the accomplishments of General Francisco Galván's revolution are taught in schoolbooks and ten-story murals throughout the Americas. The General is mythicized as an indigenous King David smiting the Yanqui Goliath. Under the General's firm and just hand, half the land surface of the nation was distributed to those who worked there. Overnight, the copper mines of Jaquemate became the collective property of the miners, the railroads suddenly belonged to those who ran them, and the country's considerable petroleum deposits were expropriated from the gabachos.

The General's projects were not always successful (the railroad workers wrecked the railroads, for example), but his most abysmal failure was the creation of the Party of the Organic

Revolution, a misguided strategy to sustain the hard, clear flame that was his vision of the national revolution, burning eternally on the altar of the Patria. Unfortunately, the General catastrophically under-assesed the perfidy of his successors. Indeed, the instant that he abandoned Los Primos, handing the scepter to a corrupt comrade-in-arms, the revolution that he gullibly believed he had left humming behind him shuddered to a dead stop. As political heirs devoured its achievements cell by cell, the General's own cells metastasized and caused him grievous suffering.

Nonetheless, an unbending string of PRO presidencies had never been completely successful in extinguishing the General's fire. Down the decades, local rebellion was as regular as the seasons wherever the General's vision had taken root. The spores he had scattered behind him still sprouted in the fertile, corpse-strewn earth of the countryside and the teeming slums of the cities. Though the PRO had self-righteously tried to co-opt the General by encasing him in metal statues and leaden speeches on the anniversaries of his birth and death, no true galvanista ever bit the big lie. For them—the sons of the soldiers of his army and those to whose families he had once given out the soil of the nation—the General *was* the revolution and the PRO the despoilers of the Patria's one glorious moment of liberty.

For years, General Galván's supporters had papered the land with life-sized portraits of his stern, smoldering features to remind the forgetful of his heroic stewardship. The ruling PRO would rip them down, paint them over, track down and destroy the presses on which they had been run, but still the posters kept showing up on the walls. Shadowy crews padded through the satin nights, slapping them up on municipal surfaces with a secret glue so adhesive that the walls had to be taken apart, brick by brick, just to remove the General's face from public view.

Now Raus and Pease spotted these legendary posters clinging to the mud-caked homes along the highway from Uchuskata to Lake Tzintzun. Next to them was plastered a second life-sized face, the eyes every much as incandescent as the father's in the on-rushing dusk: Tonatiuh Galván, the one they called The Hope, peering through the eyeholes of his jungle ski mask.

The road to the state capital was lined with the two faces. Here and there, though, the PRO had already postered over the images with grandiose blow-ups of Filemón Barcelona's tiny hands. "You're in good hands with the PRO," blurbed the slogan, a steal from some Yanqui insurance vendor. Strung from house to house in the cool, azure evening, as if to illuminate this battle of the walls, were hundreds and hundreds of Christmas bulbs.

"Bloody, frigging Christ!" blew Pease, sucking the dregs of ersatz Bombay from his paper sack. "There's only 12 days to Christmas." He began whistling carols like a manic canary.

⚐

THE INAUGURAL RALLY of Doctor Tonatiuh Galván's miracle crusade was nothing short of a disaster in the dark. At the last minute, the PRO mayor of Ciudad Real, the state capital, ordered all power and light lines cut off to the General Francisco Galván Plaza adjoining the Cathedral, where a thousand elderly galvanistas had assembled at nightfall. The black-out was a harbinger of treachery to come. Raus and the *Times* man could hardly make out the veteranos in their straw sombreros and bulky winter coats. A bullhorn had been substituted for the crippled sound system, reducing the old men's words to the braying of broken-down burros. Tonatiuh's voice resonated like he was holding his own nose. "This is a marvelous old cathedral," Horace Pease mused, appraising the looming structure from which the harmonious strains of the Christmas season's first posada procession were already reverberating. The *Times* man excused himself to worship.

Raus watched his colleague head for the Cathedral Hotel bar across the avenue and knew that, once again, he was on the road alone and unattached, far out in front of the curve. Maybe much too far out.

Even under the most idyllic lighting conditions, Tonatiuh Galván was not an impressive speaker. He did not wave his arms and his somber voice did not swoop and leap like any normal political orator. Too often, the Doctor would read from a prepared text in a monotone known to seal whole audiences into a deep sleep. In the dark, Tonatiuh's talents were even less impressive. The unintelligible content seemed to switch languages without warning, from Spanish to Nahuatl to Purepecha—the Doctor was conversant in all of the nation's 56 indigenous tongues. Raus groped around in the dark, but could not find Doctor Huipi to translate.

The response to Tonatiuh Galván Sharatanga's inaugural campaign address was nothing to hold the presses for, either. Several enfeebled The-People-United-Will-Never-Be-Defeated's rolled in from the darkened plaza. Solitary cries of "¡Tonatiuh Presidente!" and "¡Justicia!" penetrated the hum of canticles leaking from the old stone cathedral. Cristóbal Cantú Cabañas tried to warble the National Hymn, but the bullhorn would not cooperate. The rally melted into the moonless night abruptly. This was history happening?

Mickey figured he had little to lose by tagging along on this first campaign tour for a few days. He hailed the Bishop. They had met before, once, at the near-riot on October 12. Tonatiuh's aide seemed to remember.

"The *L.A. Times* is already interested in our crusade?" he marveled, offering a limp handshake. Raus noted that the Bishop, a soft and meticulous man, wore not one but two wrist watches. In this country, it is acutely impolite ever to be on time.

"One watch is set in real time, the other for the hour in which we win," the Bishop explained. Click! It was the same explanation that Subcomandante Caralampio once had given for wearing two watches: "When the times on my wrists come together, then we will have won."

"I assume you'll want an exclusive interview for your *L.A. Times*?"

Raus nodded cautiously. Both of them knew that Raus did not string for the *L.A. Times*.

The Bishop had pertinent ties to Tonatiuh Galván. The youngest of the Doctor-brothers, it was he who had sped halfway around the globe to fetch Tonatiuh when the General lay dying in the Monteca. He had been the son's shadow ego ever since. As campaign director, he controlled access to the Doctor.

"Put your things in the blue minivan and Tonatiuh will talk to you when it's time to talk." The Bishop's beautiful teeth flashed a cosmic smile. "First, you must watch..."

"Thanks, compañero." Raus backed off to get his stuff out of Pease's trunk, not quite entertaining the same thrilling sensation that his one-time role model, John Reed, must have experienced eight decades previous when he finally cornered Pancho Villa out there in the Chihuahua desert.

II

THE MEMORIES OF OLD MEN

December 16, 1999 – February 15, 2000

TONATIUH GALVÁN was born on a rainy day in August 1939, during the General's penultimate season encamped behind the presidential palace out in Chapulín Park. The General had been bivouacked in the park for five years because the splendor of Los Primos grated against his mission to abolish all privilege.

Tonatiuh's first year on earth was his father's last as president and it was swaddled in tragedy. His mother, Nana Esmeralda Sharatanga Cucu, the tall Purepecha noblewoman said to be descended from the Purepecha goddess of the moon, bled to death following the still birth of his sister, Anahuac. The women were buried out in the family plot, just west of Los Primos, on a sad summer day in a blinding rainstorm.

After Nana Esmeralda's death, life changed radically for Tonatiuh. The General left office and moved into the huge old residence on Carlos Quinto Street in the Centro Histórico that Tonatiuh still occupied 60 years later. During the colonial period, the structure had been a refuge for mad women, la Casa de las

Dementes, and the General's plan was just as deranged. Instead of donning widower's weeds, General Galván assembled a regiment of nannies and housekeepers and cooks and mistresses and began adopting orphan Indian babies, all boys, one from each indigenous group in the land until the family grew to 56 sons. With Tonatiuh included, the count was 57.

The General thought that he had fought and won a revolution against privilege and, because he was a revolutionary even in the marrow of his soon-to-be cancerous bones, his sole guiding child-rearing principle was to make sure that privilege was distributed equally among those who had formerly had the least. All the boys would be raised absolutely identically—although, by reason of being the General's only natural son, Tonatiuh was always to be the last served. The young Galván grew up thinking that maybe his father loved "the People" more than he loved his own son.

"The Patria needs physicians to heal itself," General Galván instructed his 57 sons when they entered their thirteenth year and each was assigned rigorous pre-medical studies from which they were not to stray until each had acquired a degree, a goal 56 young men diligently achieved. Many of the doctor-brothers, as they still called each other, went on to guide affairs of state, science and industry. Several followed the General when he abandoned the PRO and joined the opposition. The twins, Miguel and Manuel Niños de Galván (Huave), were thought to have been murdered by government troops under the command of another doctor-brother, Gertrudis Niños de Galván (Totonaco), present minister of defense, during the guerrilla war in the west in the 1970s.

Tonatiuh alone rebelled against the "doctor-orders," arguing that he had first to know the world before he would know what to do in it, an attitude that led to sharp disagreements with his father, even a legendary fist fight when the younger Galván took up with one of the General's favorite mistresses. One glum day in June 1960, Tonatiuh, then 22, pulled shut behind him the great oak doors on Carlos Quinto Street and hotfooted it to Havana to join a real revolution. Fidel welcomed the General's son on the tarmac. Che invited Tonatiuh to work in the ministry of health. But revolution was breaking out everywhere on the continent below. Tonatiuh worked a year setting up clinics in the Sierra Maestra and then slipped south.

Little was heard of him for years. Once in a blue moon, ghostly picture postal cards would appear under the door on Carlos Quinto, postmarked from frontier towns on the peripheries of important jungles—Cocalito, Ihuarete, Ihuantzu. Young Galván was spotted by intelligence operatives chatting up Chedi Jaagens in Guyana, with Douglas Bravo in the Guajira and Tirofijo high in the Colombian sierra. Interpol reported sightings in São Paulo, Tucuman, Iquique, the Chapare, Guayaquil, sometimes on the same day. But, although the CIA had red-tagged Tonatiuh as a Cuban agent, he was much more an agent of his own liberation.

With no plan at all and only his own curiosity to determine the route, the General's son ploughed recklessly through barely charted deserts and swamps, communing with the forest spirits and listening to the elders of lost tribes recount their creation myths. Along the way to God and back, he nibbled peyote buds and hallucinatory fungi with old men in long houses at the bends of big muddy rivers, chewed coca leaves and sipped Ayahuasca. To the day of his death, he carried a zombie-protection cross etched into his bony chest, his long ears had been slit on a tributary of the Orinoco, and he was circumcised by surviving Araucans at the southern tip of the continent.

For two full years, young Tonatiuh was lost in the Peruvian Andes, searching for Urim, the Condor of the South. Then, all of a sudden, he reappeared in the subways of Paris, at the St. Germain metro stop, playing cuica, the cane drum with a voice that cries like a man in pain, in a band that featured a real live Inca princess, Paloma Huantar.

Nearing 30, Tonatiuh seemed to have mellowed from his travels in southern latitudes. He finally heeded his doctor-orders and enrolled at the Sorbonne. His vast knowledge of native botany served him well and he earned the first of several medical degrees. Meanwhile, Paloma took a doctorate in proctology.

But the young doctor was growing impatient with exile. On

the way to Calcutta to meet and treat the real Indians, he received word that his father was dying at the top of the Monteca Mountains, in the other direction. The Bishop fetched him at the Istanbul airport. General Francisco Galván's cancers were now so severe that he had been driven into churches for temporary relief. After 13 years of wandering, the General's prodigal son returned from across several oceans, with an Inca doctor-princess on his arm, to fetch the old man from his mountain top.

Following his father's death, Tonatiuh and Paloma set up practice on Carlos Quinto Street where they treated the penniless residents of the old quarter for free, and began to build their own family. Now there were three fine, strong sons, each named for an Indian king—Cahuiri, Cutzmandi, and Cuauhtli. Each was, of course, engaged in rigorous pre-medical studies.

Tonatiuh's political life was not particularly resonant for much of the 1980s as he followed his old schoolmaster, Cristóbal Cantú, through a maze of splinter-left organizations, until he finally arrived at the dead end of the Authentic Revolutionary Party (PAR), an old folks' home for his father's surviving cronies. The PRO astutely seized upon the Doctor's political rootlessness and invited Tonatiuh to unveilings of new statuary to honor his father. A strange interval followed in which the General's son became convinced that he alone could alter the course of the party that had broken his father. The General, who for years after he left office publicly burned the Gold Card the PRO sent him every Christmas, gyrated irritably in his sarcophagus.

Soon, Tonatiuh Galván was the PRO candidate to become governor of Malinchico, the Patria chica of his father. The experiment lasted two months. The timber barons urged the President to fire Tonatiuh after he expropriated all non-Indian sawmills in the state and turned them over to the communities they had for years despoiled. Tonatiuh and Paloma went to the mountains at once and stood with the Purepechas at Zapicho against the army troops who had been mobilized to take back the sawmill of a PRO bigwig there that the Indians had communalized. The tense stand-off galvanized the nation for weeks and momentarily catapulted Tonatiuh into leadership of the splintered opposition, but he seemed disdainful of the spotlight and soon retreated back into the wings of political obscurity.

For a time, Tonatiuh and Paloma returned to Carlos Quinto and treated the victims of an increasingly damaged city. Soon after the PRO's monumental theft of the 1988 presidential election, Doctor Galván quietly dropped from public view. His appointments were canceled. "He's taking a breather," Paloma told friends, suggesting mid-life crisis. There were rumors of separation. Only Paloma and the Bishop knew otherwise.

When the rebellion came in Chiapas, "Subcomandante Caralampio" was right there, in the 31st of March Plaza of San Cristóbal—he even appeared in one amateur video. Caralampio didn't talk much to the press, leaving the communications to Marcos. He didn't fight much either. His war was against the jungle fevers, the Leishmaniosis, cholera, the hemorrhaging dengue, that wracked the rebel troops and the Mayan communities from which they came.

Subcomandante Caralampio's ski mask was a badly-designed disguise. His true identify was an open secret: *Protesto* ran deliberately leaked national security documents; photographic evidence was meticulously compared in *Mejor Nada*. When, finally, the Accord was signed and the comandantes at last removed their masks at the historic public destape in the Basílica, no one was very amazed at Tonatiuh's emergence.

But much as the unveiling of his hand-picked successor by the outgoing president has ensured the Organic Party of retaining control of the state apparatus for nearly a century now, Tonatiuh's destape in the cavernous shrine of the Virgin of Guadalupe was a starting point in the Doctor's miracle turn-of-the-millennium crusade to win the presidency of his country.

THE FIRST DAYS on the road with Tonatiuh Galván featured tiny, uneventful gatherings in backwater Malinchico hotland plazas. Handfuls of fearful attendees stood at respectable distances from the bandstands upon which the Doctor towered, rawboned and red-necked, in the brilliant sunlight. The sound system lent little substance to his words. Cristóbal Cantú Cabañas concluded each meeting with a few garbled bars of the National Hymn. Around the perimeters, husky men in stained guayaberas jotted down the names of those brave enough to gather there, with stubby pencils.

On the third night of the tour, the Galván caravan passed over the Bolsas de Plástico River, into El Horno.

The hot sun of El Horno has hatched many warriors. Cuauhtemoc, the descending eagle, was born in its mountains. Guerrilleros from Zapata to El Jinete Chueco—the Crooked Horseman—have ridden its sierras and coastal trails.

After the students were slaughtered at Tlatelolco in 1968, the survivors, thinking that going to guns could save them from the underground torture rooms at Military Camp Number One, came to El Horno's hills, filling out the ranks of the small campesino armies assembled by the rural teachers Lucio and Genaro. A few had survived and married and become cousins. By the '90s, the veterans of those campaigns had grown old themselves but, infused by the spirit of the New Zapatistas to their south, their sons had risen again. Significant massacres came next and soon one community after another was drawn into the fray until each family had a stake in the fighting because each family had lost at least one child. This latest outbreak had ended two years ago with the supposed death of El Jinete Chueco— born Luis Montes—high in the dry, cracked sierra of the south. Black-bereted U.S. "advisors," operating under the North American Security Treaty Agreement (NASTA), moved in to contain the rebellion from spreading to the Gold Coast between Acapella and Acapulco, "the Twin Jewels of the Pacific," which the DisneyMex-Century 21 Corporation had big plans to condominiumize. The young army was not ready to take on the Rambos and fled further and further into the sierra until the rebels were hardly heard from anymore. Even old-fashioned napalm couldn't flush them from the caves. Then Comandante Luis Montes—the Crooked Horseman—was lured down to Atila, the town in which the rebellion first began, under the pretext of a weapons deal and, like Zapata half a century before him was ambushed by hundreds of elite paratrooper-fusiliers, under the direction of then-captain Gertrudis Niños de Galván (Totonaco). A truce was hastily arranged with El Jinete's under-leaders, who in the months since had been assassinated, one by one, during a long skein of extra-legal executions that were always being critiqued by international human rights delegations. The Army still held El Horno under partial martial law, although in his 1999 state of the nation address, outgoing President Arturo Lomelí proudly announced that the region had once again been fully "pacified." No one else believed this. History runs underground here. It doesn't just dry up overnight.

⁕

ON THE FOURTH morning out, Mickey Raus sat down to a large savory platter of chorizo and eggs on the flower-filled verandah of a finca in the mountains above Atila. The candidate was seated across the table. Tonatiuh, five years his senior, did not appear as seamless as he had in big city traffic. The hot breath of the jungle was upon him and the ritual scars on his exposed chest and arms were rimmed with perspiration. Deep furrows dug into his brown brow.

"Jabalí," Tonatiuh announced, pointing to his own plate. "Wild boar." Raus understood that the Doctor was identifying a large chunk of meat floating in a brackish mole before him. The reporter declined a taste.

Under Tonatiuh's elbow, Raus spotted a familiar book—General Francisco Galván's log of the 1933-34 campaign that had taken him to every corner of the republic and won him the hearts of his people forever. Raus had just finished reading the diary, had it in his shoulder pack even now, wanted to find out how the first days of the Doctor's campaign compared with his father's experiences.

Tonatiuh did not wait for questions. "We need to know what your intentions are, Compañero Raus," the Doctor demanded.

"Well, they're actually sort of...historical." He had wanted to say 'nostalgic' but realized it wouldn't play. The Doctor's centered black eyes were hard on him and Raus was caught off-guard by the sudden aggressive probing.

"Writing me up is not going to please the PRO, you know. I doubt that whatever newspaper you say you string for provides catastrophic care coverage," he dead-panned, trying unsuccessfully to sublimate a smile. The man's taste for the mordant impressed Raus. He laid his battered mini-recorder out between the plates.

"May I?"

"Please do." Tonatiuh nodded cordially.

Mickey's questions followed his nose. Why was the electoral route to power now more viable than the armed option? Why should the Civil Society vote once again after years of frustration at the ballot box? Weren't the parties with their self-serving bureaucracies hopelessly outdated? Were there enough keepers of the flame out there to revive his father's revolution? Did he fear for his life? Why had he begun his campaign here in El Horno where guerrillas still scuttled through the hills and he knew the government would be watching closely?

"Eat up while it's still warm," signaled the Doctor. "It's a long road down from here; there's not going to be much lunch."

"The questions?"

"Yes, we are beginning here because we have many friends here and they invited us a long time ago.

"Yes, we will find out how many 'keepers of the flame,' as you call them, really are out there.

"Yes, the parties are useless—the PAR has lent us its name so that we could register our candidacy but they are just stupid old men. Be clear—this is our campaign.

"Yes, the Civil Society is tired of casting its ballot and losing even when it wins.

"Yes, we will find out if the people want to pick up the gun or the ballot—we think it must be both.

"Yes, we fear for my life. The PRO wants to kill me every bit as much as it did when I wore the ski mask.

"Of course, we consider that I will be killed before this task we have undertaken is accomplished, but I have many sons." The Doctor gestured to the guest house where his three boys had spent the night. "And they will have many sons.

"Compañero Raus, I know you are attracted by the nostalgia," the Doctor added sternly, "but this is not my father's campaign. Things are different now. I study this only to educate myself about the mistakes that were made." He fanned the pages of the famous diary so forcefully that the petals of the orchids on the tabletop shuddered. "I am my father's son—I share the same blood but I am not him." Raus was surprised by the candidate's personal vehemence when each previous answer had been so coolly formulated in editorial "we's."

The man with two watches cut short the Doctor's cautions. "Ya es hora…it's time to go."

Later, a lot later, Raus would learn a little of why Tonatiuh had been so insistent upon being his own man. Unlike most childhoods, his was fraught with 56 separate sibling rivalries. Painful jealousies had bruised the brothers and many remained unforgiving to this day. The only true son resented a father who seemed to love a whole people a lot more than he did his own child. It wasn't natural.

And then there was the question of the names to be lived up to—the General's own and the one which had thrust the child into the sun at the center of the Indian universe—when what the child really craved was the cool, dark solitudes of the caves.

A DELEGATION OF SMALL coffee-colored men, dressed in cottons so shabby they seemed translucent, halted the caravan on the outskirts of Atila. Each man wielded a broad-blade machete.

"¡HOOOOOSTIIIIICIAAAAA!" The familiar chant exploded from the dense banana groves that lined the dirt road down to the coast. Only now the cry was matched syllable for syllable with the candidate's name: "¡HOOOOSTIIIIICIAAAAA TOHNAATIIUHH!" The cry would echo from one end of the country to the next in the coming months and years.

A banda de guerra struck up a skipping martial tune just down the road. Hand-painted banners unfurled. School girls presented the Doctor with bouquets and formally curtsied, tripping over their pretty new shoes as they backed away.

Flanked by a phalanx of banana workers, Tonatiuh was paraded through the small commercial district to the center of Atila. Bushels of confetti were thrown by well-wishers. The rockets that announce both fiestas and funerals exploded in festive braces.

⁂

THE DISTANT BOOM of the cohetes and the band's tinny umm-pa-pahs wafted in wisps to the top of Skull Hill. From up there, the campaign hurly-burly seemed small, like the buzzing of the bloodsucking black flies. "It is nothing. It is insignificant," Captain-Major Epidemio Gutiérrez Mofo muttered to himself, pressing the field binoculars against his aviator sunglasses, an adjustment that gave an even fuzzier focus. Frustrated, "El Caimán" hurled the glasses at his adjutant, a clever boy with quick hands, named Juanelo. "Count those who are marching. Make sure that you identify everyone who went out to meet Galván. You will have the list on my desk no later than nightfall. Do you understand what I am saying, boy?"

The youth clapped his cracked, naked heels smartly together and folded a hand over his eyes: "Sí, mi Capitán." But El Caimán had already turned away, having more important work to do than acknowledge the boy soldier's response. Stomping savagely down on the gas pedal, he gunned the jeep back down Skull Hill to the command post. He had to badger the video crew. We want everything done right this time, Gobernación had warned. Gonzalo X. Davis was on his neck and the Crocodile was sweating.

The homefolks of Atila de la Jun, El Horno, jocularly refer to their town as "the little inferno," but the midday heat was no jest. Raus, bushwhacked by the scorching sun, brought a straw sombrero from an old lady crouched inside a plaza stall but he felt ridiculous when he put it on. He was already two feet taller than the banana workers who milled animatedly in the cramped plaza. Whenever Mickey scanned the crowd, he would catch eyes openly gawking at him, as if the Doctor had lured a Martian to the town. Gringos, Martians—they came from the same planet in the banana workers' geography.

Tonatiuh spoke from the gazebo in the elevated center of the square. The bananeros quietly drank in every squawk of the loudspeaker, their equally diminutive wives shaded under black umbrellas on the outer edge of the plaza. Two burly white men, pretending to be a state television channel team, were filming the event although few opposition candidates had ever appeared on television in the nation's tortured electoral history.

Tonatiuh's words blasted through the pitiful speakers like a cross between a duck quack and a dog bark. The Bishop, who faithfully recorded every speech, was fiddling with audio dials and twisting loose strands of wire together and could not be bothered to translate. Doctor Huipi was up on the bandstand with Cantú Cabañas and the three boys. So far as Mickey could divine, the Doctor's outrage was directed at the PRO government's intentions of selling off the cooperative banana groves to DisneyMex-Century 21.

"My father kicked the norteamericanos off this land once before," Tonatiuh squalled, his ideas beginning to gel inside Mickey's anglo ears, "but the PRO has let them in the door again. There are documents that guarantee the collective ownership of this land. It is not for sale and it is not for lease." There were many shouts of "¡HOOSTIICIA TOHHNATIIUHH!"

The Doctor was more rueful when he spoke of the vote, how it was a weak weapon in the hands of those who have fought the government with guns, but "first we must see how many there are of you and how far you are prepared to go." Then the speech took a curious turn that Raus would hear again—the Doctor invited the soldiers and the government spies in the crowd to join his movement to overthrow the PRO. "We know that you are here, taking notes and filming my words, and that by tomorrow morning the tapes and the complete transcribed text will be in the hands of Gonzalo X. Davis."

Two young bananeros approached Raus, flagrantly fingering the blades of their machetes. "¿Qué estás escribiendo, señor?" *What are you writing?* Mickey edged away, pretending to be a Martian.

"We ask you to reflect on what you have heard here today, what the people have said to you by their presence here. Take these thoughts home with you and consider that you are a part of the people too," advised the Doctor. The young macheteros glared at Raus; he reholstered his Rolling Writer.

"¡HOOOSTIIICIAHHH TOHHHNAAATIIIAHHH!" sang the sun-dried men and women in the plaza of Atila, over and over again.

AFTER THE RALLY, the Doctor was taken to sit with the elders, nine thin men in thin white cottons, distinguished from their compatriots in the plaza only by the blades of their weapons and the lengths of their militancies. The room off the plaza in which they met was cool and dark, and Raus slumped in a corner, relieved to be out of the blast furnace of Atila's sun and away from the two angry macheteros outside. A wiry little man passed him his water gourd and—grateful for the gesture after the flash of steel outside in the plaza—he gulped greedily.

The nine elders sat stiffly on folding chairs in a semi-circle facing Tonatiuh, the three boys standing behind their father like one strong young arm of support. Nailed up on the white-washed wall Raus recognized many portraits—Zapata, the General, Lucio, the Sup Marcos, Comandante Luis Montes mounted astride a jet-black horse.

Each of the elders spoke his concerns in turn. Many were similar—we have lost sons here before, we have other sons but we are not sure if the sacrifice will be worth it. We don't want to lose again.

One of the old men, Ismael Caracol, the wiry leader of the banana workers cooperative, was more direct.

"Twenty-four years ago, after Lucio was killed, they came for my brother Nacho. They took him, his wife, 12 children, our grandmother. We never found a trace of anyone, not even a shoe or a bone. My brother was a brave man who stood up to the government and was Lucio's fourth in command but his children, well, they were just children.

"Years passed and we waited for others to rise up with us but there was no agreement. Then came the rebellion in the south and our young men, who had listened to all our stories but who did not yet know war, were inspired again to take up the gun and the machete. The students came again from the cities and joined our struggle. But when the Yanquis let their napalm fires fall upon our villages, just as in Lucio's day, it was us who stayed and fought and the outsiders fled back to their homes in the city and some turned against us and joined the PRO in the so-called 'Pacification' campaign.

"We have been sold out here many times, Doctor. And it has made us suspicious of who it is that comes to save us now. You are the General's only true son and that is hopeful but for us, history is not enough…"

Tonatiuh studied the old bananero with those x-ray eyes of his for a long minute before he responded. His voice was small and clenched when finally he spoke, like a raw recruit amongst veterans of a war that knows no end. "Yes, the compañero is correct—history is never enough. Yes, we bring trouble to you but that is not new. They have been watching us since the moment we arrived, but they have been watching you longer. Even here in this room, they have their ears. Yes, they can kill me whenever the moment is right for them. But you must remember, I am not just the General's son. Yes, I am your son too." Tonatiuh gestured to his own sons, arms folded and unblinking, behind him. "Yes, I will bring you many more sons."

🦎

TONATIUH'S MIRACLE CRUSADE broke for Christmas. Eight days later, it was New Year's and a new century. Raus floated up to the capital but couldn't keep his mind from the campaign. His friends teased him relentlessly about it. When finally the cars began to roll, Mickey felt relieved. It was as if his life had found purpose again.

Years later, whenever Raus recreated those first months of Tonatiuh Galván's long campaign of 2000, he would find himself struck all over again by the many old men who flocked to the rallies. Sometimes hundreds of them would pour into the small town plazas from the neighboring hills to listen to Tonatiuh's solemn words and chant their demands for justice and their hatred of the PRO, and, above all, to shake the hand of the son of the man who had once given them this land. Sometimes, it would only be ten. But the numbers did not matter. Tonatiuh would stand and chat, his long slit ears drinking in their tales of misery, much as his father's had during the 1933-34 campaign. Inevitably, the Bishop would intervene, steering the candidate towards the station wagon and other old men gathered down the road.

"So many viejos, every place we go," Mickey wondered out loud to the Man with Two Watches as they tooled back across the Bolsas de Plástico River into Malinchico a few days after the New Year's break. A millennium had turned in the interval. Raus himself had become a viejo.

"We knew it would be the old people who would come forth first—they have the most to lose. They know this is their last chance." The Bishop stubbed out his Delicado in the still smoldering ashtray. "The century has run out on them."

It's run out on me too, Mickey thought.

"You know what attracts me to the campaign is how old-style it seems. How Tonatiuh has to shake everybody's hand, hear every story. How he resists the future..."

The Bishop fired up another Delicado. "That's a bum rap, Mick. We just do not forget the past..."

"Tonatiuh says this is not his father's campaign..."

"Blood says more than all the words, hermano."

THE BISHOP'S TIES to Tonatiuh Galván reached back to their fathers. Abelardo Salmón Guengoitia had been one of the thousands of Basque and Catalunian Loyalists to whom the General had extended political asylum as Franco's black legions marauded through those tormented lands. But the weight of the war back home caused the elder Salmón unquenchable draughts of depression. After his father's suicide by pulque and his mother's by rat poison, the orphaned Abelardo was forced to eke out his bread in the streets, a black-faced urchin sleeping in La Bondad market, where the General's driver discovered him one morning amidst the melons and took him back to Carlos Quinto to meet the Patriarch.

By then, all of the doctor-brothers had left home and gone off to university and Tonatiuh's father gratefully took the boy under his old wing. Abelardo Salmón Guengoitia, "the Bishop"—so named for his ability to beat the General at chess and not for any religious proclivities (which were prohibited by the Old Man)— became the fifty-eighth and youngest doctor-brother, personally attending to the General's failing health after the student massacres plunged him into lethargy. It was the Bishop who dispatched himself to Istanbul to bring Tonatiuh home.

Abelardo Salmon attached himself permanently to his elder doctor-brother once the General had passed on. During Tonatiuh's brief stint as the PRO governor of Malinchico, the Bishop served as chief trouble-shooter, traveling the Purepecha villages of the state, soliciting denuncias against the sawmill owners. And during Tonatiuh's Lacandón jungle tour, the Bishop acted as a conduit between the rebels and the family and the press, moving the Zapatistas' messages into the upper echelons of government, brokering the beginning of agreements.

Now, in the miracle campaign, the Bishop was a similar crucible, connecting Tonatiuh to those outside the inner circle, transmitting the Doctor's warnings, his prescriptions, his guarded optimism to the people, laying out the circuitry for the miracle.

It began with the wiring. At rallies, the Bishop fiddled with loose strands, soothed the fractured sound system, faithfully recorded the Doctor's speeches as if each turgid word was sacred prophecy. On the road, he kept the two-car caravan gassed and rolling along a web of backwater tracks, always moving from meeting to meeting, sometimes 15 in a day, with hardly a moment in between to pee. Even in the urinals, Tonatiuh never stopped shaking the scarred hands of the old men.

Often, speeding from one tiny gathering to the next, the Doctor would dictate to the Bishop as if assigning a treatment plan. "The man with the cataracts back there says he fought with my father. Can we see that his roof is shingled for the rain?" Or, "The woman in the market in Quetzaltero with the two sets of twins who have no arms—find out how she can sue the drug company."

All through January and February, the caravan cruised El Horno, the western farm towns of Malinchico, north to San Pancho and the breadbasket of the Bajío, pausing wherever the locals would allow the Bishop to set up his infernal loud-speakers. Meanwhile, the ruling party candidate never left the capital, Filemón Barcelona being content to communicate his vision of a happy-face Patria from the TeleVida studios on Chapultepec. Choop. Choop. Choop.

Mickey Raus tagged along from one plaza to the next, with no prearranged plan, noting the pit stops in the squares and marketplaces all across the fertile lowlands of the Bajío. The Bishop was always careful to avoid the larger cities, moving over packed dirt roads, hunting up rendezvous arranged on dysfunctional telephones long after midnight. And always there were the old men to greet them with cohetes and handshakes and the memories still brimming in their eyes.

Tonatiuh's retinue fit comfortably into a rusting Impala station wagon that finally threw a rod ten klicks from Comala on the road to El Rulfo. The Bishop drove, the Doctor on his right. In back, Cantú Cabañas, playing hooky from his duties as the lone PAR deputy in the congress of the Republic, was on board to croon the National Hymn. Next to him perched Doctor Huipi, sometimes described as Tonatiuh's "spiritual adviser." The three companions played relentlessly at dominoes.

The Doctor's princely sons, depending on school and examination schedules, rode in the far back. Their mother traveled less frequently, nailing down the campaign headquarters on Carlos Quinto up in the city. Usually, a local elder like Ismael Caracol would ride along to point out the route to the far-flung settlements and ensure a rousing welcome at the rallies.

At the wheel of the Press VAM was Don Estalin Lenin Gómez Gómez, a shave-headed, hard-rock old communist whose square swarthy features were ornamented by a bristly reprise of Joe Stalin's trademark mustachio that replicated every ramrod-stiff, Marxist-Leninist follicle. Don Estalin deployed an energetic democratic centralism to keep order on the road, wading into brothels and cantinas like a Red Carrie Nation to re-orient wayward reporters.

Covering these momentous events for the national and international press were Antonio Malcreado, a consumptive lyric poet and the correspondent for the leftish *El Machetazo*; Jesus Von Voodle (aka Don Chuchu the German), a munchkin-sized native ultimately of Teutonic descent, who was assigned to cover the Doctor's campaign by the PRO government's *El Orgánico*; and Mickey Raus, a down-at-the-heels stringer for a Northern California paper so close to folding that the slimy-limey "foreign" editor wouldn't even take his collect calls anymore.

Each week the Bishop handed Malcreado a white unmarked envelope, the contents of which were to "cover any emergency expenses." Von Voodle was on the government payroll and did not deserve the chayo. On the bottom rung was "El Mickey," who received no stipend at all and whose pathetic bankroll barely bought him a bed each night.

"They hate us," Mickey muttered morosely to himself, folding into a no-star fleabag near Ciudad Tacumán, nursing a jug of low-budget kiwi wine and the animosity his road colleagues had just radiated down in the hotel cantina. "No matter how you cut it, they just hate us."

LONG-SHOT OPPOSITION CANDIDATE CALLS FOR CACTUS REVOLUTION

Special to the North Coast Variety News

CIUDAD TACUMÁN (February 15)—This broad, fertile valley beneath a still-active volcano produces some of the world's most luscious kiwi fruit but still cannot feed its own people. Nonetheless, despite below-minimum wage scales, 12-hour days, substandard housing, and widespread malnutrition, Tacumanians are a peaceable people whose collective recollections of their nation's now-distant revolution seem limited to the day that General Francisco Galván came here to hand out land parcels to the poor and disenfranchised, more than a half century ago.

This past week, the natives' long-dormant memories were jolted alive when the General's son, a long-shot opposition candidate for the presidency of his country, came to town to ask for their vote.

As it often does these days, Tonatiuh Galván's appearance in Tacumán stirred deep nostalgias, particularly among those who originally received land from the General, and their many descendants.

Lost Land

"Things are different now, but we still remember General Galván here," farm worker Ultiminio Machain told a U.S. reporter during an energetic rally in the town plaza. Mr. Machain was holding up a tattered portrait of the General—the same poster, he says, his father held during the land giveaway 65 years ago.

Land ownership in the Tacumán Valley has slowly been ceded to corporate agribusiness since Galván's celebrated agrarian reform was decreed in the mid-1930s. Many farmers lost their plots when banks foreclosed after the 1994 peso collapse. Under provisions of the Amended North American Free Trade Agreement (NAAFTA), transnational kiwi growers and packers producing the specialty fruit for the California market picked up rent-foreclosed land from the banks for next to nothing. The discovery that kiwi enzymes may contain a cure for testicular cancer has created a mini-boom for the growers here under the still-smoking Kalimba Volcano.

Vertical Modernization

Today, Tacumán agro-industrialists produce 53% of all kiwi fruit consumed north of the Rio Bravo river, outpacing even New Zealand, for whom the fruit has become a national symbol. The kiwi boom returned almost $450 million much-needed dollars to the national economy in 1998. One downside: the former owners of the land now are day pickers and shed workers who no longer produce their own staples. Because the strategy of the past three PRO presidents has been to increase NAAFTA exports while cutting back on national food production, in order to maximize payments on the nation's swelling $250 billion USD debt, land is no longer sown with such basics as beans and corn and not with—particularly here in Tacumán—nopal and maguey cacti, once thriving local crops. This unpopular policy is expected to be continued by the PRO's hand-picked standard-bearer Filemón Barcelona, who Doctor Galván is challenging in the July 2 election. Mr. Barcelona, a former finance minister, is the architect of the export-for-credit scheme that the long-ruling Party of the Organic Revolution (PRO) touts under the rubric of "Vertical Modernization." Barcelona has already indicated that the nation's farmers will have to make additional sacrifices in coming years "so that the revolution can meet the challenges of a new millennium that is globalizing at the speed of light."

No Gardens Permitted

Here in Tacumán, "Vertical Modernization" has meant healthy annual profits for transnational growers such as UniTree and G.E. Fruit, but lower nutritional standards for the region's own populace. With all available land under kiwis, no grain has been grown locally for a decade, and yellow corn, imported from the United States as animal food, is available only on the black market here, an enterprise that Galván supporters charge is controlled by the PRO.

"We are not even allowed to grow home gardens anymore in Tacumán. When we do, the soldiers come and cut them down," complained Mr. Machain. Growers have reportedly decreed that all private plots be put under kiwi. UniTree's home offices in Galveston, Minnesota, did not return this reporter's phone calls.

Health workers at the independent "Glorious Comandante Ramona Rural Health Clinic" indicate that 70% of Tacumán's 60,000 residents suffers from second and third-degree malnutrition. "These people eat very little basic protein. They are not in good health, particularly the children," lamented Dr. Irma Guadarrama, who directs the bare-bones, concrete-block facility. The doctora pointed to hundreds of empty jugs of high-octane kiwi wine that litter Tacumán streets, complaining that "everyone drinks their lunch now."

In addition to poor nutrition, which has upped infectious disease incidents to alarming proportions (measles killed 103 children in Tacumán last winter), Dr. Guadarrama is particularly worried about generalized pesticide poisonings in the area. Chemicals—many of which are outlawed in the U.S.—used to douse the kiwis are now reaching critical levels in patients' blood systems, the doctor claims.

Cactus Not Kiwis

During his two-hour visit here, Dr. Galván, who is a medical doctor and who once served the Zapatista rebels in Chiapas, spoke often of the area's declining health. At one point during his speech to 1,500 kiwi pickers, Galván, 62, urged Tacumanians to plant food crops and medicinal herbs once grown by the region's Indians, placing special emphasis on the reputed beneficial properties of the nopal cactus. "Yes, the nopal has served us for our history as food and good medicine. Yes, it cleans our blood and our mind, it keeps our brown skins fresh and sleek, it nourishes us when we are hungry. It is native to our culture and our traditions. The kiwi is not. The kiwi is like this Barcelona, the candidate of the PRO. It comes from outside and it is not good for us," Galván warned the farm workers.

Despite the lack of charged rhetoric and elaborate body language, Galván's speech pleased Doña Rafaelita Jiji, a seller of medicinal herbs in the Tacumán marketplace, who told a U.S. reporter that "no politician has ever come and told us to plant nopales before. Doctor Tonatiuh is a true doctor who can cure our country from the poisons the PRO has put in our food and water." Part of the Doctor's appeal, Jiji—a Kichi Indian—conceded, is that "he is a brown man but a smart brown man." Barcelona, like his immediate predecessors Arturo Lomelí, Ernesto Zedillo, Carlos Salinas and Miguel de la Madrid, is of European stock.

Uphill Fight

With 71 years in power, the PRO is the longest-running political dynasty on the planet. While the PRO has sometimes faced challenges, most previous opposition presidential candidacies have been symbolic gestures, largely subsidized by the PRO itself. But for the past three months, Galván has been cruising the rural center of this huge country, encouraging rebellion in imaginative forms, such as his suggestion to sow nopal cactus on UniTree plantations here. He has also been testing his constituency for the July vote. Government internal security agents keep careful tabs on the candidate, filming each meeting and tailing the Doctor's tiny two-car caravan. "It is for his own protection," according to Captain-Major Epidemio Gutiérrez Mofo, who is in charge of the detail.

As in Tacumán, Doctor Galván often uses the nation's Indian past to connect to those who have come to hear him and voice their demand for more just agrarian policies. Sometimes switching into Nahuatl—the nation's second language—or other Indian tongues in which he is conversant, Galván celebrates past struggles and indigenous traditions in his speeches. Even his own powerful name—Tonatiuh, the sun god whose four avatars were at the heart of the Aztec religious system—conjures up the past glories of his people.

Despite his repeated allusions to indigenous traditions and his own roots as the only legitimate son of the legendary revolutionary General Francisco Galván, the candidate is adamant that his campaign is focused on the future. "But we must help people to remember their history—after all, it belongs to them and not the PRO," the doctor emphasized in a recent interview.

Doctor Galván's protestations notwithstanding, history hangs heavily over his upstart crusade. Some Indian revivalist groups, notably "The Sixth Sun Movement" and "The Warriors of Huitzilopochli," whose members danced before the Tacumán rally, suggest that the election of Tonatiuh to the presidency fulfills the prophecy of the Sixth Sun, the promised rebirth of Aztec ascendancy. Responds Doctor Galván, uncharacteristically laughing: "All we are fighting for is simple justice and that these people should have enough to eat. We are not yet demanding a new sun."

III

LITTLE MIRACLES

February16 – May 25, 2000

WINDING THROUGH MAH, Tzimah, Taneem, Yoom, and Cuim, at every step of Tonatiuh's climb into the Sierra of the Purés up to Zapicho, there had been pumping brass bands, grotesquely masked devil dancers, and winsome señoritas offering piping hot bowlfuls of choripo chili stew, star-shaped tamales called corundas, and cups of sweet cinnamon tea laced with the region's thunderous white lightning.

KAAAAAAAAAA-WOP! KAAAAAAAAAA-WOP!

A brace of rockets lifted and flared into the blue mountain sky. Everywhere along the route, jubilant crowds had come out to greet Tonatiuh and set off the booming festival rockets. Down in the hotlands where only ten tentative souls had ventured into the plazas to hear the Doctor not three months before, now there were a hundred. Where there had been a hundred in the flatland bracero belt that stretches across the Bajío, 500. In the cathedral square of the state capital where the campaign opener had turned into disaster in the December dark, 10,000 stood hat-brim to hat-brim in the blazing Malinchico noon, chanting "¡TONATIUH PRESIDENTE!" and "¡HOOOOOSTIIIIICIA!" so vengefully that the PRO "antennas" in the crowd fled in terror.

The Bishop was percolating with enthusiasm. The campaign "has at last taken off," he beamed to the ragtag press corps as they cruised towards Zapicho. "The tremendous outpouring of popular support here in Malinchico is a signal that this July the opposition will break a string of 71 consecutive years of PRO deceit and defeat," Malcreado had written in *El Machetazo* that morning. Crudely painted "Aztec Suns," circles of crimson radiating emerald rays, multiplied on the mud walls, and Raus banged out potboilers about how Tonatiuh's sun would rise in the next election. Even Von Voodle was infected—*El Orgánico* begrudgingly reported that "Dr. Galván's supporters have, at last, come out of the woodwork—at least here in Malinchico, the birthplace of his illustrious father, General Francisco Galván, the founder of the Party of the Organic Revolution."

GILDED STATUES OF General Francisco Galván populated every plaza and park in the wide western state of Malinchico and Zapicho's was no exception. Although the local Galván replica was minus an ear, lost to an errant army mortar during the sawmill stand-off a decade ago, the General was revered in this high mountain town. His blessed mother, the curandera Nana Lupita Cucu, Tonatiuh's abuela, had relatives here and his grandfather had set up business in Uchuskata, twenty kilometers west as the crow flies.

Sadik Galván, an itinerant Lebanese merchant, had been the proud new proprietor of an important tortilla factory in his adopted hometown of Uchuskata when Don Porfirio's dread rurales strung him up on a makeshift cross in the plaza, for "fraternizing with the Indians"—presumably Doña Lupita Cucu. The immigrant's furious neighbors lashed back, killing a score of the hated cops, but they could not cut poor Sadik down in time and he died in their arms.

Later the rurales returned and slaughtered those Indians who had not fled. Then they dug a quarry on the abandoned hillside into which all their bones were cast. The town of Uchuskata was obliterated from the maps. The Uchuskata that now appears on the Malinchico state map is not the first Uchuskata.

The young Galván, who was 14 at the time of his father's crucifixion, was rumored to be dead himself, or else a political refugee in Arabia or Guatemala. For five years, according to E. Krauze's official biography, the teenage general crept from ravine to ravine, scouring the hotlands and the sierra for young men who would ride behind him. On his nineteenth birthday, Francisco Galván and an army of equally enraged adolescents erupted into Ciudad Real and blew up the Government Palace. Years of guerrilla war followed, much of it here in the Sierra of the Purés, where for generations the General's spores had found receptive ground.

KAAAAA-WOP! KAAAAA-WOP! KAAAAA-WOP!

General Galván had often come to Zapicho with Tonatiuh in tow to see his great compadre, Anastacio Acuitzio, the boy's de facto godfather. Now Tonatiuh and Paloma visited here every year, an annual spring pilgrimage that usually coincided with Semana Santa vacations. It was indeed during Holy Week that the two had stood with the townspeople under the bayonets of the army after the President had sent troops to take back the sawmills. Public services were named after all the Galváns here: the Doctora Paloma Huantar de Galván Infant Center, the Doctor Tonatiuh Galván Sharatanga Rural Health Cooperative, the General Francisco Galván Primary (and Secondary) School(s), even the Sadik Galván Municipal Tortillería.

Tonatiuh and Paloma had come with their three tall sons—Cahuiri, Cutzmandi, and Cuauhtli—and young women in shiny satin blouses and long swishing skirts, their ebony tresses perfectly plaited, pressed in around the boys, fluttering their long Puré lashes, offering warm, sweet tamales, shots of chinguidi, baskets of mountain Tejocote fruit, and gales of girlish giggling.

KAAA-WOP! KAAA-WOP! KAAA-WOP! KAAA-WOP!

A gorgeously embroidered shawl was draped over Paloma's bronzed, fragile shoulders. More rockets flared. Dancers appeared in the cobbled streets—young men wearing frozen-faced wooden masks of old men stepped in merry circles around the Doctor. The band pumped and pumped. As the party mounted the steep streets to the plaza, men and women streamed out of every house to embrace the Doctor and his sons, and shyly shake Paloma's hand. Each house—wood-plank cabins the Purés call trojes—flew a homemade flag upon which had been stitched Tonatiuh's crimson sun.

"The only PROs left in Zapicho are rotting in the graveyard," boasted a gopher-mouthed man with a what-me-worry grin in his eye. "Pamfilo Ihuatzi at your orders, Don..."

"Mickey Raus, reportero. Con mucho gusto."

"Igualmente, Don Mickey Raus, reportero." The two wrung hands.

After a meeting in the mountain plaza where the "Tonatiuhs" and the "Hoosticias" crackled like rifle fire in the crisp mountain air, the candidate sat down with the elders, as was the custom. All the men were permitted to attend, but Raus lingered outside the whitewashed town hall to watch Paloma toss a plump baby amidst a pile of young, laughing wives as naturally as if she had lived in Zapicho all her life. Much later, she would confess to Mickey that she thought she had.

Inside, the Tatas were gathered on splintery benches. They had come to defend Tonatiuh's candidacy with their lives. Despite the warm spring morning, the men were uniformly wrapped in great sheepswool gavans—thick blankets which must have weighed seven kilos folded.

"We are people of the mountain and the weather changes swiftly up here," Tata Pamfilo winked. Abruptly, each man dredged a weapon out from under his long garment. Hunting rifles mostly—old Mausers, an ancient Enfeld, the usual 22s—but, here and there, automatic weapons, too. It was the first time Raus had seen long guns on the campaign trail. The Tatas raised the weapons high in their right hands. "I swear to defend Doctor Tonatiuh Galván hasta las ultimas consecuencias," the men rumbled in unison.

Each of the Tatas lined up—with their tall cone sombreros in their hands, and their guns back under their gavans—to touch Tonatiuh's palm. Raus saw that the Doctor knew them all by name; he paused to chat with each white-goateed grandfather or twisted old tío about their children and their cows, and how the spring planting was going in the valley far below.

Tonatiuh touched Tata Pedro Baltazar, the barrel-chested mayor, on the shoulder. "Is Tata Anastacio mad at me? Why isn't he here? Or has that old coyote gone over to the PRO?"

"He feels old and sad, he says. He thinks he is going to die soon. He stays up there most of the time now." The Mayor chucked his chin towards the mountain above town.

Tonatiuh wanted to climb Tarihuata and find his godfather right away. The Bishop, who had been hovering like an impatient raven all morning, pointed emphatically at his watches. "Hermano, it's a long day—we still have Cuimtzimah, Tenbem, and Uchuskata II to visit."

"We're always late anyway," the Candidate laughed, playfully nudging his younger doctor-brother uphill. Raus couldn't remember having seen Tonatiuh in better humor.

POUNDING UP TARIHUATA, the Old Woman Mountain, on the goat path leading to Anastacio's shack, Tata Pamfilo told Raus of a curious experience. "When I was up here last to visit Tata Tacho, I watched an eagle swoop down from the peak and gobble up a snake that was sunning itself in a nopal cactus right over there," the goofy little man gestured. Raus had heard this story before.

"Only, this snake had two heads and the eagle couldn't

swallow it and so he choked to death trying. He fell from the sky like a great stone, right into the Plan." Mickey looked behind him where, far below, ant-size oxen plowed furrows slim as pencil lines into the valley dust.

"You know what I think?" Pamfilo insisted. "I think it's an omen. I think Tonatiuh is like the two-headed snake and the PRO will choke to death trying to swallow him whole."

Anastacio's hut was halfway to the summit, set under an immense and crooked pino—the oldest tree in this part of Tarihuata, Pamfilo said. Tonatiuh lifted the gate off its hinges and knocked against the side of the jerry-built cabin, calling in a singsong voice for the old man.

"He's stone deaf. He can't hear you." A young buck, a teenager really, rounded the corner of the cabin. Arnulfo, Tata Tacho's great grandson, stared Tonatiuh square in the eye.

"¡Qué milagro! ¿Cuándo llegaste de California?" Pedro Baltazar asked.

"Is your abuelo here?" an eager Tonatiuh wanted to know. Arnulfo pointed and stepped aside. Raus smelled alcohol in the air.

Anastacio Acuitzi had been just a child when he rode from the ravines with Francisco Galván, but he was always more of a farmer than a fighter. Once the war had ended and the land of the village had been secured, he had returned to Zapicho and traded in his bandaleros for a plow. When Tonatiuh was himself a boy, the General would send him here during the summers for a month at a time. His father's old comrade-in-arms was as close to a godfather as the atheist General would allow. Tata Tacho raised Tonatiuh on tales of revolutionary heroism. He taught him how the Purés first walked in the forest on the day the world was created. He grounded him in the names of the myriad trees and weeds and flowers that pushed up in wild abundance on all sides of the Old Woman Mountain. The lessons had been the seed of the Doctor's lifetime fascination with the medicinal properties of native plants.

Tata Tacho stewarded his forest. Just ten years ago, when he was all of 93 years old, Anastacio had single-handedly held off a gang of UniTree timber goons who'd come to cut down the ancient pine—"la Reina"—which oversaw his property. The thugs brandished chain saws, the old man held a muzzle-loader on them, the powder and the shot tamped firmly down by his own hand. The stand-off lasted half the day and in the end the timber thieves backed down the mountain with buck-shot-peppered culos.

At 103, his life having touched three centuries and two millennia, Tata Tacho had retreated halfway to the top of Tarihuata, but his presence pervaded Zapicho down below every much as that of Tonatiuh and the General. Now, in the soft streaky light filtering through the fine fingers of the pines, Tonatiuh had come for Tata Tacho's blessing.

The old man was lying like a dark, rumpled puddle on the hard bed, the fire dead and cold on the packed dirt floor. He roused himself when the Doctor stumbled into the dark room. "¡Mierda! I must have overslept! I meant to come down for the meeting. I told the boy to wake me," he fussed.

Tonatiuh knelt to kiss the old man's hand. Raus saw that it was exactly the color of the ground here in Zapicho, the dirt floor, the floor of the valley being plowed by ants far below.

Tacho stirred the ashes in the firepit. "Dead, dead, dead—just like me..." He gave Tonatiuh a rubbery, toothless smile and began to crack twigs. On a rough pine plank at the far end of the bed, Raus noticed a cluttered altar, the spectral images of the General and the Virgin of Guadalupe strewn amidst the candle stubs, dead flowers, and wedges of copal.

Outside in the patio, the Bishop paced in small circles, staring down his watches. The three sons clung bashfully to the doorway. Tonatiuh talked incessantly as Anastacio prepared the tea of Nuriti flowers, listing all the reasons he could remember to explain why he must once more try to take the country back from the PRO.

"Now it's not just what the General wants or even your damned revolution anymore. Now it has become the trees, the rivers, the corn, the land, always the land, our history, it's all for sale. They're trying to make us disappear, the Purés, the human beings. For this mountain just to disappear, for the trees and the flowers to disappear, the flower of the Nuriti bush that grows at the feet of Tarihuata, this tea that sustains us. Desaparecidos, all of them."

Anastacio poured out a clay cupful and handed it to the chattering Tonatiuh, spooning in what looked like a half pound of sugar. The two squatted, staring into the embers on the floor, thinking about the long years strung between them.

"You know they will kill you this time," Tata Tacho finally said.

Picking his way back down the mountain, the sun still straight up in the sierra sky, it came back to Raus what the drunk boy had cautioned back there at the gate—that Tata Tacho was as deaf as a stone.

ﺣﺒﻲ

TONATIUH GALVÁN pushed north into the Altos of Plan de Abajo under an inflexibly indigo heaven from which only white stones ever fell in the name of precipitation. The austere weather had yielded a race of stoics whose only emotional indulgence was a fanaticism for the Roman Catholic faith that bordered on the psychopathic.

So many Martyrs of Christ the King had been dispatched by the cossacks of Maximato Marco Aurelio Avenida back in the 1920s that the Vatican set up a permanent office in Los Altos just to sort out the candidates for canonization. In the year 2000, although the Church and the PRO had long ago buried the hatchet, these impoverished provincials still nursed a yen to avenge the ancestral blood that Avenida and his lieutenant Calles had spilled in what was now the last century. The Martyrs of Christ the King, thought to be just the phantoms of extinct, renegade priests, were still technically at war with their government.

After the Pope and the PRO reached accommodation, the Christ the Kingers extended their jihad to the church hierarchy itself. In the 1970s, liberationist priests infiltrated Los Altos from the lowlands, bringing with them a fierce loyalty to the poor that infected the Martyrs. Class hatred soon commingled with holy wrath and the Martyrs of Cristo Rey turned their weapons upon the nation's number one prelate, the 400-pound Cardinal Santoniño Pigolino, an intimate of the liberation-theology-baiting Pope John John Paul I. There had been at least one assassination attempt.

Tonatiuh Galván was an unlikely candidate to cruise into this theological dispute. As the name his father had hung upon him suggested, the Doctor was hardly a devotee of the Christian faith. His grandfather had been crucified for being a Semite in gentile lands long ago. Tonatiuh's half-breed chromosomes tilted precipitously to the native side. He had come to understand Christianity as a two-pronged devil's pitchfork of genocide and conquest. In his view, the Virgin of Guadalupe was a ghastly trick played upon the Indígenas to steal their souls—souls that he knew to be still pure because, beneath every rite and saint and stone and superstition that the Catholic Church had foisted upon these supposed "mestizos," the Doctor's x-ray vision permitted him to cut to the ancient rituals of life-giving and taking that still vibrated in the subterranean chambers.

Whatever the candidate's religious convictions actually were, they were not Christian ones.

☆

ROUNDING A TREACHEROUS BEND in the bald foothills 30 kilometers below Guadalquiver on the first morning of Tonatiuh's swing through this inhospitable region, the Bishop nearly mowed down a group of schoolchildren who suddenly blossomed from a tangle of nettles on the shoulder of the road. The Doctor motioned his aide to brake.

Their rancho was far away—the teacher pointed west into the choking dust blowing off a shelf of saw-toothed hills far in the distance. They had trudged for half a day, she said in a trembly voice, just to catch a glimpse of the Man They Call the Hope. Virgen de las Moras was so poor, she apologized, that they did not even have paper confetti in the rancho store. Now the children flung handfuls of white rose petals instead. The storm of fluttering gossamer momentarily blotted out the blue stone sky, blurring and softening the glare. As the falling petals kissed the obdurate ground, they seemed to crystallize. Suddenly, the hardscrabble dirt was blanketed with what looked suspiciously like shimmering snowflakes.

"¡No puede hacer!"

"¡Qué pinche padre!"

"¡Qué hijo de la gran puta!"

Raus knew enough about the perverse nature of miracles not to believe his eyes. But he did, sort of.

To be sure, there were scoffers. The PRO weatherpeople denied the miraculous nature of the phenomenon, attributing the snowfall instead to a singular interaction of rare atmospheric pressures upon certain vegetable matter in an unusual state of decomposition, a one-time-only event.

Nevertheless, the snowflakes soon became generalized throughout Los Altos. It had never snowed up here in the memory of anyone's memory and now, in April, the kinkiest month, the feathery flakes were falling everywhere on everything.

By the time Tonatiuh's caravan left Guadalquiver, the snow had turned to a fine, clean rain. For ten years, the only article to have tumbled from the sky in this immutable landscape had been the useless stones that littered the tough, tilted terrain. Now rain was drilling down in slanted sheets, soil was softening, the moist, startled earth closing around seeds thrust into the ground with no hope at all. Little shoots were taking root and the humus was singing. Leathery campesinos dared to contemplate a real harvest. No corn had grown for a decade in the bone-dry Altos.

The miracles followed the Doctor into the hills like the fine rain. In Madre Madona Morena, the business end of a rainbow settled on the bandstand, bathing the candidate in a mosaic of light. In Santísima Purísima, where the proscribed sons of the proscribed Martires de Cristo Rey marched the Brown Madonna to the plaza, a boy child was born under the lopsided little stage. The 14-year-old mother claimed never to have had carnal knowledge of man or beast and the baby was christened Tonatiuh Jesus on the spot.

Crowds of true believers scuffled just to touch the hem of the Doctor's Italian suit, as if it was the Shroud of Turin. At every stop, dark women, hooded by dark rebozos, massed around the old converted combi the Doctor was now pushing to its death over the hump of the mountains, tossing real confetti, strewing flowers in his path, kissing his hand. The rallies were charismatic events, like revival meetings. Young liberation priests shepherded their flocks to the squares and some spoke in tongues. Tonatiuh reluctantly shared the platform with the Virgin of Guadalupe as the worshipers melodiously hummed their names. "Tohhhhnatiuhhh...Virgen Purísima..."

Inside the bosom of Holy Mother Church, the rebellious padres raged against Cardinal Pigolino with unChrist-like gusto. Their mission was "to accompany the poor" on their journey through this vale of tears, but all the fat cats of the hierarchy cared about were the profits. They demanded that Pigolino fork over the Church's vast wealth to succor the extremely poor. Unlike the gluttonous Cardinal, the young priests were uniformly gaunt and eager idealists, infested by the parasite of injustice.

Feeling keenly that the groaning of stomachs often drowned out the masses they celebrated, the priests had organized their own labor union and initiated a string of soup kitchens—Las Mesas de Don Samuel—named after the imprisoned Nobel Peace Prize-winning Bishop of San Cristóbal de las Casas. At each rally in Los Altos, the "pobres padres," as their order became known, raised funds for the soup kitchens, vending stamped tin images of the Brown Madonna inscribed with the legend "Tonatiuh Presidente."

The claims of purported miracles and the seditious activities of the under-class clergy on behalf of a candidate sworn to overthrow the PRO did not sit at all well in the various stomachs of the Capo di Tutti Capi.

Behind gilded screens in his discretely elegant offices under the Basílica down in the doomed capital, Cardinal Santoniño Pigolino cursed beneath his pungent breath as each report of

Tonatiuh's feats and the insolence of the liberationist clerics reached his meaty ears. He summoned his lackeys and blustered and farted and breathed sulfur and burning garlic upon them. Thank the good Christ that the possibility of Tonatiuh's victory was remote, he preached to the Bishops—the PRO administered the temporal world with a stern hand. But the deepening chasm between the Lords of the Church and its ill-paid, unionized clergy down on the ground was turning into a bothersome labor problem. As with everything that Tonatiuh touched, the Church seemed to divide between the high and the low, rich and poor, fat or thin, for or against.

"What is your pleasure, Monsignor?" the Bishop of Cuérvano finally managed to gather enough courage to ask. Pigolino had been ranting for hours now with no port in sight, alternately threatening to defrock every dickhead rebel priest in this infidel land and bring in Italian scabs, or plotting the castration of the Antichrist, Tonatiuh Galván, without anesthesia. Just 666 him and his goddamn miracles!

"Get me Gonzalo X. Davis," the fat man belched at his underlings. "We are going to nip this nasty business in the bud."

☙

AT THE TOP OF LOS ALTOS in San Pedrote de los Pedregales on the final evening up in these stark mountains, there were only more mountains stretching north, all the way to the mines at Jaquemate. The priest of this rocky perch, a wizened young padre known as Pascual El Pobrecito, had, five years before, vowed never to eat food again until all of his countrymen, women, and babies had enough food to eat. Now he lived on a thin gruel fashioned from turgid water and mountain fogs. To his followers, Pascual El Pobrecito had become a living saint.

"Our plate is full," gasped Padre Pobricito to the hovering reporters. "Our appetizer is the Poor. For the entrée, we have Jesus Christ. Tonatiuh is our postre." His saucer-sized eyes bulged with thankfulness as he offered Mickey and Malcreado a sip of his gruel.

The two reporters tiptoed out of the little churchyard where the emaciated priest—he now weighed no more than 70 pounds— was laid out in a litter, cheek by jowl with the tombstones. They pressed their mini-recorders to their ears to check the quality of the interview. But so weak was the timbre of the starving cleric's voice that when he gasped ecstatically about the fullness of his plate, his words did not even register on the tape.

"YOU'VE GONE DANGEROUSLY delusional on us, mate. You're living some bloody Gabriel García Márquez opus. Wake up and smell the napalm! The PRO's getting ready to carpetbomb your guy—and, soldier, you better find a foxhole."

Horace Pease was not pleased. Raus and the *Times* man were sampling the tamales at the Tacuba. "These are yesterday's oaxaqueños."

"I'm disappointed in you, Horace, really I am. Tonatiuh is history happening and where are you? I haven't seen you out there since Ciudad Real. Malcreado's saying that Barcelona's people put you on the payroll."

Pease was stung. He brandished his fork waspishly, thought better of it, dug it into a mess of oozing corn meal instead.

"Horace, I'm serious. The next week or so is going to have scratch. Pay attention to what happens next. See, the Bishop has Tonatiuh shadowing Filemón. They're at Jaquemate just a few days apart. It's the first back-to-back, get it? I'm heading north on the Midnight Plus."

Horace Pease was tippling straight from a tabletop carafe of Tacuba Red. "There's precious little percentage in chasing this suicidal charade, joven. You know how this bloody government rips the hearts out of messengers. It's an old Aztec communication strategy."

Raus winced. The foreign press corps didn't have a clue as usual about what was really happening out in the provinces. He knew what he had seen.

Or was it what he wanted to see?

"Still gaga over your sun god?" trilled Jane Ann Arbus cruelly as she drifted past their table in a backless frock that seemed to be fashioned out of tinted saran wrap, arm-in-arm with Big Sid Bloch, the 6-foot, 7-inch black CNN camera lug.

"Woof Woof," jammed El Sid, cupping his Shaquille-shaped hands to Jane Ann's basketball-plump rump.

Mickey's colleagues disappointed him mightily. He had played hunches since he'd first begun stringing from this godforsaken country. He'd come up with stories that Pease and Arbus and the others would never touch without first donning sterilized gloves. But the respect he earned for his efforts was as meager as the money. Too often his scoops had broken behind the Real Estate section in whatever bogus Advertiser he was offering his flesh to at the moment.

Tonatiuh Galván was just not a hunch, damnit. He was history happening.

The early polling, conducted by Disney-GallupMex (DGM), gave Barcelona a 7 to 1 edge over Tonatiuh—the diminutive ex-finance minister had a 5 to 1 lead over the disintegrating PIN Party candidate, the fascistoid Saddam Falanges de la Madrid, who had just suffered a "stroke." There were cynics in the press corps, such as Pease, who would wager $100 USD to your ten that Tonatiuh Galván wouldn't even finish the race in July. For once, Raus was determined to prove them dead wrong.

"I'll take your damn money. We're going to cream Barcelona."

"You're losing your objectivity, sonny."

The tamales had been reduced to stained husks. Pease had killed the carafe. There was little left to eat or drink or even say to each other. They shook hands out on Tacuba street.

"You worry me, Raus," Horace mumbled apologetically. "Excuse an old man his maudlin prose, but you're getting yourself into something the bottom of which you cannot see. There are crocodiles down there, Michael, they devour unwelcome guests. Always remember that you are an unwelcome guest here. They hate us, m'ijo. Never forget that."

Raus never forgot it.

Pease patted Mickey on the shoulder blade. The touch was

almost tender. "Yes, I feed off the PRO. I take their money and swallow their lies. But it's not so much the chayo as it is knowing how they can make their lies come true. They're not very life-oriented around there, you know."

Raus was weary of Pease's warnings. He had a midnight bus to catch north. He promised the *Times* man that they'd go out on the town when he got back in a few weeks. They'd shed "all their illusions," he quipped. It was a traditional joke between them. Raus backed off towards Artículo 33 Street.

It's better out on the road, Mickey decided, cutting across the dimly lit, deserted zócalo. By tomorrow night he would be in Jaquemate for the May Day march with the commies. There was talk that the fabled red-bearded leader of the miners, V. Dolores Leñero, was about to throw the weight of the working class behind Tonatiuh.

WORKERS ATTACK PRO CAMPAIGN— 7 MINERS MISSING

OPPOSITION CANDIDATE WINS MAY DAY SHOWDOWN
Special to the North Coast Variety News

MINAS DE JAQUEMATE, ZACATINCAS (May 1)—The tumultuous greeting extended opposition candidate Tonatiuh Galván today in this historic copper mining town 600 miles south of the Texas border is one more signal that the presidential election, now less than 70 days off, is turning into the first real horse race since 1988, when Carlos Salinas—now imprisoned in the U.S.—is believed to have stolen the vote count from the still-missing Cuauhtemoc Cardenas. The PRO has not lost a presidential election in the past 71 years.

Last Friday (April 29) angry miners here repeatedly interrupted a speech by PRO standard-bearer and former finance minister Filemón Barcelona, forcing the candidate to cut short his appearance. Miners, apparently infuriated by outgoing PRO President Arturo

Lomelí's decision to return this huge copper mine to the Anaconda Corporation after more than 90 years of bitter litigation, then broke out windows on Barcelona's campaign press bus and attempted to disable his private helicopter before the military presidential guard (Estado Mayor) and riot police drove them off. Seven miners are still officially listed as missing after being taken into custody by a new police agency whose agents are known here as secretos. Unconfirmed reports indicate the miners' bodies have been located in the desert east of Jaquemate.

Commie Sympathy

Today's welcome of Dr. Galván unfolded in a remarkably more distinct atmosphere than did Barcelona's. Longtime miners' leader, V. (for Vladimir) Dolores Leñero, known universally as "El Compa," began the day by leading 12,000 copper miners and their families out to the edge of this little city of 25,000 to greet the upstart candidate. Up until now, El Compa, who is also director of the nation's tiny but resurgent Revolutionary Communist Party (PCR), has been reluctant to extend his support to Dr. Galván's effort which, he charges, is tainted by alleged ties to the PRO. Dr. Galván's candidacy has been registered by a minor party known to receive subsidies from the ruling PRO.

"We have invited the General's son to Jaquemate to celebrate the International Day of the Worker with us," was as much as the ruddy, red-bearded labor leader would say when interviewed during a wreath-laying at the "One Hundred Martyrs of Jaquemate" memorial monument outside the heavily guarded gates of the mine. A source close to the Galván campaign tells the *Variety News* that Leñero's endorsement has already been made.

May Day!

The "General" referred to by Leñero is, of course, the candidate's father, General Francisco Galván, the much-respected president of the nation in the 1930s. One of the General's first acts in office was to expropriate the Jaquemate, then the fourth most productive copper mine in the world, from the Anaconda Corporation. Anaconda had been granted the concession from the Diaz dictatorship in the last century.

The Jaquemate is arguably the national labor movement's most hallowed shrine. The lengthy struggle to organize this country's workers was born here May 1, 1906, after federal troops—abetted by the

Arizona Rangers—massacred 100 miners during a May Day strike, said to have been organized by the anarchist Industrial Workers of the World (the IWW or "Wobblies"). The One Hundred Martyrs of Jaquemate, now immortalized in one hundred corridos or traditional northern border ballads, are a mandatory theme for leather-lunged orators each May 1, International Workers Day in much of the world— although the U.S., where the first May Day was celebrated on the streets of Chicago in 1886, continues to honor labor in September.

Miners Checkmated

The re-sale of the gigantic mining complex to the Anaconda Corporation (now a subsidiary of GE-DisneyMex) has generated months of intense protest by the miners, who formerly held the Jaquemate in partnership with the government. Although no details of the sale have ever been released, the mine has apparently been "swapped" for a piece of the nation's $250 billion foreign debt.

Last year President Arturo Lomelí sent 5,000 troops into the mine to take back the huge complex—which includes both open pit and underground operations—from workers who had barricaded themselves inside. After sitting dormant for the past six months due to alleged sabotage to the Jaquemate's great blast furnaces, Anaconda-GE-DisneyMex is once again digging and smelting ore—with an almost entirely new work force. The Lomelí government's ruling that contracts with Leñero's union were no longer valid under the new ownership agreement was clearly on the mind of the miners when they assaulted his probable successor last week.

Masculine Pluck

Although the PRO has vehemently condemned the unexpected attack on its candidate as "a violation of free speech," Leñero defended the miners' right to protect their jobs. "Jaquemate belongs to its miners. The PRO government sold us out like we were so much dog meat, and then they have the huevos to send Barcelona in here to ask for our votes? What pendejos!" The labor militant gruffly told a U.S. reporter, "We showed those sons of the great whore who the real huevones are here!"

"Huevos"—literally "eggs"—is a Mexican expression for masculine pluck.

[OPTIONAL CUT]
Too Many Martyrs

"Ever since the General left the presidency, the PRO government has been trying to give the Jacquemate back to the copper bosses," added a hard-hatted miner who identified himself only as Jose Cerro, as he stood shoulder to shoulder with El Compa along the first base line of the One Hundred Martyrs of Jacquemate baseball stadium. Dr. Galván later electrified the May Day throng with the still-unconfirmed report of the discovery of the missing miners' bodies.

Angrily accusing the PRO of the alleged murders, Galván told the stadium crowd that "we have too many martyrs as it is" and demanded "an end to the death the PRO brings us and a beginning of the culture of life." All over the country, recounted the Doctor, he has seen how furious people are at the ruling party. "It is time we came out of our houses and demonstrate to this tyranny that has controlled our political life for a century just how angry we are," the candidate urged his followers, many of whom held signs reading "Death to the PRO." Other supporters clutched little flags upon which were inked crimson and emerald suns—Tonatiuh's suns—as the emblem has come to be called.

Who Owns the Jacquemate?

With respect to who exactly owns the Jacquemate mining complex, Galván recalled that "you the miners took this mine—my father only signed the expropriation order" and encouraged union members "to move intelligently to recover your patrimony, which is more than just a great mine, it's a great chapter in our history, too." Later he warned the workers and their families that "what Lomeli and Barcelona are up to is not the final chapter of the Jacquemate—you will write that." If elected president, he promised, he would re-expropriate the mine from Anaconda-Disney just as his father did 65 years ago. "The revolution demands it," Galván insisted. The rescue of the revolution and the nation's indigenous traditions are often central themes of the Doctor's speeches.

PRO's Perplexed

For the past week, the opposition candidate has been directing his attentions to the mineral-rich north of the country, often following Barcelona's campaign in the region from stop to stop and inviting supporters to compare the two candidates' respective defenses of the Patria's nonagenarian revolution. According to Abelardo Salmón, Dr. Galván's electoral coordinator, the strategy has proven successful. "Before we came up here, we weren't sure what kind of reception awaited us, but just look at the size and enthusiasm of the crowds.

These are the same people who ran Barcelona out of Jacquemate last week." Salmón asserts that Galván has a real chance of beating Barcelona July 2. "The PRO knows this and they've got to be worried."

Labor Rebellion

In addition to opening up new territories and constituencies on his trips through the countryside, Galván has apparently ignited the beginnings of a labor rebellion against the PRO candidate. Although most unions still make PRO membership mandatory, rank and file rumblings have grown progressively louder as presidential elections approach and the economy—wracked by six years of steep recession, stagflation, collapsing emerging markets, and plunging oil prices—continues to flounder.

Yesterday, while Galván was celebrating a militant May 1 with the miners of Jacquemate, 300 miles east, in the industrial center of Regiomonte, railroad workers threw fruit and railroad ties and disrupted still another Barcelona campaign appearance, the fourth this week. The rally in Regiomonte's Macro Plaza had to be called off when police uncorked so much tear gas that visibility was reduced to zero.

THE WINDOWLESS MONOLITH out on Generalísimo Avenida loomed above the capital's midnight skyline like an enormous obsidian tombstone. The party stronghold was locked down as tight as a maximum security prison, the bleakness of its black facade broken only by a pulsating band of light that encircled the fenced roof garden, endlessly blipping P-R-O-P-R-O-P-R-O-P-R-O-P-R-O-P-R-O-P-R-O-P-R-O-P-R-O…

Down at street level, tight-mouthed secretos manned the video-monitored fence. Sleek limousines and Gran Marquises sped into the complex, discharging their occupants at the VIP turn-around into the arms of muscular security teams. The members of the central committee and their personal retinues were then whisked off to subterranean levels by a third line of security. So many agents were attached to each personage that they could not all fit into one down elevator. There were ugly shoving matches.

Wedged into a dry crevice directly across the broad avenue, El Torso checked off two lists. One enumerated the receipt numbers for the 104 lottery tickets he had hawked from his roller that day. The other list was much shorter and contained the names of the men who ran the PRO as, one by one, they assembled for the hastily called junta.

𒀭

SEVEN OUT OF TEN central committee members were gathered in the Persian-carpeted underground war room when, just after midnight, President Lomelí and his protégé Barcelona were ushered into the soundproof bunker. They had been driven over by electric jitney through the underground tunnels that snaked beneath Chapulín Park, connecting Los Primos to the PRO World Headquarters. There was light applause. "Gentlemen, please remain seated."

There were no women present.

A somber Secretary of Internal Security, Gonzalo X. Davis, summoned the session to order: "Compañeros, I'm not here to hash over bad news but we need to be frank. You all know why you've been asked here tonight."

The backslapping and deep coughing subsided. Momentarily, at least, Davis had the committee members' attention.

"I'm not revealing any state secrets when I confess we are a little perplexed by the Galván problem." He stressed the word "problem." Previously, the opposition candidate and his campaign had always been referred to as "this Galván thing," like the Doctor was some nasty woodtick that could be squashed with a swipe of its paw by the Big Dog Party. The elevation of Tonatiuh Galván to the dimension of a "problem" provoked serious hrrmmmphing on the left side of the table where the Popular Sectors were installed. In the rarefied air of the inner sanctum, every syllable was charged with political nuance.

Gonzalo X. Davis, a pale, aristocratic man in a silk suit, exhaled perfect, fragrant smoke rings fashioned from the clove-scented cigarette that he was always puffing. "Please, gentlemen, may I continue?" Davis fish-eyed his hrrmmmphing comrades through rimless glasses. Of all the silk suits in the room, Davis's fit the best.

Sometimes it seemed like the 20-foot long, two-ton inlaid teak conference table, around which the party Iluminati now huddled, was sustained, not by its stout legs, but by the complex, occasionally shifting balance between the crusty old hard-line "Bronto" members of the PRO Central Committee and the younger, preppier "Tecos."

The leaders of the Popular Sectors were planted immediately upon Gonzalo X. Davis' left, a row of withering old stalks and decomposing stumps. Paco Vallarta, the centenarian labor czar, bounced excitedly six inches from the Internal Security Minister's crisp white sleeve, drooling and gurgling as if he thought he had been invited to a cock fight at a neighborhood palenque. Advanced age had so shrunk Vallarta's body below the neck that now he was little more than a melon-sized head atop a doll-like body, a dead ringer for a ventriloquist's dummy, except that dummies are usually dependent on their operators for animation. Paco Vallarta's animation depended on the multiple tubes plunged into his veins and excretory orifices, and plugged on the other end to an impressive bank of medical hardware whose gauges oscillated about as much as they would measuring the brain wave of a pancake.

Despite his embalmed condition, Paco Vallarta's in-person appearance tonight was evidence of the importance he attached to the junta. Usually, the labor czar was content to communicate corrosive testiness from the comfort of his palatial Valle de los Ilustres finca through closed-circuit TV chip implants. But the rank-and-file rabble that had thumbed its nose at young Filemón Barcelona up north last week compelled his attendance.

Seated next to the vegetative union honcho was Bernabé Warmán Warmán, the mummified "cacique of all caciques" and supreme commander of the nation's campesinos. No one knew how old the campesino leader really was, but his complexion had become so webbed with crow's feet and weather lines that he now resembled a crumbling Mayan jade mask that had been spatulaed back together, shard by shard, by careful archeologists.

Despite this seeming frailty, Warmán Warmán commandeered a much-feared mafia of bloodthirsty caciques—rural political bosses with their own private "White Guard" armies, who faithfully delivered up 90% of their districts each election day in return for an unencumbered hand in enslaving and killing their Indians and moving the drugs they trans-shipped for the cartels up the NAAFTA pipeline. Don Bernabé was owed many favors that could never be refused. "You like it? You like it? I'm giving it to you," he bragged to Don Sancho de la Mancha before the meeting, stripping off an elegant leather jacket. "It's yours—I got it from Sly Stallone himself. It's black rhino. But it will cost you…"

Warmán Warmán and Paco Vallarta were the godfathers of the Brontos, dangerous retrograde dinosaurs who wouldn't die no matter what monstrous disabilities were inflicted upon them. Like the extinct large-bodied lizards for which they were labeled, the Brontos mobilized the great weight of their organisms to sit on the opposition. Aside from the traitor Tonatiuh, the Brontos' pet hate were the spineless Teco faggots who sat owlishly across the heavy teak table from them.

Sancho de la Mancha was the backbone of the Bronto operation. A compact man who affected weird pinhole sunglasses and translucent guayaberas—under which inevitably bloomed a blue-steel .357 Magnum—de la Mancha was the "Leader for Life" of the Organic Party's third sector, the "Orgánicos"—the nation's large lumpen population who had little else to sell other than their shifting loyalties: squatters from the lost cities, spoiled-meat taco vendors, scab garbage pickers, low-life rateros, cartaristas, pistoleros, ex-judiciales, crooked beat cops, suplones, madrinas, sadistic narcos who would stick their mamas between the ribs for a fix. Salvador de la Mancha did the PRO's dirty work, commanding a criminal army of "electoral auxiliaries," buying and selling voters and disappearing the opposition, with little compassion for their many families. Legend has it that Sancho once buried his own brother—a homosexual hairdresser who voted for Cárdenas in 1988—alive under a hill of fire ants, in his native Chiapas.

"I don't have to detail last week's debacle for you, gentlemen. The reasons are apparent enough: the exigencies of the 'Permanent Crisis' have forced our people to make sacrifice after sacrifice that have not always been patriotically absorbed in some sectors." Gonzalo X. Davis' perfect smoke rings looped the left side of the table. "Red scoundrels have agitated these workers for years and we have been tolerant. Now Tonatiuh Galván is further irritating this wound. First, gentlemen, let me say that I appreciate your forceful suggestions as to how to resolve this special problem, but let us understand that Don Tadeo is watching this situation closely. The White House continues to have this absurd gringo concern for democratic appearances."

Apprehension was already furrowing de la Mancha's thick brow.

"The upshot is that, like it or not, we have to forge some sort of mutually beneficial arrangement with this traitor Galván."

"He can be bought! It's no problem, buster. He can be bought! He can be bought with plata! Or he can be bought with plomo," de la Mancha rose on squat legs and bellowed petulantly. The Leader for Life's pinhole gaze swiveled the table, menacing with mayhem any maricón Teco who dared to differ. A small tense silence ensued in which the whirring of Paco Vallarta's life-support machines became the only sound in the bunker.

"Precisely how much do you calculate it would take to purchase Doctor Galván's acquiescence, Don Sancho?" interjected Victor Manuel Rodríguez Lefkowitz icily. Don Victorito was the chairman of the board of the PRO and interim director of the national bank. The youthful, curly-headed "Israelite"—a fifth generation banker-industrialist whose immense family fortune had been accumulated through a panoply of usuries, and been salted away in Swiss bank accounts long before the Revolution scourged the monied classes—was the chief architect of the "técnico" or "teco" wing. The Lefkowitz dynasty had survived dictators, populists, and 71 years of PRO cowflap, accommodating itself admirably to the re-arrangements necessitated by the Amended North American Free Trade Agreement and the globalization of practically everything.

"Don Sancho, do you have a dollar amount to share with us?" Lefkowitz hammered. De la Mancha, who was still shouting obstreperously, offered no hard figures. Bernabé Warmán Warmán had begun to pound the table in rhythm with his crony's curses. Though it was barely underway, the session was threatening to escape Davis' control.

"Compañeros, we are making a grave mistake." The rich baritone of General Gertrudis Niños de Galván (Totonaco) humored his colleagues into lowering their decibel levels. "I think I know Tonatiuh a bit better than any of you. If you recall, we were raised together. It is a serious miscalculation to think buying him is a do-able option. Tonatiuh Galván is a stubborn, pig-headed fool. He cannot be bought with money. I seriously doubt that he can be bought with anything."

Despite his feminine name, Gertrudis Niños de Galván (Totonaco) was 100-proof macho warrior. A tall, tight-skinned man, aviator glasses tilted to his tousled, jet-black locks, General Gertrudis always appeared to have just gotten in from maneuvers, his boots and jodphurs artfully flecked with mud. A passionate defender of the Revolution, whose day-by-day chronicle he had learned at the knee of his adopted father, Lomelí's defense minister had been responsible for many atrocities, particularly in El Horno and Chiapas. Whole villages had been exterminated "in defense of the Revolution."

Gertrudis straddled a tightrope between the two PRO camps, equally disdaining Brontos and Tecos. These payasos didn't have a clue. "Tonatiuh Galván answers to a higher power. It is not, I repeat, in his stubborn spirit to deal with us on the worldly terms Don Sancho has proposed."

"From our way of seeing it, there are multiple options." Gonzalo X. Davis seemed to imply that "our" way was that of the President, his hand-picked successor Barcelona, the banker Rodríguez Lefkowitz, and himself. The bloodless Minister of Internal Security began distributing closely typed sheets to his right and left. "We have never spoken exclusively of financial remuneration. In point of fact, we've taken the liberty to prepare a list of these options for each of you to review. You will note the terms of the offer sheet. The PRO is prepared to reduce its traditional margin of victory to 60.1% of the national vote. The remaining votes will be awarded to Galván and the PIN and the satellite parties. Galván and the PIN can squabble over second-party status in the congress. We will allow the opposition a total of 245 seats in the Chamber, 46 in the Senate." Such a split would give the PRO a razor-thin ten-vote majority in the lower house, but a 3-1 advantage in the senior chamber.

An audible string of epithets arose from the Popular Sectors. Their leaders noisily crumpled the proposal into golf-ball-sized wads.

"This is a charitable and democratic gesture," bolstered the foreign minister, Antonio Lomeli Cano, the President's nephew who six months before had replaced Reggio Ahumada Tamal in this position. "I believe it will play very well with Don Tadeo and the NGO community."

Don Tadeo was Thaddeus Appleton Blackbridge, Washington's ambassador to PRO-landia. The Non-Governmental Organizations were a perpetual pain in the butt. At the far end of the table, President Lomelí sat quietly, playing with his tie. He had not uttered one word since Davis had called the meeting to "order."

"¡Blxfuccbapaaboobinchaghhh!" De la Mancha was back on his stubby feet, his mouth opening and closing around apoplectic curse words, but only an unintelligible gargle spasmed forth from his throat. "You pansy bastards! We're not giving up our fooking seats!" De la Mancha's brain and vocal chords were back in sync. "¡Nunca! ¡Nunca! Do you cocksuckers hear me? ¡Nunca!"

Davis nodded condescendingly at the poor man. "And not only that, Don Sancho, you should know that we are prepared to concede Malinchico, Chiapas, and possibly El Horno to buy some peace and quiet from Galván." Davis and the elder Lomeli exchanged meaningful glances as if the latter state was negotiable. "It is our understanding that this demonstration of how our guided democracy can adapt to the new pluralism will win sympathy in Washington. We have the new North American Economic Annexation and Trade Accord (NEATA) to consider,

Don Sancho, the Double Debt Discount. The DDD will bring in fresh loans. Fresh loans mean increased cash flow to the Popular Sectors, Don Sancho. This is the best deal for you and your esteemed associates."

De la Mancha had not listened to a word since his congressional delegation had been put on the block. "No fooking way! No fooking way!" he hollered over and over again, his palms flailing at the inlaid conference table like a crazed bongo player. The soundproof room once again boiled over with venomous recriminations.

"I don't really understand. Why are they so upset? If I can live with it, why can't they? After all, Tonatiuh is the General's only real son, isn't he?" Filemón Barcelona innocently burbled at the deep end of the table. The Candidate was immediately silenced by a swift, hard kick from his predecessor beneath the expensive teak.

"Yah, let's see how long you can live with it..."

"I don't give a fook whose fooking son he is..."

"Yah, what does that have to do with it, you asshole..."

"Shaddup! Shhh, Paco's trying to tell us something..."

The rancorous sector leaders hushed their hated Teco rivals into respectful silence. A white uniformed attendant stepped forward to wipe the spittle from the melonhead's cracked lips. Vallarta's voice was so tiny that his colleagues had to cup their hands to their ears and strain forward to audit his golden words of wisdom.

"What'ssss....the...problem...com-pañ-er-ossss," the Czar leaked sibilantly like some gangrenous gas was escaping. "Jussst...burn him like we did Colosssssssio..."

"¡Que Viva! ¡Que Viva Paco Vallarta!" whooped Bernabé Warmán Warmán, turning his thumbs downwards like a mafia capo ordering a significant execution. "¡Que Viva!" his Bronto comrades cheered. "¡Que Viva!" Guttural hullabaloo filled up the underground room once again. Sitting just out of harm's way, President Lomelí whispered into Filemón Barcelona's teacup-sized ear, "Just think, all of this will soon be yours." More than a trace of irony dusted his nondescript lips.

"OK OK OK OK OK OK OK OK." Now it was Rodríguez Lefkowitz's moment to shout his colleagues down. "OK OK OK OK OK OK OK OK OK," he kept repeating in English until he had commanded enough attention to proceed. "OK, I see a series of options here. Options. The key word is options, OK? OK.

"One. We offer Galván cash. Two. He does or does not accept it. Three. We offer him votes. Four. He does or does not go for it. Five. We offer him a cabinet spot. We poison him with a taste of power. Heh heh heh." The Chairman hacked with deep satisfaction and continued with his not-so-clever delineation of the options. "Six. We offer him dum-dum bullets..."

"Not one of these stupid options is going to bring Tonatiuh Galván to this table," snapped General Gertrudis Niños de Galván (Totonaco), furious at the Israelita's smugness. "Tonatiuh Galván is General Francisco Galván's only true son. The General still talks to him every night down there on Carlos Quinto Street. If you want to get to Tonatiuh Galván, you'll have to get to the General first. And he's been dead for nearly 20 years now."

Gonzalo X. Davis blew still another pungent smoke ring, thoughtfully considering this new information.

De la Mancha had heard enough. "Fook this bullshit. I'm supposed to be in Vegas in the morning for the Tyson-Stallone fight. I got no time for you Teco maricones. Who's going to lean on this asshole?" The Leader for Life could not bring himself to fit his teeth around Tonatiuh's name.

"I can open channels with Doctor Galván tomorrow morning." The Minister of Internal Security sucked up a lungful of clove-scented smoke. "If that doesn't produce the desired results, then perhaps Gertrudis here can convince his stubborn sibling and long-dead father of the good sense in our proposals."

WHEN THE CALL that he'd been waiting for all morning finally came in, Reggio Ahumada Tamal's cramped Barrio Chino waiting room was jammed to the transoms with petitioners: damnificados who, a decade and a half after the cataclysmic earthquake, still did not have a roof over their heads; ambulantes, fuming at city inspectors for extorting five-figure permisos that allowed them to sell hairpins in the street; palm readers caught red-handed telling lies to undercover cops; lottery runners and bootblacks; door-openers and fixers; would-be bodyguards; and the usual wrestlers. All were shoehorned into the waiting room, leaving little space even to exhale.

A delegation of Zipotec Indians from some remote colony in the south of the megalopolis stopped frozen-footed on the threshold, like deer caught in the glare of RAT's bifocals. Two of the wrestlers, one of them a midget in a pull-over ski mask embroidered with little daggers and roses, pressed up against the desk to complain about a purse the Coliseum refused to fork over because management alleged the legal minimum requirement of blood had not been spilled.

"Compañeros, I need some breathing room," the portly político supplicated amiably as he breast-stroked the public toward the hallway. "Give me just ten minutes of peace and quiet and I promise to open up shop again." RAT quickly shut the frosted glass door behind him. The two wrestlers posted themselves just outside, like Mutt & Jeff sentinels.

The phone light was still flashing. He had a good idea why they were being so persistent.

"Dígame."

"Licenciado, El Licenciado needs to see you tonight," the Voice coolly enunciated.

"Look, Voz, you can tell El Licenciado that I have two meetings tonight—one all the way out in Coatlicue."

"Come by after you're done out there. He'll make time for you late. And please, Licenciado, come alone." RAT had a habit of showing up at these secret soirées in the company of certain members of the Capital's wrestling fraternity, notably the much-loved "Prince of the Streets," SuperPendejo López, and his team of masked "rudos."

"I'll do what I can," Ahumada Tamal growled, slamming down the phone in irritation at the Voz's frigid unction. Then, reflexively, he fished the receiver from the cradle and put it to his ear to make sure the damn thing was still functioning. It did not pay to smash up your own phone when it took a 5,000 peso note just to lure a PROTEL repairman onto the premises.

The phone was still working. RAT knew this because he could hear the pájaros in the Chinatown basement eavesdropping. A series of heavy clicks, punctuated by light breathing, then a segment of playback squealed into his tympanum. "Tweet Tweet, you scumbags!" RAT snarled into the mouthpiece, loud enough to dislocate the bugger's own eardrum and re-slam-dunked the receiver to the cradle as viciously as before.

Reggio Ahumada Tamal, a devious politician with an angel face whose checkered career was once again on the rebound, felt flattered that the PRO government was still bugging his phone.

RAT knew just what Gonzalo X. Davis wanted. He'd been expecting the Interior Minister to call since Jaquemate. Should he try and reach Tonatiuh—where was he today?—Regiomonte. No, there would be time enough to discuss the offer later. What was important was to hear X. Davis out, to understand what they were angling for, what the first offer weighed in at.

The masked midget perched upon his partner's burly shoulders and yelled through the transom. "Jefe, I bet it's your mamá on line two." The ghostly shapes of the petitioners were pressed up against frosted glass.

The light danced on the phone board. "Hola, Mamá—¡Qué milagro!"

REGGIO AHUMADA TAMAL'S curriculum vitae was listed in *Who's Who in Mexico and Central America*. This was not enough of the world for him. Ten years ago, during the dog days of "Perro" Portillo's regime, he had served briefly as Secretary of Gobernación, Gonzalo X. Davis's current sinecure. As president of the PRO from 1984-1985, he guided the Party of the Organic Revolution through the dank tunnel of debt crisis as if it were the best of times. In the early years of Salinas's aberrant reign, RAT bounced back from career hiatus to be appointed first ambassador to Denmark and then Fiji, far-off posts that kept him out of domestic mischief for several seasons.

To the bewilderment of many PRO watchers, when Lomeli took high office following poor Ernesto Zedillo's "suicide," RAT was appointed foreign minister. There was even mention of a presidential candidacy. But Lomeli inherently distrusted RAT, whose files were said to contain kinky bondage photos that compromised many of the PRO's elite, possibly including the president. When word reached Lomelí that Ahumada Tamal was meeting with Galván, he cut his losses and replaced him with his young Teco nephew, Antonio. Reggio Ahumada Tamal, who had snuck into the Lomeli cabinet as a dark-horse candidate for the dedazo, found himself being pointed to the door.

RAT's aristocratic bloodlines were nettled by this ignominy. His grandfather, Julio Augusto Ahumada had served General Galván as his foreign minister. His father, the late Senator Augusto Julio Ahumada, had himself once been presidential timber. Reggio had been groomed from birth by his doting mother for the dedazo.

Reggio Ahumada Tamal was, of course, the son of María Cristina Terrazas Tamal Menchú, viuda de Ahumada, the long-lived film queen. Once a teen-age temptress, la India Cristina had scandalized the nation when she openly became the widower General Galván's young mistress. Still said to retain a dark and sensual beauty at the age of 91, la India was now the nation's most ardent collector of artifacts from its pre-colombian past. Lately, she had become a spokesperson for revivalist Indians, loosely banded together by the prediction that the election of Tonatiuh Galván was the harbinger of the Coming of the Sixth Sun, a world in which the Indígenas would once again rule the land.

Despite his high-born ancestry, Reggio Ahumada Tamal fancied himself a man of the people and a leader of oppressed masses. The vehicle to which he'd hitched his star was none other than the legendary SuperPendejo López, whose super-hero exploits on behalf of the urban under-class had achieved Disney-Mex HBO status. A paunchy, old-quarter ambulante who sold candy bars outside the coliseum when discovered by RAT, SuperPendejo had metamorphosed into a slim, trim, acrobatic Apostle of the Raza.

Summoned by cohetazos to the popular neighborhoods, SuperPendejo rappelled free-fall from tall buildings to stop evictions in progress. Then, having run off the cops, he would organize the tenants to get the furniture off the street and back into the building before police re-enforcements arrived. RAT would appear on the ground, often accompanied by the press, to put just the right spin on the rescue. Together, the two packed a Batman & Robin wallop that had been instrumental in building RAT's urban constituency. Now, that constituency was being offered to Tonatiuh Galván. The price had not yet been established.

ﱡ

REGGIO AHUMADA TAMAL settled himself into the smooth sea-turtle leather lounger and tilted back easily. Once, he had commanded this same great chair, dealing nose-to-nose with his adversaries in this luxurious old palace just a few blocks west of his current cramped cubicles. Such moments of supreme power had forever permitted RAT a certain contempt for his fellow man. He understood this contempt to be the real reward of high office.

Rain was sweeping the city for the first time in months and Gonzalo X. Davis had ordered a fire set on the enormous hearth of the old marble building. Fragrant pitch pine crackled on the bubbling logs. RAT rolled a snifter of Fundador between his palms and considered that fortunes, like those inside the cookies at Mah Gong's downstairs from his shabby Chinatown offices, could change swiftly in this magic country.

The beady eyes of what appeared to be African okapis peered down from the mahogany walls. The President had personally shot a pair while on safari in the Saranghetti last spring, Gonzalo X. Davis informed RAT by way of small talk. Despite the coziness of his inner sanctum, X. Davis' tone was as glacial as ever.

"I believe it is primary to both of our fortunes that our

revolution survive the new millennium." The Secretary was tête-à-tête-ing at very close quarters—RAT could taste his clove-scented breath upon his own. He prayed X. Davis would not put his cold hand around his knee, a ploy for which the Secretary was noted.

"Licenciado, it is no news that the revolution continues to suffer Imperialist aggressions. Confidentially, we have come to agree with your friend's analysis about the NAAFTA. The Transnationals have twisted Gingrich against us, and the Gringo Banks are intent on bleeding us dry. The War On Drugs & Criminal Alien Act ("WODCA") unleashes lynch-mob law against our less fortunate compatriots. The racist Yanquis have imposed upon us a Permanent Crisis that perverts every moment of national life."

RAT lapped at his snifter and wondered where this conversation was heading.

"My government is resolved to resist the North American aggression in accordance with our most cherished national strategies. First, we shall smile them in the eye. Then we shall spit in their cocktails.

"Meanwhile, the Vertical Modernization of our economic development and the Guided Democracy of our civic life, as initiated by my party—which, I must remind you, Licenciado, used to be your party, too—will ensure that Our Revolution survives in the twenty-first century."

Zzzz. His guest was on the brink of nodding off.

"We are not going to let anything or anyone interfere with our plans."

Then X. Davis did clamp his icy hand around Ahumada Tamal's English-drape knee. RAT tensed.

"Sí, but of course, Licenciado, I remember now: the future is ours if only we can just put aside our petty differences for the good of the Patria." A devilish spit curl bounced on Ahumada's cherubic brow. He wished X. Davis would just cut to the price tag. The damned Zipotecs had called a pre-dawn march on the stock exchange.

"I'll be frank, Licenciado, your cuate Tonatiuh is stirring up expectations. We admire his pluck and we are prepared to reward it with, let's say, a third of the popular vote and perhaps a third of the congress, give or take a few seats. I should tell you that there is some thought of your Chairmanship of the Autonomous Electoral Center of the Republic (CAER). Then there is Malinchico. As you know only too well, the Left has not won a provincial election in a long time..."

"You are offering us Malinchico, Licenciado?" Ahumada Tamal was incredulous. "Muchísimas gracias, se lo agradezco, Don Gonzalo, but we are going to win Malinchico just as we are going to win this city."

"No, you will not win this city and, as for Malinchico, you have not won it, but we are perhaps going to let you win it," corrected the Internal Security Minister, infuriated by RAT's presumptions. "What we are telling you is that Doctor Galván has to lower his sights considerably. Naturally, we will lower ours in similar proportion. We welcome the new plurality. Power can be shared amicably. We must agree to do so for the survival of the Revolution."

Only then did Gonzalo X. Davis release his bloodless hand from RAT's knee. Settling back upon his own sea-turtle leather lounger, he blew a perfect smoke ring in his colleague's direction.

"Is that it?" asked RAT peevishly. He produced a foot-long Havana cigar that he promptly clamped between his feral teeth and fired up, exhaling a luxuriant stream in retaliation for the cool blast of the Secretary's own smoke. X. Davis nodded and puffed. The two sat there smoking at each other, the polished room slowly filling up with their fumes and those of the ancient fireplace which, in truth, had not been lit for years.

At length, RAT crushed out his stogie in a virgin ashtray stand and slipped on his trench coat. "We'll be back to you, Licenciado."

Gonzalo X. Davis lightly took his arm and escorted the guest to the night gate of the sprawling palace. "We'll be expecting to hear from you on this sooner than later, Licenciado." The Secretary smiled a thin reptilian smile. RAT passed through the gilded, wrought-iron gate into the shadows of the city.

The night was blustery and moonless. Remnants of the evening rain dripped from chipped cornices and ripped awnings. Pools of filthy, fluorescent water stippled the slippery streets. Ten blocks north, at the corner of Avenida Generalísimo and Plutarco Elías Calles, Reggio Ahumada Tamal paused under the all-night flashing lights that never spelled anything but P-R-O-P-R-O-P-R-O-P-R-O-P-R-O-P-R-O, and fished a few crumpled bills from his pocket. Then he dashed across the vacant, sinister boulevard and stuffed them under the greasy slab of cardboard in the crevice where El Torso guarded his nights.

WHILE FAR AWAY in the capital of the country, the PRO capos were formulating offer sheets they hinted would not be in Dr. Tonatiuh Galván's interest to reject, the object of their consternation barnstormed obliviously, rolling through the western Sierra Madre in a scarred Ram Charger bought off a narco-run used car lot after the Doctor's third-hand VW combi had blown its transmission in the baddest part of the Chichimeca badlands.

Don Estalin was now hauling the press around in a converted Cadillac hearse. Two carloads of cops completed the cavalcade. The RayBanned secretos had been tailing Tonatiuh for so long now that the two camps addressed each other with the personal "tu."

The caravan descended on arid, pitted Durazno, the fossil-filled dry lake beds of Laguna, mounted the cordillera of Zacatincas, skirted Los Altos, dropped back into the bustling little factory towns of Aguahedionde, cruised the greening plains of Quetzaltero, finally backtracking through the bursting market places of Plan de Abajo. The fine sweet rain followed Tonatiuh everywhere, sometimes an hour behind, sometimes a day. It was expected of him now to bring the rain and the townspeople laid out large concentric circles of pastel-hued plastic buckets wherever he walked, to catch the precious liquid. Out in the muddy fields, just beyond the villages, the thirsty milpas drank the moisture in greedily and, by the end of May, the corn was knee-high wherever Tonatiuh had touched down.

The little miracles continued to drip from the Doctor's cornucopia. So many babies were born under the platforms upon which he spoke that a whole generation of infant "Tonatiuhs" were suddenly a-howl in the land. The following January, the little "Tonatiuhitos" would be joined by countless baby brothers and sisters, each of them to be christened "Tonatiuh" and "Tonatiuha," all of them conceived during this fruitful season of the candidate's miracle campaign.

Besides the rain and the corn and the babies that fell in his trail, the Doctor added faith-healing to his repertoire. Always the conscientious physician, Tonatiuh could never pass up a treatable disease when he saw one, and there were many among the constituents who pushed in around him. Sometimes, the candidate did not even have to dig in his doctor's bag to treat. The faith of the afflicted was such that just the touch of the Doctor's long brown fingers was quite enough to cure. The bent straightened right up, the mute sang out, the purportedly blind claimed they could really see.

Raus saw all this with his own eyes, and believed.

At each step in the 15 stops he still made each day, Tonatiuh Galván testified to greater miracles to follow—of winning the election and of forcing the PRO from power and healing the soul of the nation. Every foot of the way was now lined with well-wishers as the Doctor retraced the route he had taken in April, the crowds growing from town to town, moving in around Tonatiuh, pressing up against the candidate so that they might protect him, when, at last, the gunfire broke out.

One softly raining afternoon, the four-car caravan winding its way back towards Ciudad Tacumán through proscribed cornfields, the Bishop anxiously chewing up one Delicado after the next because the Doctor was already three hours late, Raus sat with Tonatiuh in the front seat of the battered Charger and asked how he felt with the people drawing in so close around him.

Tonatiuh was acutely aware of the change. "They're my only protection." His dark, focused eyes were actually smiling.

"You never consider the dangers?" Since Colosio, all the candidates wore bullet-proof vests and were blanketed by bodyguards.

"Yes, but the General would never allow such things," laughed the candidate. "You see, when I was small, I used to take trips with my father. The trips were not unlike these trips. We went to give out land or inaugurate a dam or a new school— long, long trips through many regions of the country for months on end. The General did not like to be confined to the capital. On these trips, the General would never bring with him the military or any sort of guarura at all because he thought it kept him from the touch of the people—and without that touch he did not have the power to be president."

"Doctor, I thought this was your own campaign?"

Tonatiuh's usually anchored eyes were adrift in childhood memories. "Sometimes, friends would accompany us on these trips, and perhaps, you know, they would bring a weapon, innocently thinking, well, if anything happens, I'll be prepared to save the General's life. But no matter how well they were concealed, my father somehow always knew about the weapons. When the time was right, he would ask his friends to take off their guns and give them over to the campesinos.

"You know, I took a lot of trips with the General and I could never figure out, how did he know about those guns?"

꙰

LOS HUSTLERS, exuberant young men who now trailed the police tailing Tonatiuh, set up at every rally, hawking tee-shirts and the pobres padres's Virgins and cassettes of the new corrido breaking across the nation—"The Ballad of Tonatiuh Galván"—the chorus of which lilted "through whose eyes shine the General," and those mysterious crimson and emerald green Tonatiuh Suns that had first begun to pop up everywhere back in Malinchico in March. Los Hustlers, strapping young Indian youths, danced with The Warriors of Huitzilopochtli, the Aztec-Mexica revivalist group that sometimes opened the Doctor's rallies.

Between the towns, farmhouses flew Tonatiuh Suns and the

back roads were lined for miles with campesinos and their families displaying their Madonnas and their banners of hope. They had been assembled by no organization at all, really, other than the vast network of poverty that webbed the land. Mickey Raus felt that finally he had followed his nose right into the making of history; somehow he had sliced into the same vein from which old John Reed once drank.

After the rally in Tacumán City, he talked to a thin man with a long florid scar that ran from his left ear to the corner of his mouth. The man was staring dead ahead into the center of his callused hand. "The father gave me this land, put the deed right here in the palm of my hand. I don't have the deed anymore and I don't have the land—but I still have the hand. Now the son has put his own mark right there. I am a lucky man because now twice I have had history in the same hand."

Raus left the thin man with the long florid scar still staring at the calluses in his hard, brown right hand.

In the last days of May, Tonatiuh returned to the capital to gather energies for his final push to wrest the Patria from the PRO.

IV

LA CAPITAL

May 26 – June 1, 2000

BY THE BREAKFAST HOUR, the commerce of La Bondad market begins to climb towards the noonday peak. The hum cranks itself into a constant, not unpleasurable roaring. Shoppers, with their colorful plastic errand bags tightly gripped in hand, clog the aisles and gossip amidst the canticles of the vendors. Domestic animals add their voices to the chorus: growling pariah dogs and the mewling of skinny market cats, the lowing of dying cattle, and the squealing of doomed porkers, the loud scuttling of La Bondad's world-class rats. Beggars whine for the love of God.

Raus watched a thickly built man in sturdy denim overalls reel through the din, screaming repeatedly: "For-the-love-of-god-I'm-hungry-and-I-don't-have-any-work."

"But, Mickey, he doesn't look hungry and this is his work," Doña Metiche admonished the reporter before he could put a lonely leaden coin in the man's hand. The rising fumes of cow intestine soup chloroformed Raus. He retched shamelessly.

It is the air in the capital that drives men mad, Mickey concluded, trying to choke down a thimbleful of menudo just to please the Doña. No one could survive the air of this city unscathed. A half million infants were lucky enough to die each year from respiratory deficiencies before more painful syndromes set in. Countless millions more were brain damaged beyond repair by the lead accumulated in their own mother's mammary glands. The noxious effluvia took their toll on the mental health of the citizenry. Depression drove hundreds each year to leap from multi-storied buildings or fling themselves before the bright orange trains down in the Metro.

During the winter months, when cold air pressed the poisons under the windowsills and through the cracks in the slumhouse walls, old people expired in such numbers that convoys of moving vans were needed to haul the corpses away to common graves out in Mictlan. Joggers dropped dead in mid-gait out in Chapulín Park, their knees pumping, their lungs exploding.

In the spring, nasty winds rose off the hills, sending clouds of swirling hepatic shit out over the city, communicating further intestinal grief to the most susceptible, a plague that, in the end, only added to the fecal gasses massing over the capital.

Summertimes, the rains, by reason of their extraordinarily high acid content, penetrated the reeking vapors, stripping the features off statues of the nation's liberators and brutally singeing the scalps of the city's 30 million live inhabitants, no matter what sort of sombrero they might be wearing, so that now the capital of the Republic had the largest concentration of pelones (bald ones) on the face of the globe.

The autumn was reserved for mourning the dead.

Raus flicked black specks from the stinking tripe stew. Christ knows where this has fallen from. Even at upper altitudes, there was definitely something in the air. Tourists flying inside pressurized airplanes 35,000 feet above the capital gagged on the stench. By the time their flights landed in Acapella, many were already experiencing wrenching dysentery that would keep them shitting their brains out in fancy hotel toilets for the entire duration of their two-week, five-figure vacations. The plumbing was not good. Sewage oozed right up through the shag carpets.

"¿Qué pasó, mi Mickey, you don' like you soop?" Doña Metiche, a large woman with a jeweled star embedded in her final tooth, waxed indignant in pidgin English.

"No, no, it's delicious, Doña, exquisito."

Raus drew defensively upon his Negra, and picked at the broth as if his own grandmother was standing over him, wagging her stubby finger and threatening to wrap up a disgusting slab of flounder and ship it off to the starving children of Poland. Uncountable colonies of microorganisms trickled down his constricting throat.

"Wuxtra! Wuxtra! Your periódicos, Mister Mickey..." The Flea dropped the newspapers on the tabletop with a sort of a splash, crossed himself reflexively, and pocketed the coins Raus had piled there. He shuffled from one foot to the other as if he had an embarrassing question to ask.

"What's up, Pulgacito?"

"Mr. Mickey, is it true that you are with Tonatiuh now?"

Raus was surprised that the pious little voceador even knew who Tonatiuh was. Flea thought the newspapers he sold were "all sins and lies." He never even glanced at the headlines.

Raus was delighted at the question. "Yes, I've been traveling with Doctor Galván."

"That's good, Mr. Mickey, that's very good," the Flea smiled mischievously, and darted off.

The headlines snarled darkly.

WATER RIOT SNARLS CITY

Led by the urban avenger, SuperPendejo, and the activist environmental group Patria Verde, 100,000 citizens marched through the city for five hours yesterday to protest the sale of the capitol's dwindling water supply and services to the Tokyo-based transnational International Water..."

El Machete reported that the giant traffic jam had raised noonday pollution to over 300 on the IMECA scale, the 67th Red Alert emergency of the year. To break up the milling protesters, the granaderos had been forced to turn water cannons on the mob, further depleting the capital's fast-disappearing water supplies.

Hopeless. It was hopeless.

Patria Verde marched every day through the already dangerously overrun streets, hoarsely shouting jeremiads like "Live together or die together!" Mostly they were upper middle-class youth from Culocán and El Rolex, ritzy neighborhoods in which the residents lived their entire lives inside, only venturing forth from climate-controlled townhouses through portable clear plastic tunnels that piped them into the next hermetically sealed environment.

Raus poked at the suspect menudo. Hopeless, really hopeless.

The Great 1985 Earthquake brought catharsis. The extremely poor lost in the Lost Cities had little to lose and delighted in the leveling of the posher districts. The panic of the PRO government only fed the general merriment. As city officials leapt into their limousines and fled the crumbling city for safehouses in the fashionable suburbs, the extremely poor eagerly filled the vacuum, digging out those crushed under the jerry-built apartment buildings, nursing them back to health in patchwork tent hospitals, feeding the damnificados with stores expropriated from government warehouses. Tonatiuh and Paloma threw open their doors and their hearts and hundreds found refuge in the former House of Demented Women on Carlos Quinto Street.

RAT had been the first professional politician to understand this new empowerment. The rush of popular energy had built him and SuperPendejo an enterprise that was now to become the spinal column of Tonatiuh's campaign here in La Capital, control of which, all parties knew full well, meant control of the nation.

"¡Ya Viene! ¡Ya Viene!" Suddenly, Doña Metiche was leaping onto the greasy, newspaper-strewn table, recklessly kicking over sugar and salt, jalapeño chiles, chopped onions, oregano and little wedges of lemon to get a good look at whoever the hell was coming.

"Who's coming?" Raus asked, removing his bowl from beneath the Doña's platform heel. Hopeless…

"¡Ya Viene! ¡Ya Viene!" Metiche pointed over the excited crowd at the Man They Call the Hope.

✦

YODELING MARIACHIS accompanied Tonatiuh through the slippery, festooned passageways of La Bondad as a storm of pastel confetti drizzled down from the ceiling of the great, dim market shed. "Thruuuu whooose ayayayays shayayayan owwwwr Generrrraaaallll."

The aisles were stacked high with the new fruit—to which Tonatiuh himself had contributed mightily—of a rainy season.

"No-o-o-o-o descansarayyy haasta qque Tohhhhnaatiuhhhh SSea Nueeeessstro Prrreyyyys…"

SPLAAAAT!

De la Mancha loyalists who controlled NAAFTA-town, the aisle that exclusively featured U.S. produce imports, blocked the Doctor's advance and fruit began to fly. A barrage of rotting papayas retrieved from the steaming garbage pits out back was unleashed. Cantaloupes catapulted from barricaded stalls, watermelons smashed down from the eaves.

But Tonatiuh's people were armed too and responded in kind, with hard tubers: potatoes, calabashes, turnips, huge purple beets, cabbages big as cannonballs. "¡Tohhhnaaatiuhhh Prrrreyyyysiiiidenteeee!" the tubers crooned, driving de la Mancha's goons into retreat. Through it all, the Doctor stood resolutely above the market fracas, picking strands of tropical mamey from his Italian suit.

✦

WITH THE PRESS scuttling right behind, the Man They Call the Hope toured all of the capital's 49 still-public markets (Se Fue and K-Mex had bought all the rest). "We're driving the PRO bananas," Bishop boasted. Tonatiuh visited the encampments of the last damnifacados out in Mictlan cemetery, the hillside caves of the old people further west, and the Lost Cities of the southern districts, impossible thickets of hovels—the light outside diminished into darkness the deeper you traveled inside so that Raus thought, "I will never return to the surface again."

Wherever the Doctor moved in the capital that week there were converts.

"¡¡¡Hooooostiiiiiciaaahhhhh!!!"

Out on the sad, moistureless lake beds of Nuevo Chalco, east of the city, the newest newcomers were just setting up campsites. Here, Sancho de la Mancha's water trucks "PRO-vided Life!"—or so read the sides of the Party tankers. Nonetheless, the Doctor's presence stirred wild defiance. Brass bands pumped away just like back home in the villages of Malinchico, El Horno, Huajuco and Chiapas from which the settlers had been driven. Rockets flared and thudded. Little flags with crudely sewn Tonatiuh Suns fluttered from every refrigerator-box home.

"¡Tohhhhhnaaaatiuhhhhh Preyyyyyyysiiiiidenteeee!"

Out in the industrial north of the capital, the mohawked Chavas Bandas that RAT and Super had assembled shook their spike-braceleted fists and stained the walls with graffiti, some of which was written in blood. War had broken out between de la Mancha's PRO-Youth and Tonatiuh's young people, and the combat was fierce for the hearts and minds of the rough-and-tumble kid gangs that prowled the appalling chemical factory district, ripping apart elderly pensioners for small change, furiously fighting to stay stoked day and night (there was no difference out there). Dope was their only defense against the black poisonous helplessness in which they had grown up and which was their only future.

The PRO brought them the dope—gallons of industrial paint thinner—with which they burnt out the final embers of their brain cells and became PRO-zombies for life. Tonatiuh brought them hope and planted a tree, a slender flash of green amidst the chemical pall—it was the first tree that many of the Santo Pachecos, the most predatory pandilla in the north of the city, had ever seen. "¡Grueso!" the wild boys laughed savagely. "This Tonatiuh's re-grueso!"

Flanked by RAT and the crimson and scarlet-caped and masked Prince of the Streets, Tonatiuh marched through urban hells like a triumphant liberator. His retinue grew long. The

Bishop, Dr. Huipi, Cabañas Cantú, the three boys and their mother formed the second line. The mariachis and the bandas de guerra came next. Local leaders, block captains, squatter organizers, young parish priests, neighborhood curanderas joined the parade. Don Estalin marshaled the capital's ravenous political press pack. A pepper and salt-bearded gentleman with a pirate patch pasted to his right eye melded into the line of march. Everywhere, he proclaimed heavy doom: "Genocide! Ecocide! Live Together Or Die Together!" Raus deduced that he must be José María y Cruz Patadas, the eccentric papá of Patria Verde. "Gimme Five!" the eco-pirate confirmed, as they slapped hands high in the sooted air.

Only at one stop in this jubilant, swelling procession through the capital was the welcome muted: the San Valentino garbage dump, the great, rotting cordillera of debris that smoldered evilly for miles along the eastern edge of the metropolis. RAT backgrounded the delicate situation for the choking reporters. Montec Indian pickers out here were organizing against Sancho de la Mancha's PRO Garbage Kings and the ambiance was, well, rare. "Cuidado, compañeros and, ehhh, compañeras..."

Jane Ann and the compañeras held their noses delicately.

Descendants of the proud cloud people of the western Oaxacan sierra, the Montecs were now reduced to picking through the flotsam of a throw-away civilization. A handful of Indians met the Doctor at a kicked down side-gate. Their welcome seemed very tentative. There were no brass bands or mariachis out here. Just holding this meeting could get them all killed, Malcreado whispered. PRO spies hid behind every slimy hillock.

Tonatiuh moved from one crazily slanted lean-to to the next, trying to shake bony hands that were so limp he had to raise them from each crushed lap. Others averted their gaze, reflexively jerked away from him, as if contact might brand their fingers for life. Tonatiuh tried to talk but no one talked back. Outside, buzzards circled in a sky smudged by ten years of smoldering tires.

"This is really creepy," muttered the mop-haired colombiana Tania Escobar, taking Sasha Vigo's arm.

"Hermanas y hermanos, we have come to express our solidarity with your struggle against the PRO Kings of the Garbage," the Doctor declared somberly to a group of small ragged men and women who picked at freshly hauled mounds of decay, taken from the city that very morning, the best stuff. They didn't look up.

"We come to ask your vote in July but we come too because we want to tell you that together we have a common enemy and now we must join hands if we are ever to overthrow the PRO."

Large black flies massed ominously, their smeary buzzing the only response to Tonatiuh's mournful overture. Even the gaudily garbed SuperPendejo failed to arouse the curiosity of the humbled pickers. "It's pretty bad out here, alright. Maybe we've seen enough." The Urban Avenger didn't like the look of the light.

Suddenly, a deranged woman lurched over a tottering garbage mound and uttered a frightful, throttled scream. She pointed the butt of her bottle right at Tonatiuh and, for an instant, froze there at the very crest, taking aim. Then she just seemed to sag, like all the air had gone out of her, and collapsed helter-skelter down the rotting hillside, pulling orange peels and melon rinds, tallow bones, eggshells, soiled Pampers, broken glass, and two dead rats down with her. The woman rolled comatose right to Tonatiuh's feet, where she rested, her legs spread grotesquely, exposing her bleeding, violated vagina. The Doctor knelt instinctively and measured the woman's pulse. "She's dead," he whispered.

"If you ask me, all of these people are dead," Tania Escobar side-mouthed to Mickey, as the representatives of the international press stepped briskly back to the car.

"A TOAST OF THIS filthy worm-water for Warren here—pass him the little critter, Jane Ann dear, like a good girl," Pease commanded. "The poor boy needs red meat. We have to fatten him up for his Oscar."

Raus had been the obligatory butt of big-time foreign correspondents' depreciating jibes for decades now. Excoriated by his own colleagues, who treated him like the last pigeon in the pecking order, Mickey Raus mechanically martyred on. Now he held the embalmed maguey worm in the palm of his hand as if he was about to perform a prayer service for the dead. He had been drinking all afternoon but he was not very drunk.

"¡Cómatelo, Mickey Maus, come tu gusano!" Tania Escobar hooted from across the Illusions saloon. The unwritten rule of this sanctuary was that the native and the gringo press corps never sat at the same table if they could possibly avoid it. "The filthy woggos," as the *Times* man stigmatized them, thrusting fingers over his seersucker shoulder, sat to the left of the zinc counter, at the one gouged table on that side of the grubby room, generally imbibing Cuba Libres and guffawing at the latest gaffes of the ignorant outlanders, whose retainers they greatly envied, weeping copiously into Poncho's already diluted Coobas about how us pobres nacionales were forced to grovel for bribes named sobres and chayos and embutes, doled out to them each Friday by the very people they were assigned to be covering. Oh, the shame of it. ¡Qué vergüenza! The Patria's self-esteem was at stake.

"C'mon, Warrencito, down the hatch," coaxed Jane Ann Arbus. The Pease-Arbus clique had taken to confusing Raus with "Warren Beatty," an American actor who once championed the journalist John Reed in a sentimental old flick entitled "Reds." Mickey Raus was a card-carrying John Reed junkie.

"Good Christ, Warren, this Reed-bugger was born with a silver spoon up his arse. Ten Days that Bored the World! Even the part about being buried in the Kremlin wall was bloody bull-doody. They couldn't even locate hide nor hair of his frigging bones when they tore it down to build the new Howard Johnson's last year."

"Pease Pease Pease," Raus pleaded with his tormentor, "let the man rest in peace. Besides if Reed was alive today, the government would throw his culo right out of Mexico under Artículo pinche 33."

"Watch you don't get 33'd your own self, buddy," clinked Bloch, chugalugging a triple margarita, and trying to strip a mini-camcorder simultaneously. Pinche Artículo 33 of the local constitution decrees immediate expulsion for any foreigner who is adjudged by the PRO government to have taken a too active interest in the welfare of the Republic and those who dwelt therein.

"Sid, Sid, Sid, being part of Tonatiuh's campaign is like being, like, well, like, a part of history," Raus the Red warmed to the black cameraman's challenge. "Do you know how history smells? How it tastes? Well, you can smell it and taste it out there. You do not forget what you see. It makes you take sides. Just the way the people press in around Tonatiuh, as if to protect him from the PRO. It can make you cry. It can give you hope."

"I dunno. This is their dogfight—not yours or mine. Mick, you step in the way, your little Rolling Writer there won't stop the slug when the time comes, and believe me, brother man, that time will come."

Sid Bloch's startling footage from the frontlines in Salvador and Nicaragua were fabled in the region during the late '80s. Then he got himself caught in a murderous Contra bus assault on the road north from Esteli, surviving only because his enormous frame was pinned beneath a dozen innocent corpses. Ever since, he had limited his graphic activities to shooting talking heads at press conferences in Latin American capitals. On long flights now, he dreamt that he was heading home to Tulsa, Oklahoma at last, where he would arrive on a hot Sunday afternoon, his dad hunkered over the barbecue, burning pork ribs. He never went home, of course.

Bloch, like Pease and Arbus, was booked to fly the country with Barcelona for the next month, 31 states and the Federal District in 32 days. "Hey, they feed fucking good, lots of booze, blow till you drop, five-star hotels every night, freaky little ladies to suck your dick when the speechifying gets stupid, no gunfire." The CNN man laughed and then, remembering Colosio at Lomas Taurinas, corrected himself. "Well, *almost* no gun fire."

El Sid had a point. Where would Raus be when the Heavy Shit came down? What would he do when they finally opened fire on Tonatiuh? He wanted to think that he'd instinctively pounce upon the would-be assassin and worm his way into history. He tossed back the mescal with macho flourish. "What the hell? I've got no future in this business anyway. I might as well let you creeps collect your Pulitzers writing my obit."

"Warren, you are definitely losing your objectivity," Ms. Arbus smirked, patting her definitely downwardly mobile ex-lover, matronizingly, on the knee.

"¡Tiempo!" Malcreado whistled, like a soccer referee, already slanting for the door. The *Machete* Man, Von Voodle, the spidery blonde Sasha Vigo—Tania Escobar on her heels—abandoned Las Ilusiones. The Bishop had scheduled a press briefing for 7 PM, Tonatiuh's strategy for the final month of the campaign. It was already 7:35.

Pease signaled Poncho for the cuenta. Bloch slammed heavy coins on the tabletop and dropped both halves of the dissected camcorder back in his bag. Ms. Arbus made a face into a hand-held mirror, illustrating that even jaded foreign correspondents agonize over zits. Without muttering even a prayer for the dead, Raus' gums closed around the bitter worm that, for the past half hour, had been detoxifying in the cup of his hand.

THE PRESS CORPS shouldered through the wall of well-wishers packing the narrow sidewalk in front of No. 2 Carlos Quinto Street. The crowd of supporters was a permanent fixture 24 hours a day, there to salute Tonatiuh and Paloma when they sallied forth to campaign before dawn, and there to welcome them home when they returned, dog-tired, long past midnight.

Save for the mobs out front, No. 2 Carlos Quinto was not distinguishable from block after block of gloomy, termite-infested colonial buildings, many now hopelessly subdivided into damp, cramped half-room cubicles where 12 people slept on the rat-shit-peppered floor each night and there was no running water. The interiors of the former Casa de las Dementadas had fared better; however, its 27 drafty rooms, still attended to by porters and maids, were supervised by the doddering Nana Ninfita Cabeza de Vaca, once wet nurse to a half a hundred doctor-brothers.

Much of the nation's history had been written in and under this neighborhood, once Tenochtitlan, the seat of the Aztec empire. The buildings themselves had been deliberately plastered atop the malignant temples and sacrificial wheels of the Aztecs, as if European architecture could somehow seal off forever the blasphemies of an Indian past. Under the former House of Demented Women, the National Archeological Institute's excavation crews had unearthed evidence of an Aztec ritual bath house and sometimes, during dull hours awaiting press conferences, Raus found himself fantasizing about the Aztec priests, stinking of gore and the excremental discharges of the dying, sudsing their blood-matted hair down there in the gurgling catacombs below the basement.

The decaying old manse had one other phantasmal feature. For decades the General had inhabited these musty rooms and his death did not much diminish his presence on the premises. His fully clothed ghost was said to be still cruising the cold hallways of Carlos Quinto #2 in a Great Depression-dated, double-breasted suit and wide polka dot tie, his hair slicked down around his prominent ears, like a farm boy dressed up for a Sunday night dance, barking orders at his son and his daughter-in-law, his three princely grandsons, and doddering Nana Ninfita.

WHEN NOT SUCKING up the worm water at Las Ilusiones two blocks east, reporters had taken to lounging around Carlos Quinto, trying to look blasé enough to provoke the candidate or his campaign manager—or anyone at all, for that matter—into a newsworthy remark whenever they passed in the moss-green hallways.

Tonatiuh's house vibrated with visitors at all hours of the day and night. With the election just five weeks off, a steady stream of supporters from many regions of the nation moved through the thick oak doors that were carved with the faces of startled, mythical beasts.

Small men from the provinces came, ate, argued, agreed,

strung up their hammocks or crashed on straw mats, went home in the half light of early morning with documents designating them as Tonatiuh's captains in all the electoral districts in the land. A meeting seemed to be always underway in some nook of the old stone nuthouse. Raus spotted many faces from the campaign trail: the red-bearded Compa; his sidekick, the miner Jose Cerro; the banana worker, Ismael Caracol from down in Atila; an earnest, attentive Doctor Guadarrama from Tacumán; the barrel-chested mayor of Zapicho, Pedro Baltazar; and goofy Tata Pamfilo. Padre Pascual Pobrecito had been carried into the patio. SuperPendejo and RAT were on hand for the tardy press conference. So was La India Cristina, RAT's spookily glamorous mother, whom the PRO press wagged had become the "court astrologer to the Sixth Sun."

Amidst this familiar hubbub, Tonatiuh paused to take council and strength for the remarkable days to come. Now he was ready to roll.

ꚃ

THE MAN WHO Wore Two Watches wedged a Delicado between his handsome teeth and swiveled away from the insanely cluttered desk. "The way we see it, the Doctor is now running well ahead of Barcelona in the 11 states we've already visited, and pretty much neck and neck in the rest of the country. Our straw polls show the capital, where the campaign is being organized by SuperPendejo and Reggio Ahumada here, to be ours, all 30 districts. What we've learned in the past few months is that wherever we go, we pick up votes, and we're going to cover so much ground in the next 30 days that we will win this election by such a large margin that the PRO will not be able to deny us victory."

One of the quainter features of Tonatiuh Galván's Miracle Crusade of 2000 was that it, quite literally, was run right out of his own kitchen—an enormous, ramshackle colonial kitchen off the courtyard on Carlos Quinto that the Galváns had long ago, converted into one of the most cluttered offices on the American land mass.

"Excuse me, señor Obispo, but did you say that you are actually going to win the July 2 election?" Pease asked, as if this was the most preposterous assumption that he'd ever audited.

"Not me, señor Pease, the Doctor is who is going to win."

"Compañero Salmón," Antonio Malcreado sliced in, cutting Pease off before he could ask for a 'precision.' "You say Tonatiuh will win by a margin so large that the PRO won't be able to steal the election. But how will you force the PRO to count the votes honestly?"

"That's a key question, compañero. I think I'll wait and let the Doctor respond in more detail."

"What, sir, you are saying is that there is going to be fraud at the polls—that the Party of the Organic Revolution will try to steal this victory you already prematurely claim, and that, somehow, you will stop them from doing this, am I correct?" Pease persisted, the incredulity encrusting his lips like fermented saliva. The pear-shaped *Times* man's ties to the PRO were no secret.

"The PRO has committed fraud in 14 straight presidential elections and we don't think they've turned a new leaf just because the *Times* editorial board says so," the Bishop smiled through those beautiful teeth.

Pease's alcoholic fog was a cover for a coldly clicking brain. "You speak of 14 fraudulent presidential elections, sir. This would mean that the General himself was elected by fraud, as was his successor."

"Those are your calculations, my friend, not mine." The Man Who Wore Two Watches hurriedly recognized Jane Ann Arbus.

"Mister Bishop, how do you think this fraud will be committed? Can you give us an idea? In the polling place? When they count the totals? At the district tallies? On the computers? At the CAER? Just where?"

"Gracias, compañera. We think it will happen in all of those places and at every level. In fact, we think it has already happened, that the PRO government has been buying votes and obligating voters to cast their ballots for Barcelona ever since Tonatiuh announced his candidacy. The PRO has placed its operatives inside the CAER and the PRO controls the electoral machinery. We think they have already erased the names of Tonatiuh's people from the voting lists and we think that this new computerized Gold Card that is being used for the first time to access the ballot has been engineered to keep those who want to vote for Tonatiuh from casting a countable vote."

Computers had been used before to steal elections here. In 1988 the PRO government claimed that a huge Unisys system had "crashed" on election night. No results were available for eight days and half of the polling places were never reported. The much maligned Salinas took power although most voters still believed that Cuauhtemoc Cárdenas, who vanished into thin air ten years later, had won the presidency. Now electoral reforms had produced a purportedly tamper-proof ballot in the form of the computerized Gold Card that the PRO was handing out at every street corner.

"Yeah, but how do you stop computer fraud?" Raus wondered out loud.

"Good point, compañero." The Bishop tugged at a yellowing newspaper clip wedged into the trash pile atop his desk and, abruptly, a slag heap that included crumpled gas receipts, crushed Boing-g-g cans, a week of Delicado butts, and last night's half-eaten supper of enchiladas suizas slid sickeningly to the floor.

"Leave it there, compañero." The Bishop stuck a fresh ciggie between his teeth and handed Raus the clip, which was in English—something about a computer virus, Baltimore, the Peruvian insurgency...

"¡Compañeros!"

Tonatiuh sauntered into the kitchen, the ruddy, red-bearded Dolores Leñero right behind. Mickey folded the squib into his breast pocket. The Doctor and El Compa shook hands all around.

"Yes, you were asking how we can stop the PRO from stealing our victory? Only by making sure our vote is so big that it will be impossible for them to lie to the people about who won."

"And then, we must organize those who voted for us to defend their vote. To stand at the polls and the district tallies and the CAER and not go home until the PRO has admitted our victory," the Compa added. Raus noticed that Leñero's left hand was folded into a fist.

"For the next 30 days, we are going out in this country to spread the message that we have already won the election and will not let them take it away from us," Doctor Galván announced. This was for publication. "We are going to speak to millions of voters from the Guatemalan border all the way to the northern frontera, and we are going to organize them to defend their vote as has never been done before in our history."

"But, Doctor, what if, no matter how big your edge is, they steal the election from you on the computers?"

"Compañero Raus, you're a good old-fashioned Maoist," chuckled Tonatiuh. "You should remember that people are mightier than the machines they build."

Transportation would be provided by the miners of Jacquemate, who had donated two buses: El Martillo (The Hammer) and La Hoz (The Sickle). Don Estalin, of course, would navigate The Hammer and his son Lazaro, The Sickle. The Bishop promptly parked the buses over at Earl Scheib-Mex and contracted a painter to rechristen the vehicles El Sol and La Luna. Dolores Leñero was piqued at the name changes, not a good sign for the socialist future.

Tonatiuh's caravan would head east over the turrets of Citlaltepetl and hook into the old Caribbean Coast highway, driving south through Julapa and east again, circling the flat Mayatán peninsula, then southwest, through the swamps of Kukulkan and Cocodrillo, and into the jungles and bleak highlands of deeply Indian Chiapas and Huajuco, turning north across the narrow isthmus, where the Pacific laps the land, into the Monteca Sierra, down to El Horno and on up the Pacific Coast road, whistle-stopping San Pancho and Amapola, across the great Yunqui desert, touching the U.S. border at Tijuana before flying south back to the capital, with the campaign's close set for the evening of July 1 on the shores of Malinchico's sacred Lake Tzintzun.

Such a route and pace was patently cockeyed and logistically impossible to accomplish in the 31 days remaining before election day. The Man Who Wore Two Watches proposed to cover General Galván's entire Long Campaign, a trek that had taken him over a year to complete, in just a month. What the Bishop needed was rocket-propelled magic carpets—not two broken-down motorized mules formerly known as The Hammer and The Sickle—to move Tonatiuh up and down the nation from south to north and east to west. While Filemón Barcelona winged into one state capital after another in the presidential jet, Raus calculated that the crowds along the highways would be so thick that Tonatiuh would never even get out of Julapa. The watches, Raus decided, had finally driven the Bishop mad.

ON THE EVE of his departure from the capital, Tonatiuh paid a call on the most powerful doctor-brother still in the service of the nation. Brigadier General Gertrudis Niños de Galván (Totonaco) had once been surgeon-general of the military before transferring to more belligerent theaters of operation, and his surgeon hands still mesmerized his colleagues at meetings of the Estado Mayor.

The white-gloved guard posted outside Gate #3 of Military Camp #1, a secretive fenced-in enclave on the western flank of the city, had been forewarned and passed Tonatiuh's Shadow through without questions. General Gertrudis himself came to the surveillance gate that encircled his incongruously gingerbread-like house to greet the Doctor. The two embraced and pounded each other on the back cautiously, as if each were acutely aware that small, sharp blades could be concealed between fingers during this ceremonial pat-down.

As a child, Tonatiuh had always been envious of Gertrudis' (Totonaco's) easy relationship with the General, his precocious military talents, his deft hands and good looks. Gertrudis, older and unconcerned with the jealousies his favored position provoked, protected Tonatiuh from the juvenile cruelties heaped upon him by the 55 other pseudo-siblings. But the two were not really close. In the past 30 years, they had seen each other socially on rare occasions, usually the commemorations of the General's feats in bronze, when the surviving doctor-brothers would gather for what amounted to family reunions. The Doctor and the Military Man followed each other's public careers in the press, of course, assiduously combing the political columns each day for mention of one doctor-brother or another—but there had been no real contact between the two since Tonatiuh ran away to join the Cuban Revolution. Even now, General Gertrudis had not invited the Doctor to his home.

"So if what we are hearing is to be believed, it sounds like Tonatiuh Galván has launched an active candidacy. ¡Salud!" The General lifted his Johnny Walker Black half an inch and did not clink glasses.

"We are going to win."

"Electoral campaigns have much in common with military ones. The long-range strategies, the tactical surprise attacks from the flanks…," General Gertrudis continued, waving his beautiful surgeon hands and pretending that his adopted brother had not just said what he thought he'd heard.

"I said, we are going to win, brother."

Gertrudis closed his eyes. "Ah yes, that…" He pronounced the word *that* as if the subject was a chore, like a fence that needed mending somewhere on the periphery of the military camp.

"Hermano, I have come to ask you what the Army will do when we win the election on July 2," Tonatiuh insisted.

General Niños de Galván (Totonaco) pressed his fingertips together in a thoughtful gesture. "As you must remember, hermano, the Army is a politically neutral institution."

Tonatiuh fixed his laser stare on the still-dashing officer. "The PRO has sold off the Revolution," he said bluntly. "It has murdered what our father stood for."

"Personally, I share some of your views in this respect, hermano, but it is not my function as the commander of the Revolutionary Army to criticize the Party. As you know, the military is sworn by the Constitution to uphold the revolutionary government."

"We have no revolutionary government anymore," Tonatiuh

blurted blackly. "You are living a lie."

A painful silence descended over the dully paneled room. The conversation had come to its predictable dead end. "Will you shoot us down when we rightfully demand our victory, hermano?"

General Gertrudis had had enough of this absurd chitchat. "Our Army does not commit massacres. Nor is it responsible for crowd control—that is a function of civil authority. You know all this, Tonatiuh, and you have come out here only to needle me into placing the General's concerns over those of the government that I am constitutionally sworn to defend," he said sharply, seeking a way to extract himself from his doctor-brother's brooding glare. The leaden silence was broken only by the drumming of the military man's fingers, marching against the wooden rests of his armchair. He drained his glass and stood up stiffly.

"They are watching you closely, Tonatiuh. The time is coming when they will have to make a decision about allowing you to proceed. You must be very careful now, more careful than I have ever known you to be." Not without feeling, General Gertrudis gripped his younger brother's sharply boned shoulder as he accompanied him to the surveillance gate that encircled his tightly barricaded gingerbread home.

V

INTO THE SOUTH

June 1 – June 13, 2000

NUT-BROWN MEN in pressed tan uniforms were posted at 10-foot intervals along the shoulder of the Caribbean highway, bouncing stout batons against the flats of their hands—the Julapa State Transit Police. Contrary to Raus' forecast, crowds of Tonatiuh's followers did not slow the caravan's progress. In fact, there were no crowds. Those who had wished to welcome the Doctor were kept penned up miles away, on both sides of the roadway.

The rally was scheduled for Laguna Negra, 60 kilometers east of the Julapa state capital, on a meadowed peninsula that juts lazily out into the green Caribbean. With its rich quilted pasture lands, Laguna Negra had once been the dairy of the nation. Now it was a national disaster. Laguna Negra #1, a decaying nuclear power plant, had been spewing its black magic for a generation now. Radiation slithered out of the cracked containment building and out of a thousand leaky pipes and valves, so poisoning the grass and cows that the milk could not be sold publicly anymore.

The Mothers of Julapa had protested this catastrophe to the last four presidents, all of whom had been so dazzled by this claptrap symbol of Progress that they could not hear the Mothers' message. Instead, they sought to silence the messengers. The Mothers of Julapa's famous Nursing Breast logo was banned as pornographic by "El Chango" Chiringo, the present governor, and the group's offices were shut down after being deemed a public nuisance by health inspectors. Mothers began disappearing into the dismal chambers of the secretos, and the movement itself had gone underground last spring. Nonetheless, the Mothers of Julapa enjoyed widespread support from nursing mothers all over the Americas. Their blockbuster exposés of the contamination of the nation's milk supply were widely distributed in plain brown envelopes from gulf to ocean and border to border. A recent Mothers' investigation, published in a *Machetazo* supplement, measured radiation levels both in the milk that flowed from their own breasts and that which spilled from the udders of the thousands of black and white Guernsey cows that roamed these radioactive meadows. The Iodine 131 count was so high in the moo juice that the Lomelí government was now holding all milk on site in lead-lined safe storage. Meanwhile, the radiation count in the breast milk of the farm women who lived on the perimeter of Laguna Negra #1 now measured well above maximum levels for plant employees, amongst whom thyroid cancers were epidemic.

The Doctor was headed for Laguna Negra to offer his medical services and invite the Mothers of Julapa to join the Miracle Crusade.

※

AS THE TWO BUSES glided down the flat coastal highway, the passengers pressed their noses to the polarized glass, counting the cops and trying to pinpoint distant supporters on the horizons. At the Laguna Negra turn-off, the Transit Police barricaded the roadway with boulders. Outside, 3,000 state cops—twice the number actually on the Julapa public payroll—massed shoulder to shoulder to block Tonatiuh's progress onto Laguna Negra, each banging a big baton into a nut-brown palm. "There's not going to be any rally," affirmed Jesus Von Voodle, the government's man, as if the matter was quite decided. A mile down the road, behind the massed police and the black and white cows peacefully grazing on the poison grass, Tania Escobar spotted military vehicles hidden in the palm trees.

The Bishop dismounted to talk to the Comandante, a man built like—and the color of—a used tractor tire. "This is a security zone," the tractor tire barked. "Get back on the bus!" The Man Who Wore Two Watches glanced at them both. "¡Quítate de aquí, payaso!" Bishop got back on the bus with a disgusted shrug.

A stand-off that would persist for many hours had begun. Cantú Cabañas, a professor of law, dismounted to debate with the legal authorities what the constitution of the country had to say about the right of free transit. Malcreado stared through the tinted glass and muttered, "He's got the wrong country if he thinks that's going to work." Up ahead in El Sol, Tonatiuh skulked in the back of the sweltering bus and slammed down dominoes with his three sons, Dr. Huipi, and El Compa. The impasse extended past lunch time.

Around four, the Caribbean greened darkly and began to show its teeth in tiny white caps. A squall blew in from the east in slanting bands, soaking the Julapa State Transit Police but hardly melting their tightly packed formation. The pilgrims on this stalled crusade dozed disconsolately against the streaming panes—all except the tiny German. "We're not going anywhere, anywhere at all," Von Voodle burbled singsong-style. "We're stuck, stuck! Stuck! Steckengeblieban!"

"Shut your pinche spy yap or I'll shut it for you, Don Chucho," snapped Tania Escobar. She looked like she was eager for a round of dwarf-tossing. Mickey liked her spunk. Scuttlebutt had it that she had been in the M-19 leadership before picking up the pen.

The rain fell in white sheets.

Just before nightfall, Tonatiuh's caravan was visited by emissaries from Laguna Negra. The couple had bravely circled ten miles around the police lines. Raus recognized the dripping pirate-patched Patadas. They slapped slippery fives. The large, wet, handsome woman with him was Consuelo Concepción, the main Mother of Julapa. Fifty-one apprehension orders had been issued in Concepción's name, and she was constantly dodging secretos.

The two reported, breathlessly, that 10,000 steaming supporters ahead in Laguna Negra had been penned up all day by the police. The rain had not dampened their anger a bit and feelings were running high. They feared a confrontation with the authorities was brewing. "There are many hotheads back there. We do not want this to get out of hand, Doctor. There has been trouble before from government provocateurs. People have been hurt. One young boy was killed. He was only five." Consuelo Concepción's large breasts undulated like the damaged sea. "We are peaceful people, Señor."

The big damp woman was clearly trying to tell Tonatiuh something.

"What Consuelo is trying to say, Doctor," Patadas laid it out, "is that we're afraid that violence is going to break out back there and Green Fatherland and the Mothers of Julapa cannot be parties to violence in any form, from whatever source, for whatever reason. We are disciples of Mahatma Gandhi inside here"—he pointed to his pot-bellied navel—"and our movement cannot risk any transgression of its principles. Therefore, we have come these many miles, through a driving rainstorm, to plead with you to consider canceling your appearance here tonight."

Don Estalin signaled his son Lazaro to turn his bus around.

TONATIUH'S CONVOY headed south through the sticky Julapa night. The cloying scent of jacarandas blended with the stench of the distant refineries on the slim Caribbean breeze. Young Lázaro, aka "El Nene," hunched over the wheel of The Moon, chewing the fat with his father on the CB. A half mile up the road, "Papa Sol" did not like what he was seeing—or not seeing.

"Do you read me, Nene? This is no good. There's no one on our tail. There's no cops on the road. I don't get it."

Raus peered through the polarized glass into the dim first light of a southern dawn. The highway was completely unposted. The Julapa State Transit Police had evaporated with the night.

All morning, the caravan moved towards the distant plume of the refineries, the Julapa sun cooking the macadam roadbed under them. There was little traffic on the Caribbean coast road. There were no police.

The day's events were anchored to a dissident oil workers' rally in Ciudad Lomeli, a smoldering boomtown the natives still called Cocotitlan, because—once upon a time before the PRO government installed its rusting refineries and pernicious petrochemical plants—this region had been the coconut capital of the country. Now there were no more coconuts or any kind of fruit for that matter, and the coastal jungle that had once thrummed with vibrant ribbons of life was now discolored by brown stains, the by-product of a witches' brew of vinyl chloride and 21 other volatile solvents that consumed the canopy at the rate of a kilometer a day like a plague of filthy giant land crabs. In the industrial sections, the sirens wailed day and night.

The once crystalline Cocotitlan River—a stream so transparent that 50 years ago one could watch the shrimp mate ten meters below its swiftly moving surface—now ran ocher and sometimes belched flames around the PROMISH (Pro-Mishubishi) refinery, the DowMex pesticide complex, and the MierdaMexa fertilizer loading docks.

What river fish survived this toxic bouillabaisse mutated into bulbous one-eyed lumps so saturated with mercury and benzene that the government sent in the Navy to keep the populace of Cocotitlan from fishing for the mutagenic monsters. Still, driven by habit and hunger, the natives did digest the illicit carcasses of the contaminated fish, and when slow death finally overcame them, sometimes on public streets, scavenger birds settled in and partook of their flesh.

So contaminated had the food chain become that now there was hardly a vulture aloft circling the skies above Cocotitlan to clean up after the dead.

␡

THE BUSES ROLLED unimpeded down the off-ramp into the outskirts of the oil town. The absence of anything but a token public security force was, indeed, disconcerting.

Tonatiuh huddled over lunch in a downtown "fish" parlor with Chon Yaa, the hard-hatted leader of the Mayan contract workers who had recently been expelled from the official oil workers union. Chon Yaa brushed his dark bangs away from his narrow little eyes, and Raus could see that he was apprehensive. He had just learned that Sancho de la Mancha was in town. All morning, burly men in stained guayaberas had been arriving in rented buses. They said they were "educators," come for the union beisbol tournament. "Chorro" Vallarta, Paco's 88-year-old kid brother and lifetime leader of the "Sindicato Orgánico de Petroleros Patrióticos" (SOPP) had personally greeted each "educator." Chon Yaa was worried about the rally. "There could be a lot of trouble, Doctor."

The Bishop tugged at Tonatiuh's sleeve to make it clear that canceling another rally would send the wrong message to the PRO. Chon Yaa agreed. "We have lived here under the threat of violence before Vallarta took over the SOPP. Remember, this is our land. It was our land long before PROMISH showed up. Years ago, we would say it doesn't matter what they use this jungle for, that in the end we would get it back. But then we saw what they were doing to the jungle and we were not so sure that we wanted the land back any more. I don't know. We are organized now to stop this destruction, but we do not see any way to do that without first destroying the PRO."

"As you wish. I am your servant," the Doctor offered graciously over the spoiled "fish."

RAUS REALIZED there would be serious trouble the moment he stepped onto the speaker's platform. Several thousand contract workers had gathered in the unfinished boomtown plaza, a mass of little brown men in hardhats. Behind them, on all the streets feeding into the square, beer-bellied men in stained guayaberas wielded clubs that looked very much like Louisville Sluggers.

The Bishop spotted it right away too and warned Tonatiuh. The candidate was about to step forward to speak when the goons attacked like a wave of Huns, unmercifully clubbing at the Mayans as if they were so many baby harp seals. Hard hats flew as the contract workers were beaten into the unpaved street. A handful of Julapa State Transit Police stood to one side of the stage, riveted to little true crime comic books, unconcerned with the real-life carnage transpiring right under their noses.

SOPP!

Raus gasped in horror as a grotesquely fat teenager in a New York Yankees hat and Snoop Doggy Dogg tee-shirt swung from the hip like Bye-Bye Balboni and made clean contact with Chon Yaa's hard-hatted brown skull. Little scarlet beads flew off the rebel leader's ears, like water off a boxer who has just been pasted square on the button by Iron Mike Tyson in his prime. But Chon Yaa did not go down.

"¡Vamos, Mickey!" Antonio Malcreado and Tania Escobar were pulling him away, pointing towards the buses parked just north of the plaza. "Vamos, Mickey, you've seen enough. We've got to get out of here," she pleaded. But Raus was mesmerized by the sound of skulls shattering beneath him, the little *ufffs* of men whose lives were leaking away through their crushed scalps. He turned slowly, like he was trapped inside a Saturday morning cartoon, and saw the Bishop dash from the platform, followed by Tonatiuh and the boys. He heard the crunch of hickory splintering bone behind him, the little *ufffs*. He marveled at the sound, flipped on his mini-recorder to capture it for history. Tania yanked him rudely from the platform. "You are such an asshole," she yelled. "C'mon!"

Now a comandante ran up to Tonatiuh in the street and Raus saw that he was offering an escort to the highway. Behind him, the baseball bats kept grand-slamming the busted hardhats. SOPP! SOPP! SOPP!

"Why don't you stop them?" Raus hollered at the fireplug-sized comandante. "Stop what, gringo? We don' see nothing. You see something? You want to show it to me?" The cop shoved Mickey hard in the small of the back and he stumbled into the bus now called the Moon. El Nene had the motor running.

Raus slumped down in the seat in front of Tania Escobar. "Thanks," he puffed.

"Man, you sure got some slow reflexes," she whistled softly.

ON THE THIRD MORNING, the caravan breached the wide, flat limestone tongue of the Mayatan peninsula—the route of the Maya. But, judging by the public force dispatched for the Candidate's "own protection," Mayatan authorities did not plan for the Doctor to do much hands-on sight-seeing. Sometimes the uncurving highway, running between ant-sized foothills, was empty of all vehicles save for military and police transports. But sometimes the road was lined with the newly sworn recruits of a hitherto unknown elite corps who bore the dollar sign patch of the "Fiscal Police" on their burly upper arms.

The Mayatan Fiscal Police kept the "protective cordon" up all the third day. The campaigners could see knots of little men, with Chon Yaa-like haircuts, waving their arms way off in the anthills but Tonatiuh was allowed only to pass through the state, not to actually talk to anyone who lived in it.

That evening, the frustrated convoy was ordered to put in to a many-gabled hotel, awash with purple bougainvillea, out in the deep suburbs of Mordida Hermosa. The Doctor and his entourage were to be confined to the hotel grounds "for their own protection," of course.

Polite men, in freshly ironed guayaberas and pencil-thin

mustaches, large blue pistols wedged into their waistbands, escorted the travelers to their rooms and locked them in from the outside. The guayaberas patroled the hallways to prevent inter-room fraternization.

When Malcreado tried to send 1,200 words up to *El Machetazo*, spelling out this bothersome adventure, the phone system died on him. He picked up his cellular but it too had ceased to function. He called Mickey two rooms down the hall and it sounded like he was talking from Venus—before the phone went mute in Raus' ear. Then the lights went out, imprisoning the press crops in darkness.

On the far side of Mickey's stripped-down single, Tania and Sasha Vigo were banging on the thin hotel walls, calling for help. Tania and "Miss Blonde Ambition" lit each other's ciggies, held hands at breakfast, and were always in each other's ear. They disappeared into the same hotel room each night to do who knows what to each other. The possibilities aroused Mickey's interest.

Raus tapped on the wall, contemplating what sort of hanky-panky was up on the other side of the sheet rock.

"Tania, it's Mickey, can you hear me?" She tapped back. He found himself excited by the erotic possibilities of percussive conversation.

"Mickey," Tania breathed through the hotel wall. Was she in her underwear? "We're locked up in here. The lights blew. And those men out there in the hall. I'm scared."

"Did you check the balcony?"

"There's no balcony. The windows are locked," Vigo hissed.

"This is a human rights violation, don't you think, Mickey?"

"I hope that's all it is," Raus muttered to himself. Leather heels clicked against high-shine linoleum tiles out in the hallway.

"Don't worry—I think we're okay. They're not going to fuck with the press. I mean, we're Internationals, right?" This last supposition, he had to concede, was a little upscale for the *North Coast Variety News*.

"You're right, I suppose—but we have the door booby-trapped just in case." Booby-trapped? He heard Vigo giggle. "Mickey, look, I've got to go. G'night, sleep tight."

Raus did not sleep tight. The rhythmically shifting bed and the coos of lovemaking in the next room pestered him into an enormous hard-on. He masturbated—short, hard, painful pulls that did not bring much relief. Outside in the hall, the guayaberas walked the tiles until dawn.

꧁

THE FOURTH DAY got off to an equally dismal start. An exceedingly polite troika of Fiscal Police commanders informed the Bishop that the meeting in Mordida Hermosa would have to be postponed. The city had been designated a disaster zone due to the arrival of a virulent strain of African Killer bees. Partial martial law had been proclaimed. Any kind of excitement could provoke the bees to riot and attack. The triumvirate also strongly advised Tonatiuh not to put in at Kukulkan because of a similar problem with venomous Guatemalan snakes. But, since the luxury resort was now leased to Kleenex-Fantasia Americana (a division of GE-DisneyMex), it was really out of their jurisdiction and they couldn't stop the Candidate from trying to hold a rally there, not even for his own protection, could they now?

꧁

THE LOMELI REGIME had just ceded Kukulkan to DisneyMex in exchange for the write-off of a little less than 0.07% of the nation's zooming foreign debt. Now this shining slab of aluminum, glass, and limestone, over which bone-white beaches had been artfully salted to accommodate the bone-white tourists, was leased, managed, mortgaged, and visited exclusively by jet-setting North Americans and their European guests. The natives who once fished this sleepy Caribbean shore named for the Mayan version of the Plumed Serpent now needed special photo I.D. just to come to work.

Mayan laborers had constructed Kukulkan's splendid hotels, step by step, to replicate the pyramids and astronomical observatories of their ancestors. Once the hotel-temples were built, the hod-carriers and their families stayed on, providing international hoteliers with hordes of minimum-wage chamber-maids and dishwashers and ditchdiggers, in the event of new hotels and condominiums.

In contrast to the sumptuous surroundings that the servants vacuumed and polished and walloped and hauled cement to all day—under the hot sun, in leaky buckets—their own quarters were set in a malarial swamp. The contrast between life in the Fabulous First World of Kleenix-Fantasia Americana and what was here closer to the famine-struck Fifth was so stark that the Secretary of Tourism had declared the slum off-limits to prying photographers. Although only separated by a mile of sewage-infested swampland, the slums of Kukulkan could have been at the other end of the universe from the resort's soaring hotel-temples.

In these forbidden swamps, the WHO had recorded virtually every known tropical disease in the manuals and a few with patents pending, including seven strains of malaria and three yellow fevers (one was actually jonquil). It was this desperately ill Kukulkan that the Doctor intended to visit.

The rocks and bottles began to fly ten yards into the Kukulkan enclave. Drunken little men lurched in and around the buses, hurling construction materials and drained Presidente bottles and hollering belligerently for the maricones inside to come out and fight like a "macho." Who was it they had been told was in the bus?

One obsessed borracho was now climbing up the Nene's windshield, hacking at it with a short ax—but each time that he swung, the weight of the weapon all but tore him from his precarious perch. "Papa Sol, Papa Sol! Do you read me, Papa Sol?" the shaken kid appealed to his father up ahead.

Through the splintering windshield, Raus saw a large chunk of concrete disappear into the rear window of the Sun, scattering terrified domino players but ultimately severing no arteries. "Out of here!" bellowed Papa Sol on the CB. "Do you read me, m'ijo?"—hand-signaling frantically out the window just in case the kid had missed it.

Raus felt the bump. He knew what had been struck was less brittle than a bottle and softer than a stone. The drunk with the short ax was no longer clinging to the windshield.

Two klicks down the highway, the convoy was cut off by a swarm of red-flashing traffic cruisers and the reporters were instructed to descend from the La Luna with their hands high in the air. Young Lázaro had flattened his attacker, an open-and-shut case of hit-and-run vehicular manslaughter. The sallow, pinch-faced kid, undefended by his pop's bristling facial hairs, was ordered to "spread 'em." In the flashing lights of the cruisers, camou-wearing DisneyMex cops frisked the Nene for weapons. A husky officer forced a breathalyzer into the kid's mouth. Another stood by with the Mason jar for the mandatory urine sample. Old Cristóbal Cantú Cabañas limped over to volunteer legal counsel and was arrested for interfering with an officer. The cuffs were snapped on and he and his client led off to a waiting cruiser. The Moon was to be impounded. The DisneyMex cops ordered everyone back up into the Sol and encouraged the campaigners to continue west across the state line into the treacherous bayous of Cocodrillo. The Stringer's temples throbbed. Where was he heading?

꙰

DAY BY DAY and hour by hour, what was billed to be a miracle crusade through the republic's Indian South was tail-spinning towards witless disaster. The PRO had carefully undermined the route every speed bump of the way, de la Mancha and Warmán Warmán traveling a day in front, suitcases filled with silver Centenarios and South African Krugarands, rough jute sackfuls of paper pesos leaking from the trunks of their limousines, spreading the wealth around to their people and their people's cousins, along with the weapons and the uniforms to create spurious police forces. The concept was to keep Tonatiuh's caravan rolling through the region but to deny him much quality time with the voters.

Meanwhile, the "People's Choice," Filemón Barcelona, campaigned in the grand PRO manner, jetting to staged meetings in state capitals aboard the red, green, and white presidential airbus, although he had not yet been elected to its usage. Fleets of U.S.-supplied military helicopters lifted the little Candidate from airport to rally. Security was thorough and intense. Barcelona drove down broad avenues, waving to the bused-in multitudes from the bubble of a domed PROmobile—the Colosio Syndrome still worried planners. The Army cleared the roads over which Barcelona traveled of possible land mines and the Air Force kept all aircraft from the skies when the presidential jet (and the press jet with which it flew in tandem) lifted its silvery wings into the wide blue yonder.

Each magnum event was meticulously plotted. There was no room for fuck-ups. Rivers of patriotic red and green and white bunting—the PRO's colors, as well as those of the national flag—were draped over the facades of every public building from government palaces to the pissoirs in the parks. Enormous outlays of cash—the PRO made little distinction between public monies and its own campaign war chest—were expended to ensure the attendance of the Popular Sectors. Every possible vehicle in the anointed state of the day was commandeered to ferry the populace to Filemón Barcelona's tightly orchestrated bacchanals. A free lunch (usually green "bologna" on white Bimbo bread, a genuine U.S. Ho-Ho, a can of classic strawberry Boing-g-g!) plus double a day's wages were one enticement to attend. One could lose one's job or one's land or even one's life for failure to pass muster. Everyone had to wear weird tri-color assemble-it-yourself cardboard Barcelona hats. PRO Gold Cards, with direct access to the July 2 ballot, were distributed at the gates of the streamlined portable stadium the Party had designed to accommodate its masses with maximum surveillance. The stadium itself was adjustable so that it could fit around a crowd snugly enough—to transform even the most disappointing turnout into a standing-room-only triumph on the despicable Abraham Mongo's nightly "news" cast, "Abajo de la Noticia."

ABOARD THE DAMAGED SOL, Tonatiuh's 11 surviving fellow
travelers hunched defensively, convulsed in dreams of doom as
the bus limped through the vibrant green muck of Cocodrillo,
swamps in which 19-foot crocodiles were still said to lurk despite
the PRO government's program to convert them all into luxury
export shoes.

"Next stop, the PROs feed us to the crocs," Raus jived Tania.
She frowned, her curly head propped against Vigo's shoulder.
No one much wanted to hear Raus's graveyard commentary. The
quintet of reporters snoozed fitfully. The dominoes had been scattered in the Kukulkan scuffle. A solemn Tonatiuh, who had opened
his mouth less inside the bus than he'd been allowed to open it
outside, was leafing through his father's old campaign diary.

Raus figured the next move would be a phone call up to
Carlos Quinto Street to confer with the ghost of the Old Man
himself.

But Cocodrillo, and the Pantano Rico region where the
Bishop's star-crossed itinerary was taking the Candidate today, was not a PRO stronghold. The Putan Mayas of Pantano
Rico were on the warpath against the government, which, in
its thirst for Black Gold, had drilled and abandoned hundreds
of uncapped wells into which Indian children kept vanishing
with annoying frequency. A World Bank scheme to introduce
tens of thousands of heads of white Sebu cattle had given the
region a kind of Hindu ambiance, that is, until the herds were
all sucked up by the mud or plummeted, clumsy-hoofed, into
the open wells with which PROMISH had pocked the landscape, like encrusted sores on the soft surface of the once
smooth-faced swamp.

The cacao bean was another commodity endangered by
mindless oil greed. The cacao trade had roots here that were as
deep and as rich as the chocolate fashioned from the bean was
bitter and sweet. Mayas and Aztecs had traded for the beans;
they became so valued that for centuries cacao was the

currency of their empires, linking the center and south of the nation into one indigenous subcontinent.

As much as the loss of their children and their Sebus, it was the encroachments on the cacao trade that united the populace. From the lowest chocolate picker to the King of Cacao himself, Pantano Rico stood up against the PRO government. Indeed, it was the King himself—a heavy man carried in a sedan chair, his fleshy chops and several bellies eerily recalling the images of Mayan kings preserved in the ancient murals at Polanco—who would personally welcome Tonatiuh's bedraggled caravan to town.

WITH ITS SLOW-AS-MOLASSES air, tropical drawl, and down-home hospitality, Pantano Rico was to be the next chapter in this souring chronicle. The old colonial port, laid out on the bank of a lazy delta plied by steamboats and packet barges, seemed oddly benign at first. Marimbas ponged in the plaza and feathery palm trees swayed like graceful hula-skirted dancers. Mickey sucked up a long, cool glass of iced chocolate and white rum, and tuned into the King of Cacao, Magnesio Brondo, as he opened the rally with a few introductory remarks.

"Compañeras y Compañeros, Camaradas, Hermanas y Hermanos, Señoritas, Señoras, and Señores, Amigos and Enemigos, My Fellow Workers..."

An hour and 40 minutes later, the Monarch was still intro-ducing his remarks; his long-suffering subjects, all of whom had been coerced to stand hours for such ramblings before, grew fidgety. Perhaps it was the mosquitoes. Kamikaze squadrons dive-bombed the 3,000 wildly swatting citizens. As the war between man and mosquito drew blood, torches and smudge pots were lit. Sweat glistened on the brows of the swatting Putans. Between attacks, Raus distinguished the crackle of walkie-talkies at the corners of the plaza.

The meeting in Pantano was the first on this thus-far disas-trous tour of the south at which the Doctor was actually permitted to speak. Dwarfed by the King of Cacao's extravagant introduction, Tonatiuh's words sounded formal and parsimonious.

"We have already won this election," he announced to the slapping audience, "but only if you confront the PRO with your voice, as well as with your vote, will our victory be known..." The "¡Muerrra Elll PRRRROOOOs!" and "¡Hoooostisssiahhhhs!" were matched decibel for decibel by the industrial-level buzzing of the swamp mosquitoes. El Compa stepped forward to issue instructions for defending the vote at the polls and in the district tallies. Raus could not tell whether the applause was for the candidate or against the mosquitoes.

THE GALVAN PARTY was invited to pass the night behind the walls of the King of Cacao's majestic palace. The feed was a royal one. Platters of giant iced prawns laid out on saw-toothed palm fronds in the Grand Salon, tureens of oysters and mussels and clams, trays laden with Caribbean lobster and Pacific crayfish, long red snappers swimming in coconut milk, stuffed turkeys and turtles and the King's personal peafowl, glazed oinkers simmering in chocolatey sauces, whole sides of Sebus barbecued golden on mesquite fires. The press corps washed the free chow down with crystal goblets of Spanish champagne.

"So, Mickey Maus, I want your story, the whole story, and nothing but the story."

Raus stood champagne glass to champagne glass with Tania Escobar. Her long-legged companion chatted with Malcreado beneath a garish mural that covered one entire side of the Grand Salon, the history of the Patria or the Brondo family—in the King of Cacao's self-obsessed imagination, they amounted to the same saga.

"Your story, please, Mister Maus. I'm on deadline!" she urged mischievously, flashing a street-urchin smile. In Colombia such children are called gamines. She eyed Raus with what, in his increasingly lubricated state, he fancied to be a wanton orb.

"Mine has been an obscenely long and tortured story..."

"Yeah, I've heard that one before," she leered.

Raus was flustered by Tania's attention. Across the room, Sasha Vigo glared white heat. He segued into politics.

"Well, for one thing, the Left. In my country they call geeks like me 'red diaper babies.' I was born on the Left and I stayed on the Left until I left the states." A Mayan Indian in a starched linen tunic refilled their glasses.

"But why did you leave? Why didn't you stay and fight?"

Mickey retraced his motives. He trotted out old John Reed and touted international revolution. He talked, at some length, about the event that had immediately triggered his decision to head south nearly 28 years ago now: the mining of Haiphong Harbor by Richard Nixon on May 9, 1972, and the wild, running battles that exploded on the streets of San Francisco the day after. Some lunk in a suit had yelled at him to go back to Russia and Raus grabbed for the suit's hair, which came off in his hand. Mickey wore the toupee all day, dangling like a scalp from his belt.

Tania, who was six years old in 1972, nodded like she understood Mickey's stream-of-consciousness babble perfectly. Or maybe whatever story he told her didn't much matter.

He had the chilling sensation that Tania was intentionally trying to provoke Sasha Vigo into a jealous rage.

After the street battles, Raus went home to watch himself on television and found the Mission District flat, dark and silent. Cassandra, the scat singer he'd been shacking with for a year, had split to the north country where the real revolution, the internal one, was taking place in tie-dye teepees, under the dripping redwoods. Raus hated the near north woods—the coastal damp that rotted your dope, the chipi-chipi of the rain no one could fix, the lethal depressions of the rednecks living under the belching pulpmills. Six months later Minnie Raus's "red diaper baby" was waving his arms helplessly in a ghastly airport terminal at five in the AM, watching his typewriter disappear into the chilango dawn. But that was a long time ago. A long, long time ago.

The real question was, What was he still doing here?

The two gulped at the champagne greedily. It was Raus' turn to probe. Tania was supposed to be M-19: Bolivar's sword, the incineration of the Supreme Court. "What year did you leave Colombia? Why did you leave?" Her eyes smiled covertly. They were green. "I'm going to tell you all that later." The way Tania said *later*, it sounded like she meant *sooner*.

She took his hand and they tiptoed off towards pink piles of shrimp. Raus was a lot drunker than he remembered being. So was Antonio Malcreado.

"To the King of Cacao! Long may his chocolate words put Pantano Rico to sleep," the *Machetazo* man toasted, missing Raus's glass entirely.

"To the King of Cacao! Long may he shit all over himself in public!" Raus hiccuped by way of small talk.

Now the two sloshed newshounds connected, clanking their glasses into smithereens, drawing hysterical giggles from Tania, a snort of disgust from Vigo, disdainful stares from the Indian servants, but little notice from the butt of their toasts, Don Magnesio, who, like an overly hospitable giant squid, had draped his steaming underarms over Tonatiuh's shoulders and would not let go.

Mickey looked up from the stem of his busted goblet and observed Tania Escobar being dragged off to the upstairs bedrooms by her piqued blonde paramour.

🦎

BUT THE NIGHT, as Tania had hinted, was yet young. When Raus heard the soft tap at the door, he suspected right away who it was and why. The alcohol in his belly had distilled into pure, glowing lust. Tania turned the knob and tiptoed across the threshold, feigning drunkenness. "Oh, I must be in the wrong room."

"Sure you are." The mop-haired urchin had already stripped down to her panties. She fell upon him like a carnivore, tonguing and tearing his flesh. Raus, starved for sex and love since Jane Ann had moved on, grew huge, and Tania kissed his cock greedily, even as he shredded her wet panties with his few remaining teeth. An old stallion straddling the squirming, squealing Tania, it took Mickey many thrusts to reach climax.

Later, she smoked a joint and he floated joylessly on the stained sheets. "Weren't you going to tell me why you left?"

"No no," she giggled, "why I came..."

And still later, stumbling to the tall window of the spinning guest room in the faint light of the dawn to sneak a pee, Raus almost urinated all over a small man with a Chon Yaa-like haircut who was perched atop the high hacienda wall. The little man jumped soundlessly into the jungle below before Mickey could even file his face for future reference.

By morning, everyone was back in their proper beds. After a breakfast in a garden blazing with parrots, the Doctor prepared to shove off for the long, sad haul through Chiapas, a rendezvous with the phantoms of the Zapatista rebellion. The good news was that young Lázaro and old Cantú Cabañas had been released by the Kukulkan authorities, under orders from Hollywood. DisneyMex wanted to avoid the appearance of involvement in the coming Mexican presidential election.

And eighteen full hours after the King of Cacao kissed Tonatiuh good-bye on both cheeks, his magnificent hacienda burnt dramatically—if unspontaneously—to the ground. On the morning after the morning after, the cinders of Magnecio Brondo's chocolate-covered empire fused with the rubberized shards of splintered champagne glasses and shredded panties left behind by Tonatiuh's pickled paparazzi.

EL SOL CRUISED the main drag of Polanco, sandwiched between U.S. Army surplus Humvees. After years of rebellion and massacre, Chiapas was again ruled by a military man, General Archibaldo Absalom Ramírez Ramírez. Although General Ram Ram's mandate was restricted by the Treaty of the Basilica to those areas of Chiapas outside of the Zapatista autonomous zones (ZAPs), he ruled the rest of the state literally with an iron hand—the General's left hand had been blown apart in the Army's final, failed assault on the Zapatista caves. In its place, Ramírez Ramírez had installed a steel claw.

"Death to Tonatiuh!" it said in loopy spray-painted letters on the pastel blue walls of Polanco. Curiously dressed natives studied the fast-drying paint. Don Estalin did not stop. Instead, he drove to the edge of the tourist town and continued south towards the world-renowned ruins of the long-lost Mayan wizard city, where the autonomous zones commenced.

Raus had never been to Polanco before. These days, the far-famed temples drew appreciable numbers of European Community tourists. Some, pretending to be freelance archeologists, just moved in for good. Germans with long, tangled blonde dreadlocks took up residence in the turreted precinct of Zotz the Bat God. Naked Frenchwomen cavorted in the catacombs where the Jaguar Gods prowled the night. Italians in loincloths on vision quests tried to break through the fading friezes on the walls of the sacred precincts into the Old World. The English had set up camp in the Temple of the Magicians. Each Guy Fawkes Day, the Brits would blast off rockets from the steep steps of the Pyramid and some fell drunkenly to their deaths. This annual sacrificial rite delighted the Polanco Mayans clustered around the base of the temple, begging the foreigners for small coins. Nowadays even the foreigners were panhandling visitors.

Tonatiuh's party brushed aside the small-change artists and crossed the broad grassy avenue that had been etched from the jungle more than a millennium ago. Beyond the Temple of the Magicians, to the south, the jungle resumed dominion. Two men—Moises, Marcos' long-time adjutant, and a barefoot old shaman—met the Doctor under the sole surviving ceiba tree in the east of the forest. Tonatiuh and the heavyset Moises embraced fondly.

"Doctor, we have been expecting you ever since your mule returned," Major Moises smiled. Tonatiuh saw that the smile in Moises' eye was a tired one, eaten away by the jungle fevers that afflicted the True Zapatistas year after year in this disease-ridden zone the rebels had finally wrested from the PRO Government after many angry years of struggle. "This is the same mule you rode when we had to pull out of Tepeyac in February '95. We abandoned it in Agua Azul after the bombing, do you remember?" Moises coughed and spat. "It hasn't been seen since. We only found it last week, grazing in the jungle—here, in back of the temple."

They took Tonatiuh to the mule.

"It is the same mule your father rode when he visited us in the other time," the Chilam—who, like his village, was called Chamul—whispered into Tonatiuh's long ear.

"How can it be the same mule?"

"Your father's mule had the star of the morning upon its forehead. So does this one."

"But such a mule would have to be older than I am now."

The grizzled beast nuzzled Tonatiuh, as if an old fond memory had been stirred. Chamul insisted that Tonatiuh mount the prodigal animal. "Come, we will take you to Marcos," smiled Moises wanly, leading the mule deeper into the Lacandón.

Raus and Tania, Malcreado, and the others followed behind, discretely stumbling headlong over twisted jungle roots. No one had interviewed Subcomandante Marcos in two years, since soon after the Treaty of the Basilica was signed, when he finally removed his ski mask—to reveal a second ski mask. Marcos had chosen to stay with the "sin rostros"—those without faces—deep inside the autonomous zone, besieged by disease, with General Ram Ram encamped on his perimeter. Renouncing all pretensions to political office, the Sup had settled in the bat caves of Zotz, a haunted, hermit-like figure, attended only by Moises and his longtime lover, the former Tequila Minsky, an ex-L.A. talk-show host who had made his story her own.

It was said that Marcos no longer spoke.

Moises and the Chilam led the Doctor through the collection of stone huts that was Chamul, across a swiftly moving stream and down into the deep green, fog-shrouded canyon sunk between the blue mountains. The representatives of the press were soon swallowed up by jungle vegetation. Giant flaming macaws broke from the emerald canopy as the procession passed below. From inside its hollowed-out lair, the reddened daylight eyes of the jungle's last jaguar traced the interlopers as they trampled down the ferns. A weird gooning vibrated through the forest. "Howler monkeys," Tania whispered. She had lived in tropical mountain jungle before, during her last years in the guerrilla back home in Colombia. Mickey Raus, on the other hand, had never gotten much past Tarzan and Jane.

ALTHOUGH THEY WERE comrades-in-arms, Subcomandante Marcos and Tonatiuh had served distinct wings of the armed struggle. Marcos, the brilliant, brash strategist, embodied the EZLN's unquenchably combative spirit. Tonatiuh, a usually morose man, fell victim to the solitudes of the jungle mountains. The wizened, infirm Indians he treated only saddened him more, and he grew taciturn and invisible under his ski mask as he made his way from one Zapatista village to the next, tending to the sick, a sole silent figure treading the jungle paths.

Now their roles had turned upside down: Tonatiuh was the speaker and the Sup had retreated into unreachable silences deep within the caves of Zotz. Wary of the brainless babble of national politics, Marcos, like Maher Baba before him, had sworn his tongue to silence and no words now left his lips—Tequila had publicly stitched them together so that now only his ever present pipe fit between the sutures. He did not give interviews anymore.

The domed cavern was artfully camouflaged by a matted curtain of lianas and jungle creepers. One hundred masked True Zapatistas barred passage to all except the Doctor, Moises, Chamul and the mule. The Bishop smoked and fumed. The press sniveled and begged to be allowed to accompany Tonatiuh into the inner sanctum.

"We're accredited journalists, don't you dumbos understand?" Von Voodle demanded, fishing out plastic cards. Tania nearly hung a fat lip on the munchkin reporter.

A pale, spectral figure—the same old Sherlock Holmes pipe

pluming from the mouth-hole of his pasamontañas—material-
ized in the dim jaws of the cave, blinking at the harsh noontime
rays flooding the jungle floor. "Marcos!" the reporters gasped.
"It's Marcos!" The Sup did not seem to acknowledge their shouts.
Instead, Tonatiuh and his Zapatista comrade embraced warmly,
the Doctor bending down to clasp the increasingly crookbacked
Sup.

As the two vanished arm and arm into the cave, Marcos could
not resist hiking up his pants cuff and saucily kicking out his
leg behind him like the good old days—"showing pierna" they
call it, what starlets do at movie premieres.

Who knew how long they would have to wait now, Raus
wondered. Tania took his hand and fastened her happy green
eyes inside his shaded lens. They hung there, pendulous and
fused, transfixed by the transient magic of the moment. No one
could say for just how long. No one could calculate just how
long Tonatiuh and Marcos, Moises, the mule and the wizard
were gone or even where they had gone. The Bishop kept shaking his watches. They had both stopped hours before.

When, at last, Tonatiuh and Marcos emerged, they were preceded by a great fluttering of bats or birds—Raus could not say
what dark, winged creatures flew first from the cave mouth and
soared into the speckled sunlight. Now, both the Doctor and the
Sup were emitting that same soft, spectral glow Marcos had ex-
uded when he first appeared.

"We have talked," was all Tonatiuh would say, never men-
tioning what the self-silenced Subcomandante had said back.
And when the reporters sought out the Sup for clarification,
Marcos had dissolved into memory.

ALL THAT DAY and into the night and the morning again,
Tonatiuh rode the old mule to the caves of the True Zapatistas.
The Doctor greeted each of the Indians by his or her nom de
guerre, checked the pulse and the color of the tongue of each
one, patted them on the back, and traveled on—never asking

for their votes because the candidate knew the True Zapatistas believed only in themselves.

Tonatiuh and his ancient mount plodded slowly up the rutted track towards the mountains. Behind them, Don Estalin maneuvered the campaign bus out of the sweltering jungle zones and began to climb for the highlands. Now, in some villages, the men wore short white skirts. In others, vivid ceremonial ribbons dangled from their wide sombreros. "The ribbons are the four corners of the earth where the Bacabs hold up the world," marveled Tania. The women of each village were swathed in huipiles so complexly embroidered that it seemed as if the universe had been emblazoned in magic threads upon their bosoms. "The opening for the head is where the sun rises," she breathed into his ear. "The opening for the arms points north and south."

Everything up here in the highlands had been transformed into an object of devotion: the threads of the huipiles, the tall, green crosses by the sides of the road, the wild totem animals in the forest or up in the ghost corrals at the summit, the color of the candles, how long they burned, what the Saints said, what the Talking Stones said, what the posh said because "posh makes you listen to your soul"—the Orange Crush or Boing-g-g, the flavors favored by the Saints that they mixed with this clear, harsh white lightning. All of these objects radiated prophecy.

The spiritual life of the Zotzils was as old as the bat caves. One Christian Bishop after another had sought, without success, to domesticate the drunken Indians. Even Don Samuel, the beatific former bishop of San Cris who was now imprisoned in the Vatican basement, had failed to quench the Zotzils' spiritual thirst.

The ceremony was the same in each highland village: Tonatiuh, the ski-masked Moises, and the shaman Chamul would ride through the town, pausing to pay homage at the roadside crosses and the shrines of the saints and the hidden temples of Zotz, listening to the Talking Stones concealed in locked, felt-lined boxes that the elders held for safekeeping.

Then the compañeros would take the visitors to the massacre sites. Each village had one somewhere, hidden in the gullies at the edge of the houses or far out on the damp meadows, blooming with sage and summer flowers—the killing fields that General Ram Ram and the terratenientes and their White Guards had always selected to execute those suspected of not being dead enough yet. Each secret graveyard had been consecrated and camouflaged, the bones of the dead Zotziles marked by a pebble or a branch or a single drying petal, so that once the murderers had moved on, only the villagers would know what lay under the earth.

The light dipped low over the highlands and a steady rain beat in from the east. The visitations to the killing fields now were accompanied by melancholy chanting, prayers rendered in a softly clicking tongue, the serious women in their huipiles like little wet birds, carrying candles and wildflowers, eggs and incense, the men gulping down the posh and crying out their desperate longing for the dead. Amidst the rain and the lamentations, Tonatiuh spoke in the secret graveyards.

The Doctor had said little for days. Now, his tongue loosened by the potent spirits, he spoke what troubled his heart. As always, he remembered first the past. His father's visit here during the Long Campaign, a journey that had filled the General full of wonder. How the General's revolution had expired before it ever reached Chiapas, picked clean by the vultures of the PRO. "Now the people are being taught to forget their history. This is why we have come to you, little sisters and brothers—to reclaim our true history."

He had begun to speak in a softly clicking Indian tongue. The Zotziles understood every word.

Tonatiuh kept marching further and further back in history. He recalled that dread morning when the pink-skinned conquerors came with spiders on their faces to eclipse the Fifth Sun of the Aztecs. He reached back to when the fierce Aztec-Chichimecas carried their bloody Humming Bird god to the center of the One True Heart, there, in the nopal cactus, where the Eagle dined upon the Serpent. He remembered when Quetzalcoatl-Kukulkan, the young Lord of the Morning Star, reigned peacefully over a gleaming white empire so burnished by time that no one could quite conjure up its name anymore.

"In all these different suns, our emissaries walked with the Maya. Quetzalcoatl himself came and was transformed into Kukulkan. Treaties were forged and signed and sealed with amber and beeswax, blood and seed.

"But that was in another sun. In this time, I come again as an emissary from the North. We are, like you, a subject and humiliated people, but our prophets still read the comets and the stars. They see signs. They see conjunctions. They say we will soon cast off the darkness the PRO has brought upon us. Only then will the world return to its rightful Sun."

Raus had heard the India Cristina expound her crackpot theory of Aztec revivalism on the talk shows, and even flipped through the paperback pages of her best-seller *The Age of The Sixth Sun*, never once imagining that Tonatiuh Galván might believe these loony predictions.

Did the Doctor really believe?

AND, IN THE DAYS AFTER the campaign descended from the highlands to the Pacific, a buzzing louder than a cloud of killer bees or homicidal mosquitoes could be audited over a huge region that extended from Chiapas past Mordida, all the way east to the tip of the Mayatan peninsula, and north half the length of the state of Julapa, an area roughly the dimensions of the old Mayan territories.

From room to room and house to house, cooking pit to marketplace, rancho to town, jungle to milpa, mountain to mountain, across the narrow neck of the isthmus from one coast to the next, the message traveled on the stormy wings of summer squalls and in the daily afternoon drops of rain and the soft, wafting tropical breezes that bless the old kingdom. And to those who could hear it, the words came in loud and clear. The Sixth Sun will soon rise. Watch for the signs. Then the old treaties are to be honored, and after a half millennium of enslavement, we will join together as one people again against the common despoilers of our destiny.

OPPOSITION CANDIDATE'S AIDE GUNNED DOWN AT HUAJUCO CAMPAIGN RALLY

GALVAN SUPPORTERS HELD

Special to the North Coast Variety News

GRAN HUAJUCO, HUAJUCO (July 13)—A key aide to Mexico's chief opposition presidential candidate, Dr. Tonatiuh Galván, was shot and seriously wounded last night during a campaign rally in this sultry provincial city, located on the Huajucan Isthmus, 400 miles south of the nation's capital. Cristóbal Cantú Cabañas, 72, had just stepped forward to sing the new national anthem, as is the custom at the close of Galván election rallies, when the gunfire broke out to the left of the speaker's platform. Cantú Cabañas, a deputy for a minor political party in the national congress and childhood mentor of the candidate, was hit ten times by small-arms fire in the stomach and legs. His condition is listed as grave in a local public hospital.

Although Galván was standing unprotected some six feet from the victim, the gunmen—or gunwomen, as the case may be—apparently made no effort to fire upon the candidate.

"The PRO writes us a message in the blood of our friends. We are not impressed," an unsmiling Tonatiuh Galván, who is a medical doctor and was the first to attend his old teacher, declared to the *Variety News* immediately after the shooting.

The acronym to which the Doctor was referring is that of the long-ruling Party of the Organic Revolution, which has not lost a national election in the 71 years that have elapsed since the founding of the state party. The shooting of Cantú Cabañas is widely interpreted by Galván supporters as a warning to the opposition candidate not to claim victory in the July 2 polling. Galván appears to be running strongly in many regions of the country and has often said that he has the votes to win—if the PRO is prevented from committing massive electoral fraud.

Gunwomen Guilty?

Despite Galván's assertion that the PRO was behind last night's gunplay, State Preventative Police Chief Edgardo Bobolobo, whom Governor Inocencio Mu personally assigned to protect the candidate during his two days here, announced this morning that two women, apparently affiliated with the Galván cause in Gran Huajuco, are being held, after signing confessions admitting that they fired the shots that wounded Mr. Cantú Cabañas. In copies of the women's statements, distributed to the press by Bobolobo, the pair purportedly said their intended target was Galván "because he is spreading false prophecies among the Indian peoples."

The accused, Olivia Xandani and Lourdes María Xuhlub, were presented to national and international news media during Bobolobo's press conference, but remained mute when reporters asked them to confirm their confessions. The two large women, both dressed in the typical native garb of the isthmus, exhibited contusions on their faces and arms.

In response to reporters' questions about the weapon or weapons used, Bobolobo repeatedly answered that his men were "working on locating one."

"The arrest and torture of these women compounds the outrage we feel at the attack on our compañero Cristóbal," a visibly shaken Abelardo Salmón, Dr. Galván's longtime adviser, commented following the police chief's presentation of Xandani and Xuhlub. The aide confirmed that both the accused are activists in the Galván campaign.

Large Political Ladies

Gran Huajuco, a commercial capital of 200,000 situated on the Pacific rim of the isthmus, is famous for political participation by women. It was, in fact, the woman mayor of Gran Huajuco, Mirasol Xixi, who personally invited Dr. Galván here to conduct the rally, which drew upwards of 20,000 mostly Zipotec women, the largest public event the candidate has been able to convene since he began a swing through the nation's heavily Indian south two weeks ago.

Gran Huajuco has a long-standing tradition of political independence. In the two most recent national elections here, many large, militant Zipotec women blocked access to all polling booths in the city in an effort to prevent the PRO from declaring victory. The official party, nonetheless, claimed 89% of the vote in both elections.

The shooting of Mr. Cantú came at the end of a tense rally during which occasional scuffles broke out between plainclothes federal secret agents and long-skirted municipal police officers assigned by the mayor to keep order. Mayor Xixi later told the *Variety News* that the agents known as secretos were trying "to provoke our women into a 'balacera' (shoot-out)" in an effort "to discredit the first feminist-run city in the land." Gunshots were heard earlier near the packed, bird-filled plaza in which the rally was held.

Bronto Hardliners

Prior to the shooting, the state's half-Zipotec, half-Chinese governor, Inocencio Mu, a member of the PRO, guaranteed Galván "the right to free speech anywhere in Huajuco." This morning the Governor's office issued a statement "deploring" the shooting of Mr. Cantú Cabañas—and said his offer of "free speech" still goes.

Governor Mu's pronouncements were known to ruffle feathers among PRO "brontosauri," or old-guard hardliners such as farmers' confederation chieftain Bernabé Warmán Warmán and Salvador "Sancho" de la Mancha, a leader of the PRO's popular sector, both of whom were present in Gran Huajuco today. Both men accused Dr. Galván of "setting up" Mr. Cantú in order to stir sympathy "for his failing cause."

Warmán Warmán and de la Mancha were reportedly dispatched by the PRO central committee to counter the opposition candidate's surprising success during forays to various parts of the republic.

Rocky Road

Governor Mu's conciliatory message contrasted sharply with those of neighboring PRO governors through whose states the Galván caravan has passed in the final phase of his campaign. In neighboring Chiapas, Military Governor General of Brigade Archibaldo A. Ramírez Ramírez refused to grant Dr. Galván rally permits in the state capital of Uxtla Ramírez, explaining that "national security matters" took precedence over the airing of "minority views" in the conflictive region where rebel Mayans fought the government to a stalemate in the 1990s. Dr. Galván spent several years as the rebels' medical chief.

Last week, on the Mayatan peninsula, police refused to allow the Doctor permission to conduct a public meeting because killer bees were said to be hovering in the area. When events have been allowed to proceed, Galván's supporters have been set upon by club-wielding PRO thugs, such as occurred in Ciudad Lomelí during a dissident oil workers' rally.

During the past 12 days, the candidate has been stoned by intoxicated locals, apparently in the employ of the ruling party in the resort of Kukulkan; and the home of a wealthy farmer who housed Galván and his party for an evening was burned to the ground in Pantano Rico, Cocodrillo state.

Indian South Strategy

Capturing the largely Indian South of the nation is one of Galván's key strategies for dislodging the PRO. The official party has never taken less than 89% of the vote in the region and, despite the difficulties the Doctor has faced in the past few days, there has been enthusiastic contact when he has been permitted to interact with the citizenry.

Support among Mayan Indians was perhaps most palpable when Dr. Galván returned to his old haunts in the jungles and highlands of Chiapas, where he served as a member of the guerrilla Zapatista Army of National Liberation (EZLN) from 1991 through amnesty in 1998. The candidate met with the legendary "Subcomandante Marcos" and other old comrades-in-arms and was received warmly wherever he traveled. The Doctor journeyed through much of the region on mule-back.

The size of the meeting in Gran Huajuco, the seat of the 400,000-strong Zipotec nation, underscores that Galván's message of "taking our history back from the PRO" has wide appeal among distinct Indian constituencies.

Not Over Yet

While Galván zeroes in on the Indian vote, his heavily favored rival, Filemón Barcelona, a former finance minister, has been drawing large crowds of his own as he jets to rallies in state capitals around the country. A poll released yesterday (June 12th) by Disney-GallupMex (DGM), indicated that the PRO standard-bearer will capture between 75% and 80% of the total vote July 2.

Up until his current swing through the southern provinces, Galván was clearly narrowing the gap between himself and Barcelona and was thought to have the lead in several states. Although the Doctor, who is the son of one of the nation's most beloved presidents, risked losing momentum by choosing to conclude a crucial phase of his campaign in a part of the country that is not much in the public eye, the impressive rally in Gran Huajuco indicates that, despite PRO violence, less than three weeks to election day, Galván continues to gather strength.

VI

HEADING NORTH

June 14 – June 29, 2000

THE MOON-FACED Tata-mandones stood watch outside as Tonatiuh inspected the little box of a room placed like a museum piece right in the center of the plaza of Cuacua. He ran his long fingers over the rough wooden desk, tested the narrow tin cot and sat down on it, afraid that the only other article of furniture in the austere room—a straight-backed chair—might splinter under his weight. The single dim light bulb swayed gravely in the mountain breeze. Except for weekly dustings by the town clerk, the room had not been altered since Tonatiuh had come to Santa Eulalia 25 years ago to fetch his father. The Tata-mandones had preserved it exactly as if the General still lurked here in the dark, trying to remember God's name.

There are always so many old men, Tonatiuh despaired, everywhere I go, everywhere I've been. Old men trying to show me what's in their hand or teach me the name of a rock or a flower. Old men who fought with my father or against him. So many elders, teachers, abuelos, Tata-mandones waiting outside in their white kotones. Tata Anastacio at the top of Zapicho. Cristóbal Cantú, the life oozing out of ten exit wounds down in Gran Huajuco just two nights ago...

The old men all died in the end, defeated by the darkness after ungraceful, excruciating battles with the Gran Calaca, never slipping quietly away with famous last words framed on their lips. No, his old men were repositories of regrets, shouting and sobbing, drooling and pissing, pleading for you to seek revenge. He sat by the death beds and asked them questions about what they had done, why they had fought in the revolution, what battles had been won, anything of value to pass on, to teach those they were abandoning how to find the right road, and they could only remember what they'd lost. His father, sitting here in the dark like a silent monk, trying to remember the name of God.

The candidate could hear the Bishop pacing outside, the faint tick of his watches. Outside, time was running out on him, he knew that, but he continued to campaign in here, among his ghosts.

Tonatiuh no longer had many childhood scores to settle with the General, but for a long time he had thought that he did. When all 57 doctor-brothers sat down to eat, he was always served last and least. Why? There were always seconds for everyone but him. "You've already had your seconds, son," the General hushed him. But 25 years ago, Tonatiuh knocked timidly on this scarred board door in the plaza of Santa Eulalia Cuacua and realized that the father who lay knotted in fetal sleep was not the one he'd left in charge on Carlos Quinto Street. Tlatelolco had come at him like a swift, sharp kick to his gut and each new massacre bit deeper. His insides bled copiously. In the end, he had taken to huddling in the back pew of the little chapel here, holding his hemorrhaging belly while he tried desperately to remember God's name.

The General quite simply wanted absolution. Before he allowed himself to die, he craved God's forgiveness for the sin of having created the PRO.

THE TATA-MANDON they call Anecleto meekly interrupted the Doctor's reverie. "It is time to eat now, m'ijo. The members of the councils are waiting." Anecleto lured him into the harsh light of the High Monteca, the brutal sun finding its reflection inside the glint of rock surfaces. The great flinty slabs of stone were the only fruit of this cracked mountain moonscape.

The Tata-mandones sat at long tables outside under the eaves of a rambling town hall. They had come from each of the three Montecas to touch his hand and carry the message back to the many other Santa Eulalias that hid bashfully in the threadbare folds of this bare, eroded sierra.

For the fiesta the Tata-mandones of Santa Eulalia Cuacua had killed and barbecued a sheep, and the scent of the roasting meat had been an additional incentive for the elders to walk the many stony miles to attend the banquet. It had also brought out hordes of small, swollen-bellied children, who squatted in the street swatting flies and fighting skinny dogs for the bones the old men tossed over their shoulders.

"We do not get to eat like this everyday," joked Anecleto, mowing down a rack of ribs despite a mouthful of badly de-pleted teeth. "We haven't killed a sheep here all year."

"In the Low Monteca, it is better because it is nearer the sea down there and the fog helps the corn grow. Way up here, we've had no corn crop since your father was president," explained a Tata-mandón from Santa Eulalia Triko, sucking noisily on his fingers.

In the time of the Fifth Sun, the Montecas had occupied a fertile kingdom where these gentle people of the cloud forests fed not only themselves but the gods above and the poor devils down below on the scorched isthmus. Then came the Christians, who taught them to kneel before the image of the Blessed Virgin and gave them axes to chop down the tree gods. They say Tlaloc ran in fright before the blades and it had only rained six times since, once when the General died.

In Santa Eulalia Cuacua, 150 out of each 1,000 births died in their first months and became angels, lethargically haunting the smoky kitchens of their mothers forever. Those children who escaped into adolescence left quickly for the north in the rusting buses the Garbage Kings sent for them. Others hitchhiked to the big cities and rented accordions while their baby brothers begged passersby for coins. Villages like Cuacua were inhabited only by old people and infants, whom absent parents had sent home because it was hard to travel from dump to dump with so many kids too young to pick garbage or play accordions strapped to you.

"Our sons have traveled far in the world but we do not know them anymore," Anecleto was explaining mournfully. "When they come home for the fiestas, you can see the disappointment in their faces. They look at us and can't remember why they came. Up in the cities they say people come by and drop stuff on the ground, if just by accident. Here, there is not even that."

Beyond these barren mountains, Monteca families had become the garbage pickers of the nation. It had happened gradually—first, one would be allowed to pick, and then his cousin. Now they lived and picked in all the dumps of the capital. Colonies of Santa Eulalians lived in garbage pits all over the country. The largest population of Montecas anywhere on the planet now resided in Tijuana, where all the refuse of the kingdom of California right above it bottomed out. And now the Montecas were migrating further north into the industrial wastelands of California itself and could even be found clear across the U.S., digging in the garbage cans on the lower east side of Manhattan.

"They do not come home so much anymore," old Anecleto sighed forlornly. "I think it is because we are too poor to make garbage for them." Tonatiuh put his arm around the broken-hearted old grandfather, as if to say, *Wait, wait, abuelo, they will be coming home soon...*

PADRE LUIS had grown older than all the rest. The priest was now so curved with arthritis that he could only talk to you through the tops of his eyes. The priest had been a callow novitiate when he first came to Cuacua looking for the poorest parish in the Monteca in which to install himself—which was how he found the General, who was also searching out the poorest place in the poorest mountains in the land in which to die.

Santa Eulalia is a tiny town, drained by the emigration of all its citizens between the ages of two and 75, so the General and the priest had plenty of space and time to argue in the one cantina in the plaza that remained open then. For years, they tippled good greasy mescal while Francisco Galván demanded photographs of the Holy Ghost from the good father and Padre Luis got drunk enough to toy with redeeming the old infidel's soul. "But the sin of having given birth to the PRO ate at him and every day he went far away into himself. Towards the end, we had many drinks but few words. Then he started coming to the church when no one was around. He always sat back there. All day. Sometimes he didn't eat. Right through the Mass he sat there, holding his belly. That's when we knew something was wrong and sent Abelardo to find you," the bent old priest recalled.

"He was trying to remember God's name," Tonatiuh said abruptly.

"It's all so long ago, son. Sometimes, I can't remember His name myself. But tell me, Tonatiuh, what is going on out there beyond the Monteca? We get no mail here anymore and there are never batteries for the radios. The only newspapers we read come with the dried fish and are months old."

"You must have heard that I am challenging the PRO to become president..."

"And that you are traveling the whole country, just like your father, asking old men like me for their blessing." Luis removed the Brown Madonna's medal from his own neck. The stamped metal image felt cold as a fish scale against Tonatiuh's dark, spare flesh. "I do not trust much in the Virgin of Guadalupe, you know, Padre."

"Think of her as Tonantzin, son," cackled the crooked father, enjoying his last laugh, at last.

☙

THIS IS A SAD AND TIRED PLACE, Raus considered. Don Estalin and the Nene revved up the buses. There are no votes here and Tonatiuh has lost half a day looking for the General. La Luna moved through the earthen streets, past row after row of boarded-up homes. Santa Eulalia Cuacua is a ghost, he thought. Tomorrow, the campaign would descend to the troublesome coast of El Horno, where there was news that fighting had broken out near Atila.

Raus and Tania stared through the dust-caked window panel, the town becoming a dot on the map behind them.

"Mickey, did you feel it?" she shuddered.

"Feel it?"

"It's going to be bad up ahead."

☙

JUST NORTH OF ACAPELLA, the Pacific Jewel highway was studded with military checkpoints. Only after lengthy wrangling was Tonatiuh's caravan allowed to proceed. But near Atila, the convoy was brought to a dead stop. Don Estalin was informed that they could not continue north.

The killing had begun again in Atila—twenty-four banana workers slain in a "confrontation" with the military.

Tania flashed white heat. "It's a set-up," she spat. "It's a massacre."

On the eve of Tonatiuh's arrival, DisneyMex surveyors had suddenly appeared to stake out ejido land for the expansion of the Twin Jewel tourist complexes. Ismael Caracol led the workers out from town to demand that the gringos leave. A hundred army troops, detailed to protect the North Americans, were hidden in the trees. When the gunfire subsided, Caracol and 23 others were dead or dying. Another dozen were left unattended, bleeding in the banana groves for hours. The playboy governor, Coco Fernández, sent his people to offer them money for their silence, and those who refused to accept the blood money were given the coup de grace to the base of the skull.

Now military intelligence had sighted the late Luis Montes riding through the hills of Atila on a black stallion, calling upon the campesinos to dig up their guns. Further up in the sierra, Lucio's people were said to be moving.

The Bishop stepped down from El Sol to discuss the holdup with whoever was in charge. Ten minutes later, he was back, exasperated. "Necesito tu ayuda," he lip-synched to Raus. Mickey was flattered to be deemed of some use.

He pumped the Captain-Major's hand enthusiastically. "Miguel Raus, *Los Angeles Times.*" He whipped his credential past Epidemio Gutiérrez's highly mirrored shades. El Caimán was a slow reader and his eyes hurt anyway. Mickey explained the deep interest of the U.S. public in the coming presidential election— this interest was particularly keen in Los Angeles, California, where so many compatriots were concentrated. President Lomeli had personally encouraged the *Los Angeles Times* to cover the election campaigns and help his government communicate the new democratic spirit afoot in the land. Raus had clippings to substantiate the invitation. "Look at this one, mi Capitán—PRO's COMMITMENT TO DEMOCRACY QUESTIONED." He wagged the clipping under Epidemio's snout.

El Caimán remembered this smart-ass gringo from his first trip through town and wanted to shoot him on the spot. Instead, he got on the field phone, clapping a paw to his exposed ear so he could get the instructions down right for once.

"Sí...sí...sí, mi General. Hecho." Gutiérrez hung up hard and handed Raus back his credential. The orders had been revised: the caravan could proceed on to Atila. "No hay problema." Raus asked about reports of a confrontation up ahead. "Didn't I just say there's no problem, señor?" el Caimán snapped.

THE FUNERALS OF THE massacred banana workers had begun. Raus and Tania followed Tonatiuh up into the wooden, pine-scented church. The funeral Mass was the first that Mickey Raus ever attended in Tonatiuh Galván's company, but would not be the last. There would come a time when the funerals would become the Doctor's most frequent political platform.

The dead needed to be buried quickly in Little Infernillo. There was already a gassy odor when you came near the coffins, despite the ice that had been spread around the punctured corpses to keep the evidence intact until the Doctor got there to bear witness to the infamy. Raus saw that each man was being buried with his machete slung across his breast. He studied the honed blade of Ismael Caracol's machete, and remembered how Caracol had passed him a water gourd on the morning that the stringer felt like a Martian in Atila. The banana worker's words that day came back to him: "We have been sold out many times here. For us, history is not enough." Up on the rickety altar, a priest droned the rosary. Quiet, steady sobbing filled the packed church house. Raus saw the big tears dribbling into El Compa's brick-red beard. The Doctor's three sons stood straight as rifles in front of the coffins.

"I am your son. I will give you many sons," Tonatiuh had responded to Caracol.

MANY HUNDREDS OF banana workers had come out of the hills and up from the coast to accompany the dead to the graveyard. They had come tramping the old guerrilla pathways that criss-cross the hot lands, avoiding the military patrols. Now they clustered in front of the church, waiting for the mass to be done and holding up portraits of Lucio and the Crooked Horseman and Subcomandante Marcos and Tonatiuh Galván.

From atop Skull Hill, the Captain-Major saw the mourners

as so many ants. "¡Qué mierda!" he barked, glaring through the wrong end of his binoculars. This assembly was clearly illegal. Yet he'd been ordered to let Galván and this pinche gringo reporter and the rest of these commie mierdas through the lines. And here were these cabrones outside the church, showing off Montes and all the rest of these other red shitheads. This was defiance of his authority, a violation, goddamn it. He snatched the field phone from his barefoot adjutant. "Listen, Cabo, I want you to tell these pendejos that this is an illegal assembly. They have five minutes to disperse. Prepare the francotiradores. ¿Me entiendes, papito?"

THE COFFINS CAME tumbling out of the church door. Tonatiuh and his sons were so much taller than the other pallbearers and the casket of the compañero Caracol was trundled out at such a steep slant that the dried-up little man nearly slid right out of his box onto the steps. El Compa, Don Estalin, El Nene, the Bishop, Cuauhtli, Cahuiri, and Cutzmandi steadied their corners.

"You have three minutes to disperse. This is an illegal assembly," crackled the pubic address system, mounted atop a U.S.-supplied light tank parked just up the street. Tonatiuh stood somberly on the top of the church house steps and surveyed the terrain. "We are going to the graveyard, compañeras y compañeros. We are going to put our people down in their own ground. The Yanqui DisneyMex will not dispossess them of this land, even by death."

"¡HOOOOOOSTIIIIIICIAAAHHH!" the banana workers rumbled back. "¡TOHHHHHNAAAAATIIIIUHHHHH! ¡HOOOOOOSTIIIIIIIICIAAAAAHHH!"

The Doctor led the mourners and the mourned down the rutted, sunbaked road. At his side was a stout brown woman, Nacha Caracol, her machete raised like a steel flag over her thickly braided head. Behind Ismael's daughter, nearly a thousand banana workers lifted their machetes in uniform defiance.

"¡HOOSTIIIIICIAHHHH! ¡TOHHHNAATIIIIUHHHH!"

A picket of soldiers was strung out 50 yards ahead, barring the fork to the Atila cemetery. One more order to disperse was issued and ignored.

"You have one minute to leave this area."

Raus and Tania followed the line of march, watching the distances between the mourners and the soldiers vanish pace by pace as if they were reviewing videotape. The soldiers raised their weapons. Tania, who had seen this movie before, jerked the Stringer's arm, and both belly-whopped into a shallow road-side ditch. When they looked up, the troops had lowered their Galils, allowing the mourners to pass. Somewhere up the chain of command, El Caimán's order to fire had been frustrated.

AFTER THE MEN had been put down in a graveyard filled with the markers of dead comrades and the wild chanting of the live ones, Nacha Caracol invited the Doctor back to her father's palapa, the thatched open houses in which the banana workers live along the Costa. Raus was astonished to see that Ismael Caracol's palapa was full of books. Rows and rows of homemade bookshelves were stuffed with ancient, ragged volumes. Cardboard boxes spilled back issues of yellowing magazines. Crumbling stacks of news-papers lined the reed walls.

"When my father wasn't defending our community, he read these like a glutton. It was his vice," Nacha Caracol explained. She sounded almost apologetic. "Even when we had nothing to eat, he would go to Acapella and bring home these books. All night he would sit here, picking up one book, then another. That is how we would find him in the morning, with a book in his hand, studying the texts. I never knew him to sleep." Her large hands fiddled with a torn paperback. "Here," she said impul-sively, handing Tonatiuh the book. "My father was reading this just before they killed him. He never got a chance to finish it."

Raus leaned over to view the title: Doña María Cristina Terrazas Tamal Menchú viuda de Ahumada's *The Age of the Sixth Sun.*

"I will finish what our own two fathers have begun," the

Doctor murmured gently. After that Nacha Caracol, the banana worker's daughter, always traveled with the caravan.

TICK TOCK. The Bishop glared at his watches, revised schedules, dates, routes, sped the Doctor through one hasty rally after another. Outside the Sol and the Moon, huts, hamlets, towns, cities, whole states became a solid blur of sombreros and flags, victory speeches, "¡TONATIUH PRESIDENTE!", handshakes, embraces, and pudgy men in RayBans who dogged the caravan as it groaned towards Tapatitlán. Then, in San Pancho, like broken-down mules, the buses gave up the ghost. The brakes went out on the Sun and the Moon just died in her tracks, the probable victim of a heavily sugared gas tank.

Tick Tock.

The Bishop sucked up Delicados and sent Tonatiuh and his entourage up ahead on public transportation for meetings and rallies in Tapatitlán. Tick Tock. Just when the campaigners least needed temper tantrums, Vigo and Tania finally had it out on the run-up to that big western city.

The spat began, as usual, with snide insinuations about who was sleeping with whom and escalated into a screaming brawl in the labyrinthine bus terminal. Raus tried to stay out of firing range and got whacked twice.

Whack! "You asshole! You fucking coward asshole! You just clam up when I need your support!" Tania left the marks of her taut little fingers hot on his stubbly cheek.

Whack! "Yeah, you dumb fucking asshole, why you no defend her like a man?" Vigo snarled. The two stomped off, hand in hand. Oh well.

Tick Tock.

Raus checked into the Golden Phoenix with the rest of the retinue. Antonio Malcreado was solicitous out in the hotel hallway. "Tonight, we will go to the Zona de Tolerancia and find some real whores. ¡Qué chinga estas pinches lesbianas!" Sure, the putas, just what the Doctor ordered. Mickey slammed the door tight behind him. They hate us. They really hate us.

All the hotels in Tapatitlán are owned by the drug cartels. So are all the banks and the casas de cambio, the department stores and the shopping malls and the nightclubs and the bars and all the working girls in the Zone of Tolerance. The taxi cab fleets that take you there, the bus companies, the travel agencies, the airlines, the car dealerships, the city council, City Hall, the Princes of the Catholic Church (they had even assassinated a Cardinal once to prove this point), and the municipal, state, and federal police. Theirs. All theirs.

Raus lay back on the queen-size bed in the heart of the narco capital of the nation, kicked off his shoes, flicked on the vibrating fingers and picked up the Gideon Bible. A complimentary gram of cocaine slipped out.

Mickey could taste the set-up. He bolted into the bathroom and was poised to flush the fat packet of white powder when the room door just about came apart. The dope went down the commode, he pulled the chain.

"Mickey, let me in, you asshole." It wasn't a bust at all, just Tania, wildly apologetic. "It's over. I put her on the plane. She'll be okay." She threw herself at Raus, bit him savagely on the neck.

"Damn, bitch, that fucking hurt." Raus was pissed. "I thought you were the police—I just flushed a gram of good cocaine down the goddamn toilet. It fell out of the Bible."

"Out of the Bible? No problema, mi Mickey. I've been shopping." She fished a baggy, two tight grams at the bottom, from her training bra, hunkered down by the marble bed table and started chopping.

The sex was sweet, urged on by the rush of barely stepped-on, freshly flown-in, Santa Fe de Bogotá coke and a room-service-supplied vat of Courvoisier. Raus entered her mouth, her ass, her cunt, and Tania sucked him in greedily, closing wet and tight around his scarred old cock as they pumped on into the dawn.

Tick Tock.

The buses had come up from San Pancho. They were waiting downstairs. Tania and Raus snorted up the dregs of the blow and sent the bellhop out for two grams more. "This will really speed up this movie," she grinned. But Raus was already feeling uneasy. He was leery of the blow. It was too alluring. It immersed you in its rhythms, ran over you before you had a chance to get on top of it. Worst of all, cocaine convinced you that everything was coming up roses just as you sailed right into the shitstorm of your life.

The phone binged with urgency. "Les go, les go, Mickey, you guys are keeping Tonatiuh waiting." It was the Bishop.

Tick Tock.

AS THE BUSES pushed off at last for the Pacific Northwest and the border at Tijuana, Mickey scented new paranoias on the horizon. A teeth-grinding intensity ran like a short fuse through the multitudes that greeted Tonatiuh as he whistle-stopped north towards Amapola and Desierto de Yunque, a high whine of straining circuits, electric white static in the shimmering, unmarked heavens. Malcreado put his finger right on it during a pit stop in Alacrán. "Vitamina C," he offered, snuffling heartily from two thick lines cut out on the enamel toilet-tank top.

The snow was falling so thickly inside the press bus that it seemed like El Nene was plowing through the Alps. Tania was the snow queen. She always knew where to buy it. She was neat—she kept mirror and razor blade in her wallet and never flubbed a flake. She was discreet. Back in Colombia, it paid off to be discreet. Too many of her friends had blown it, been blown away, if not by the blow, then by the lead poisoning that inevitably came with it.

"In the guerrilla, there were no questions asked. We did what we had to do to grow strong. The capos paid us in cash or in product. We moved the product and both causes advanced and got healthy." But as the guerrilla began to come apart, the comandantes carved out zones of influence. After the Wall of Berlin came down and the Sandanistas lost the elections in '90, drug greed replaced Marxism-Leninism. Dreamers like Tania lost currency and friendships began to unravel. Comrades disappeared in plain daylight, committed suicide, went crazy and killed their whole families. "The polvo confused it. I couldn't sort it all out. This why I left. Why I'm here." She squeezed Mickey's hand.

The capos and their drug of choice had preceded Tania north. In the 1980s, the cartels fashioned Amapola into their own private Rancho Grande. The Colombians' knowledge of the terrain was limited to (a) the fact that the region bordered the country to which they wanted to deliver their goods, and (b) the syrupy strings of mariachi music that filtered through their shortwave radios. Soon they were addicted. Now the South American capos dressed like Pedro Infante and pretended to be silver-plated cowboys with hearts of gold.

Similarly, their confederates—the native-born bumpkins of Amapola and Desierto de Yunque—transformed themselves into snap-brimmed, cumbia-dancing, tropical capones capable of a style of mayhem, cruelty and mass murder at which only the Policía Federal de Estupificantes (PFE or Estupificados) were more practiced performers. Indeed, the Stupefied Ones were often drawn from the ranks of the narcos they were assigned to combat and vice versa. Despite the interlocking directorates, the confrontations between these various cartels, bandas, mafias, drug families, judiciales, secretos and estupificados was anything but fraternal. Innocent bystanders were swiss-cheesed en masse in the streets of Maravillas de Malverde. Unmarked airplanes dropped live bombs on civilian populations. Brutal torture was how directions were asked. Many roadside corpses were collected each morning. Although the capos and the cops squabbled fiercely over control of the drug pipeline, their legendary bloodbaths had less to do with the legality of the product being moved to the northern border than with who was going to move it.

The cartels spread the money around to make it all work. They had paid Barcelona off handsomely and the PRO candidate limited his visit to Amapola to the airport. The capos did not appreciate the attention that public events like presidential campaigns focused on their industry. Now, as Tonatiuh Galván crawled through the state inside a slow-moving bus, lingering here and there to actually listen to the people, the Mafias watched nervously and studied their opportunities. Pushpins were inserted into road maps. Small fortunes were wagered as to when and where the fusillade would be unloosed.

☙

AMAPOLA MADE ITS first drug fortune in brown and black tar heroin, distilled in rough mountainside laboratories from opium scraped off the blood-red poppies that gave the state its name. During the Second World War, North American pharmaceutical corporations, who did commerce in morphine with the U.S. military, paid local campesinos to cultivate and score the poppies. When peace closed down this sudden windfall, the gomeros—those who collected the sticky gum—went into business for themselves. Simple barefoot country boys became the occupants of marble mansions overnight. Their cousins and their brothers and their compadres were converted into trafficking armies. Las bandas wheeled the smack north to Texas and California and protected the home turf with enough firepower to ignite a third world war.

The production and sale of these potent drugs to the norteamericanos brought rewards beyond expectation—creature comforts like Doberman pinschers, champion boxers and enormous diamond pinkie rings, private zoos, legitimate businesses, government contracts, political clout. In Amapola, you could not tell the PRO from the narcos and the PRO narcos from the police.

One downside of the drug economy was that Amapola got hooked on what gringo junkies injected into their veins, and heroin—a very '50s drug—faded fast from popularity up north in the more sprightly 1960s, leaving the region with tons of pretty but unsaleable poppies. Then, miraculously, the cowboys from Medellín showed up to rent the state out as one enormous landing pad for their fleets of Turboprops, Caravels, and DC-7s. This new economic miracle was inevitably attributed by the locals to the ministrations of their saint, an old embalmed bandit known as Jesus Malverde—Malverde, because he once robbed well-to-do travelers by leaping from the underbrush clad only in banana leaves.

⁂

THE GOMEROS FLOCKED to welcome Tonatiuh Galván to Maravillas de Malverde. Their leader, Flavio Flaco Farina, embraced the Doctor and insisted that Tonatiuh receive Malverde's blessing. The procession to the old bandit's shrine down by the railroad tracks was led by a ten-man tambor, belting out raucous corridos that chronicled the exploits of the region's antiheroes, gallos like Caro Quintero, el Señor de los Celos, and General Jesus—country youth turned narco-czars. "He was ju-u-ust a poo-o-r country boy-y-y-y who the gummint tri-i-i-ied to crucify-y-y-y," the Banda de la Mafia Platiada yodeled, lionizing Opigomio Cobranza—"la Oreja"—a cocaine-crazed monarch now imprisoned in a luxury suite of a penitentiary on the outskirts of the capital, after personally cutting off the ears of a dozen dead DEA agents.

Thousands joined the parade to Malverde's tomb. Many were aproned women carrying a single poppy in one hand and an arm baby in the other. A platoon of one-legged beggars hopped into line—Malverde is the patron saint of the one-legged. The whores and rateros of Maravillas poured from the cantinas—Malverde is their patron too. So did the braceros just steaming into town atop freight cars down by the railroad track.

"Thru-u-u who-o-ose ey-y-y-yes, the General shi-i--i-i-nes..."

"They're watching us, Mickey. Don't you feel it? They're all around us here," Tania fretted. Raus eyed the bystanders on the sidewalks, knots of street vendors, razor-thin farmers with smashed straw sombreros, cholos in Bermuda shorts, lots of guayaberas.

Malverde's sanctuary was a crazy-quilt Plexiglas tower leaking puddles of melted candle wax and plastered with throw-away trusses and crutches and shorn hair, gifts given to thank the sainted bandit for good lovers and new pick-ups, the lucky number on the lottery, a light sentence from the judiciary, and the load that got across to El Otro Lado.

"Touch him—you have to rub his head if you really want to beat Barcelona," Flavio Flaco urged, and Tonatiuh followed custom by fingering Malverde's embalmed head mounted in a glass case. Then Flavio Flaco led the candidate to Malverde's tombstone cross and Tonatiuh tossed a symbolic pebble, a ritual simultaneously performed by the thousands of devotees who had accompanied the Doctor to this funky holy place.

"¡TOHHHHNAAAATIIIUHH! ¡HOOOOSTIIIICIAHHH!"

Flavio Flaco had brought the rank-and-file gomeros on board the Galván bandwagon, but their bosses, the capos, did not tip their hand until Tonatiuh had moved up the road.

Tick Tock.

The next midnight, a spectacular fertilizer-bomb blast ripped through Malverde's shrine, spraying shrapnel for miles around and sending such a torrent of candle wax rushing over the tracks and the adjoining highway that traffic north was slowed for days. Miraculously, no one was killed (an unlucky street woman was cold-cocked by a flying crutch). Another miracle: the embalmed head of Malverde survived intact inside its shattered glass case. Guilt-ridden local comerciantes announced they would build it a cathedral.

THE PARANOIA SEEMED to recharge itself as Tonatiuh's caravan climbed through the Yunqui desert for the northern border. You could almost hear it out there, a sort of psychic ack-ack across the vast, dry expanse. Helicopters buzzed like large desert flies on the horizon. Small planes droned overhead but you could not locate them in the bottomless sky. Clusters of police and military vehicles swarmed around the buses and then, suddenly, orders would be emitted from some indefinable command post, and they would race off across the achingly flat and arid landscape to rendezvous with incoming aircraft.

Here and there, the desert was broken up by barbed wire and ornate iron gates, with grillworks curled and scrolled to read Rancho de los Panchos or some such hokum—infinite tracts, extending to the foot of the Yunqui buttes. The ranches appeared to be exclusively populated by bony heads of cattle.

"Feedlots," Tania explained. "They fill a thousand head of cattle full of cocaine and drive them across the border. It gets under the Pentagon radar set-up every time."

It suddenly occurred to Raus that his girlfriend knew much too much about this business.

ﮊ

OUTSIDE YUNQUI CITY, up against the desert bluffs, Tonatiuh spoke to a swirling nighttime encampment of Indians. His father had come here during the Long Campaign and later returned to divide up the huge waterless haciendas among the once-feared, now increasingly lost, Yunqui nation. As in so many places that Tonatiuh had visited for an hour or two on this protracted per-ambulation across the map of the Patria, the Yunquis considered themselves galvanistas because of the General's long-ago con-cern for their welfare. No one had cared much since.

Raus and Tania plied the edges of the disorderly camp. What breeze there was came in hot, dry spasms off the bluffs and then just stopped, as if it had met a dead end in the desert. The sweet, sickening smell of mesquite-wood fires, decaying insects, and human feces scented the airless night. Half-clad Yunquis squat-ted against the gritty desert floor in the torchlight, nodding slowly at Tonatiuh's words, as if they were very drunk or stoned.

The Doctor wanted to speak to these down-at-the-heels war-riors about their health—how badly they were eating—the gringo junk food franchises fanning out everywhere in the land, even here, to the desert. The Golden Arches of Yunqui City were the tallest man-made structure in the region.

"The fields where the marijuana is grown," Tonatiuh said, pointing to the mountains, "that is land you should use to feed yourself, not to grow mota to make the Yanquis even crazier.

The maguey was your mother. Nopales will grow well here and nopales clean the blood."

The Doctor looked north to the border, now just a few hundred miles off. Raus had never heard him speak so directly about the United States before. How sick Tonatiuh thought that gringo society was and how the drugs that moved through the Yunqui were used by the white oppressors over there to keep the poor black and brown and yellow peoples of the ghettoes and barrios and chinatowns in bondage slavery. "It's no different than when they were kidnapped from Africa and China and Aztlán and brought to North America to pick the master's cotton and build his railroads and do his dirty work. We should not help the Yanquis enslave our brothers and sisters."

Mickey found himself nodding in affirmation. Tania snuck under his arm. After the rally they watched stoned Indians watching them. Many of the spectators were still squatting on the desert floor, rocking slowly back and forth, nodding heads folded onto their chests. Others had simply passed out in the makeshift street. Plastic syringes and empty shortdogs of cheap wine and little brown vials crunched underfoot. Raus and Tania discovered one old man dressed in a hand-me-down military jacket, looking for his shoes. He wore no pants.

"At your orders, mi jefe," the Yunqui general mumbled. Mickey flipped through his notepad.

"Sí, the narcos are the bosses now. Sí, they came and threw us off our ejidos. Sí, they make us pick the marijuana for them and feed the cattle condoms stuffed with cocaine. They do not even pay us money anymore."

"They don't pay you money?"

"Now they give us these little rocks to smoke. They say they keep us from being hungry." He displayed an empty brown vial. "But they only last a little while."

Mickey made a note: CRACK COMES TO THE YUNQUIS.

Then Don Estalin blew twice, and Raus and Tania jumped for the buses. "Please, jefe," the Yunqui general trembled, holding out his empty crack pipe, "you don' have any of those little rocks for me?"

OPPOSITION CANDIDATE LEADS HUGE MARCH TO U.S. 'WALL OF SHAME'

U.S. TROOPS ON ALERT AS CAMPAIGN WINDS DOWN SOUTH OF THE BORDER

Special to the North Coast Variety News

TIJUANA (June 28)—Opposition presidential candidate Tonatiuh Galván today led tens of thousands of his countrymen and women to the "Wall of Shame," the 20-foot high, electronically charged barrier that marks the dividing line between north and south on this stretch of the border. The march featured a noisy protest against the deaths of 107 migrant workers killed attempting to penetrate the wall during the first eight months of the year.

Galván, the son of one of his nation's most respected presidents, later accused the government that has long been run by the Party of the Organic Revolution (PRO) and its presidential candidate, Filemón Barcelona, of "having blood on their hands. They are as responsible for these deaths as the Yanqui army. The Gringos," Galván charged, "are only the material assassins."

Thirty-three of the shooting deaths here this year are attributed to the U.S. military, which now coordinates interdiction defenses with the U.S. Border Patrol and other civilian police agencies. The Border Patrol, or "La Migra," as it is universally known in the region, has been adjudged responsible for another 36 victims. Between 12 and 15 would-be migrants (the two countries do not agree on the total figure) have been gunned down by members of American Border Light, a racist vigilante group also known as the "187s," thought to be headed by Pete "Pete" Wilson, the fugitive former governor of California. Twenty-five additional victims have either been electrocuted trying to climb the Wall or drowned in the moats that line the U.S. side.

The chaotic situation in and around the Tijuana border is often compared to the 14-year-old Palestinian intifada. Both Amnesty International and the Organization of American States currently monitor tensions; blue-helmeted U. N. peacekeepers have been proposed to maintain order in an explosive atmosphere where stone-throwing youth clash nightly with heavily armed U.S. soldiers and police.

Jumpy Military

Although kept discreetly out of sight, U.S. combat troops flown in from Fort Bragg, North Carolina were placed on full alert this morning as Galván led 50,000 followers over the surrounding bare brown hills, north towards the border. As Galván approached a section of the high-voltage barrier less than a mile west of the frenetic Otay border crossing station, a combined force of 800 Border Patrol agents, California highway patrolmen, and San Diego County sheriff's deputies were ordered to position their weapons. But Doctor Galván defused the tension when he halted the marchers 20 yards short of the Wall of Shame.

The opposition candidate then set fire to both a U.S. flag and a state of California Golden Bear flag in a symbolic gesture he called "an interactive history lesson. The Yanquis have forgotten their own history. They have forgotten how they stole California and 12 other western states from us. I am burning these flags to remind the North Americans that California still belongs to us," Doctor Galván explained to his supporters. Only when the galvanistas had been marshaled away from the wall by well-organized monitors, coordinated by the Monteca Indian Union of Garbage Pickers, did the combined U.S. force stand down.

The so-called Wall of Shame now extends 1,952 miles from Tijuana-San Ysidro on the Pacific, to Matamoros-Brownsville, Texas on the Gulf of Mexico.

Traitor to the Future?

Galván's appearance on the border—and particularly the burning of the U.S. and California flags—contrasted sharply with Filemón Barcelona's visit here last week. Accompanied by U.S. ambassador Thaddeus Blackbridge, whom he impulsively embraced, the PRO candidate announced plans for the total economic integration of the two neighbors, including the substitution of the U.S. dollar for the almost valueless peso. Barcelona, a former finance minister, labeled Galván "a traitor to our nation's future." Rather than burning the U.S. flag, he accepted from the ambassador an historic "Stars and Stripes" that had once flown over his nation's capital following the 1847 U.S. invasion. The heavily favored PRO standard-bearer made no mention of the daily violence that colors life and death on the Tijuana border, but he was under heavy military protection at all times—six years ago, another PRO presidential candidate was slain in a slum colony here in a bizarre political plot involving two former presidents.

Speaking later on the same hillside from which Barcelona spoke eight days ago, Galván turned again towards California and called the U.S. "a sick society where the poor are drugged to keep them docile." The Doctor reiterated his nation's ancient claims to the Golden State and declared that it was "the drugs that have made the gringos forget what history means." The forces of history are a common theme in the candidate's speeches.

Galván then invited his compatriots on "the other side," who, he maintains, have been driven over the wall by "the barbarian economic and political policies of the ruling clique," to return July 2 and cast a ballot "to overthrow the PRO." An estimated three million voters with political rights in their own country are currently thought to be working in California.

Doctor Galván's father, General Francisco Galván, founded the Party of the Organic Revolution more than seven decades ago.

Ballots or Bullets?

The assassination six years ago and the violence that has marred the Galván campaign in the past weeks was on the minds of many at the Tijuana rally, and Mr. Galván was blanketed by heavy volunteer security all day. Protection was provided by supporters, including the indigenous dance troupe known as the Warriors of Huitzilopochtli, rather than by local or federal police. "We all remember what happened to Colosio right here," explained one volunteer. The rally was held less than a mile from the Lomas Taurinas colony where the official party's candidate was gunned down by government security agents under orders from former presidents Salinas and Zedillo. Salinas is now incarcerated at the U.S. super-maxi federal penitentiary in Florence, Colorado. His successor hung himself late last year.

The Doctor was joined at the microphone today by militant leaders from both sides of the border, including V. (Vladimir) Dolores Leñero, head of the miners' union and an official of the Revolutionary Communist Party which is supporting Galván's candidacy; José María y Cruz Patadas of Patria Verde (Green Fatherland), the nation's number one environmental organization; Ignacia Caracol, a peasant leader from the south of the country; Miguel Rambo Fitzcaraldo, the bespectacled U.S.-born leader of Tijuana's huge Monteca Indian population; and the venerable Carlos Lechuga, the silver-haired California farm labor organizer who accepted Galván's invitation to bring his members "back home" to vote in next Sunday's election.

The turnout of 50,000—while smaller than the numbers reported for Barcelona's stop here last week—was one of the largest audiences Galván has drawn on a difficult 30-day, 10,000 kilometer trek, during which he was the target of a failed assassination attempt. Shootings, beatings, police harassment, and vehicular sabotage have also enlivened the tour.

Campaign Winding Down

Nonetheless, the size of the crowds lining the highways and filling the plazas for the Doctor's rallies has grown considerably in the last ten days. While Barcelona remains the odds-on favorite, the opposition candidate, whose campaign stalled momentarily in the Indian south of the country, now appears to have regained a head of steam.

Galván will now fly back to the capital for a final rally there June 30 that his campaign manager, Abelardo Salmón Guengoitia, says will be "historic." The candidate closes his eight-month odyssey on election eve (July 1) on the shores of Lake Tzintzun in his home state of Malinchico. The chain-smoking, affable Salmón, the Doctor's long-time aide and an adopted brother, was jubilant at today's turnout, predicting that the PRO's 71-year-old dynasty will end "Sunday afternoon, July 2, at precisely 18 hours"—the hour the polls close.

The PRO has never lost a presidential election.

(Note to Editor: Optional cut)

From the viewpoint of a reporter who has personally tracked the campaign since Tonatiuh Galván first threw his hat in the ring last December, the Doctor's crusade has been an educational experience. Without a formal political movement to back him up, and officially enrolled as a candidate of a minor political party that has never achieved more than .009% of the national vote, Galván has run an aggressive campaign that has enjoyed exceptional contact with the grass roots. His appeal has been particularly strong among Indians and mestizos, who comprise 97% of the total population. Combining his dark skin and famous name, Galván has generated powerful nostalgia for the past in a nation where the past has at least as much weight as the future. In many recent speeches, Galván, whose given name Tonatiuh is that of the Aztec sun deity, has taken on an almost messianic tone, as if the defeat of the PRO will usher in a new millennium for the nation. One group, the Sixth

Sun Movement—a network of revivalist Indianists and activist indigenous peoples—has even predicted that Galván's election will
bring about an Aztec renaissance here.

Washington is Watching

The PRO's own prophets calculate a 70 – 80% plurality for Barcelona
next Sunday, citing earlier DGM (Disney-GallupMex) polls taken in
31 states around the republic. In previous presidential elections the
PRO has often awarded itself 80 – 90% of the popular vote.

But, in this reporter's view, the pollsters' predictions do not much
reflect the virulent anger at the ruling party that Tonatiuh Galván
has Galván-ized in months of travel to the remotest parts of his
nation. The July 2nd results may indeed surprise and anger the
always confident PRO, although, given the Organic's lengthy history of electoral fraud, the official tally may not reflect the true
outcome of the impending election.

Galván's response to possible PRO fraud could well trigger civil
strife south of this conflictive border, with its inevitable spillover
into the U.S. This is one reason why, according to embassy sources,
Washington—in the person of Ambassador Blackbridge—has
sought to open back channels of communication with the charismatic opposition candidate, at the same time that the interim
Gingrich administration has bestowed its blessing upon Barcelona.

VII

VISPERAS

June 30 – July 1, 2000

MICKEY WAS MUCKING IT UP with a lizard-faced Tania Escobar in the tar pits of a steamy dream when the phone's searing ring tore the dawn into shreds. Her little lizard claws grabbed at his swollen rod, red and thick as the trunk of a madrone and he screamed. They were sinking into the sweet molasses morass and no would could save them.

Save us! *Don't save us…*

The phone did not stop ringing.

When he could finally pry his caked lids open, the daylight was not broad. For an awful second, things got very green. The phone was still drilling into his brainpan. Tania the Gekko snuggled into his armpit. He grappled for the receiver.

"Raus, are you up?"

"Para nada…"

"Lo siento, mano—listen! They've taken the Bishop…" Malcreado paused dramatically.

"When? How, man?" Oh shit.

"Sometime around midnight as close as I can figure. They got Estalin too."

"Who has them?" He knew.

"Who else?"

"You down at Carlos Quinto?"

"I just walked in the door. You better wake Tania and get over here."

He let the receiver slip to the littered rug and stumbled blindly out of bed. It felt like some malevolent morning deity was driving a foot-long railroad spike right through his forehead. He fumbled at the little paper, spilling precious grains of glittery white powder everywhere, his fingers trembling so fearfully that he missed twice just trying to stab the rolled thousand peso bill up his nose.

"What's shaking, Mickey Mouse?" Tania smiled brightly. Asleep or awake, she had this uncanny radar for detecting cocaine entering user bloodstreams within a five-mile radius.

Raus reached for the mescal to back him up. "I'm not ready for this." Mickey just wanted to climb back between her scaly little thighs and nest like a frog prince for the next two billion light-years.

Tania jumped from the bed, her pubes rasping at his levitating cock. "You're not ready for what, Maus man?" she breathed.

"The Bishop and Don Estalin have been disappeared."

"Oh fuck," she clucked, cutting herself a neat, fat line and wiggling her ass deliciously. "You never have enough time to get your rocks off in this racket."

THE PRESS GATHERED like a pack of sleepy buzzards on Carlos Quinto, quietly sipping liquids from Styrofoam cups and thumbing the morning columns for clues. Antonio told Raus and Tania what he knew: "The Bishop leaves here just after 10 p.m.. He takes Estalin with him because Tonatiuh says no one goes anywhere alone. He's supposed to be going to a meeting at La India's with

RAT in Coatlicue, out by the cemeteries. He never shows up."

Tonatiuh remained closeted all morning. More representatives of the national and international press appeared—Jane Ann and Big Sid, Sasha Vigo with stilettos in her eyes, a half-bombed Pease. "Do you believe any of this, really?" Pease asked Mickey, incredulity puckered on his lips like sulfuric acid. "I mean, this is the eve of the bloody election and the PRO is supposed to have disappeared the opposition candidate's campaign manager? ¡Por favor!"

"Who else then, Horace?"

Pease rolled his beady, bloodshot eyes around the gloomy mansion. "I would think the occupant of this dank structure is a good place to begin asking those questions."

The sympathetic and the curious were already gathering outside in the street. A major rally was scheduled for mid-afternoon in the Zócalo and the leaders of many contingents were already banging on the carved door of the House of Demented Women, wanting to speak with whoever was coordinating the event about their place on the plaza. The Bishop was in charge of such logistics. Raus felt a sudden chill, like he was looking into the cockpit of an airplane and no one was at the controls. He intuited that the Bishop was not coming back.

Tania goosed him back to terra firma. "C'mon and watch Mongo, Mausito." He could see the blow percolating in her eyes. He didn't much feel like playing.

Auditors universally dubbed Abraham Mongo's midday news broadcast "Mentiras del mediodía." You watched it not because Mongo told you what was going on but because he told you what the PRO wanted you to think was going on. At sticky moments like this one, you learned to stomach his smarminess for a glimpse at the Byzantine thinking of the rulers he served.

The item was the third one into the broadcast. The smirking Mongo led with a brainless barrage of Barcelona's last-minute campaign quips and an urgent bulletin from the Labor Secretariat about record low unemployment that sent peals of bitter laughter lofting over the bedraggled nation. Tania touched him from in back, secretly frottaging his meatless behind. "This is not appropriate behavior, mi vida." He stared down at the Bishop's hyper-cluttered desk: hacker manuals and diagrams, how-to-do-it guides, *Computer Ethics, Politically Correct PCs, Hot-Wired, Break-In,* and *CoreWar.* The Bishop was really getting into this computer stuff. The Bishop, he remembered, was not coming back.

"—*Federal District Security Director Florentino Zorillo told 'mediodía' this morning that no warrant had been issued for the Galván campaign aides and, we quote, 'so far as we have been able to determine, we do not have them in any kind of custody.'"* A still photo of the bloodhound-like physiognomy of the police chief lingered on the screen, his words transcribed in electronically transmitted yellow ciphers underneath his sagging jowls. Mongo's enunciation of the two syllables that compose "Galván" was the first time in nine months of miracle campaigning that the Doctor's name had been pronounced on "High Noon Lies."

"—*President Arturo Lomeli personally instructed Secretary of Gobernación Gonzalo X. Davis and, we quote, 'to leave no stone unturned.'"*

"Not even this one?" cooed Tania, her little lizard hands stroking the bulge now threatening to break out of Mickey's fly.

He tried to shrug her off. "Why don't you go molest Sasha for a change?"

"—*Meanwhile, Victor Manuel Rodríguez Lefkowitz, chairman of the PRO)...*" The still photos switched. "*...extended his sympathies to Candidate Galván, that is, and we quote, 'if Abelardo Salmón and Estalin Lenin Gómez Gómez are really missing...' Other PRO headmen were not so charitable. According to veteran labor leader Don Paco Vallarta, Salmón and his driver are probably out drinking, and, we quote, 'in some house of ill-repute in Tepito or La Bondad.'"* A familiar melon-head loomed on the screen.

"Tonatiuh's coming out," Malcreado hissed at the dry humpers. She slid off Raus with a delicate tremble. Mickey oscillated for a minute in the dim recesses of the kitchen, staring at the hydrocephalic labor czar flickering on the Bishop's dying tube and wondering where to hide his hard-on.

TONATIUH'S LONG FACE was frozen into an extended frown, his deep coloring turned ashen. Paloma accompanied him, but still he seemed to list to one side, as if he could not quite balance himself without the Bishop there. A pale, chubby Ahumada Tamal, his veiled mother on his arm, followed the Candidate into the open patio. RAT ran a chronology of the last hours.

"A few minutes after 10 p.m. last evening, we received a phone call from Abelardo Salmón. He said he was leaving here in Tonatiuh's Shadow, license number SOL22X103, to go to my mother's home at 6666 Lomas de Huesos out in Coatlicue and that Don Estalin Lenin Gómez would drive him. We don't like to go out alone these days. The Bishop and Estalin never arrived at my mother's home. At midnight, my mother called Tonatiuh here at Carlos Quinto and we drove in together, retracing the route that Abelardo and Estalin always take out to the end of the park. We found no sign of the Shadow.

"After 2 a.m., we called Secretary of Gobernación Gonzalo X. Davis to inform him that there is reason to believe our compañeros have been kidnapped. Tonatiuh has spoken with the Bishop's wife, Florida Ferrando, in Malinchico and she has heard nothing. Don Estalin's son is here with us." The Nene raised his hand. "He has received no telephone calls from the missing men or their captors either. Abelardo Salmón and Estalin Lenin Gómez have been missing for 15 hours now. We do not know where they are or what condition they are in. We fear for their lives."

Tonatiuh took over. "We demand the immediate presentation with life of our compañeros and colleagues. Failure of the PRO to do so will have grave consequences for the fragile future of democracy in this country." He raked the two dozen reporters and camera people assembled in the courtyard with eyes that burned like funeral pyres.

Von Voodle waggled his hand. "Señor candidato, Don Paco Vallarta has suggested that the Bishop and Estalin are drunk in a neighborhood whorehouse. Do you have a response?"

"Yes, you must tell your bosses for me, Don Jesus, that when they open their mouths, they stink of death. This campaign is about life. Next question."

Jane Ann jumped up. "Doctor, have you received any communication, any word from the kidnappers? Do you have any clues as to who, you know, has taken Mr. Bishop and Mr. Gómez?"

Tonatiuh forced a wan smile. "Only the usual suspects, compañera."

Pease wedged in an unctuous index finger. "Doctor Galván, you seem to be suggesting that this abduction—if it is that—is the work of the PRO."

"Yes, I am certainly suggesting that, señor Pease, and I sincerely hope *The Times* will quote my words correctly in that respect tomorrow, if you are filing."

"Compañero Tonatiuh, do you really think the Bishop and Estalin are still alive?" Tania Escobar asked abruptly.

"If they have taken them for information they believe the Bishop and Don Estalin have, then they may still be alive. The problem, as you must know from your own country, is that many people whom the authorities think have information die during the interrogation procedures, from—how do they put it—'cardiovascular insufficiency.'"

"Excuse me, Tonatiuh," Raus interrupted ingenuously, "but what information do they think the Bishop has?"

"When we know this, we'll know if he and Estalin are alive or not," the Doctor shot back, his eyes reaching through to the back of Raus' brain stem.

"But Chief Zorilla says that Salmón and Gómez are not in his jails," Chuchu Von Voodle persisted.

"Not in the jails we know about anyway. One more question."

"Sí, compañero, in a few hours you are scheduled to hold a rally in the Zócalo that Abelardo Salmón told us the other day would be historic. Has anything changed because he is not with us today?"

"Compañero Malcreado, yes, things have changed greatly because the Bishop is, as you say, 'not with us today,' and, yes, at 1600 hours, there will be an historic rally in the Zócalo of this city, and, yes, we are going to be there, as we have always intended to be. Yes, I repeat: this campaign is about life."

꙳

THE GREAT FLAT ESPLANADE of the Zócalo is stuck at the heart of the One True Heart, an enormous esplanade that has been the setting for some of the most spectacular bloodlettings in the gory history of the Patria.

Once the Zócalo was Tenochtitlan's central square upon which towered the twin temples of death and rebirth—the voracious warrior hummingbird, Huitzilopochtli, on the left hand, and Tlaloc, the bringer of rain, to the right. A hundred meters west rose the pyramid of Xipe Totec, whose priests donned the flayed skins of virgins each spring to speed the new corn on its way. Where the metro stop is now, stood the precinct of Tezcatlapoaca, the smoking mirror lord of the underground, its culverts and drains clotted crimson with the hemorrhaging victims of a thousand "flower wars."

Later, the death-colored conquerors came in their gleaming body armor and tied unrepentant infidels to high-strung horses. Under cruel whips that drove the straining steeds to the four cardinal points of the Zócalo, they tore the old ways apart. Mestizo liberators, generals, despots, and dictators next stained the Zócalo floor with the bodily fluids of the ever restless pueblo. Soon, it was the revolution's turn to transform this sterile stone square into a bed of blood. The Indian armies rode down the elegant, stuck-up "capitalinos," trampling their fashionable bones under inchoate hooves, the firing squads setting up shop on the side streets as José Guadalupe Posada sketched macabre portraits.

These days, the great plaza was filled up with sentient humanity only for patriotic holidays, the president's inauguration, and the campaign closer of his hand-picked successor. At least once a year, the opposition tried to pull its collective anger together and claimed to stuff the space to capacity but, when viewed from the terraces of the five-star hotels above, there were notable bald patches in the mob. Never before June 30, 2000

AD, had an opposition candidate so jammed this monumental plaza. As the Bishop had predicted, the rally was historic.

How many souls were actually crammed into the Zócalo that day has been a subject of intense speculation ever since. Raus calculated six citizens to a square meter, multiplied by architectural estimates of 60,000 meters, and figured the crowd conservatively at 350,000. Malcreado and Tania insisted on twice that number, arguing that there were hundreds of thousands more of Tonatiuh's people out of sight lines, on the feeder streets. Horace Pease, a pear-shaped cynic, rounded the rabble off to 100,000 in his *Times* piece the next day. Preventative Police estimates did not top 15,000. Popular culture and a few years' distance put the attendance at well over a million.

۔ﺟﻴ

THE MULTITUDES POURED into the Zócalo from every flop and floor space in the capital. RAT's "roots" committees swept the popular barrios clean. Damnificados streamed out of the caged camps beyond the cemeteries; colonos from the festering hillsides and parched lake beds out in the misery belt strutted down the parallel streets, propelled by brass bands; bent and blinking denizens of the lost cities of the south tramped into the sunlight smiling down upon the Zócalo; a handful of Montec garbage pickers shuffled in from the San Valentino dumps; raucous brigades of street vendors hauled Virgins and potatoes just in case, the market mariachis ululating the Ballad of Tonatiuh Galván, "thruuuu whooooose eyes shayayayayns the General's."

SuperPendejo ushered a contingent of masked wrestlers into the plaza to wild applause. Behind their eternally adolescent leader, Aquiles Plantón, pimply-faced students from the Autonomous University and its swarming high school system dashed lickety-split into the steadily filling square, uttering their arcane "boolas" and "goras" and flying their incoherent demands for reforms like "cellular democracy" from staffs stout enough to batter down the doors of the National Palace.

On the students' tail slouched those who never had a chance

even to go to school—the doomed, mohawked Chavas Bandas from the city's industrial north: first the dreaded Santo Pachecos; then their spike-headed rivals, the Red Chemos; and the skinhead Calacas Unidas.

The workers' entrance was more subdued—solid blocks of men and women marching in disciplined cadence as hardly anyone does anymore. The dissident delegations had come on 10,000 rented buses from many corners of the land. Flying the red banner at the head of the labor contingent was the flame-bearded Dolores Leñero and the miners of Jaquemate, their fists raised high and tight. They had cast the first stones at Barcelona. Then came Chon Yaa and thousands of small Mayan men in hard hats, their fists similarly extended in salute. The railroad men and the bus drivers who had tramped through the capital every single day since public transportation had been suspended five years ago displayed clenched, callused hands too. So did the women garment workers who had toiled for a decade without a contract in underground sweatshops where the rats scuttled around the women's ankles; the teachers, whose salaries did not even pay to get them to and from school each day; auto workers, whose Japanese managers so speeded up the assembly lines that 6.6 comrades were being mangled every day; furious government workers, whose dues and pensions and Christmas bonuses were pocketed by embezzling PRO union bosses to pay for Barcelona's campaign.

Their voices booming through the stone canyons of the Centro Histórico, the campesinos, commanded by Nacha Caracol, her machete still raised like a steel flag, marched into the surging plaza. Banana workers, kiwi pickers from Tacumán, and Flavio Flaco's gomeros stepped onto the esplanade. The campesinos came from farms and ejidos, communities and collectives all over the nation. Faces flashed by that Raus had seen everywhere in the land during many months of miraculous campaigning. Tania never let go of his arm.

Not a large number of news gatherers had mounted the press platform to record this magnum event for history. Outside of Sid Bloch, who was filming for GE Disney-CNN, no national or international TV network would cover Tonatiuh's campaign finale.

"You can bet they'll be here when Barcelona closes tomorrow," Tania snorted. "Pinches vendidos."

"But, honey, there are so many people here. They can all see each other. They don't really need TeleVida or TeleVersa to tell them this is happening."

Beneath them, the immense crowd pulsated and seethed like living lava. Chants rose in unison from all sides of the stage, far back in the throng, in a thousand scattered pockets in the belly of the mob.

"¡¡¡TOHHHHHNAAAAAATIIIIIUHHHHHH!!!"

"¡¡¡HOOOOOSTIIIIICIIIIIAHHHHHH!!!"

And still the Capital disgorged its guts into the Zócalo as if Coatlicue, the snake-skirted Aztec earth mother, was trying to concentrate all life here at the center of the One True Heart. Despite all the homicides past and to come, this campaign is about life, Tonatiuh had insisted.

The Indians arrived, wearing antlers and pounding deerskin drums, burning sage and copal, blowing conch shells and flying white doves on long golden strings. On their shoulders they carried the heavy metal corpse of Columbus, their first trophy in this miracle-laced campaign.

The ecologists filed in, moving under hundreds of yards of organically dyed green cotton cloth, elegantly inscribed with the Patria Verde logo in which the nation's map was made to look like a leaf. The clandestine Mothers of Julapa dared arrest as they trundled a great papier-maché breast, a logo their governor had declared feloniously obscene.

Now it was the liberation clergy's time to shine. Emaciated priests from every slum in the capital hoofed into the square. Behind them, Christian-based communities struggled with back-breaking crosses and crooned socially conscious canticles. Padre Pascual Pobrecito, the Guinness Book of Records hunger striker, was carried in on a stretcher by the proscribed "Martyrs of Cristo Rey."

And in back of them came platoons of gaudily garbed gay men, led by a rumba band with no less than 20 Carmen Mirandas, piggy-backing Robespierre de las Rosas, their militant transvestite commander-in-chief. Not to be outcamped, "the Doñas of Lesbos" sat Doña X, their cigar-chomping chairwoman, up on a sedan chair.

Tania eyed the dyke platoon, winking at ex-lovers.

The back end of the pageant was taken up by the hosts, the residents of the old Centro Histórico, striding proudly into the record-breaking mass of humanity that had just marched onto this slab of stone at the hub of the nation and their neighbor-hood: housewives and icemen, brick masons and sweet potato ladies, laundresses and organ grinders, putas in baby dolls and shifty-orbed pimps, table dancers, till tappers, pickpockets, paleta men, a legion of beggars and fire-eaters and traffic clowns and other assorted street scammers. The last marcher to roll in, El Torso, was picked up bodily by his wheels and handed all the way to the front of the stage.

An ocean of brown faces had assembled itself drop by drop under the very nose of the PRO. Inside the National Palace on the east flank of the Zócalo, the gathering had not gone unno-ticed. "The crowd's well above 300,000 already, sir," the young lieutenant whispered into his cellular phone.

"That's enough." X. Davis hung up on the other end.

Beneath the balconies of the palace, a rainbow of insignias, banners, mantas, demands, and secret signs bobbed up from the brown sea. Huge block letters called attention to radioactive cows at Laguna Negra and the Hundred Dead who had tried to cross the Wall of Shame. Some of the demands were inked in Mixtec and Montec and Zipotec and Zapotec and Maya. Many were written out in Aztec Nahuatl. Thousands of big and little Tonatiuh Suns unfurled in the small breeze. Hammers and sickles and Virgins and sacred Aztec swastikas, portraits of the General and the Son, the Centaur of the North, the Caudillo of the South, Lucio and Marcos, Luis Montes and someone who might have been Kim Il Sung, popped out of the colorful tide. Across the proscenium of the stage, an enormous swatch of white linen was writ big in carefully traced letters: WE DEMAND THE PRESEN-TATION WITH LIFE OF ABELARDO AND ESTALIN!

"¡¡¡VIIIIIIIVOOOOOS!!! ¡¡¡VIIIIIIIVOOOOOOOOS!!!"

Music preceded the speeches: a Montec accordion band, the oldest member of which was no more than five; a norteña conjunto, "Los Rodinos"; "Los Mariachis de la Esperanza"; jarocheros and huapangueros; even an Andean combo, "Los Condores de Gonzalo" to serenade Paloma.

The Warriors of Huitzilopochli opened the program, leaping in hypnotically fluid steps from one edge of the stage to the other—stalking, gyrating, balancing their fancy footwork against the heartbeat of the skin drums, the exultant trumpeting of the conches, the precise flailing of bone rattles fastened to the dancers' high-stepping calves. Tania and Raus locked into the timeless rhythms that throbbed from the very umbilicus of the national body.

Down below, deep under the Zócalo floor, amongst the ruins of the blood-spattered temples, matted priests compulsively fed the fresh hearts of the captured flower warriors to the sun, to keep it warm and floating aloof across the inflexible heavens—his Sun, the Sixth One. Today it was Tonatiuh's.

A gargantuan roar, unlike any human tumult Raus had ever experienced, exploded over the plaza, every throat tuned to its own personal pitch of primal affirmation. Tonatiuh surrendered to the ovation, encircled at the microphone by Paloma and his three princely sons, a void at his right hand where the Bishop always stood.

"¡¡¡¡¡VIIIIIIIVOOOOS!!!!! ¡¡¡VIIIIIIIVOOOOOOOOOS!!!"

The Doctor held his palms out flat in a small bid for silence. The chanting slowly shuddered to a stop.

"Compañeras and compañeros, I am not going to read a long speech today. Many months ago Abelardo Salmón, who you all know as the Bishop, said to me that he was going to show us how to beat the PRO. He has. You are the proof that we have won this election. The Bishop always knew just what to do and he would know just what to do now, if he was with us. But he is not with us. They wound us where we hurt the most when they take our comrades and brothers, our sisters and fathers, our mothers and our kids.

"But what they cannot understand is that we are no longer afraid of them. Long ago, Abelardo and myself swore to endure this burden of disappearance, torture, death, as the price we must pay to save the Patria's glorious past from the depredations of the PRO.

"Make no mistake about it. The PRO has taken Abelardo and Estalin as hostages. They will try and exchange them for our surrender. Let this, then, be a warning to Barcelona and his gang: the people do not disappear with the disappearance of one or two men. Let them understand that we will not negotiate victims or victories.

"We will not disappear before we vote, and we will not disappear afterwards. We will stand there and watch our votes be counted and we will not disappear even then. We will not disappear when the votes are validated in the districts and we will not disappear when the so-called Autonomous Electoral Commission refuses to acknowledge our victory. After we vote, we will come right back here, to the one true heart, and we will sit here in judgment of those who rule there in the National Palace. We are history happening and they had better get out of the way!"

"¡¡¡TOHHNAAATIIIIUHHHH PREESIIIIDENTEEEEE!!!"

Then old Cristóbal Cantú Cabañas, minus his right leg and still enfeebled from the shooting in Huajuco, hobbled on his silver walker to the microphone and hushed the pandemonium with the first pure notes of the national anthem.

A million voices joined as one in an apogee of exaltation that Raus would always remember as the most resonant moment of the miracle campaign, the one that felt the most unified, that found the deepest echo, a rich, true voice that suspended itself inside all who were there that day and never went away.

Even as Tonatiuh's people left and came and went home again, the sound stayed behind, penned between the four far walls of the Zócalo, rattling the windows and the PRO administrators behind them in the National Palace like a fearsome tuning fork, a noise that never let them forget where it had come from and that it would never, never again, be silenced.

THE LIGHT NARROWED to unpolished silver upon the water; the encircling mountains were daubed a solemn purple. The Purés of Lake Tzintzun, from which the sacred hummingbird drinks, cast their last winged nets of the day upon the slate blue surface. Tomorrow they would cast ballots instead. And after the voting?

The future stalled at dusk. Centered by the cone-shaped peaks of the sierra, the lake was as serene as God's right eye. The Indians peered into its muddy pupil and extracted plump whitefish they sold on sticks up in the town.

The cold solitary beauty of the sacred lake was antidote to the euphoria of yesterday's rally up in the capital. A melancholy damp permeated the stone textures of the lakeside colonial town. Even the thousands and thousands of Indians who filled the cobbled streets and decaying plazas seemed muted, exhausted by nine grueling months of roller-coaster ups and downs. Or maybe they were only catching their breaths before the heavy shit began to fly in the morning. Raus couldn't figure out which.

The Bishop and Don Estalin had been gone for 45 hours now. The pain of their disappearances pulsed like an abscess. The chambers of Mickey's heart, which yesterday had boomed with hopeful resonance, today were strangely hollow and unloaded.

Tania reluctantly had stayed behind in the Capital. Bogotá had insisted that she cover Barcelona's big rally although she had badly wanted to come out to the lake. Mickey felt diminished by her absence. They had shouldered through every minute of these last months of the campaign, elbow to elbow, whispering into each other's ear what they had seen and what they had felt. The sex between them was still fresh and full of exploration. He mistrusted her drug but he had to concede that he had fallen for her. Hard.

As the hours mounted, the PRO was growing more defensive about the fate of the missing men. Speaking in the same Zócalo that Tonatiuh had packed 24 hours earlier, Barcelona accused his opponent of staging the disappearances in "a desperate effort" to stir "last-minute sympathy." It was the first time in nine months of campaigning that the PRO candidate ever acknowledged in public that he actually had an opponent.

The PRO padded out the crowd with the usual incentives: intimidation, a bad lunch, double a day's pay. De la Mancha drummed out tens of thousands of lumpen Orgánicos and Paco Vallarta's gorillas ensured the attendance of tons of working stiffs. Everyone had to register the number of their Gold Card on a check-off list held by a PRO goon. Because the meeting was held on a huge square with many ways in and out of it, those who had been forced to attend made list and slid off through unguarded side streets and alleyways so that Sid Bloch had to shoot really fast to get any film from the Zócalo before it emptied out completely. With the throng evaporating before his little pop-eyes, Barcelona spoke very quickly so that it sounded like his speech was being read by one of the Chipmunks. It was like the plug had been pulled and the PRO was disappearing down the Zócalo drain.

Tania told him on the phone that she had seen many familiar faces. Then she realized that she had just seen them yesterday. Many people who had been "obligated" to attend the Barcelona rally had come out for Tonatiuh the day before of their own free will.

THE PUREPECHAS poured into Tzintzuncuaro, the colonial town by the sacred lake, from every cuaro and picho and rancho and hamlet and ravine in the steep state. The delegations from the heroic Puré municipalities of the sierra roamed the stage, the tatas' breasts thumping with pride under their wool gaváns, just to be up there with Tonatiuh, their "Native Sun." Clever, very clever, Raus. Mickey jotted down the descriptive for future publication. His hands felt heavy, his fingers without feeling, like they'd said all there was to say long ago about this campaign.

The tatas from Zapicho clustered around Tonatiuh, demanding to have their photos taken with "nuestro presidente." Goofy

Tata Pamfilo flashed a gap-toothed grin. Pedro Baltazar swelled up like a powder pigeon. Tata Tacho came dressed to kill in a brilliant new gaván, waving his muzzle-loading mauser and slapping his godson on the back. "Haven't they shot you yet, hijo?" the old man jibed.

It was an innocent but ill-timed joke, born of Tacho's creeping senile dementia, but it put a chill on the day for Raus. He didn't much like Tzintzuncuaro anyway, a monk-stained place where long ago the Church had beaten the Purés into proper Christian submission with its clubs and its tough love.

Tonatiuh reiterated yesterday's incantations: how the election had already been won, how his people were not going to disappear after they voted, how we would all return to the Zócalo to throw the PRO out of the National Palace. Raus wondered how many of those who had traveled to Lake Tzintzun to see Tonatiuh today would really vote tomorrow or stay late at the polls after they'd closed to count the ballots—let alone trudge up to the capital to overthrow the PRO.

With Florida Ferrando at his side, Tonatiuh talked haltingly about the Bishop, whose Christian name he could not bring himself to invoke. The Doctor-brother recalled long years of dedicated service, how the Bishop had cut short his medical studies to take care of the General, how long ago the General's driver had found the young boy asleep in La Bondad market atop the melons. The Doctor spoke as if the Bishop's life was oozing irrevocably away in some subterranean cell he could not locate on any map. The "¡Vivos!"—so vibrant in the Zócalo sun—seemed like a death sentence today. Florida was already wearing widow's weeds.

The final syllables of Tonatiuh's nine-month miracle crusade spread into the silvery dusk, a flat echo floating eerily out over the becalmed lake. To the west, lightning danced over the Sierra of Zapicho and thunder dimly trembled. It was July, the time of the great storms, when blue stones and black ice could fall from the sky above the saw-toothed mountains. A bone-chilling rain would soon be upon the lake, driving everyone home to sit by smoky wood fires and sip hot cinnamon tea laced with aguardiente.

LONG AFTER MIDNIGHT, Malcreado and Raus sat up under the dripping eaves in the empty plaza of Tzintzuncuaro, chugging down the chinguidi against the cold and listening to the frogs croak under the muddy bank of the lake. Neither had been able to file for hours because the storm had disrupted telephone transmissions and deadlines had been deferred. Both were traveling far in their heads, each retracing his own fork in the long campaign trail that had brought them here, making stops along the way, remembering faces, the color of the skies, the way the earth smelled that particular day.

"Remember that school teacher in the flower-print dress by the side of the road on a day that it snowed in the Altos?"

The two exchanged hints of where they were journeying.

"The chocolate caca king of cacao..."

"Marcos shimmering in the mouth of the bat cave..."

"Ismael Caracol's wonder library..."

"A man in Tacumán staring into the palm of his hand..."

Neither knew what to expect next—the Bishop had always prepared the itineraries. But each knew that they were going to be a part of this story for a long time to come. They drank to it.

The monster rose out of the lake after 2 a.m., stumbling on muddy stumps up from the docks. Muffled in ghostly spumes, it careened through the old stone town, frightening alley cats and growling curs, waking the burghers with its war whoops, mariachi yowls, and baleful retching.

Raus and Malcreado, both their heads nestled to their chests, were startled gaga by a lurching, fire-eyed Nene, sucking the dregs from his final jug. The mud-spattered kid dropped loopily to the bench on which the reporters nodded. His angular face announced the agony of certain loss.

"You hear them?" he pointed, suddenly animated, crazy fear flooding his blood-red eyes. "Don't you hear them chewing on my father's heart?" His head crashed into the oilskin-covered tabletop.

Raus and Antonio listened like good reporters but all they could hear was the drip of heavy, precisely formed drops sliding from the colonial eaves and the croak of many frogs under the banks of the sacred lake.

VIII

THE HEART OF THE MATTER

July 2, 2000

DAWN BROKE CLEANLY over the lake. The early rays stroked the silver-blue surface and the mists cleared to reveal the fishermen spreading their first gossamer nets of the new day. Steam lifted off Raus's coffee-con-chinguidi and cleared his nose for news. His head was thinning out. He had barely slept.

Tonatiuh drove back to the capital to vote and await some sign from those who had taken the Bishop and Estalin. Mickey handed Malcreado a mash note for Tania. He was going to spend the day cruising Malinchico with Dr. Huipi. What happened in the state today would be like the small smooth stone he skimmed now, breaking the surface of the sacred lake, sending progressively larger ripples across the surface of the land.

Mickey hopped into Dr. Huipi's Ranchero. "You ready for the first day of the new sun?" the gaunt, Leon Trotsky look-alike asked cheerfully. Ezekial Huipi was a native of this sacred place, having been birthed on the island of Las Muertas in the dead center of Lake Tzintzun. To Dr. Huipi, Las Muertas was the control panel of the universe. This steep threadbare island was crowned by a 40-foot neon-lit likeness of Cuyacahuiri—like the Aztec Tonatiuh, the Purepecha deity for the sun's fusing energies. Dr. Huipi had hooked up the neon.

Ezekial Huipi was not a doctor-brother. In fact, around the lake he was known to labor less at doctoring than tinkering. At the bottom of his being, he was really more Rube Goldberg than Albert Schweitzer. Once he had outfoxed a nuclear test reactor proposed by some supercilious presidential commission for the shores of the sacred lake by harnessing up enough appropriate energy from the methane gases emitted by cows grazing on Tzintzunzan's brackish weeds to power 100-watt lightbulbs in all 12 lakeside towns—proving, once and for all, that organic output is a lot more powerful than nuclear bullshit.

Ezekial Huipi mistrusted the cities of his country with millennial disgust. He wrote off the capital, its poisoned air, venal politicians, and irresponsible populace as beyond redemption. To Huipi, the end was nigh. He was a committed practitioner of the tabula rasa school of politics—the worse the better, sweep the table clean, start all over again. Of all those close to Tonatiuh Galván, Dr. Huipi was the purest revolutionary.

TONATIUH'S "SPIRITUAL ADVISER," as he was often identified, wheeled his lovingly rebuilt '62 Ford Ranchero around the 12 towns of the lake on election morning, as heavy-footed and horn-handed as any cowboy drug lord. "Out of my way, pendejos," he admonished three straight brand-new pickups, deliberately driving them onto the shoulder. "¡Pinche PRO punks!"

The polls were to open by 8:00 a.m. That's what the law says. By 9, the town halls had still not been unlocked. Seventy-one voters waited outside the General Supo in Rancho Mistu, PRO Gold Cards on display. All of them were women, lined up serenely under blue-ribbed rebozos. Although guaranteed the vote since 1952, women around the lake did not much vote without their husbands' permission. Raus and Ezekial bailed out of the Ranchero, and Mickey pressed a young broad-faced Puré for her preference. Dr. Huipi asked her again in Purepecha. She giggled in something that sounded like Russian.

"She says to tell you that the vote is secret but she will let you know soon enough, that you should wait around until it's dark."

"Where is her husband?" Mickey persisted.

Her thick braids jiggled merrily. "She says she doesn't need a husband to tell her how to vote."

The long lines of women had caught the PRO off guard, and the local caciques stalled for time. The lines only grew longer. Finally, orders came to unlock the doors. One by one, the town halls reluctantly opened for business; by mid-morning ballots were being cast in all 12 lakeside towns. Huipi headed west into flat irrigated country that California restaurateurs put under Belgium endive and other nouvelle cuisine delicacies during the winter months. Every summer for a century, the men of the region had migrated to work off California contracts.

Chirimoya was the soul of the Bracero Belt, studied and re-studied by social anthropologists from both sides of the border, who relentlessly tracked the Malinchicans' migratory patterns as if they were so many geese. All agreed that in mid-summer in these towns there were no men—other than cripples and babies—to be counted here. Nonetheless, on the second day of July in the year 2000 AD, at the height of the California picking and canning season, Chirimoya was filled with middle-aged men in Stetson hats and pressed Arrow shirts, standing in line outside the Palacio Municipal, Gold Cards in their callused fists.

Raus stuck the mini-recorder in Jesus Cuate's face. "Don Jesus, isn't this the time of the year when most of the men of Chirimoya are up north for the chamba?"

"Bueno, we just came back for today to vote. Our leader up there, Carlos Lechuga, says the Madre Patria requires it."

"Hell, we came back to vote for the General's son," a bow-legged old bracero yapped. The men on line shushed him. "It's a secret ballot, you old fool." After that, the migrant workers clammed up. Raus could almost touch the mistrust. Anyone who wasn't them must be the PRO.

They hate us.

Huipi and Raus climbed into the sierra in the early afternoon. The nanas and the tatas were queued all along the windy road from Uchuskata to Ma, Tzima, Yum, Taum, Cuim, and Zapicho. The voting was being conducted in the clear mountain air of the plazas. A jubilant Tata Pamfilo explained that the PRO election officials had arrived the night before with "pregnant" ballot boxes and locked themselves into the courthouse, refusing to open in the morning. But the Tatas didn't have time to wait. They broke down the doors, cleaned out the thieves, dumped the pre-stuffed ballot boxes, and were now holding their election out here in the healthy mountain air so everyone could watch each other vote. What would happen when the polls closed at 8 p.m.?

"Why, we will count the votes and then we'll take them down to the Uchuskata district office and guard them right there," the little man insisted, mountain fire in his eye. Tata Pamfilo did not seem quite so much the goofball now.

DR. HUIPI HEADED the Ranchero south, dropping off into the hotlands, the 3 p.m. sun baking the scorpion-infested ravines. Drug bosses from Amapola had moved operations down here and their pistoleros held the sparse population in thrall. Dr. Huipi and Raus eavesdropped outside a school house in Aguja Negra as, one by one, the campesinos silently presented their PRO Gold Cards and were handed a ballot to X, along with instructions as to where to make their mark.

"The colors of the flag, señor. You put it right here, see, or else the ballot won't be counted," a Fu Manchu-mustachioed "auxiliary" explained to the farmers.

The ballot itself was a rambling list of choices for federal offices. Deputies, senators, and—ultimately—the president would be selected today. Each candidate was lined up behind his party's colors and insignia to facilitate voting the party line. At the top of the ballot, there were three options for the President of the Republic. The first column was demarcated by the pale blue hues of the PIN, whose candidate, Sadam Falanges, had suffered a "stroke" early in the campaign and was now in a vegetative state. The second column featured the red, white, and green colors of both the PRO and the flag, under which the name "Citizen Licenciado Filemón Barcelona de Ocelli" was crisply inscribed. The third column depicted a smudged Tonatiuh Sun. "T. Galván," it was succinctly subtitled.

Each weather-worn farm woman and man presented their Gold Card without a word, listened unblinkingly to the instructions, and retired to check off the ballot. Raus had underestimated the power of the Gold Card. The credit-like card had been designed as unimpeachable voter ID by the PRO-controlled Autonomous Electoral Commission, but the Party had bypassed the CAE and handed out so many of them in order to inflate its shrinking numbers that the little gilded swatch of plastic was now universally known as the "PRO Gold Card." There were probably 60 million of them loose in the land. A quarter had been legitimately sent to voters by election authorities, and a quarter were doled out indiscriminately by the PRO at Barcelona rallies. The rest were stolen from government printing offices and sold on the street corners of the country or else manufactured in Centro Histórico basement sweatshops, the computer strip that backed the plastique unfunctional but hardly necessary, since the machinery didn't exist to receive the cards anyway.

The card was multi-purposed. It served (1) as personal identification (it was helpful to have a PRO Gold Card in your possession when accosted by the forces of public order); (2) to purchase discount bus fares (holders got 10% off on long-distance hauls); (3) as a national health insurance card, providing access to free hospital care (the public hospitals were knee-deep in so much human suffering 25 hours a day that there were often more corpses in the waiting rooms than in the morgue); and (4) to entitle its holders—but not to encourage them—to exercise their franchise in national and state elections.

In its tunnel-minded determination to maintain itself in power by any means necessary, the PRO had never seriously considered that the Gold Card might one day be used to rip the throne right out from under its posterior.

༜

AS THEY COMPLETED the wide loop of the state back up past the lake to Ciudad Real, Huipi and Raus pieced together what they had seen so far. "Hay muchos votos por el Doctor. Many more than I expected," admitted the Trotsky facsimile.

"But can you make them count the votes?"

"I believe so. There are really a lot of people voting and I think they'll stay to watch the count. It's when the district modules take possession of the ballot boxes that worries me more."

"What will they do with the ballots?"

Dr. Huipi chuckled cadaverously. "Burn them—just like they did when Ingeniero Cárdenas won, back in '88." He pushed the Ranchero against the oncoming night. They wanted to be in the state capital when the counting began.

There were military vehicles on the road. "We shouldn't worry about the army. The troops will vote for us," Raus's guide assured him. "Tonatiuh is the General's son."

I wouldn't bet on it, Raus thought. If the small rebellion at the polls they had seen today was happening everywhere in the land, a military coup was not just a science fiction scenario.

Ezekial Huipi was more concerned with the logistics of statistical collection: how the raw results were being transmitted to the CAE's computers. "What we don't have yet is access to the raw data flowing into the computer banks at the CAE. The PRO does." According to protocol, the parties and the 21-member Autonomous Electoral Commission would have access only to processed results. Tonatiuh had been granted three representatives on the Commission—two old geezers from the PAR and Reggio Ahumada Tamal—and they would be overwhelmed on every substantive issue by the combined bloc of the PRO and the PIN, particularly when they demanded access to the raw data. Meanwhile, explained Ezekial Huipi, PRO "alchemists," housed in the bowels of the windowless monolith on Avenida, would be prowling the numbers on the CAE screens, moving great loads of votes around from one candidate to the other with cybernetic forklifts, rounding off the results to meet the whims of their managers, making the whole package suitable for international viewing.

Mickey flashed on all those *Break In* magazines on the Bishop's desk. Everyone around this campaign was suddenly very interested in computer intrusion.

"How will you deal with their black magic, Ezekial?"

"We have to get inside their system and stop them."

"But you can't do that without the password!" Raus was starting to log on.

"Not just one password, a rather long and complicated pathway—designed by very expensive Yanqui programmers—that the PRO considers impenetrable."

"Did the Bishop know that pathway?" Raus was using the past tense now.

"I wish I knew," Dr. Huipi blew. "Watch it, culero!" The thin man balled his fist at a passing lumber truck and gunned the Ranchero for the glowing lights of the state capital. "I really wish I knew."

THE GOATEED DRIVER navigated to the wrong side of the Ciudad Real tracks—the General Francisco Galván Popular Colony, established by railroad men and their families during the 1940s, one of the oldest in the provincial capital, where many residents still lived in homes fashioned from abandoned cabooses and freight cars. In the "Galván," the kindergarten, the grade school, the secondary, the football stadium, the health clinic, the post office, all of the streets, even the chicken rotisserie and the wash house proudly bore the name of General Francisco Galván.

Despite the General's lifelong feud with the party he had mistakenly founded, the PRO claimed election after election in the Galván in his name, bagging 90% of the votes 100% of the time, although no more than 40 out of the 917 citizens inscribed on the precinct voting list even bothered to check in each election day.

On this election night, however, Ezekial Huipi had to park his steaming machine two whole blocks from the General Francisco Galván Secondary School gymnasium where the balloting had just concluded. A quiet crowd, perhaps a thousand neighborhood residents, pressed in around the gym. Those who couldn't actually get in the door spread out beyond the chain-link fence that encircled the grounds. All were gazing fixedly ahead, even if their sight lines did not include a window through which they might catch a glimpse of the events transpiring within. Through steel, brick, stone, asbestos, concrete, wood, shingle, plaster, and glass, the colonos of the Galván were watching their votes being counted.

"Por favor, ¿nos dejan pasar?"

The PRO thugs at the schoolhouse door sneered down their Fu Manchu mustaches and refused to allow Mickey and Dr. Huipi into the jam-packed gymnasium. Raus flashed his famous credential. "Por favor..." The Fu Manchus nudged him back with their broad bellies. TV lights were flooding the gym. "TeleVida's inside," Raus complained loudly, almost ramming his press card up one lout's nostrils. "¡Que los dejan pasar!" The railroad families outside began to chant. "Let them pass," echoed those already inside. "Let them pass!" Mickey saw the goons' hesitation and slid between two beer bellies, the knife-thin Huipi right behind.

A trio of shirt-sleeved auxiliaries were tallying the votes cast that day in the Galván. One would unfold the ballot, a second would interpret for whom it had been cast, a third would write in the vote on the CAE tally sheet. Normally the procedure went unobserved and served to ensure hands-down PRO victory in every district in the land. But what was unique about the count in the Galván was that the three auxiliaries were hemmed in on all sides by the civic-minded voters of the Galván, who were hip to every false move they might make. In so vigilant an atmosphere, the auxiliary charged with announcing the person for whom the ballot had been cast found it inadvisable to enunciate "Barcelona" when the paper was clearly marked "Galván." The few times he had attempted to do so, the disputed ballot had been firmly removed from his mitt, inspected by the galvanistas, and instructions given to the tally man to mark the vote for Galván. Similarly, efforts by the triumvirate to disqualify Galván votes because the required "X" overlapped the little box or because one leg of the letter was longer than the other were soundly neutralized by the neighbors.

"We are defending the vote just like Tonatiuh told us to do," Fidencio Rojas, the old railroad man who was the Doctor's captain in the Galván, told Mickey. The count stood at 843 for Tonatiuh, 17 for Barcelona, and 11 for the PIN's paralyzed offering, with about 60 votes still to be sorted. Raus and Huipi caught the drift.

OUTSIDE, THE WITNESSES pressed in to watch the final counting. Raus stopped a plump railroad wife bulging up out of a shiny rose-colored dress—Verónica Virginia Valdez.

"Can I ask you who you voted for, señora? And why?"

"I guess we really fucked the PRO this time," Verónica Virginia exploded, her vermilion mouth pulling apart in what Mickey Raus could not describe, in a family newspaper, as a shit-eating grin.

Doctor Huipi directed the pickup towards the state house. They wanted to see what was going on in the middle-class neighborhoods around the cathedral. There were more military convoys in the street now, canvas-covered vehicles carrying troops. Ezekial continued to insist that the army would soon respond to Tonatiuh's invitation to join his crusade. The soldiers made no effort to halt the Ranchero. "He is the son of the General. Just watch the polling stations around the military camps," the driver argued, in spite of the show of force in the streets just on the other side of the windshield. He looked exactly like Leon Trotsky in the dim light.

Raus flipped on Radio Miel. All day, the national news network had been playing sticky ranchero music. The newscasts had not even mentioned the presidential election, choosing instead to broadcast bulletins from ministries about the decline in both tooth decay and armed bank robberies. Now a strident voice was trying to tell the nation urgent news.

"Police tonight recovered the mutilated bodies of opposition campaign workers Estalin Lenin Gómez Gómez and Abelardo Salmón Guengoitia. The discovery came shortly after polls closed in today's national elections. Investigative Police Chief Florentino Zorrilla has just confirmed to Radio Miel that an area around opposition candidate Tonatiuh Galván's downtown residence, where the bodies were found, has been cordoned off for investigatory purposes."

There it was. It had happened. Raus had expecting this moment ever since the men had been taken.

Ezekial Huipi braked ferociously, checked the gas, stomped down on the pedal and fishtailed the corner by the cathedral on two wheels, burning rubber due east, all the way out to the vacant 12-lane expressway that ran up to the capital of the country—its 10,000-peso tolls kept it free of traffic. As the Ranchero sped out of Ciudad Real, Raus saw many young Indian recruits impaled upon the high beams, their sharp cheekbones blackened for combat as the troops moved into the streets.

⚚

THE ABSENCE OF ANY election-night news on the Ranchero's garishly glowing dial was a dead giveaway that Tonatiuh was way ahead at the polls. The local chieftains and the PRO honchos had been caught napping and were at odds about what to do next. Sides were shifting now, the lines between the factions blurring, deals were being cut. This was the kind of situation journalists described as "fluid." The Party had been in power way too long. In its infernal, eternal arrogance, the PRO had never considered that it could be beat and might actually have to concede defeat.

A malevolent odor was spreading over the capital. Mickey could smell it from two states away, welling like swamp gas out in the Chapulín Park, filling the underground passages beneath Los Primos, seeping into the metro and the telephone grid, leaking from the water faucet drip by drip. He wondered where Tania was. Who was close to her?

The Bishop and Estalin were already accounted for. It was old news. There was no further word on the subject from Radio Miel. The first notice of the election finally came at 10:10, riding the coat tails of the Japanese Mariachi Hiroshima's syrupy rendition of "Cielito Lindo." Dr. Huipi was storming over the butterfly-plagued ridges of eastern Malinchico.

"The Autonomous Electoral Commission announced tonight that it has suspended the issuance of preliminary results due to computer problems occasioned by seasonal electrical disturbances in the provinces. Interior Security Secretary Gonzalo X. Davis, who chairs the commission, told Radio Miel just before 10 p.m. that incoming results had temporarily disappeared from the technical staff's terminals, but predicted that the computer flow would be functioning normally by morning."

This is going to be a very long night, Mickey considered.

"The suspension of the issuance of preliminary results" was Radio Miel's cruelest joke. Later in the evening, if the scenario hung true, the PRO would proclaim its own victory, then the commission would divulge "preliminary results" to confirm Barcelona's triumph. The district computations, days after election day, would seal this finding in lead. The PRO always celebrated its victory this way, taking its time to rub salt into the public's wounds so that the people might more easily become used to the pain of the next tyranny.

Now the computers had crashed, not a good omen for the nation's success in the 21st century. Or else "electrical disturbances" out in the provinces—where it was a hot July night notable for an absence of seasonal thunderstorms—had broken off connections.

Or...

Raus imagined himself blade dancing on the lip of a black hole.

"It's begun," Doctor Huipi said in his best voice of doom.

"What's going on? Did the computers crash or what?"

"They crashed their own computers."

Raus had a Cro-Magnon understanding of cybernetic flim-flam. Why would the Commission close down its own computers if the PRO held the only access to the raw data flow and needed to move the numbers around and quickly prove that it had won?

"You still need a password to get in?"

"A series of passwords..."

"That means..."

"Someone else has gotten in..."

Dr. Huipi whipped out his cellular phone but the battery was dead as a dumbbell. Cursing the fiendish aparato, he parked and the two hunted down a functional public phone. Ezekial punched in Tonatiuh's cellular but it too was down. The five inside lines on Carlos Quinto rang busy. Raus took over and dialed his house. Babs González's bebop babble spilled into his tympanum: "Ooo bop sha bone, the Raus ain't home." Where was Tania? He tried Malcreado's. The phone tolled emptily. "I have an idea," lightbulbed Ezekial Huipi and dove back into the phone booth. Mickey waited under the warm blanket of stationary tropical air that had invaded the broad industrial valley that surrounds the capital. Once, the Aztec-Mexicas had reaped bountiful harvests of maize from this devastated plain.

Dr. Huipi was trembling when he climbed back in behind the wheel. "It's worse than we think," was all he said for the next 20 kilometers. Then: "They were thrown up on the doorstep on Carlos Quinto a few minutes after seven. They'd been mutilated." Raus figured he'd know soon enough how they had been mutilated.

"They cut their hearts out of their chests," Doctor Huipi said thickly, 20 klicks later.

They were moving through the heavy industrial belt now—auto plants, churning turbines, steel mills, acre after acre of industrial wastes.

Listen, Mickey remembered El Nene's moan. *Can't you hear them chewing on my father's heart?*

"Their hearts?"

"It is a message from the PRO saying they too remember something about the past."

A millennium ago, upon this very landscape they were speeding through, the Aztec-Mexicas had waged a peculiar sort of arranged war in which the victor carried off many captive warriors, whose hearts were subsequently ripped from their chests so that the suns of the Mexicas, collectively called Tonatiuh, might continue to wheel through the heavens. These wars were called "guerras flóridas" or "flowery wars" be-cause—once the battlefield activities had been completed—the victorious lords and the vanquished ones alike hunkered down behind curtains woven from wild flowers and watched the losers dispatched by blood-soaked priests on the temple mounts below them. Then, together, the nobles feasted on the exquisitely roasted haunches of the sacrificed warriors.

Now Tonatiuh's spiritual advisor was trying to tell Raus that the flowery wars had begun again.

COMING DOWN INTO the capital from the ring of hills above, the largest urban nightmare on earth seemed an unrumpled bed of symmetrically strung streetlights. But the order darkness imposed upon the city's excesses was eerily deceptive. "God, I hate this evil place," Ezekial Huipi muttered. To him, the capital of his country was Sodom pi'ed.

The Ranchero sped into the northern suburbs where the chemical mills loomed, the sultry air pressing down upon the greenish bile billowing from unscrubbed stacks. Acetylene torches licked at the night. The rusted-out General Francisco Galván Refinery blazed noxiously. The stench was insufferable. It permeated the cab, Raus' clothes, his hair, his damaged nostrils. He stifled a gag and checked his watch: 12:45. He had barely slept for two days now. I'm getting much too old for this abuse, he thought. What he needed most was a drink. He scanned the industrial avenue for an illuminated storefront.

The neighborhoods out here were deserted. Off-duty cops

stalked the shadows of the warehouses, ready to pillage and butcher anyone who stopped between streetlights. Dr. Huipi glued an eye to the rearview mirror. There was no sign of the military yet. Radio Miel announced that Filemón Barcelona had won the presidential election.

"According to preliminary results obtained by Radio Miel from high-level Organic Revolutionary Party sources, former finance minister Filemón Barcelona has won 75% of the popular vote around the country and is the president-elect of the republic. Licenciado Barcelona's closest challenger, Tonatiuh Galván, received a surprising 14% of the total ballots cast. In announcing the victory, PRO party co-chairman Bulmaro Marrano invited the general public to a pre-dawn celebration of the party's triumph at PRO headquarters, at which the President-elect himself is slated to appear."

Ezekial Huipi whistled reflexively. "Pinche marrano—¡Qué mierda!"

"El Gacho" Marrano was de la Mancha's main man. Raus had just read yesterday how the famous fixer was still doing hard time in Aineedaloya Federal Penitentiary for appropriation of party funds in some hapless drug-money laundering scam. What was El Gacho doing out on the streets, calling himself co-chairman of the PRO and announcing that Barcelona had won? Proclaiming PRO victory was a jealously guarded protocol of Party chairman Rodríguez Lefkowitz.

"They are splitting much faster than we anticipated." Dr. Huipi was genuinely alarmed. "They will fight over how to deal with Tonatiuh. How to preserve their own little empires. The Tecos and their computers will go up against the Brontos and their hired killers. Many hearts are going to be taken before this is over."

Both men saw the headlights closing in on the mirror. Huipi gunned onto Avenida. The tail slipped behind again, blending into the sparse traffic, but never letting go.

Dr. Huipi was driving straight through to Carlos Quinto. Raus was fried, flying on no octane, but his nose kept urging him to follow it to the source of the bad smell that permeated the night. Trotsky's ghost dropped him off near the PRO compound with a caution: "Be watchful, amigo, this is where they do the surgeries."

Mickey was unnerved by the PRO's chutzpah, one minute claiming there were no results, the next announcing a victory party.

"Welcome aboard, m'ijo. The booze is on the house." Pease handed him a brown paper bag twisted tightly around a liter of "Brandy Presidente." What else? He guzzled deeply.

"You've heard about the Bishop and Estalin?" Raus wiped his mouth with the back of his wrist.

"Don't blame me, Mick, mi boy. I'm entirely heartless myself." Horace Pease was very drunk, circling around the sidewalk outside the compound on Avenida, looking as if he was about to crashland on the concrete.

Despite the lights that kept flashing PRO-PRO-PRO-PRO-PRO ad infinitum from the roof garden and the sizzling sound of a salsa band in the compound courtyard, the party seemed suspiciously over. Large numbers of poorly dressed people were pressing up against the inside of the video-controlled gate, apparently trying to get out. Others were scrambling up the tall spiked fence in their eagerness to exit the premises, oblivious that rent-a-cops were beating them around the shins from below. Raus watched horror-stricken as one women fell straight-legged from the fence, smashed into the sidewalk with a sickening thunk, picked herself up, dusting for broken bones, and ran off hollering, "¡Que muera el PRO!" A soiled man came hobbling past on busted stumps and Raus pushed his mini-recorder at him. "The PRO made us come. They sent police trucks to our colony and made us come. We didn't want to come here. In the Jinete Chueco colony, we all voted for Tonatiuh." Then he clammed up. "You're not going to use my name, are you, sir?" the lame man pleaded.

☙

RAUS SAW THE TAPE of El Gacho's victory celebration at Carlos Quinto an hour later. TeleVida and TeleVersa kept repeating it over and over again all night long. The skinheaded, big-nosed Gacho was waving his arms around like an insane orchestra leader, honking, "We've won! We've won!" and urging a bunch of lethargic Indian women in aprons to dance. A white-tuxedoed orchestra struck up a sizzling beat. No one danced. In the very rear of the screen, there seemed to be a small disturbance, or perhaps it was only the celebrants being carried away by the intoxicating triumph.

"Barcelona didn't show up," Malcreado pointed out.

"¿Y Tania? Has she been here?"

"She said she was going back to your place. She got real sick when she heard about…the news."

Raus dialed the house. Babs González reiterated the zany rap. Maybe she was asleep.

"The funeral service is at noon at Payaso's by Parque Solomán," Antonio reminded Raus as he pushed through the oak doors.

Outside, night and day were blending—a foul, suffocating dawn welling up after a rainless night—as if all weather was suspended until further notice. The teary, bloodshot eye of the sun peeked over the horizon through the stagnant industrial residue, promising a new day of stomach-wrenching disasters. Raus stumbled home towards La Bondad, stepping gingerly through hepatic gutters filled with floating fruit and human turds. On every corner, solitary pedestrians gnawed from stained paper sacks. Raus stopped to listen. Now he could hear them chewing, their incisors tearing into the viscera of his friends.

CAPITAL TENSE IN WAKE OF HIGH-LEVEL KILLINGS, POSSIBLE ELECTION UPSET

Special to the North Coast Variety News

TENOCHTITLAN (July 3)—The discovery last night of the mutilated bodies of two high-level aides to opposition candidate Tonatiuh Galván, and the possibility that Galván won an upset victory in yesterday's presidential balloting, has this sprawling capital on a tense string this morning. Army troops are reported poised at Military Camp #1 on the western edge of the city in the event of disturbances today, and partial martial law has been declared in Galván's home state of Malinchico, where he apparently has won a lopsided victory over the long-ruling (71 years) Party of the Organic Revolution (PRO) and its candidate, Filemón Barcelona.

The PRO has won every presidential election here since its formation by General Francisco Galván, the opposition candidate's father, seven decades ago.

Crashing Computers

Confirmation of a Galván victory was muddied when, shortly before 10 p.m., the government announced that its vote-tallying computers had "crashed"—just as preliminary results were being received. Although the Autonomous Electoral Commission (CAE) had promised to begin releasing preliminary results within hours of poll-closing, Secretary of Internal Security ("Gobernación") and commission chairperson Gonzalo X. Davis declared last night that "the numbers have just disappeared from our terminals," attributing the system crash to "electrical disturbances in the provinces."

Later this morning, the Internal Security Minister, who had earlier predicted the computers would be functioning by today, conceded that it may be a week before the system is up and operating again.

"We are checking the whole system for leaks," one anonymous Autonomous Electoral Commission technician told the *Variety News*.

As news of the computer "failure" spread, hundreds of Galván supporters began gathering outside the CAE's 22-story skyscraper on downtown Reforma Boulevard, claiming that the PRO had deliberately shut down the computers because "Galván was winning." Outside the CAE skyscraper early this morning, Galván's representative on the commission, Reggio Ahumada Tamal, declared that "the PRO is holding the nation hostage."

Despite galvanista optimism and the computer breakdown, the ruling PRO insists that Barcelona, its heavily favored candidate, has won 75% of the national vote, at least 5% less than the party's traditional margin of victory. "We have won! We have won!" party co-chairman Bulmaro Marrano cheered at a pre-dawn "victory" celebration at PRO national headquarters here in the capital. Marrano, who was apparently released from prison on election eve, where he was serving a 40-year sentence for looting party coffers in a drug laundering scheme, noted that Galván had taken nearly 15% of the vote, a share he called "the largest any opposition candidate has ever achieved in 71 years of the PRO's guided democracy."

According to the government tabloid *El Orgánico*, Marrano based his projections on reports received "from our citizen committees throughout the nation." The PRO candidate Barcelona failed to appear at the PRO victory celebration.

Galván Sweeps Capital

Galván campaign sources also base their calculations of an upset on telephoned reports from their captains around the country. According to temporary press chief Antonio Malcreado, Doctor Galván has won stunning victories in such disparate regions of this huge country as Tijuana on the California border and Chiapas, the southernmost state fronting Guatemala. The Doctor has apparently swept the western states of Malinchico and El Horno by mounting margins and is showing considerable strength in the center of the country, where he campaigned extensively during the early phases of his grueling nine month-long crusade for the presidency. Throughout the night, in the capital—where a sixth of the nation's voters reside—galvanista captains have been presenting signed copies of CAE tally sheets showing the opposition candidate winning all 30 of this gigantic metropolis' election districts.

The upset, if allowed to stand, was achieved because of "the first honest vote count in the nation's history," Malcreado told the *Variety News*. Voters throughout the country gained access to ballot boxes by presenting "Gold Cards"—credit card-like voter ID widely circulated by the PRO—and then voted for the opposition candidate Galván. The galvanistas ensured a clean vote count by refusing to leave the precincts until the votes had been tallied to their satisfaction. Despite his anticipated triumph, Dr. Galván, who has been closeted since learning of the deaths of his aides, has made no claim of victory himself.

Grisly Aztec Rites

An hour after polls closed last night, the mutilated bodies of Abelardo Salmón, 39, and Estalin Lenin Gómez Gómez, 63, Galván's campaign manager and transportation director respectively, were tossed from a fast-moving car in front of the Galván residence-campaign headquarters in the former colonial section of the city, known as the "Centro Histórico." Police immediately cordoned off the zone but could not locate the vehicle, which neighbors described as a late-model gray Gran Marquis with no license plates, a car popular with ranking government and PRO officials.

Both men disappeared three nights ago, on the eve of a mammoth Galván rally here in the capital, and Galván has repeatedly accused the PRO of responsibility for the kidnapping. PRO candidate Barcelona, in turn, has accused Galván of staging the disappearances to win "last-minute sympathy."

The bodies of the two aides bore signs of torture, and the hearts of both men had been cut out of their bodies in a grisly reminder of ancient Aztec sacrificial rites, a gesture that has shocked even veteran reporters inured to brutal political killings. The Galván aides are to be buried today in the Galván family plot in the capital in a ceremony that is certain to heighten the tension level here.

Perpetual Session

One potential flash point for violence is the CAE itself. The Autonomous Electoral Commission has declared itself in "perpetual session" until all results are finalized. The body, upon which the PRO holds an 18 to 3 majority over the galvanistas, immediately declared a recess last night after Davis's announcement of a computer "crash." Galván has often called upon his supporters to "defend the vote," and the gathering outside the commission's offices continues to grow.

"The Doctor is prepared to summon all those who voted for him in every region of the nation to come to the capital if the district computations do not confirm what we saw yesterday at the polls," declared Antonio Malcreado, a former reporter who has replaced the murdered Salmón as the candidate's link with the press. Dr. Galván is expected to announce the national mobilization at today's double funeral.

Under the republic's baroque electoral system, autonomous electoral commissions in the nation's 300 federal election districts (CAECITOS), meet anytime between 48 hours and a week after the voting to certify the results gathered from the polling places in their jurisdictions and declare a winner. Traditionally, the PRO has used the interval to "cook" the vote so that it appears credible to outside observers.

Troubled Washington

On the morning after what could be the most startling political upset in Latin America since the 1999 victory of "Presidente Gonzalo" (Abimael Guzmán) in Peru, this sweltering, polluted capital sweats out a potentially explosive stand-off that could paralyze the government, send the stock market into the toilet, and cripple commercial relations with the United States for months to come. Galván, the son of a military man, has often encouraged the army not to act on behalf of the ruling party, but the use of troops in Malinchico, following the opposition candidate's clear victory there, leaves doubts as to the effectiveness of his exhortations.

Meanwhile, the Doctor's proven powers of convocation are known to be troubling Washington, where Acting President Gingrich is only two weeks from a Republican convention that will rubber-stamp his candidacy. Gingrich's probable opponents—Democrat Hillary Clinton and the independent Party of Christian Faith candidate, Pat Buchanan—have both declared they will make the threat posed by Galván to U.S. internal security an issue in the brewing campaign.

Although U.S. ambassador Thaddeus Blackbridge publicly endorsed Barcelona, he is reported to have opened channels to Galván as it became evident that the Doctor would run strongly. Galván heatedly denies that he has had any contact with "Yanqui functionaries."

Whether the U.S. might intervene if the chaotic situation here deteriorates further appears to be more a domestic political call than a foreign policy consideration for Gingrich. Washington's recent incursions in Peru and Suriname were both widely unpopular in the U.S. Nonetheless, the national security implications of the worsening situation here—which threatens to spill over the very volatile border—could push Washington into taking rapid preemptive action before the U.S. election season is in full swing.

Extending from the Pacific to the Gulf within 60 miles of the border, the U.S. maintains a string of 63 military installations, many of them equipped with advanced tactical nuclear weaponry. Twenty-five thousand troops, mainly concentrated in the San Diego and El Paso areas, back up 10,000 Border Patrol agents and an undisclosed number of DEA and Customs operatives, who work the region in the Gingrich interim-administration's War on Illegal Drugs and Aliens.

IX

A FOUL TASTE

July 3 – 5, 2000

THE FOUL TASTE SPREAD from the bottom of Raus's tonsils to the tip of his tongue. Maybe it was just the afterbirth of the fried brains he'd gobbled at 3 a.m. from a taco wagon near the PRO metro stop. Or maybe it was the whiff of political malevolence he had first inhaled on the road in from Malinchico. Most probably, the bitterness that made him spit like an agitated llama was only the fruit of breakfasting alone on three fingers of mescal and a petrified worm.

Home had not been where the heart was. Tania had left a scrawled note on the kitchen table. "I'm scared. I don't want to be alone. When are you coming home? I'm over at Sasha's. Call me there." He hadn't.

Raus donned a rumpled sports coat, the closest article of clothing he owned to a funeral suit, staggered through the old quarter out to Reforma, and headed towards Parque Solomán. The bad taste did not go away. Under the fancy ice-blue canvas awning of Pavarotti Payaso & Sons' fastidious funeral home by Parque Solomán, a wave of uncoiling nausea sent him retching to the gutter.

Pavarotti Payaso & Sons, "undertakers of class," buried anyone with bucks enough to afford their deluxe services, regardless of race, creed, sexual or political orientation. "The House of Payaso" was an ice-blue, temperature-controlled, 10-story funerary tower subdivided into many tastefully decorated minichapels, akin to the multi-cinema concept of the motion picture exhibition industry. The chapels varied in price from the splendors of the penthouse to the minimalist squalor of the basement cubicles. The Bishop and Don Estalin were laid out on the ground-level floor, or planta baja, not so much because a more prestigious suite was not available, but because if serious trouble developed during the lamentations, Pavarotti Payaso & Sons wanted to contain it on the lower levels of their shiny funerary spire.

The ice-blue chapel and its tiny anteroom were packed suit to suit with prominent rumormongers. Raus could barely circumnavigate through the tsk-tsking cliques. He made a beeline for the press corps, which occupied a wedge in back of the biers. Antonio, Sasha Vigo, Arbus, and Sid Bloch fraternized around the open coffin. Despite the expensive filtered-air system, the smoke of hundreds of carbonizing cigarettes assaulted his guts. Raus hid his dry heaves inside a colorful handkerchief.

The Bishop and Don Estalin were displayed in dark suits as if they were mourners themselves. It was the first time Raus had ever seen either of the men so formally attired. Their heartless chests had been stuffed with sponges and sewn smooth by Payaso & Sons' NAAFTA-trained staff. Despite the application of thick layers of rouge to hide the bruises and the vexations he had received at the hands of his torturers, Abelardo Salmón seemed unnaturally serene, his watches softly whirring, as if he was about to sail out on the campaign trail for one last encore.

Raus' eyes grew blurry. Probably just cigarette tars or an evil ozone count, the once-hard-boiled reporter sniffed.

Adios, compañero, goodbye.

"You're back!" Tania touched his arm. "Thank God, you're back..."

Mickey turned into her large green eyes. "They're dead..."

"I know. I know," she whispered.

They collapsed into an urgent embrace, nearly tumbling into the twin biers.

Adios, compañeros, goodbye...

Both men displayed an unhealthy puffiness on exposed skin surfaces. They had been tortured for several days, Antonio said, alternately beaten and burnt with lighted cigarettes. "You should have seen them before they put their clothes on." Jolts of raw electricity had blackened their testicles. They had been mock-drowned in filthy cesspools, a technique the police call "going to the well."

Whatever their abductors were looking for, Malcreado thought they had not been satisfied. "Why else would the Bishop and Don Estalin still be smiling?"

Pease was smashed and kept blabbing about the bloody necrophiliac dago undertaker. For the past 48 hours Horace had been hovering like a turkey vulture around the PRO, scavenging drinks and gossip. The skirmishing between the Brontos and the Tecos was heroic. There had been fistfights. Ambulances had taken away the wounded.

"X. Davis arranged for the Gacho's provisional parole. Apparently, Don Gonzalo's thrown his lot in with the Brontos. The dinosaurs don't even care about the appearance of the election. They just want X. Davis to declare Barcelona the winner. Why bother with the bloody numbers? That way only leads to destabilization! The duplicity of these bloody woggos has no name."

Tania was in tears. "They are going to take out Tonatiuh. They will have him killed or disappeared. They will take his heart too..."

"I quite disagree, Msh," Horace slurred. "The new NEATA treaty means they must be more cosmetic. They'll drive him from the country. Blackbridge is already making Tonatiuh offers of safe conduct..."

"They can't put the genie back in the bottle," Raus interjected.

Arbus and Bloch had just taxied over from the CAE, a mile up Reforma. Thousands were now encamped on the open esplanade. There were busloads of police on the back streets but no troops in the vicinity yet. No numbers were running on the screens upstairs and the commission was still in recess. X. Davis could keep it that way for as much time as the PRO needed. Jane Ann's sources inside the computer room had told her the system was shut down due to the suspected introduction of—of all things—a computer virus!

Raus doubled up in peristaltic agony. "Mickey, you are in pain," Arbus said indulgently. "Yeah," he muttered, turning verdant. Tania stroked the back of his neck. He was experiencing what James Joyce used to call an epiphany, one of those luminescent instances when unrelated phenomena hook up to produce a solid fist of understanding. Sometimes such illuminations get caught in the curl of one's intestines.

In the breast pocket of the rumpled suit jacket he had not worn for the past five weeks was the remnant of a folded clipping concerning computer virus contamination in the city of Baltimore, USA. The Bishop had put it in his hand before the campaign buses had shoved off for the south of the country. Actually, the AP story was about the threat of a virus—a teenage hacker had offered to unleash a crippling, information-devouring "worm" into highly secret Pentagon weapon systems unless the U.S. withdrew its troops from Peru.

"The virus story is being floated by El Gacho. He's shut the computers down by spreading it," snapped Malcreado. "The big vote for Tonatiuh is the only virus attacking their system. You can quote me on this one."

Blood pounded at Raus' temples. What had been the question he'd asked that had prompted the Bishop to hand him this clipping? The question? What the hell was it?

"Of course you knew that Payaso is a blinking fag necrophiliac, didn't you?" Pease was trying to interest Ms. Arbus in a rancid tidbit. "He only likes to do it with dead little boys."

"Horace, you sound absolutely jealous," Arbus smirked haughtily.

TONATIUH ARRIVED an hour behind schedule with his three darkly suited sons in tow. Paloma, in muted mourning, trailed behind. The Doctor was as grim as Raus had ever seen him. The mourners squeezed into themselves so the family could pass through to view the caskets.

Tonatiuh studied the victims clinically. The Bishop was his closest friend, if this angry, solitary man in an elegantly cut Italian suit could be said to have friends. His smoldering x-ray eyes tracked the scars of torture accumulated under their Sunday-best duds, the routes of excruciating pain etched into their hollowed-out cadavers.

Then the Doctor planted himself, like a solid brown oak, in front of the coffins, for the traditional standing of guard. The three princely sons fanned around him, Paloma—like a dark mother swan—at their side. Tonatiuh's eyes slashed on out the door and up the boulevard all the way to Los Primos, pinpointing those responsible for these unspeakable deaths. The room was stirred only by the whir of the air filtration unit and the final ticks of the Bishop's watches. At last, the Doctor stepped forward and broke the deadly stillness.

"We have won the election, compañeras and compañeros, but we have not won the war. They have taken two of our best warriors and many, many more will fall if they do not count our votes. Although our crusade has always been a peaceful one, they are forcing us to fight back to defend our victory."

Then, as Raus had seen him do before, the Doctor addressed the government spies in the chapel, fingering them as couriers to the ruling circles. To those who reported to the generals, he reiterated his message that the military had a constitutional duty to uphold his vote. "We are just one step from power," he instructed the PRO antennas. "You must tell your jefes to let the computers run the raw data and give our representatives on the commission equal access to the terminals. Not to do so will be injurious to the health of the nation."

Ooof. Raus was mule-kicked by his memory. He had asked the Bishop how you could stop the PRO from stealing the election on the computers?

The Bishop's answer had been to hand him a clipping about threatening vital systems with a computer virus.

Now Tonatiuh invited the mourners to please accompany him "to bury our dead." As effortlessly as if he were in a wooden church on a banana plantation in Little Infernillo, where the dead must be put down quickly, he and his three sons plus Malcreado and Nacha Caracol lifted the Bishop to their shoulders. El Compa, Jose Cerro, the Nene, SuperPendejo, and two tubby masked wrestlers from the Communist Grapplers Guild (M-L) levitated Don Estalin. It was a prescient moment: the diminutive, swishy funeral director leaping up and down, trying to communicate to the pallbearers that his expensive services included transporting the bodies to the hearse for the decorous drive to the final resting place, Tonatiuh assuring Signore Payaso that the hearses would not be needed today and directing the funeral procession down the cold marble steps, through the elegant crystal portals, out of the air-conditioned hush of the ice-blue funerary tower, and into the steaming, stinking hurly-burly of the capital's streets.

☙

THE CORTEGE DEAD-MARCHED on leaden feet down Reforma, under the lifeless palm trees and bored stares of the office workers up in the skyscrapers. Hundreds of exasperated, gridlocked motorists jabbed at their horns like Rubén "Barbed Wire" Olivares. The din obliterated all conversation.

"And this is a culture that venerates death?" Raus shouted at Tania Escobar as she fell into step alongside him.

"What did you say?" she screamed back.

Still, the local culture's fixation with the deceased quite probably rescued the Bishop and Don Estalin from being murdered again, many times over, by the occupants of ten lanes of idling automobiles. The somber passage of the funeral procession excited respect from pedestrians. Some whipped off their hard hats and paused in dignified tribute. Whether from fear of exploding radiators or a desire not to miss out on a little bit of history, dozens of drivers jumped from their stalled vehicles and joined the slow train of mourners. Contingents from RAT's neighborhoods fell into step. Plantón and the students trudged in from the university. Raus watched the Paseo de la Reforma disappear under their feet. What had been a few hundred close friends and mostly hostile reporters on the sidewalk outside of Payaso's were now thousands of pairs of sweaty footwear blanketing the boulevard from curb to curb.

The stinky August dog-day noon was compounded by the unusually stationary air mass that had anchored itself over the city. Raus had, literally, to push the atmosphere aside in order to advance. The exhausted pallbearers wavered and buckled under the weight of the metal caskets but many reserves rushed to the rescue, shouldering up the boxed galvanistas, as honored to be hoisting the corpses of martyrs as the Shi'ites of Iran. Bathed in perspiration that burst through their soot-plugged pores, the throng stopped to pray along the way.

"Fuck the fucking PRO!" the mob ranted at the foot of the untopped 112-story Tower of Vertical Modernity. "¡Chinga tu pinche madre!" The marchers shook their fists at the billion-dollar bubble-dome and pinnacle of the DisneyMex Global Stock Exchange.

Down Reforma near the park, many thousands more were gathered on the flat gray esplanade of the Autonomous Electoral Commission. Tania spotted the soldiers immediately— young, crew-cutted men slouching around the fringes of the gathering. Dim uniformed troops stood poised on the inside of the commission's polarized revolving doors.

A little city had begun to construct itself upon the esplanade. Pup tents and plastic sheets stanchioned improbably inside the cracks webbing the concrete provided crude shelter from future weather. Greasy, gangrenous taco stands opened shop. A first aid station was already attracting victims of the heat. Los Hustlers set up their souvenir shoppe under a torn sheet. Portable toilets had been installed. The galvanistas were settling in for an extended stay.

The new city was building itself around the esplanade's significant monument—a curvaceous slab of jet-black onyx draped in what some saw as a see-through nightie. In the avant-garde art mags, its detractors sneeringly labeled the piece Señorita Electoral Democracy.

This black elephant had been designed by overcharging South Koreans and sold at an outrageous commission by some deadbeat New York third-world monument broker. The PRO blithely passed the bills on to its benefactors at the National Endowment for Democracy-Adenhauer Foundation, Inc., the philanthropic arm of the World Trade Organization, who subsidized this trophy to the official party's perverted vision of "electoral democracy" in the interest of free trade and preferential access to national markets.

The beautifully draped, curving black shape on the esplanade was matched by the luxurious interiors of the CAE's glass palace. The computer rooms were ultra-bright, sanitized work spaces. The orderly banks of advanced high-speed micro systems were polished to a fine patina each morning and midnight by armies of Indians in blue overhauls. Despite the shiny surfaces, the systems really did not work very well. Fuses blew, data erased itself, unexplained short circuits caused frequent fires, embarrassing glitches occurred even without the heavy hand of the PRO "alchemists," garble was constant—in short, the systems often crashed.

All over the nation, the PRO managed similar enterprises—gleaming banks of computers with sexy six-story statuary out on similar gray esplanades—that did not work. While the licenciados and the ingenieros and the técnicos and their ill-paid staffs sat protected only by the ironed white smocks they were permitted to wear as a badge of their elevated station in life, the mechanisms they thought they controlled generated bone-softening radiation and killer smogs that suffocated a hundred babies in a single night. Sparkling control rooms ran industries that were causing citizens serious grief, much as this glove box of a skyscraper was now contaminating the presidential election in the name of "electoral democracy." Those who sat hunched all day over the computers could not have cared less. They were upwardly mobile. They were insulated from the poor and the germs and the past and the systems they ran. They were modern. They were the future of the nation.

⚕

THE CASKETS HAD BEEN set down at the enormous feet of Señorita Electoral Democracy and opened to the sky. Effusive floral offerings flooded the esplanade: enormous wreathes of roses and margaritas and claveles, golden mountains of Cempaxuchtl, irises and alcatrazes and gladioli fetched from the distant provinces of the republic by the miners of Jaquemate and the kiwi pickers of Tacumán. A woman in a flower-print dress placed garlands of white snowflake roses upon the martyrs' brows. Nacha Caracol burnt sage and spread pine boughs. The Tatas of Zapicho bore crowns of the blue fairy San Miguel Tzatzuki blossom. From every place name the Bishop had plotted and Don Estalin had driven, those they had visited came now, and they came with flowers.

Tonatiuh, normally a tall man, was dwarfed beneath the draped goddess. Now the soldiers were linked up in front of the CAE to repel any urge to seize the premises. Their gaze was fixed on the Doctor's back. Tonatiuh had spoken with troops at his back before. It was a posture that seemed to say, You can shoot me from behind like a coward, compañero soldier, but I'm going to keep on talking until I drop. Tonatiuh's cojones impressed his public. It was what convinced the gomeros of Amapola and the banana workers of El Horno of his valor. Maybe it could even convince the crew-cutted soldiers poised right behind him that they had the wherewithal to cut off the PRO's balls.

The Doctor's constituency did not have a very clear idea of the next step in this unlikely crusade. But Tonatiuh's reaction to this craving for direction was eccentric. Upon occasion, as he had in the secret graveyards of the south, he rose to the moment, mesmerizing his auditors with allusions to the past that they did not always understand. These dense, visionary moments were enigmatic. Was the Doctor suggesting that the past was the model for action in the present? Or was he merely giving vent to his burning nostalgia for revenge?

Most often, Tonatiuh took a less scintillating route, discussing health or nutrition or technology, rounding his discourse off so that he seemed to be telling a sort of singsong parable. Raus thought Tonatiuh did this because he was uncertain of the people. He was not sure how far they wanted to go. He didn't want to yank them very forcefully because they were like mules, and they would balk at being hauled forward by someone other than themselves. He said as much to Tania.

"But he also wants to make sure he has enough room to step out of the way when the mob crashes the Palace gates," she contended. Tonatiuh understood only too well the depths of the rabble's terrible rage but still wasn't quite sure how to channel it to bring change.

With the corpses of his lieutenants laid out at his feet, the Doctor spoke to the swelling, disorganized throng about computers and how they conveniently crashed when the numbers did not fit the PRO's plans. But technology was neither good nor bad, he stressed. It depended on how it was used, who manipulated it, and who had access.

In a thousand nefarious ways, the PRO had aimed its computers right at the people—dissolving their names from the voting lists, aborting their birth identification numbers, erasing their land registration, telling the world how well-fed they were when they went to bed hungry every night, delineating how productively they produced when they loathed their minimum wage jobs, lying about how happy they were with their lot in life when they were immensely dissatisfied with it, denying them the bitterness of their daily existence. In short, disappearing them from the nation.

But Tonatiuh suggested that the computers could bring benefits in the hands of the people. They could measure the Patria's real needs and desires, really open up social institutions to serve those who the PRO would rather just went away, really ensure that everyone had a vote and a voice that counted. Computers could even unify and heal disparate indigenous cultures into one linguistic and political confederation that could legitimately be called a nation. It was a novel concept but the thousands of enraged galvanistas pushing onto the already packed esplanade did not seem to catch the nuances of the message.

"¡QUE SE MUERAN LAS PINCHES COMPUTADORAS!" the mob shrieked, a momentous eagle screech against the stagnant heavens. "That the computers should die! That they should die! The Fucking Computers! Die! Die! Die!"

An aroma of revenge spiced the foul afternoon. The galvanistas' anger surged like leaping wild fire back and forth across the esplanade, their furious lungs exploding in chanted tantrums:

"THAT THEY SHOULD DIIIIIIIIIIIIIIIIEEEE!

"¡¡QUE SE MUERRRRRA EL PRRRRRRRROOOOOOOO!!

"¡¡¡HOOOOOOOSTIIIIIIIIIIIIICIAHHHHHHHHHHH!!!

"¡¡¡¡TONNNNNATIIIIYUHH PRESSSIIIIIDENTEEEE!!!!

"DIIIIIIIIIIIIIIE! DIIIIIIIIIIIIIE! DIIIIIIIIIIIIIIIIIE!"

Hour after hour, they shouted at the tall glass building, trying to shatter it with the vibrations of their indignation. The galvanistas had become one raw red throat, giving furious voice to the vengeance that had been caught in the public caw through decade after decade of electoral fraud.

By 3 p.m., the rays of Tonatiuh's namesake had many of the protesters stripping down to their bare brown skins. The formaldehyde loaded into the Bishop's and Estalin's veins began to boil as if the dead men were being simmered on low heat. Only the distant threat of thunder promised to dampen the hot doggy pant of the fetid afternoon.

Just to tighten up this edginess, it was lunch time and the tortas and the tacos and the tostadas and the sopas and the huaraches and the hot dogs, the chescos and the palomitas and the paletas and the aguas frescas had run short. The irritation level rose perceptibly. Everyone knew there was going to be big trouble. Knots of young men, ambulantes from La Bondad, the

Santo Pachecos, crew-cutted army recruits too, scoured the esplanade for empty pop bottles.

Arbus emerged into the glare to report that X. Davis was now predicting that raw data would be flowing again by midnight. There were many conflicting versions of just what the "problemita" was. Her source swore the system was being examined cipher by cipher to pinpoint possible gateways through which a virus might sneak.

The PROs were taking the galvanista threat very seriously.

Ahumada Tamal rode the elevators between the darkened commission auditorium and the jumpy esplanade like a yo-yo, his two old geezers from the PAR on either wing. Like Malcreado, he did not buy the virus story at all. "This gringo technology of yours is against our nature. My compatriots are not patient enough to plot such sinister programs. We are colorful, carefree people, Mr. Raus. This is all a PRO bad joke."

Mickey and Tania rode to the top with RAT. The lights had been pleasantly dimmed in the abandoned commission chambers. There was no sign that the "permanent session" might ever be convened again. Pease was snoozing in the dark, an empty flask of gin peeking out of his seersucker suit pocket. He came to in a rage. "What a bloody circus! Where's my bleeping battery acid? Thief! ¡Socorro!" The *Times* man dug out the empty bottle, inspected it for clues, lobbed it into a CAE trash recycler, and launched into a withering tirade.

"We must cut through all this bull dung and crown Barcelona president no matter how sordid his perversions may be. Let us get on with the killing! I've got my own personal list. You want to see it, señorita?" Pease unzipped his fly.

"You can't piss here, Horace," Tania admonished—he was already dribbling against the Commission's upholstered walls. "C'mon, let's go find you the little boy's room."

"My dear, do you know where your new president is spending his siesta? Hiding under his comfort blanket in the master bedroom of his mother's estate in El Rolex, thas where. She is changing his stinking diaper. Later, she will make him play toilet games. Or maybe you had not heard that Filemón

Barcelona is a frigging sexual psychopath who raped and strangled his nanny with her own panties whilst still a small child?"

"Pease, the walls have ears..."

The *Times* man pooh-poohed the PRO's eavesdropping capabilities, saucily farting into the hidden mike. "I have it on good word that the little prick has become a raving schizoid, sometimes catatonic as a bloody stone or else so maniacally convinced that he is the president that his keepers have to tie him down in the rubber room."

"Pease, there are a lot of soldiers out front."

"They are harmless, my dumpling, it's all a little show. The troops all voted the Tonatiuh ticket—although they were ordered to vote for Little Choop Choop Choop. Seems like Gertrudis is having this disciplinary failure and now General Ram Ram wants to ram it up his culo. Archibaldo's already been in to see Lomeli to complain because Tonatiuh's doctor-brother appears to be losing control of the bloody frigging glorious revolutionary arm..."

Pease ran out of gas in mid-epithet, blanched dead white, and collapsed face first into the armrest of an auditorium seat. "It's only my blood sugar," he croaked through cracked teeth to Tania as she cradled his damaged cranium in her lap. "Quick, my sweet, let's you and I go out for a little drinkie."

THE THREE REPORTERS dropped 22 stories in the luxurious, leather-lined elevator. The piped-in mariachi muzak kept speeding up and slowing down comically like a calliope on a bad acid trip.

Downstairs, the matter was no longer a laughing one. Bricks and coke bottles flew from the perspiring, bare-chested crowd, mostly from a pocket under the gossamer-garbed goddess where Don Estalin and the Bishop were laid out. Many people were jockeying to "stand guard" over the fallen comrades and Tonatiuh had made no move to call off the confrontation and continue on to the cemetery. The reporters watched the nerve-wracking ballet from behind an expanse of tinted glass.

Framed in front of the CAE's fragile facade, helmeted soldiers tried to hold the barbarian hordes at bay. A brick bounced harmlessly off the reinforced glass—then a bottle and the pop of exploding gasoline blackening the window. A futile bayonet thrust answered the Molotov cocktail. "DIIIIIIIIIIIIE! THAT THE PRO SHOULD DIIIIIIIIIE!" the masses spasmed back.

Tania and Raus watched the troops don rubber gas masks that made them look like human flies and raise tear gas launchers, squeezing softly at regular intervals. Pow! Pow! Pow! The canisters arched gracefully into the afternoon smog and plummeted earthwards, exploding in fast-rising white billows in the midst of the protesters.

The picture in the window began to get cloudy. Gas was backing up into the lobby. Tania, an experienced riot-goer, had readied handkerchiefs soaked in lemon juice. They wrapped them around their faces like fragrant Zapatistas. The soldiers clicked off one round after another; Mickey could no longer see the esplanade for his tears. Suddenly the rhythm of softly exploding shells was embroidered by automatic weapon fire, one short burst, then another. Then two big booms that sounded like mortars. Tania's eyes locked into his.

"Oh Christ, the tanks!"

There was no choice for either of them now. Compañeros were being gunned down out there on the esplanade beyond the marred tinted glass. History was happening and they needed to get the story. They plunged through the revolving doors, Tania's little lizard hands clasping his coattails just to steady herself.

"You've both lost your bloody objectivity," Pease boshed behind them.

🦎

TANIA AND MICKEY duckwalked along the top ledge of the esplanade, hand over hand in the billowing smoke. "I'm going to fuck you so good tonight, if we get through this, mouseman," she hummed in his ear. "¡Aguas!" Mickey yelped. Murky figures charged the building, hurling back dud tear gas canisters that had fallen into the crowd and failed to detonate. But there was no response from the troops this time—the line of soldiers strung out in front of the Institute seemed to have dissolved into the gaseous haze. The gunfire had ceased—the two short bursts had been the only ones. There were no more mortars. Now the esplanade was deathly quiet. Mickey reached for Tania.

"I'm right in back of you, mausito."

Bodies twitched on the concrete. As the stinging vapors began to fray, Raus could make out familiar shapes: Leñero and the miners of Jaquemate uncurling from the human pile-ons, El Torso righting his roller, Plantón's students stumbling to their sneakers, masked wrestlers calling out for missing companions. A resurgent rumble rolled across the esplanade.

"¡QUE MUERRRRRA EL PROOOOOOOOOO!"

"THAT THE PRO SHOULD DIIIIIIIIIIIIE!"

Miraculously, no one had expired nor had anyone even been wounded by the gunfire and the mortars. In fact, the only victim appeared to be Señorita Electoral Democracy whose gossamer gown had been shredded by the barrage, leaving her stark naked, a slab of shiny, curvaceous onyx above the littered esplanade.

An army tank hung crazily off the median strip on Reforma a hundred yards away, the muzzle of its cannon still sheepishly smoking. The tank crew had abandoned ship and joined the party.

Tonatiuh was boosted onto the wildly slanting tank by SuperPendejo and his comrades. Don Estalin and the Bishop had been stashed in the first aid tent during the melee. Now the brown, bare-chested throng passed their caskets from shoulder to shoulder towards the tank. "¡Que Viva El Bishop! ¡Que Viva Don Estalin!" the mob sang. "¡Que Viva!"

Precariously perched on the tank's errant turret, the Doctor hoarsely called upon the protesters to accompany him out to the Mictlan cemetery at the end of the Park where the martyrs would be buried in the Galván family plot "because they are our family."

And as if they too were part of that same family, tens of thousands of furious rioters transformed themselves into hush-faced mourners and fell into step behind the cortege, moving down Reforma towards the hotel district and the scorched greenbelt. Los Primos lay beyond.

And as the galvanistas marched towards Mictlan, the tensions of the day felt like they had unclenched. The sky itself was already darkening to the south and cooler air calmed ardor. A fleet of newly stocked torta vendors descended upon the procession and fresh frozen fruit paletas arrived to slake the many thousands of thirsts. Tania and Mickey walked up the dead tree-lined avenue, arms tied around each other's waist. They were on their way to the graveyard but they were possessed by the prospect of no-holds-barred sex after death. After an afternoon of high decibel riot, marchers moved all around them, wrapped in the gauzes of sad, thoughtful silence.

ﮊ

LIKE TANIA AND MICKEY, thousands of marchers had covered their faces with Zapatista-like kerchiefs, los sin rostros. Still others tied spare articles of clothing around their jaws to prevent the utterance of an accidental word. Adhesive tape requisitioned from the first aid tent was stripped across many mourners' lips. Marchers forced bizarre gags within their cheeks or simply topped their tongues with their own hands to keep them from talking. The silence was a purposeful one. The muted demonstrators would graphically communicate to the world how the PRO was stifling the voice of the people.

The absence of chanting topped the most gargantuan ovation Tonatiuh had ever received. The muffled, slowly cadenced tread—ruffled only by the clicking of cameras—cloaked the funeral procession in a majestic solemnity that Mickey savored like a long drink from history's gourd. John Reed had sucked on that same straw.

Blue-black thunderheads scudded up swiftly from the volcanoes, their scalloped edges gilded in silhouette by the sun

lowering in the west. Damp chill blasts of wind gusted eccen-
trically, whipsawing the signs and the banners and the flags
and the skirts of the mourners. The stillborn tropical air was
moving at last. Huge pear-shaped drops slowly splattered the
cortege. Tlaloc hurled spears of charged white lightning onto
the horizon towards which the grieving marchers journeyed.
Thunder crackled and boomed in long, rolling detonations.
Raus surveyed the surrounding hotels for falling balconies.

The funeral train tramped silently through the bright
canyons of the luxury hotel zone. A ring of towering Gran
Turismos blotted out the sky. Strobe lights burped above the
classy discotheques. Bejeweled casinos flashed ten-thousand-
watt walls of neon, beckoning the players to step inside. All of
the glitter was somehow diffused and softened by the deepening rain and the sadness of the day.

The mournful demeanor of the enormous procession
through this flashy, fashionable district even quieted the chattering tourists for once. The North Americans and the Germans
and the Brits and the Japanese turned from the solid oak bar
and the bulletproof glass-protected cafe tables and lifted their
lime-soaked Coronas and Tequila Sunrises and Piña Coladas
in passing respect for the dearly departed.

The mourners skirted the curve of the park. Los Primos
loomed up ahead. If the military or the police were going to
beat back this indignant wave of humanity, the fortress-like presidential palace would be the place. Mickey and Tania nodded
so-long to the sweatshop women they had been marching with
and took to the slick pavement. She mounted a park wall and
peered into the rain-streaked distance. Tania calculated about
100,000 mourners were now moving in the cortege—"dos
chingos, like the Sup says." To the west, in the mouth of the
underpass that runs in front of Los Primos, the sharp-eyed
Colombiana picked out the dull glint of steel-helmeted soldiers,
handling automatic weapons and kneeling to the wet pavement.

Mickey and Tania dashed to the head of the serpentine procession slithering through the city. Tonatiuh and his family, El
Nene and the widow Flórida slowly stepped, arms linked just

in back of the drenched pallbearers. Raus accosted Dr. Huipi, who was laboring under a corner of the Bishop's casket.

"Hermano, there are troops in the underpass by Los Primos," Mickey whispered through his lemony handkerchief and then was ashamed to hear his own hushed white voice, alone, in a damp brown sea of silence. Ezekial Huipi gestured him to seal his lips.

Under his own paliacate, Dr. Huipi was not worried. The troops were falling into line behind Tonatiuh as he had predicted—voting for the son of the General on Sunday; today, pulling back from the confrontation on the esplanade after emptying two comical rounds into Señorita Electoral Democracy. Now, too, the battalion attached to protecting Los Primos retreated deeper into the underpass and made no move to block the mourners' passage.

Outside the gilded gates, volunteers sped up and down the line of march to remind the mourners of their unspoken vows of silence, even before so-hated a symbol of the PRO monarchy as Los Primos.

Set off across a deep moat on a sculpted knoll, Los Primos seemed abandoned. Indeed—save for the customary picket of Beefeater Gin-style hussar-guardsmen, backed up by 30 or 40 patrol cars full of flush-faced secretos trying to stay out of the rain—the presidential palace seemed eerily unprotected. It looks haunted, Raus thought.

Now is our chance to take it. But Tonatiuh's people made no move to do so.

Instead, they took more immediate action and Mickey had to admit that when exhibited the next morning on CNN DisneyMex Headline News, Sid Bloch's footage of 100,000 middle fingers extended like stiff candles of outrage before the darkened mansion equaled a billion of his words.

ARTURO LOMELI and his hand-picked successor were insulated from the people's wrath inside the strong box of Los Pinos.

Huddled in the lamp-lit presidential study, Lomelí, his arm thrown casually over his trembling protégé's padded shoulders, sought to assuage his successor's sudden fear of the street, his panic at meeting a public he knew had not chosen him.

"Look at me, licenciado, you are like a son to me. I was your poor dead dad's best friend. I've looked after you since you were in stinking diapers. Pewww, what a mess you made. Fili, would I steer you wrong?"

The big-eared little "president" wagged his head disconsolately. "No, never, Papa Turo."

"Then you'll do what I say, boy. We're going on Mongo tomorrow at noon. You are going to tell the people that you are their president and you are going to do this with all the confidence and conviction that your little pipsqueak soul can summon up. The nation needs you, Fili."

Filemón Barcelona did not look very convinced.

"Come with me, young man." Lomelí took his arm and yanked the President-elect through salons lined with rusty portraits of the Great PROs: Calles, Avenida, Galván, El Perro Portillo, Colosio... Carlos Salinas had long been unhung. Filemón Barcelona inserted his little thumb in his mouth and followed meekly behind. Choop choop choop.

"You are not going to let these great men down, are you?" Lomeli demanded, seizing his thumb-sucking surrogate son by the lapels and shaking him rudely. "You are not going to let our great party down, you little twirp. And stop that with your thumb. You know how I can't stand it."

"No, Papa Turo," whimpered Filemón, retrieving his thumb; the President let go. But the shame of being his party's first presidential choice ever to have actually lost an election drove Barcelona under the covers and into fetal sleep from which he would not emerge for days.

🦎

THE THUNDER WAS STUNNING in the cemetery district. Raus' ears ached with the echo of the echo of each detonation.

The rain pelted down like a biblical deluge upon the water-logged mourners as they silently entered into the sinister grave-yards, a district in which one was cautioned never to walk alone. It was not only the ghosts and the Lloronas and the Chocaciuatles who drifted wailing through the tombstones that made paying respects to the dead a risky undertaking. There was something else out there amidst the miles and miles of crumbling graves piled helter-skelter everywhere—something else bedded down in the moldering plots of large extinct families nestled together with cracked tombstones for pillows, dead babies at the feet of dead abuelos, worm-eaten aunts and uncles and family canaries wedged into narrow troughs of spare chalky ground so that everyone could sleep the long night together.

The living moved out there too, they said, in the listing mausoleums, under the tumbled angels and prophets toting concrete bibles. Some were the last damnificados left from the Great Quake who eked out a living stealing the flowers bereaved relatives left behind and reselling them at Mictlan's gates. Others offered to guide innocent tourists to the tombs of the Great and Near-Great, but slit their throats on the way. Ghouls plied the freshly planted beds, digging up rookie cadavers, extracting re-sellable organs, pocketing the gold teeth, vending the flesh to pet food manufacturers for five pesos a kilo and the newly vacated cemetery plot to the next sucker. Still others out there in the twisted trees beyond the tangled tombstones were known to dine nightly on the faintly beating hearts of freshly butchered victims.

The sopping citizenry stumbled amidst the grave markers, sloshing and slipping down mud banks, spike heels and Nikes and huaraches being washed away by the rivulets that ran between the tilted tombs and spooky crosses. Fat fingers of lightning attached themselves to the brick tower of the Mictlan crematorium just as if they were in a Frankenstein flick. Thunder thudded like cannonballs from the Crypt of Terror. Mickey and Tania nested to each other against the beating storm behind a cracked figure of Moses and his chipped tabernacles.

The Galván family plot was in the section that featured a once-eternal, now extinguished flame. The General himself was the property of the nation and resided in the Monument of the Revolution downtown. But Nana Esmeralda Sharatanga Cucu, Tonatiuh's long-forgotten Purepecha mother, and her dead daughter Anahuac were entombed here in this unkempt, mud-packed subdivision, along with the 13 doctor-brothers who had already gone on to their rewards, several family retainers, and the General's horse, Homero. Raus was appalled by the dinginess of the place.

The rain and the oncoming evening had narrowed visibility to zero. The crash of the heavens obliterated the audio. When Tonatiuh at last broke the silence that had sealed 100,000 lips, all Mickey could make out was that he was hailing Tlaloc for the fine storm he had brought.

Mickey and his lover found sanctuary under Ezekial Huipi's umbrella. The caskets were, at last, being lowered into the puddled earth. Raus apologized for his gaffe back down the road. Tonatiuh's spiritual advisor smiled kindly: "I told you the soldiers would come over."

Then Mickey posed the $64 billion new new peso question: Whose virus was loose inside the computers?

"I'm not really the computer expert," Ezekial laughed bashfully. "You need to talk to her." He pointed his dripping goatee in the direction of the graves. La India Cristina ladled a shovelful of mud on top of the waterlogged coffins as they sunk into their final resting places.

The light was fading fast in the streaming dusk. The stately former film queen—a veiled, ramrod-straight black shadow under the black umbrella held by her pudgy son RAT—passed the shovel down the line and each hand seized the slippery handle and nudged the sodden earth in over the Bishop and Don Estalin, a spoonful at a time, until finally they were covered and quilted by the ground, slipping into exhausted repose forever and ever under the breath of the living earth. It had been a long day for them both.

AS ELECTION COMPUTERS FUNCTION ANEW, PRO PROCLAIMS A DISPUTED VICTORY

Special to the North Coast Variety News

TENOCHTITLAN (July 6)—Fifty-four hours after they ceased to function, vote-counting computers resumed operations here early this morning amidst high political tension, shrill allegations of fraud, and an apparent bitter split in the reigning circles of the long-ruling (71 years) Party of the Organic Revolution (PRO).

Secretary of Internal Security (Gobernación) Gonzalo X. Davis, who chairs the Autonomous Electoral Commission (CAE) which is charged with overseeing the presidential election, called the body back into session a little after 4 p.m. this morning to announce "our computer problems have been resolved and the data is moving again." The commission, which is in "permanent session," has been recessed since the computer system "crashed" election night.

An hour after announcing the resumption of operations, Davis returned to the commission chambers to read, without comment, what he called "preliminary results" from 31 states and the federal district that seemed to assure the victory of PRO candidate Filemón Barcelona, the former finance minister, who has not been seen in public since last Sunday's election.

Who Won—Really?

Davis' early morning ciphers conflict sharply with those reported by field captains of opposition candidate Tonatiuh Galván, the son of one of the nation's most respected presidents, General Francisco Galván. With 91% of all ballots accounted for, according to Dr. Galván's press spokesperson Antonio Malcreado, the candidate has a considerable lead in 19 states and the capital and is winning six other states by smaller margins, with six more states tilting towards the PRO. Malcreado's numbers are substantiated by copies of CAE-issued tally sheets from more than half the 102,000 polling places in the country.

Both the PRO and the Galván forces appear to agree that the Doctor has won his home state of Malinchico where federal troops enforced martial law up until yesterday. Although neither the government nor the parties have released absenteeism data, the July 2 election appears to have drawn between 70 and 80% of the electorate to the polls.

Surreal Election

Final results could be available as early as Sunday, July 9 when so-called "autonomous electoral commissions" in the nation's 300 electoral districts meet to certify the tally sheets from the individual polling stations. The district computations are expected to be complicated by the discovery yesterday, by Montec Indian garbage pickers, of tens of thousands of partially burnt ballots in garbage dumps around the country. Most had been marked for Galván.

The computer breakdown and subsequent confusion about who won the presidency of the country is unprecedented here where the PRO has not lost a presidential election in more than seven decades. For the first time since the 1910 revolution, newspapers have begun to use terms like "constitutional crisis" and "interim government" in print. In anticipation of a prolonged political crisis, housewives are emptying the shelves of shopping centers and public markets, and long lines are forming at gasoline stations. The Global DisneyMex stock exchange (DisneyMex Ex) has lost 6% of its total equity since Monday.

Bronto Bash

The public absence of the PRO's proclaimed victor, Filemón Barcelona, remains shrouded in mystery. The former finance minister was scheduled to make his first television appearance yesterday in an interview with pro-PRO newscaster Abraham Mongo but canceled at the last minute without explanation. His predecessor and mentor, outgoing president Arturo Lomeli, has been seen only at diplomatic functions in recent days, where beefy aides have shielded him from reporters' questions.

The hermetic postures of the president and his hand-picked successor have fueled reports of deep conflicts within PRO ruling circles between hardliners known as "Brontosauri" ("Los Brontos") and young professional technocrats ("Tecos") who claim to be modernizing the image of the party that was founded by Dr. Galván's father nearly three quarters of a century ago.

Inside sources tell the Variety News that the debate over how to deal with the results of the election has become so heated that fistfights have broken out at emergency Central Committee meetings. Both the Brontos and the Tecos control groups of professional thugs who have sometimes physically battled each other over party offices.

The in-fighting is underscored by the PRO's reticence to announce

any results since election night, when Bronto party co-chairman
Bulmaro Marrano claimed a landslide victory based on first estimates from PRO informants around the country. The Tecos, headed
by investment banker Victor Manuel González Lefkowitz, are known
to be opposed to announcing the margin of Barcelona's victory until they have negotiated an agreement with Galván's forces not to
contest the results. The figures released by X. Davis tonight seem to
be carefully culled from polling places in PRO strongholds and tend
to confirm the Brontos' count.

Army Splitting

Sources indicate that the PRO's difficulties have reached even into
the military where Secretary of Defense Brigadier General Gertrudis
Niños de Galván (Totonaco) is on the verge of being replaced by the
hardline military governor of rebellion-torn Chiapas state, Archibaldo
Absalom Ramírez Ramírez. General Niños de Galván (Totonaco) has
had difficulty maintaining troop discipline since the election—exit
polls around army bases indicated a heavy vote for Galván, who is
the son of a general.

On Monday, troops under Totanaco's command pulled back from
a near-bloody clash with the galvanistas outside the Autonomous
Electoral Commission. If General Niños de Galván (Totonaco) is removed from command, the PRO government will lose a valuable
conduit to Doctor Galván. The General is his adopted brother.

Galván in Person

Unlike the PRO candidate, Doctor Galván has been highly visible
since Sunday's election, leading a huge funeral march through the
city for two slain aides and making daily visits to the growing encampment of galvanistas who have pitched tents on the esplanade
of the CAE. At impromptu press conferences, the Doctor updates
the vote count from the provinces and the 30 electoral districts of
the capital which he claims to have swept.

Galván has also laid out plans for the district computations
Sunday, which he considers vital to his victory, calling upon those
who voted for him to march on the computation centers to prevent
further fraud. It is anticipated that the Doctor will invite his supporters to continue on to the capital should the district tallies not confirm
his triumph.

Expressing concern over the discovery of large numbers of partially burnt ballots marked in his favor and now in his possession,

the candidate indicated that his followers will attempt to introduce this evidence of fraud during the district computations.

Missing Hearts

Doctor Galván has also bitterly criticized the PRO government for failing to develop any serious leads in the election-eve ritual murders of his top campaign aides, a crime he has repeatedly blamed on the ruling party. Police sources indicate they have discarded the theory that a "homosexual love triangle" was the motive for the killings of Abelardo Salmón, 39, and Estalin Lenin Gómez Gómez, 63.

Because the hearts of both men were removed from their bodies in a manner reminiscent of Aztec sacrificial rituals, police investigators are now focusing on the mysterious "Movement of the Sixth Sun," an Indianist revivalist group closely associated with former film star María Cristina Terrazas Tamal Menchú, viuda de Ahumada, the mother of Galván lieutenant Reggio Ahumada Tamal. "La India Cristina's" new bestseller *Revenge of the Sixth Sun* prophesies mass destruction if Tonatiuh Galván's victory is not recognized. Several members of the Sixth Sun Movement's alleged paramilitary wing, the "Warriors of Huitzilopochli," have reportedly been held for questioning in connection with the ritual killings.

A similar ritual killing was registered late Wednesday in the Pantano Rico region, Cocodrillo state, where the body of Cacao magnate Magnesio Brondo was discovered in the town plaza minus his heart. In a telephone call to one national daily, a previously unknown group, the "Caballeros (Knights) of Tezcatlapoaca" took credit for the killing—Tezcatlapoaca is the Aztec god of the underground. The 400-pound Brondo, known as "the King of Cacao," played host to Galván in Pantano Rico during Galván's tour of the state in June, after which Brondo's hacienda was burnt down.

Which Glitch

Meanwhile, the 54-hour vote-counting glitch remains unexplained. Interior Secretary X. Davis has stuck by his account that "the numbers just disappeared from the terminals" due to unspecified "electronic disturbances." Another theory has the system being shut down because of the threatened introduction of an information-munching computer virus allegedly designed by Galván technicians. Galván CAE commission representative Reggio Ahumada accuses the PRO of shutting down the system because the opposition candidate was winning the election by so large a margin. There are even some who speculate that the computer "crash" was a Bronto ploy to gain the upper hand in their battle with the Tecos.

What is certain is that the nation's first election of the 21st century has turned into a fiasco with the government's credibility sharply reduced. For the first time in national memory, no one here knows who the next president is going to be. In a nation that is dependent upon an imperial presidency for political structure, the cloudiness of the future is generating fears of a PRO collapse, even among long-time international supporters.

L.A. Asylum?

Washington has been seeking to defuse the tense situation for weeks through the diplomatic efforts of ambassador Thaddeus Blackbridge. The ambassador is said to have communicated to the Galván forces that their victory "is not possible at this time" while offering political asylum to Doctor Galván in Los Angeles. Galván insists he has received no such offer from the U.S. ambassador and that, if he did, he would immediately request Blackbridge's removal from the country as a violation of Article 33 of the Constitution which prohibits interference in domestic politics by foreigners.

The renewed crisis here comes at a particularly delicate juncture for interim U.S. President Newt Gingrich who next week will be nominated by his party in Miami as the Republican candidate in the November elections. For Gingrich, who became president follow-ing the still-unexplained crash of Air Force One and Two over the Andes last February, this will be his first presidential election. The Democrat and Christian opposition seem determined to make the resurgence of instability south of the border a major national secu-rity issue during the coming campaign.

Washington is particularly jittery about disruption of the oil flow to the U.S. and galvanista agitation in the "maquiladoras"—U.S. and Japanese-owned border assembly plants—where many vital de-fense components are now manufactured.

In this respect, U.S. embassy spokesperson Kip Herring denied today that the surprise start-up of maneuvers by 25,000 Army and Marine troops in the desert just north of Yuma, Arizona, has any connection "whatsoever" with the current political crisis here.

X

THE ORACLE OF COATLICUE

July 6 – 8, 2000

THE TUBE PULSATED blue rays off the bureau. What time of day or night was it? Raus fished for the Mickey Mouse watch Tania had given him for his Saint's Day—ten past the midnight hour on the semi-luminescent dial. She was crashed on the couch. He slugged down a third of a tumbler of stale mescal but turned up his nose at the blow lined out on the desktop. He stared into the blue tube.

Doña María Cristina Terrazas Tamal Menchú viuda de Ahumada stared back. La India was on little Lulu and Mongo's midnight charlathon, chatting up her hot-off-the-press *Revenge of the Sixth Sun*, 600 pages of doom and gloom based on real life Aztec-Mexica prophecy detailing a dozen plagues that would befall the nation if the Sixth Sun was not allowed to take His rightful place in the Universal Balance.

"In case you don't get it, Tonatiuh is the Sixth Sun!" the old woman jibed from behind her see-through veil. She began to enumerate the plagues: "Nuclear Holocaust! the Poisoned Nig…"

"Doña María, let's talk about your film career," Lulu cooed. Mongo looked seasick.

Raus drained the mescal. La India Cristina made his flesh crawl. In her ninth decade on the planet, she still had perfect olive skin, her hair was jet-black, her own long teeth were still rooted in her own firm gums, her eyes were chiseled out of hard onyx, and her slender, ballerina body was as lithe as a young girl's. What pact had she made with which devil? La India herself attributed eternal beauty to infusions of soothing nopal cacti. "I bathe in warm nopal juice twice daily, inside and out," she oozed to Lulu.

Raus had watched La India occasionally when she hosted her own late-night, fluff-brained gabfest, "Chulos Chismes," on TeleVersa. That was before she was silenced for openly supporting Tonatiuh's candidacy. Now she had returned to TeleVida, where she still appeared as a house eccentric for the insomniac set, discussing her most recent *Sixth Sun* bestseller or pushing her chain of Aztec health and beauty spas.

The glamorous old woman's books drew upon her lifelong fascination with ancient prophecies; the booming renaissance of Indian culture throughout the land had brought her new audiences. La India's embrace of her race's pre-history was said to be personal penance for the simpering Christian martyr she had portrayed for over 40 years in the La India Cristina films. Now her known patronage of militant Indian revivalist groups like the Warriors of Huitzilopochli was subversive enough to attract a police tail every time she left Coatlicue.

Raus browsed his mental dossier on La India Cristina, a classic rags-to-riches telenovela. A mestizo Mayan servant to fabulously wealthy European collectors, from whom she inherited a fortune in pre-Colombian artifacts when her masters fled Mordida Hermosa street mobs at the height of the revolution. A raven-haired temptress who earned national notoriety, openly gallivanting with General Galván on scandalous junkets to Europe. Her liaison with the General had been a lengthy one, outlasting at least one of each of their marriages. There was delicious chisme of a similar liaison with the son.

La India's political connections opened up doors to a film career. Although her roles ran the gamut from femme fatale to farmer's daughter, Doña María was levitated to national cultdom with 43 La India Cristina films in which she portrayed a devoutly Catholic Indian lass subjected to trials, travails, tortures, and treachery by male low-life scum, from which only her simple faith in Jesus Christ would redeem her. Her tormented, prayerful face as she was being gang-raped by mangy burros or impaled on a living maguey cactus blade by sadistic hacienderos became—for the battered and bruised women of the nation—a symbol of their facility for aguantando the most painful abuse.

In the film clip that Lulu and Mongo were now unreeling, a very blue India was having her arms sliced off by a psychopathically jealous lover, a knife-thrower in a fleabag circus.

Disgusted with such regurgitated victimization, María Cristina Terrazas Tamal Menchú viuda de Ahumada unexpectedly quit show business, took a degree at the Autonomous University in anthropology, then rotundly rejected this white man's science (emphasis on the man) by burning her books at graduation exercises. Instead of "studying" them, she plunged into the cosmology of her ancestors, immersed herself in their belief systems, learned the secrets of their rituals stone by stone and sanguinary drop by drop until, some said, she had become a priestess of the blood rite herself.

"And do you practice white magic or—tee-hee—black devil magic, Doña?" Lulu gushed. Mongo was hunting for the barf bag.

"I don't practice any magic, Lulu," La India snapped, "I interpret prophecy. Through me speaks the Voice of the Forgotten Past. Now it is the Voice of the Remembered Future."

La India had married well, first the courtly old General Joaquín Terrazas, an early confederate of General Galván who, as ambassador to the Soviet Union, suffered a fatal heart attack in a Stalingrad hotel room—some say La India's boudoir repertoire got a little too torrid for the old gentleman's ticker. Don Agustín Julio Ahumada, her late second husband and the father of Reggio, was himself the son of a man who had twice been the chancellor of his country. RAT's own checkered political career had been ruthlessly advanced by La India. In the privacy of her Coatlicue cloister the seeress was said to swear on a stack of codices that her progeny's dream would one day come true.

Doña María had begun to rant again: "This is the Time of Tonatiuh, do you hear me out there?" The TV oracle looked transfixed under her flimsy veil. "You cannot hide behind the computers." She shook a sheaf of papers at the cameras— computer printouts. "We have the proof right here!" Lulu and Mongo were waving bye-bye now. "Through my mouth speaks the Voice of the Dark Goddess," La India croaked. "If you steal this election, the plagues will be cast down upon our people. Dancers, take heart! Nuclear Holocaust! The Poisoned Night! A Rain of Fir...," Good-bye cumbias belched in over the ranting India. Then the Himno Nacional, the old version, without the "yankee dogs." Then both Raus and TeleVida faded into the comforting hum of the test pattern.

THE NEXT TIME Raus saw daylight, there was a boom inside his skull and Tania was spooned to his back. The Picapiedras were bashing each other with rocks on the TV and, outside, La Bondad drummed and burped like an intergalactic hip-hop convention. Boom boom, his head said, beep beep. Beyond the ache, it was hatching a nest of Raus's infamous hunches.

The hunches unscrolled.

Hunch #1: The Bishop comes into possession of the passwords and protocols that open the gateway to the CAE's mainframe. The galvanistas can now counter the PRO's expected alteration of the vote count and maybe even steal it back. He and Don Estalin are captured somewhere between Carlos Quinto and Coatlicue and prevented from delivering the codes to La India, Tonatiuh's computer whiz.

Hunch #1, Variant A: Bishop and Don Estalin are seized after they have delivered the passwords to Coatlicue.

Hunch #2: The Virus. El Gacho is not just floating the rumor of a virus to pay back the Tecos. There is a real virus loose in the system and it is controlled by:

A) The galvanistas, who are threatening to destroy all results unless the real results are publicly posted;

B) The PRO, who wants all the results destroyed because they control the system and will only issue new ones no matter what the galvanistas say; *or*

C) No one at all—*or* at least a cannon loose enough not to be beholden to anyone else in this life-and-death struggle for power.

La India's was the place to begin.

RAUS DIALED HER Coatlicue number non-stop all day. Sometimes it was busy, sometimes the lines crossed, sometimes the phone rang endlessly on the other end and no one ever answered. Sometimes the number never rang, the little bell tones just disappearing into the ether each time he punched. On four occasions, someone did answer but it was the wrong number. Twice, he did manage to reach the Tamal residence but not her ear, each time leaving a carefully worded message—his name, his pretend journalistic affiliation (*French Vogue*, *MacWorld*, the *L.A. Times*), his great interest in both her computer skills and her gift of prophecy, his number at home, and the number at the press room on Carlos Quinto.

Mickey hung around the phone for a callback like he was attached to it. He was afraid he'd miss La India if he so much as strolled across the street to Doña Metiche's for a cold Negra. "We really need to pick up a cell phone," he flashed, forgetting how poorly they performed. His message machine now played Charlie Parker's "Little Suede Shoes" impeccably but didn't record shit. He fretted that the Prophetess of the Sixth Sun would check in and his blinking phone would be on the blink. Every time it trilled, he would jump across the room and grab it by the throat. Tania saw how antsy he was and wondered why.

"Nada, nothing, sweetmeat, I'm just a little jumpy. Every time I have a hunch, I get like this."

But he didn't say what the hunch was.

ﺝﺏ

AFTER 24 HOURS of drawing blanks, El Mickey went proactive. Raus found Taxi Andy asleep in La Putanera, a chipped stucco, powder-blue pulquería adjacent to La Bondad. Taxi had just popped back into town after six months on the lam in L.A. from his mother-in-law, a heavyweight wrestler to whom he was hopelessy in hock. He hadn't left La Putanera since.

Taxi came to with a sour yawn. "H-h-hey b-boss, th-they st-ill g-got s-some m-mean s-s-sounds up-p th-there i-in G-Gavacholandia." Mickey hired him to drive out to Coatlicue for the day. Taxi Andy was not eager to drive to the cemetery district. Bad things happened to people and worse things to their fake taxis in that corner of the park. He called the district by its old name.

"Th-that's o-one b-bad k-k-kalpulli o-out th-there..."

Raus paid Andy's bar bill and slipped him 20 bucks USD.

All the way to the park, Taxi Andy's eyes stayed glued to the rearview mirror as if they just wanted to go back home. Mickey tried to cool out his reluctant driver: "Who'd you catch in L.A. anyway, man? Horace Tapscott still in town? Red Holloway still around?"

"Gh-gh-osts," burped Taxi Andy. Raus didn't know if he was talking about Tapscott and Red or the ghouls in residence out in the graveyards.

The idea of waiting outside La India's—which was only separated from the nearest cluster of tombstones by a ten-foot-tall stone wall—was not real appealing to Taxi Andy. "S-s-suppose I-I j-just dr-dr-ive a-around, B-boss?"

"Hey, chill out. It's broad daylight and the calacas don't start their floor show until after midnight. Besides, I don't even have an appointment. They'll probably throw my culo out of here in 50 seconds flat."

Taxi Andy took a long pull on the pulque jug he held between his legs, tacked the earphones to his lobes, switched on "Love Supreme" and crawled under the front seat.

꙳

RAUS SOUGHT TO convince the little man in the gatehouse that his appointment had been confirmed late last night by Antonio Malcreado, press secretary to Doctor Tonatiuh Galván. Why else would he have run out here at this ungodly hour of the morning? He was a busy man, he couldn't wait all day.

A call was made up to the main house, and the main house knew of no such appointment. Mickey remonstrated huffily, pulled out a dozen expired press cards, pointed to the fake cab that was costing him a fortune and suggested that whoever was conducting the appointment calendar up in the main house should call Malcreado, who he prayed would cover for him. The phone conversation about phone conversations went on for a while between the two houses. At length, Raus was escorted up to the main house by a small Indian servant with a Chon Yaa-like haircut.

The celebrated Tamal Menchú collection of pre-Colombian miscellany was housed in a reconstructed monastery balconied by living quarters on the second level. The large, arched upstairs windows were heavily curtained. Down below, rough stone walls hemmed in a maze of artifact-cluttered patios. Raus was ushered through a niche-bejeweled vestibule into a large open space in the center of which a fountain softly played. The servant told him to wait.

Beveled chac mools and enormous lava-lipped Olmec heads were arranged around the perimeter of the courtyard. Jaguar stelae were posted like guardians at the four corners. The elephant-trunked Mayan rain god Chaac reigned over one alcove. Raus could see glass cases hung with jade masks of reptile gods, all eyes and teeth, in the softly lit display rooms running off the patio. The house was occasionally opened to visiting collectors and scholars.

Raus plunked down on a reclining chac mool and reviewed his pitch. He would butter up La India with questions about her prophecies, Tonatiuh, the Sixth Sun. Then he would play his hunch about the computers and the virus. He was probing for confirmation of what he already surmised and clarification of what still did not fit.

Mickey ran through his catechism, wrote the questions down, numbered them, tested his tape recorder and read *El Machetazo* cover to cover for an hour. A small Mayan servant—he could not be sure if it was the same one—brought him fragrant yerba buena tea in a mug glazed with green turtles. The fountain bubbled peacefully on a day wiped clean for once by the resumption of the rains. Iridescent hummingbirds and white butterflies hovered like divine messengers above the vines that greened the patio. What appeared to be still another small man with a Chon Yaa haircut sat against a stone wall and played solitary notes on a stout bamboo flute. Raus' lids dipped deep.

۞

A SALLOW, SQUAT Indian man, taller than the Chon Yaas, shook the reporter firmly: "The Doña will see you now." Raus gawked at his Mickey Mouse watch. He had been asleep for nearly three pinche hours. What had been in that tea? His mind felt like it was wrapped up in flypaper.

"My name is Ramón. You will follow me please," the squat man instructed.

Raus followed Ramón on rubber legs through one of the museum rooms and into a second, darker patio, the stonework danker, more solemn, the space more cluttered with stelae of serpents and jaguars, sacrificial pedestals and eagle-winged cuauhxicallis—deep stone basins in which the hearts of warriors were conserved. "This is the Mexica patio," Ramon explained, asking Mickey to once again wait. He disappeared into an office off the courtyard.

La India had designed the Mexica patio around a 14-foot sacrificial wheel, very much like the altar piece to the moon goddess, Coyolxauhqui, in the Anthropological Museum, the one that was uncovered beneath the Zócalo in 1978 by workers laying new electric lines. The wheel was divided into four panels, each expounding the dualities that Aztec theologians judged to be the mechanism of universal balance. One quarter depicted the birth of the Plumed Serpent, Quetzalcoatl, the Lord of the Morning Star; a second the lair of the dread Tezcatlapoaca, Old Smoking Mirror, the Boss of the Night Sky; the third quarter belonged to Huitzilopochli, the terrible left-handed hummingbird of the Sun in mid-flight; the fourth panel, like a glyph in a comic book historieta drawn by R. Crumb, was that of the One True Sun, Tonatiuh, the sum of all the parts. Tonatiuh was engraved as an enormous tongue lolling thirstily for the warm blood of warriors.

Mickey traced the sharp angles of the pictographs inscribed on the horrific wheel, his fingers running along the ritual drains, separating the panels, from which the sacred blood of the victims was collected to nourish and sustain the sun. Tonatiuh's Sun. Raus found himself shivering although it was a warm summer day.

"Madam will see you now," Ramón beckoned.

AS RAUS STEPPED from the gloomy Aztec courtyard into the uncannily bright office, it occurred to him that despite all the talk about computer hijinks in the wake of the election and the murders, he had never actually seen the galvanistas' setup. The Bishop had not even kept a PC on Carlos Quinto and Tonatiuh was not known to be a hacker. Now he discovered where the computers were kept.

In contrast to the ancient barbaric relics that freighted La India's mansion with millennial blood rites, the computer room was a blazingly white and antiseptic space. A Cray ultra-fast dual processor hummed efficiently against one gleaming wall. Shelves of expensively bound codices lined the other. La India worked off a Pentium 666 display at a big metal laboratory desk. Despite the balminess of the afternoon, a perfectly laid fire snapped and crackled in the neat hearth at the back of the rectangular room.

Swaddled in a flowing white huipil, La India punched keys energetically, coaxing her machine to do her bidding with extravagant body language, like a bowler egging on a long spare. She did not acknowledge Mickey's presence for some time.

"Ah yes, the reporter—disculpa." She uncoiled from her console and apologized perfunctorily for making him wait four hours. Her long polished hand was as cold as a catfish to the touch. "Coffee, tea, Pepsi, Orange Croosh or Coca?" La India offered graciously, but, after his prolonged snooze, Raus wasn't drinking any more liquids served in this house.

She conducted Raus to an upholstered swivel chair, re-sat herself at the console, and riveted her onyx eyes inside his as intensely as Tonatiuh ever did. With her black hair pulled severely back against her seamless skin, La India's beauty was positively spooky.

"Now what can I do for you, Señor Ross?"

"Raus, m'am."

"Señor Ross, you say this appointment was made by someone named Antonio Malcreado."

"Yes m'am," Raus mumbled back. Despite La India's perfectly preserved schoolgirl beauty, Mickey found himself answering her like he answered his own grandma.

"Well, it's impossible, Señor Ross," decided the glamorous old hag. "I have had no message from him. I barely know the young man. And besides, I have much, much work to complete." She patted the PC fondly, as if it were a young live-in lover. "I'm not doing interviews just now…"

Raus was flustered, his face reddening as if he'd just been caught with his fingers in his sister's panty drawer.

"But since you're here and have waited so patiently like a good boy, I don't see why we can't have a little chat about the Prophecies and my new bestseller *The Revenge of the Sixth Sun*. I hope you've brought your copy with you."

The time trip from the museum patio into the computer age had tossed his game plan right out of Raus's head. The first question popped from his lips without warning.

"Doña María, isn't all this technology, uhh, a little removed from your, uhh, era?" He fished a mini-recorder from a trash-filled pocket.

"No, please. Those things steal your voice," La India objected, genuine alarm welling in her dark pupils. "Through my voice speak many others. We would have to take a meeting first." Raus stuffed the offending machine and pulled out a notebook.

"You have seen the Tonatiuh wheel, Señor Ross. It tells you He is the sum of many parts and prophecies. You must remember that before Tonatiuh there were four Suns. Each was destroyed when it had outlived its ordained time, first by jaguars, then by monkeys, then a rain of fire, then the great flood. But the White Conquerors never extinguished the Sun of Tonatiuh. Instead He hid in the obsidian night cellar of Tezcatlapoaca where He has slept until now, when the morning star of the new millennium will usher in the Sixth Sun—actually a fusion of the first five. No one can detain this movement, Señor Ross. Anyone that tampers with it will severely trouble the balance and tempt catastrophe for the planet and the nation. You can read all about it in my brand-new *Revenge of the Sixth Sun*."

"I don't get it, Doña. Where do the computers fit in?"

"The Prophecies tell us that we must turn their tools against them. See the Humboldt Codice 3:5. In this equation, Señor Ross, the PRO is the enslaver. They are using their computers to steal the election and further enslave us. Thus, we use their tools against them, Señor Ross, and the old prophecy is congruent. All the old prophecies are congruent." La India grew shrill and distant when she quoted prophecy, her burning eyes focused on a point just beyond Raus' vision.

"Do computer viruses have a place in your prophecy, too?" Raus deadpanned to the Oracle of Coatlicue.

"Señor Ross, the only true virus in their system is Tonatiuh's winning vote." This sounded like evasive action to Mickey's practiced ear. RAT and Malcreado had been pushing the identical line.

Raus attacked on a second front. "We know the Bishop had the password. He was bringing it to you. This is presumably why he and Don Estalin were killed. Did you get the password, Doña?" He went up against La India eye to eye.

"Yes, the Bishop knew how to get into their system, but they took him before we could debrief him and feed it to the machine.

They tortured him and the old man, and they were murdered by the PRO when they wouldn't talk. They were warriors."

"But if no one else but the Bishop and the PRO had the password, why did the PRO have to shut down the system?" Mickey grilled.

"Because someone else does have the password."

"And who is that?"

"Because someone else has gotten into their system."

Raus swiveled on the edge of his seat: "Who, Doña?"

"Me!" La India's onyx eyes leaped merrily.

"But how did you get in without the password?"

"They gave us a gift when they sent us back the Bishop and Don Estalin. Their hearts had been cut from their breasts by someone wielding a sacred obsidian blade—the técpatl. This is a blood sacrifice instrument associated with both the priests of Tezcatlapoaca and Huizilopochtli. Huitzilopochtli is ours. We sacrifice and dance for him and he smiles upon us from the noonday sun. Tezcatlapoaca, the dark night, is theirs, the PRO, but they are divided and not thinking as one. You cannot understand prophecy unless you accept the duality of everything—the day and the night, the blood and the dove, death and resurrection. That is why we used the dual processor to unscramble the mystery.

"We saw the killings as a sign and gave every combination of every noun and verb associated with Tezcatlapoaca to the dual processor. Then I turned to how the men were sacrificed. I punched in the técpatl but this didn't lead us anywhere until I tried other accepted phonetic spellings. I finally was able to unlock the code when I moved the accent to the last syllable. The PRO's operators had punched in the false accent mark. What idiots they are at the Anthropological Museum!" La India seemed truly offended by the scholarly mistake.

"What did you see when you got into the raw results?"

"Plenty. Fifty-two Quezaltero districts. Tonatiuh was leading in all of them. In 23, the PRO didn't have a single vote. Results from the Mayatan, Chiapas, Huajuco, the autonomous zones. Tonatiuh was leading Barcelona in every district but two, and one of those is a desert. As everyone knows, we won all 30 districts here in the Capital. We have the complete printouts."

"What happened next?"

"Our screens went blank."

"Just like X. Davis says?"

"He should know."

"He pulled the plug?"

"After dispatching Tezcatlapoaca to devour the raw results," snapped the batty Doña. Tezcatlapoaca, Old Smoking Mirror, was now committing computer fraud?

"Davis says the numbers are running again."

"They are fabrications. But we have the true results. We captured them before they were ordered consumed."

"What will you do with them?"

"We will use them to destroy the system and usher in the Age of the Sixth Sun."

"There is a virus inside. Is it yours?"

"Correction. There are three viruses inside…"

"Who controls them?" Raus pushed.

"The PRO introduced the first virus, the Tezcatlapoaca virus, in order to obliterate the raw results—but not before we downloaded them. Then we introduced a counter virus, which we have code-named 'Huitzilopochli' to honor the Lord of the Sun at High Noon. With it, we intend to destroy the false results. We have decided to force the PRO to count the paper ballots."

"And the third virus?"

"It is the True Virus. The Healing Virus. The One who has Won," cackled the Oracle of Coatlicue.

La India's pronouncements were more difficult to decipher than quantum calculus or liberation theology. "What will you do next?"

"We have done what Prophecy instructed us to do. We have turned the tools against the enslaver. We have checkmated their technology. Gonzalo X. Davis is announcing this even as we speak. He is again suspending the count. He will blame it on our computer virus, but the bottom line is that only the paper ballots remain as proof of Tonatiuh's victory. We will make them count them tomorrow."

Raus's wrist ached. He had filled up an entire steno pad and he had what he'd come for. He definitely did have that. "I don't want to take up too much of your time, ma'am. My driver's waiting outside." He had to get to his machine before the scoop slipped through his fingers. La India seemed miffed.

"Señor Ross, I had expected to be interviewed about the Prophecies." She waved a copy of her new book to remind him. Raus sat back down. "Please tell me about the Movement of the Sixth Sun, ma'am."

"Señor Ross, you must distinguish between the Movement and the Prophecy. The Movement of the Sixth Sun is a network of like-minded souls who are convinced that only a return to ancient ways can redeem our nation. Our past is strong, like a beating heart, Señor Ross. We hear it calling us in the drums of our dancers." La India's eyes closed tightly. "The Sixth Sun of Tonatiuh shines bright as beaten gold. It is His time again. The stars tell us that Tonatiuh will be born a sixth time, more perfect than ever, in a geyser of blood."

She put particular emphasis on the blood part.

"Eh, Doña María, do you have any comment on the police investigation of the Movement of the Sixth Sun or the so-called Warriors of Huitzilopochli? Florentino Zorrilla suggests they are connected to the Bishop's murder."

"Señor Ross, just today they have carried off two more of our warriors: the Tlamatlan Adolfo Becker Schultz and Conchero Manuel Bravo. Zorrilla says he is only holding them for questioning but we await their bodies back without their hearts. The flowery wars have come again, Señor Ross, the PRO fuels the smoking mirrors of Tezcatlapoaca. Señor Ross, the Priests of Huitzilopochli must respond. Other gods are growing hungry in their sleep."

La India rubbed her catfish hands excitedly—in the gesture Raus saw the Crone of Coatlicue, girdled by a skirt of snakes, that lived beneath her unblemished flesh.

"It is all in the Prophecies, Señor Ross, they speak through my mouth: 'The flowery death must come again to warm the heart of the New Sun.' The Budapest Codex 6:4. You could look it up."

"Ah yes, the Prophecies."

"Señor Ross, you scoff as the White People always do. Tonatiuh's victory is the culmination of many signs, many messages from the Grandfathers that you do not want to understand, Señor Ross, because they upset your egocentric conception of what the Universe is. These signs were initiated with the discovery of the Moon Wheel near the Great Temple under the Zócalo by those who were looking for the light…"

"You must mean the electrical workers."

"So it is written, Señor Ross (Borgia Codex 3:1). The earthquake released new signs: Tonatiuh's Wheel"—she gestured towards the patio—"once swallowed up by the lake, has come back to us again. 'The Gods will appear from below' (Cholula Codex 7:1). In this respect, Señor Ross, we have the great Metro Blackout of 1998: 'The moles will cease in the underground' (Ibid). The mass murder at Bhopal and the start-up of Laguna Negra fulfill these prophecies: 'They will pass out the poisons of their own destruction' (Ramírez Codex 4:6). The Harmonic Convergence in the sacred city of Teotihuacan on August 16, 1987 was another prologue to the Age of Tonatiuh-Quetzalcoatl. Remember the duality, Señor Ross. 'He shall rise in the east like the Morning Star'(Borbonicus Codex 9:1). This text, of course, refers to both Lord Quetzalcoatl (Kulkulan to our Mayan brethren) and to the Mayan Neo-Zapatistas who first rose up in the east not on January 1, 1994, but on October 12, 1992—the 500th anniversary of our first 'encounter' with the Europeans. 'Consume the fruits of our enemy with caution'— a clear warning against NAAFTA, Señor Ross."

"It's Raus, ma'am."

La India was now racing around the room, opening and shutting volumes, codices, thrusting bibliographies at Raus. "How do you spell your name, Señor Ross?" she asked, signing a paperback copy of her *Revenge of the Sixth Sun* with a flourish. The old woman, imprisoned in her ageless beauty and fundamentalist faith in the prophecies of Aztec butchers, was still chattering non-stop as Raus backed out of the computer room with a respectful, "Thank you, ma'am."

"Ramón will show you to the door—Yoo-hoo, Ramón!" She shook a large brass bell. "And please, Señor Ross, you will send me the clippings like a good boy, won't you?" The nutty old lady's icy hand pumped Raus's. "¡Mexica Te'auhi!"

Outside, Taxi Andy was still cowering under the front seat. "B-b-boss," he sputtered, "y-y-ou kn-know how th-they s-say th-that th-they e-eat human fl-flesh o-out h-h-here i-in th-the gr-graveyards?"

"I believe them," Raus trembled in the back seat. "Let's get the hell out of here."

Taxi Andy floored the battered green Vochito; they spun off through the park back towards the sanctuary of the old quarter without ever daring to look back. They probably should have checked. Near the Arcs of Bethlehem, a gray Gran Marquis with tinted windows and no license plates slipped in four cars behind Andy's ersatz taxi and stayed there.

SIX DAYS AND NIGHTS after the election, the nation still had not been assigned a new president. On Friday afternoon, X. Davis recessed the Autonomous Electoral Commission and shut down the computer count a second time, advising the nation in a two-minute pre-recorded address that government computers had been threatened with an alien virus infiltrated into the system by unidentified "subversives." He did not give a name to the subversives but indicated arrest warrants were being sworn. X. Davis gave no date for the resumption of the vote count.

In Washington, Gingrich's pundits predicted nasty power failure south of the border. The convention was less than a week away. They needed a new game plan. Caspar Weinberger was brought in. The old spook trotted out long-treasured preemptive invasion plans.

Despite the prolonged absence of any reliable results, most of the electorate remembered who they had voted for and were not amused at the PRO's sham. The cybernetic hocus-pocus had gotten out of hand. *Let them count the ballots like we voted*, the voice of the people muttered. *Let them count each piece of paper one by one just like we marked them. Then we'll know who really won.*

X. Davis's sub rosa announcement that arrest warrants were about to be served on his own mother for holding the election results hostage sent the portly RAT scurrying down to the CAE esplanade where he declared himself on a hunger strike. Seven thousand galvanistas flattened themselves out on the concrete to join him.

Tonatiuh had come each day thereafter to praise the starvers, hauling sacks of burnt ballots the Montec garbage pickers had rescued from dumps around the nation. There were over 500,000 of them at last count. Despite the ballot burning, the Doctor held out hope that tomorrow's tallies of paper ballots in 300 electoral districts would somehow confirm his victory. "On Sunday, we will show our face, and it will be the face of a starving nation, a nation starving for justice. Let them understand up there that this is their final chance," he thundered above the rumbling stomachs of thousands of hunger strikers stretched out at the feet of the recently denuded Señorita Electoral Democracy.

On the eve of the ballot tally, nerves were frazzled raw across the length and breadth of the land. Reports of dark deeds kept filtering in like shrouds from the provinces. They said dead men with vacant chest cavities had been strewn along the El Horno Costa. They said that corpses stripped of their most vital organs had been scattered on the roadsides of the Bajío. They said the Tlamatlan Adolfo Becker Schultz and the Conchero Manuel Bravo had been returned to the Warriors of Huitzilopochli without their hearts in the right place.

The PRO and the galvanistas had embarked on a collision course in which there was little room for last-second flinching. Although those who had cast their fortunes with the contenders in this titanic struggle turned down their bedcovers, plumped up their pillows, and prepared to sleep, few caught any real winks on the eve of the battle for the heart of the nation.

꙳

ARTURO LOMELI was slathered into a fashionable Dior bath-
robe and matching monogrammed silk pajamas. He paced his
enormous dressing room on fawn-skin slippers. He could hear
the First Lady snoring on the other side of the flocked wallpaper.
The President took a languid draught from his warmed Chivas
and milk and congratulated himself on preserving the tranquil-
lity of the nation he was entrusted to command for just a few
hours more now. General Ramírez was a fine choice to head the
military. The Butcher of Tuxtla knew how to command respect
from his troops—that iron claw act was priceless! Oh, Gertrudis
wasn't a bad sort, mind you, but he was tainted by Tonatiuh.
How to get his troops out of town was still going to be ticklish
but we won't have a fifth column inside the Golden City. Don
Tadeo is right—we can't let the revolution be taken hostage by
these romantic relics of another age, marching backwards into a
barbaric past, thumbing their noses at the New World Order. The
Revolution must adjust to the Global Millennium or die! *Long
Live the Revolution! Long Fuck the Revolution!* The President toasted
his own mastery of nationcraft and then smashed the drained
highball glass against the dressing room wall.

"Are you okay in there, honey?" the first lady purred on the
other side of the wallpaper.

꙳

DOWN THE HALL, the Pretender to the Throne was already
under his quilt, safe here in the snugly dark from the prying
eyes of his tormentors. Since a child, Filemón Barcelona had
sought sanctuary under his mama's hand-sewn quilt. He brought
it with him whenever he spent the night, comforted by its frayed
texture and the strawberry scent impregnated by the soap she
always used. Poor Mama. She must miss him tonight.

He had been allowed to spend the weekend at Los Primos
because Papá Arturo said he must get used to sleeping here,

and, besides, he needed to be fresh as a daisy for tomorrow and the Nation.

He couldn't sleep. His nerves were shot. Someone was out there in the dark, mocking him. He could feel the scorn, like a burning mark on his forehead, right between the eyes. He wanted to cry.

Filemón was spooked that he'd been assigned Tonatiuh's old room. Los Primos had been remodeled many times since the General's day. Had Tonatiuh slept in this very bed? Was he hiding in the closet? Was this Papá Turo's Personal Aversion Therapy to rid him of his monsters?

It wasn't working.

Filemón had this creepy sensation that Tonatiuh was watching everything he did now. That was why he didn't want to go out there where the Doctor would be able to see right through him. He was obsessed that Tonatiuh would see him naked, would see right through his clothes and his skin with those x-ray eyes of his, right down to his puny little heart and shrunken, undescended testicles, and tell the nation that he just didn't have "the right stuff" to be the Tlatuani.

He didn't.

Filemón Barcelona had begged X. Davis to strengthen security, to line the walls with lead, to scan for eavesdropping devices and hidden cameras. The Interior Secretary humored him by doubling the number of cars in his motorcade. The bathrooms were swept for bugs. But the more that Internal Security closed in around him, the more vulnerable felt the President-elect. That's why he had to haul this absurd quilt around with him wherever he slept. It was the only real way to keep Tonatiuh out of his dreams.

🦎

AMBASSADOR THADDEUS BLACKBRIDGE took morphine. He took it at the most secret hour of the night, and it was the darkest, most secret secret in his top-secret dossier. He didn't take very much, really, two four-grain tablets before retiring, to sleep and dream. It helped him to be a better public servant, he thought, it gave him vision where others performed by rote. He had picked up the habit long ago in Laos—it was a common vice of the diplomatic corps there. His masters knew of his predilection and, indeed, kept him supplied. He understood they were buying his absolute allegiance by providing him the morphine, but his class and patriotic commitments didn't give him any other buyers to sell himself to. Blackbridge was a quite willing victim of his own addiction.

Still the strings attached annoyed him. There was endless haggling over potencies and weight. This damn business with the War on Drugs hadn't helped his bargaining position a bit, and, besides, the stuff just didn't pack the wallop it once did.

Oh, tonight he'd had a fine old time, hallucinating into the dawn, staring into the sad, beautiful eyes of the White Tiger—the opiates with which he was supplied were, per contractual arrangement, all distilled from Golden Triangle poppies in which the Tiger thrives.

Junked out on the balcony of his penthouse tower above the park, the Ambassador offered his prayers like a narco muezzin as the first dull blue traces of dawn smudged the east over the San Valentino dumps. "Bless the Tiger! Bless the Tiger!"

A foul breeze wafted off the garbage pits and brought Blackbridge crashingly back to earth. He stood there on the balcony, clad only in his socks. "More mierda," he whiffed, bracing himself for another day of nasty shit. He sealed the glass doors behind him.

Neither side had budged an inch despite Blackbridge's persistent meddling. The PRO was determined to release the phony results, declare the election over with, and send the army into the streets. But now they could no longer even back up their claims with the computers. Tonatiuh's virus had shut them down. The Ambassador bemoaned the introduction of Western Technology into this barbaric land. "Whatever were we thinking about?" He bit his lip deep enough to draw blood.

Now—in this age of ciphers and blips—the only certifiable count was on smudgy little scraps of paper inside cardboard ballot boxes, and today the blockhead Party of the Organic Revolution will commit mass mayhem to keep the galvanistas from opening those boxes and counting the contents piece by piece. This could go on for days. The run on the DisneyMex Ex will be worse than Montezuma's revenge.

Despite his entreaties that U.S. national security was at stake, that damn fool Tonatiuh had refused to call off his marches. Latin hormones would finish him off yet. Blackbridge was convinced that it was the high testosterone level that made these savages so damn macho and complicated his job endlessly, no matter which insolent principality in this hemisphere they sent him out to civilize.

The cellular beeped. A nasal female voice told him that President Gingrich would talk with him now. "It's very early here, dear," he mumbled into the handset.

"Ted, sorry we're on so early. We're an hour ahead of you here. Are you ready for the New Game Plan?"

🦎

NO ONE KNEW HOW or even if Tonatiuh Galván slept each night, not even Paloma who had slept next to him for nearly 30 years. When she awoke in the mornings, Tonatiuh was always perfectly awake. Most mornings, his eyes would still be closed, but his responses to her usual questions were always appropriate, as if he had been lying there all night just awaiting her voice.

When asked how he had slept, the Doctor always laughed that he had slept very well—"the sleep of the dead"—which is what he told Paloma this morning when she rolled over into his long arms, but she could see the worry lines, tracing them gently with her index finger from the tip of his strong mouth up his lean, brown jaw. She knew that he had spent the night weighing the deaths—the ones already counted, the ones to come—questioning the value of what he was trying to do that was beginning to cost so many lives.

She knew too that in the deepest pocket of the night, Tonatiuh had arisen to consult with the General, who was always underfoot at that hour, pacing the old doctor-brother barracks. And she knew what her father-in-law's ghost had told the Son too: "Put on your pantaloons, boy! Stand up to those bastards! Counter-punch when they come at you. Jab! Jab! Jab! Always seek vengeance." It was the same bloody speech every time.

How many more will be sacrificed today? She closed her eyes and tried to hold back the rising sun. How many more corpses and funerals must there be before the peoples' thirst is satisfied? Would all the blood spilled be worth it if they just gave Tonatiuh the Judas kiss as his reward for redeeming them from the PRO? Tonatiuh always told her that the price of victory was treason.

Maybe she thought the price was too dear only because this savage land was really not her native country.

MARIA CRISTINA TERRAZAS TAMAL MENCHU viuda de Ahumada, was dreaming about dinner. Moctezuma I's warriors had just fallen upon the Huejotzingos and taken 25,000 of their finest soldiers captive to be fattened for the flowery feasts. She cackled herself awake at the spectacle and found that she was still alive inside a young woman's body. She lit copal and burnt candles, thanking Coatlicue for having permitted her this beauty for one more day.

The time on the console terminal read 6:55:13. La India did not sleep alone. She sat down at the keyboard, autodialed 200 CAE mainframe computer numbers until one registered online. Then she fed 51,976 possible password combinations of the word "tecpatl" into the government's twin Terraflops at blinding speed. The avalanche of information overwhelmed the system. Bingo! The electronic gateway opened wide before her.

La India settled into the console seat poised like a fighter pilot ready to fly into the rising sun. Today was a fine day for kamikazes. All the offerings had been made. The PRO still doesn't know it is playing with the fire of the Sun. "We will spread their own dung in their own machines. Let the Yanqui reporter suspect what he wants. Now the other side of the blood will flow."

She punched fiercely at the keyboard—the entrance protocols, the first password, the program code, the second password—marching her viruses right into the system she had swept clean just yesterday.

Ciphers suddenly came up flowing left to right across the screen. They listed series of numbers divided into 300 sections. The series were running over and over again. La India saw that they were labeled line by line: PRO, PIN, PAR. In each section, the line labeled PRO had eight times as many numbers as its nearest competitor, the PAR.

"Cabrones!" she whooped, "I thought we wiped this all out already." Now each time Huizilopochtli's virus munched up the phony results, the PRO Tezlcatlapoaca virus replicated them. She reprogrammed her own worm to blow Tezcatlapoaca off the screen. The Ultimate Bomb. It would short-circuit the Terraflops, permanently cripple the government's backup systems.

Now at last there would only be paper to confirm Tonatiuh's victory—the printouts of the real results, rolls and rolls of them. *And today, the ballot boxes will be opened by Tonatiuh's people and the paper ballots will proclaim our triumph to the nation. The fate of the Mexicas has been reduced to paper, and paper is pulped from trees. Funny how we always return to the forest.* La India made a note to research this strange twist of events in prophecy.

La India switched into her electronic mail. The bad news about the Tlamatlan Becker Schultz and the Conchero Bravo was all there, in neat encoded paragraphs. The Oracle of Coatlicue tapped in instructions for retaliation, encrypted in prophecy: "The butterfly floats into the obsidian night. Técpatl party at High Noon. RSVP." She signed off. She was pleased with her terminal cleverness.

There was one more loose end to wrap up before the day took command. She punched in a call to the Widows: "Your Mother Coatlicue summons you. The men have had time enough. We must liberate our own germ, the One True Germ: Coatlicue's Virus."

Oh sí, that pinche gringo reporter…

"P.S. Be on the lookout for an alleged male Yanqui 'corre-spondent' who answers to the name of Mickey Raus. Aka El Mickey, El Gringo, or El Gavacho. Suspect CIA ties. 1.8 meters. No teeth. We must punish the Stranger."

"Buenos días. The time is now 7:00:00," chirped the computer. "Have a nice day!"

XI

THE LONGEST DAY

Sunday, July 9

TANIA YAWNED, stretched, retched. She didn't like the way this day looked already. She bailed out of the sack, robed only by her emaciated birthday suit, cut to what posed as Raus's kitchen, and threw on a fresh pot of java. The pilot light blew out with a soft sucking woosh. No, she did not like the way this day was shaping up.

Poor Mickey was already in the shower. He had spent the whole night filing the India Cristina interview. The slimy, limey copy editor in Ukiah wondered if the *Variety-News* had an up-to-date obit on him.

Just after dawn, the limey rang back—the San Francisco Sunday paper had picked up the piece. It was running on the front page today, with Raus's byline.

Radio Miel chimed 7:15. They had wanted to get an early start—this was going to be the longest day. Raus rushed dripping from the shower and kissed her on the lips. "I'm on the front page in San Fran!"

"I'm happy for you, Mickey." She looked worried. She was working color for *El Machetazo* and sending back to Bogotá every day.

"We're both working too hard. We need to get out of here for a while once this is all decided. Maybe go to the States or Spain, somewhere else. What do you think, Tania?"

Let's get out of here right now, she thought, before something really bad happens.

They hit the streets early, walking north towards the Zócalo. The stalls around La Bondad were already popping. Flea hopped up with the Morning Blats. "CLEAN BALLOT COUNT OR BLOODSHED IN THE STREETS?" hollered *El Machetazo*. "BALLOT COUNT TO CONFIRM BARCELONA VICTORY," proclaimed *El Orgánico*. "Tonatiuh is the president," El Flea opined, crossing himself. "Today, we're going to make them count all the votes."

The sun rose red-eyed and wobbly over the Centro Histórico, as if it were hung over from a month of draining days. "When this is all over, honey," Mickey promised, "I'm going to take you away to the Redwood Forest." The cool Redwoods of California's North Coast that he had always despised now seemed the other end of the sewer in which they were stewing. Raus imagined them walking hand in hand through fragrant groves, making love on the piney forest floor.

This was never going to be all over.

They strode into the Zócalo, sweaty palms pasted together, already soaked by city soot and smut. The perimeter of the plaza was ringed entirely by visored granaderos, placed every two feet, like pieces in a board game. "Vamos por la otra," she tugged, and they shot down Catholic Kings. Malcreado was waiting for them outside the 5th Electoral District "Computation Center" on Holy Ghost Street just north of the Templo Mayor and conveniently located right around the corner from Las Ilusiones.

"There are cops all over the Zócalo," the reporters reported.

"There are soldiers in the parking garages," Antonio added. There were also soldiers in the doorway of the CAE Computation Center, their bayonets prepared to lunge.

The Computation Center was just an empty rented office on the second and top level of a shoddy commercial building that housed a crucifix store downstairs. But this was Tonatiuh's district, the one in which he lived and voted. How the PRO attempted to deform the vote here would be of interest to the nation and, perhaps, the world. Raus high-fived GE-DisneyMex-CNN's Big Sid Bloch: "Is this history happening or what, man?"

At 8:17 AM on Sunday morning, July 9, in the year of our Lord 2000, Holy Ghost Street, a modest crevice in the most incorrigible urban swath on the continent, was jammed from mouth to mouth with Tonatiuh Galván's neighbors, eager to confirm how they had voted seven days previous. The vecinos were particularly encrusted around the steps leading up to #62 where SuperPendejo López was trying to persuade a platoon of combat-ready Indian troops, black battle slashes under their frozen eyes, that the electors of the 5th District ought to be permitted to witness how their own votes were being counted.

"You're blocking the doorway, Pendejo."

"Don't be calling me a pendejo, pendejo," SuperPendejo yapped at a granite-faced lieutenant.

"You're the one who's calling you a pendejo. All I said is that none of you pendejos are getting in here and that includes even a pendejo like you."

There was already skirmishing up and down the line of soldiers, short bayonet charges followed by showers of potatoes and Tequila Sauza bottles. Not good, Raus signaled to Tania, peeling potato skins off the back of his neck. "¡Prensa! ¡Prensa!" the two reporters trilled a cappella, wildly waving press credentials signed by President Arturo Lomelí himself. The solders remained implacable. The international correspondents had no more luck cracking the military barricade than the Masked Prince of the Streets.

Raus ran back and forth, up and down the line, for an hour, flashing his famous credential and jabbering about how President Lomelí had personally invited the international press to judge for themselves the PRO's democratic intentions. The troops were not concerned with public relations. The Lieutenant

252 / JOHN ROSS

coolly inhaled Virginia Slims behind the fixed bayonets and avoided Mickey's pitiable beseechings.

Tania's strategy for gaining admittance was more desperate: she would seduce the soldiers by exhibiting larger and larger swatches of her scrawny flesh. Although she worked her way down to short shorts, the pronounced outline of her nipples highlighted by a form-fitting tee-shirt that read "¡Periodista! Don't Shoot," the troops never flinched.

"This is not going to happen," Malcreado commiserated with the reporters. All over town, Gertrudis's troops were stonewalling the galvanistas, shutting out the press. Only the representatives of the three parties and hundreds of "electoral auxiliaries" were being allowed in and out of the Computation Center. Malcreado's cellular was going nuts. He headed back towards Carlos Quinto to sort it all out.

The "counting" upstairs had been underway for several hours and Mickey didn't have a clue as to how to get inside. "If we can get into their computers, there has to be a way to get into their buildings," he told Tania. "I've got to develop a strategy. You stay here and cover. I'm going to reconnoiter."

"Mickey, what if we get separated?" She looked at him with big green frightened eyes, her tough gamin demeanor suddenly touchingly vulnerable.

"Vida, we're not going to get separated, ever. We're in this together. Colleagues, remember?" Fog drifted through the cool redwood forest. "Look, if we don't find each other back here, we'll hook up on Carlos Quinto for lunch."

They kissed full on the lips. She lingered. "Don't drink too much," Tania fretted.

BATTLE-SMEARED SOLDIERS were posted on the rooftops above Holy Ghost Street. Around the corner, Las Ilusiones was not technically serving—the Dry Law had been decreed for the vote count—but business was booming nonetheless. The bar was full of electoral auxiliaries with Fu Manchu mustaches and cops posing as reporters. Mickey pushed his way to the inside corner of the zinc counter and tried to hide. Poncho slid a slimjim of Gusano Verde across the bar and begged him not to get drunk. "Por favor, amigo." He thrust his chin at the cops.

Raus poured himself a brimming shot and promptly forgot. I'm tired of buttoning my lip, he told himself, and poured a second. These guys don't scare me anymore. He surveyed his drinking partners. There was, indeed, a lot of heat in Poncho's little room.

Bathed in sunlight seeping in from the street, an old woman wrapped up in the shawl of her own thick gray hair stroked a fine fighting cock at a corner table. The rotgut touched bottom, warming Raus' belly, reviving his curiosity. The old woman blew gently to ruffle the sooty gold feathers on the back of the fancy bird's neck. "Salud," Mickey toasted the cock. The old woman blew him a toothless kiss. Raus sat down by her side and they finished the bottle together. "So this is your gallo?" Raus admired.

"Es mi gallo, sí, señor."

"Does it have a name, your gallo?"

"That is his name exactly, señor, El Gallo!"

MICKEY TOTTERED OUT of the Ilusiones still without a plan, police eyes glued to his back. Halfway back to Holy Ghost, Raus surrendered to an urgent need to relieve himself and cut into Sacrilege Alley, a traditional Catholic open air urinal. No one followed him in. He splattered the stained, 400-year-old wall and considered the total volume of urine expelled by 20 generations of pissers on this exact spot over the past four centuries. Archbishops had tinkled against this wall; nuns had squatted here—maybe even Sor Juana herself.

The thought titillated him.

"Pssst." A hoarse whisper from a neighboring rooftop interrupted his chissing.

"Pssst, up here, Prensa." Raus looked up. The soldier looked down. "You are the Yanqui reporter, no?"

"Sí, soy."

"They still won't let you into the building?"

"Para nada." Raus zipped up his fly and shook his head no.

"Look, we think Tonatiuh is a good man." The soldier was speaking to him in bracero English. "In my division, we are all Purés from Malinchico. Our fathers remember his father." The soldier had Raus' attention now. "If I let you up here to see how it is inside with the counting, you will tell the gringos what is really happening here, sí or no?"

"Por supuesto." Raus was already scaling the reeking wall which deadheaded against the rear of the 5th District Computation Center. The soldier grabbed his hand and hauled him up to the tarry roof.

"Felipe Roque Chuspata, a sus órdenes," he bowed. "If you slide yourself under that water tank, you can see right into the office. I'll patrol the roof so that nothing looks out of the ordinary. If someone starts to come up here, I'll cough twice."

Raus eased himself into the crawl space under the cool concrete tank. "Gracias, compañero," he nodded to Felipe Roque. He had a perfect sight line right into the room.

"Look, just tell Tonatiuh that we all voted for him in our division. He can't win without us."

FROM RAUS' UNEXPECTED vantage point, he could see the drama unfolding as if it was mounted on a theatrical stage. Cristóbal Cantú Cabañas was the PAR representative in the 5th district and he was waving his metal crutches around like he'd just gotten off the boat from Borneo. His backup, the old blind geezer Raus had seen with RAT at the CAE, Artemio Laguna, was foaming green around the mouth. The object of their wrath were short-sleeved functionaries seated at a long table across the room.

On the functionaries' right, a smooth-shaven, jowly licenciado seemed to be defending the PRO from the calumnies of the two furious old men. On the left side of the table, a bony woman wearing a modified nun's habit sat silently twisting her rosary beads: "Mother María Magdalena Magaña, PIN," it said on her nameplate.

Darting through this tense diorama were the fabled auxiliaries, the electoral gangsters who roamed the Union, working short-term contracts under De la Mancha. Their job was to physically control the ballots, stuff the boxes, alter the tally sheets, burn the evidence, and move on to the next election. The computers had almost put them out of business. Now, once again, they were the guardians of the paper and the key to the PRO's victory.

The Fu's routine was a circular one. One Fu Manchu yanked the cardboard ballot box from a closet that had been sealed with masking tape since the urns first entered into their possession. The first Fu hurled the ballot box across the room to a second Fu who ripped open the also-sealed-with-masking-tape container like he was Perro Aguayo stripping SuperPendejo bone by bone. Inside each urn, like a beating heart, were the ballots. They were bagged up in a see-through plastic membrane, the official tally sheet stapled to the neck of the bag. It was this tally sheet that was torn from the neck of the bag and thrust at the functionary assigned to read the results. Two other Fu's stood behind him ready to receive the sheet and reseal the violated ballot box with masking tape. The box was then hurled back across the room to the original Fu Manchu who stuffed it back in the closet. It was impossible to know if the Fus were not just opening and re-opening the same ballot box over and over again.

"¡No más! ¡No más!" howled Don Cristóbal like a decrepit Roberto Durán. "This is nonsense! None of your numbers are right!" Cantú Cabañas had copies from each of the polling places in the district. He flapped them around like they were bats out of hell. Raus's vision was clear but—from underneath a water tank that gurgled uproariously whenever anyone in the building flushed—he couldn't hear much. It sounded like the totals on the tally sheets held by the silver-haired old fossil bore no resemblance to the ones being recited by the functionaries. The differences smelled as funky as the water leaking from the valves just above Raus's head.

In Precinct 41, copies held by the galvanistas had Tonatiuh triumphing by a score of 111 to 14, but the auxiliaries had tacked an extra zero onto the PRO totals to steal victory. In Precinct 007, where Tonatiuh had won 66 to 6, Barcelona now led 666 to zip. In 13 straight instances, the vote was simply turned upside down by switching the PRO and the PAR columns.

"¡Rateros!" Don Cristóbal hurled one of his crutches right through the open window. His complexion darkened to Concord grape as the barefaced fraud and his own apoplexy grew.

Number 34 Bis was the polling place in which Tonatiuh and his family had cast their ballots, a musty Masonic Lodge around the corner from Carlos Quinto on Catholic Kings. Cantú Cabañas's tally sheet had the precinct 74 to 9 for Tonatiuh—six of the opposition votes had been cast for the paralyzed PIN man, Falanges. The head functionary reported that polling place #34 Bis had been won 83 to 0 by Filemón Barcelona.

Don Cristóbal lunged at the shirt-sleeved official and was restrained by a muscular Fu Manchu. In spite of the gurgling pipes, Raus could hear the one-legged old man screaming, clawing his way across the floor, trying to grab the plastic bag of ballots, to tear it open at the throat, and yell out each vote one by one—if just to prove that, at least, Tonatiuh had voted for himself in this election.

"Open the packages, for godsake man, let me open the packages!" the old orator croaked with his last remaining breath, as he fell from sight under the feet of the Fu Manchus. Even as Cantú Cabañas sank to the cigarette butt-strewn carpet, blind Artemio Laguna was stumbling over chairs trying to get at the Fu's and the functionaries. The possibility of having two crazy old coronary victims on their hands seemed to panic the auxiliaries, who began furiously barking into handheld walkie-talkies.

An ambulance wailed urgently in the distance. Outside on Holy Ghost Street, the decibel level of the crowd rose markedly. Moving across the roof along the wall of the meeting room, Mickey came out directly above the brawling crowd. Just below him, a woman in torn aprons was clubbed to the sidewalk by the rifle butts of the troops guarding the front door. One man wielded a clutch of crucifixes as if they were tomahawks. Paving stones crashed around a shuttered second floor window. Raus scanned the hurly-burly for Tania, thought he saw her under Sid Bloch's big protective wing: "¡Periodista! Don't shoot!" Then he spotted SuperPendejo with what looked like a manhole cover held high above his spectacularly masked and crested head. The chanting increased as the ambulance drew near. Attendants jumped out and fought their way through the mob to jump-start old Cristóbal's pump.

"¡Que Se Abren Los Paquetes!"

Now, a U.S. surplus Bell 212 locked in on the surging tempo of the turmoil on the ground and buzzed the rooftops in a slow, earsplitting sweep. Raus rolled for cover against the hot, tarry roof. Someone threw a Sauza bottle at the helicopter but the missile dropped harmlessly to the rooftop ten feet from Raus, not even shattering.

Out on Holy Ghost Street, he heard heavy treaded machinery clattering into place. Mickey belly-crawled back across the roof. Giant bulldozers revved up their engines at both mouths of the alley and began inching forward. Trapped protesters scaled walls, dove into basements, and crashed through storefronts to escape as the monster machines clanked down their broad steel blades and swept toward the center of the narrow street, penning in hundreds. Many had been caught with stones and bottles and manhole covers in their mitts.

Behind the bulldozers, a train of yellow school buses slid into formation. Troops separated out those who had been corralled by the machines and dragged them to the transports. From his perch, Raus watched a bloodied SuperPendejo hauled off to a waiting schoolbus. His canary colored tights sagged dangerously beneath the wrestler's paunch. On the fringes of Holy Ghost Street, the stubborn mob began to melt away, muttering to itself, a few neighbors at a time.

Tania was nowhere in sight.

Soon orange-colored street sweepers in orange jumpsuits were brought in and the sanctity of the neighborhood was restored. Vacated by the moiling rabble, it was suddenly a silent sunbaked Sunday afternoon in the Centro Histórico again, the surrounding barrio echoing with the solitary footfalls of old men shuffling home to lunch. It was as if nothing had happened for centuries here on Holy Ghost Street.

Mickey stumbled back from the ledge, past the open window of the empty Computation Center. The old men had been whisked off to intensive care units by the Red Cross, and the Fu Manchus had broken for box lunches and brewskis. Felipe Roque Chuspata appeared to have abandoned his post. Mickey lowered himself down into stinking Sacrilege Alley and hotfooted it for Carlos Quinto.

THE HOUSE OF DEMENTED WOMEN seemed ominously empty. Raus found Malcreado lurking in the cluttered kitchen.

Antonio hadn't seen Tania since he vacated Holy Ghost Street.

"I missed her after the bulldozers came. They picked up SuperPendejo, maybe 300 others," Raus babbled, "I'm worried about Tania..."

"We figure they've taken 5,000 prisoners in the city. It's coordinated. Gertrudis has them all at Campo Militar #1. We'll have a statement in about an hour." Malcreado mounted the stone steps to Tonatiuh's quarters.

Raus tried the house. Monk whacked out "Little Rootie Tootie," but Tania didn't answer. She hadn't left a message on the machine. Raus dialed the city room at El Machetazo. "Whoa boy, what you say?" political editor Ruy Chaparo drawled when he called. "We thought she was with you."

Had anyone seen Tania? Raus questioned his colleagues as they trooped in from various points in the city. The bad smell drew the press to Tonatiuh's like red ants to overripe mangoes.

Bloch pushed through the big oak doors. "She was right next to me for a while but when the shit began to fly after Super hurled that dumb manhole cover, I lost sight of her. Sorry, man."

Pease drifted in from Military Camp #1. He had been counting the captured galvanistas ("no more than a hundred"). No, he hadn't seen her in the pens. He didn't remember seeing her at the PRO either. "I hear you've been hanging out in Coatlicue, old man. Are you in the market for a heart transplant?"

Arbus had been at the CAE. Seventeen thousand hunger strikers were now splayed out on the esplanade. "Beat me to the front page for once in your life, you old drug-guzzling blood-hound." She pecked him on the cheek. "They just read me your India interview on the phone. How did you get hold of her? Her phone machine says she's out of the country indefinitely."

"What phone machine? Listen, have you seen Tania?"

Jane Ann gave him the fisheye. Ever since he'd taken up with the colombiana, Jane Ann had been giving him the fisheye. "Oh look, isn't that Chip Wallace over there. You know, Mickey, GE Disney NBC Chip Wallace?" She sashayed off to rub elbows with the Great Man.

As the possibility of PRO defeat boomed up and down the continent, the international media circus had descended upon the capital. Famous talking heads in safari jackets, tough chain-smoking lady correspondents, and teams of broad-shouldered dyspeptic cameramen who manhandled the print media to the back of the pack now prowled the halls of Carlos Quinto. Who needed them? Raus groused. Who is Chip Wallace anyway?

Where the hell was Tania?

The world-famous correspondents had reached that lull in their stories when they begin to interview each other.

"So what's the agenda, Horace?"

"It's the same scenario as last week, Chip—X. Davis will go on TV after six to confirm the PRO victory. Then we're supposed to be treated to little Filemón at long last, but I seriously doubt that he'll show his fear-crazed mug in public."

"Who is in charge at the PRO, Horace?" Pease was pleased at all the attention GE Disney NBC was lavishing on him.

"It's a bloody mess. The Brontos had the upper hand until the computers were running again but now the virus demonstrates just how vulnerable the Tecos are. Lomelí gave Gertrudis up to the dinosaurs to chew on, but General Ram Ram can't get to the capital without murdering half the country. There are a lot of long knives walking around these streets. I'd watch my bloody step, if I were you, Chipper."

"Are we looking at civil war then, Don Horacio?"

"The Army is split, which is never a good sign for domestic tranquility. Gertrudis is still here in the capital with his troops; so long as he remains, the PRO has a big PROblema. His troops voted for Tonatiuh and he himself is Tonatiuh's frigging half-brother although, in this game, blood is thinner than power.

"But don't count General Ram Ram out. They don't call him the Butcher of Tuxtla because he sells spare ribs on the side. Pay attention to what General Ramírez does. Pay no attention whatsoever to what he says. Keep your eye on his steel claw. And watch your culo, matte."

ANTONIO MALCREADO motioned for attention. The former *Machetazo* correspondent-turned-Tonatiuh-mouthpiece had returned with a prepared statement. The Doctor would answer questions later in the afternoon.

"As many of you who witnessed events here in the 5th District already know, the social warrior SuperPendejo and 300 supporters of Dr. Galván were physically brutalized and arrested when they sought entrance to the Computation Center on Holy Ghost Street to demand that ballot boxes be opened and each vote be recounted. What has happened in the 5th District has been repeated in the 7th, 13th, 26th, 29th. In every electoral district in the city, our people have been prevented from viewing the tallies, and when they refused to disperse, they were taken away by military bulldozers. Our estimate is that over 5,000 prisoners are now in custody at Military Camp #1. We appeal to General Gertrudis Niños de Galván (Totonaco) to release them immediately."

Malcreado then read from dispatches phoned in by galvanista captains around the nation:

"The Mothers of Julapa and their infant children are blocking the coastal highway to Laguna Negra to protest the PRO fraud. Thus far, General Ramírez has proven too soft-hearted to shoot 1,000 unarmed, bare-breasted nursing mothers.

"That's the good news.

"Miguel 'Rambo' Fitzgeraldo and 11 Montec garbage pickers, wielding only garbage bags of burnt ballots, have been gunned down by army troops in Tijuana after a march on the 293rd District Computation Center.

"In Cocotitlan, Julapa, early this morning, De la Mancha's thugs, armed with double-pump shotguns, killed seven dissident oil workers led by our compañero Chon Yaa and wounded dozens during a siege of the 177th District Computation Center.

"In Ciudad Tacumán, in the center of the country, the 93rd District Computation Center was set afire. There are reports of what the government is calling 14 'looters' killed so far, with four more hours of daylight remaining. Curiously, all of the so-called 'looters' are galvanistas.

"In Chiapas, General Ram Ram's liquidation teams have eliminated the entire village of Chamul near Polanco. This was all the information we could gather before the phone went dead.

"Just ten minutes ago, we received reports of a missile attack on galvanistas gathered in the main plaza in Gran Huajuco. Scores are said to be dead and wounded. This just happened. We'll know more within the hour.

"Finally, in El Horno, military helicopters have dropped what is being described as a 'satchel bomb' into a Pacific Jewel One hotel room where a group of masked gunmen calling themselves the 'Ismael Caracol Justification Junta' have been holding the playboy governor's playboy son for the past three days. The number of dead has not yet been confirmed.

"This is what we have up till now, compañeras and compañeros, but the situation is accelerating rapidly. The Secretary of the Interior has issued six bulletins already today to the effect that the district computations are being conducted in 'perfect tranquility.' Many of you have seen with your own eyes what 'perfect tranquility' means in the 5th District. We hope you will write what you have seen. That's it for right now. Tonatiuh will be out in a little while."

THE REPORTERS DASHED for the phones. Raus had no one to call but his own number. When he did, Tania was still not home. He stood there, listening to Monk's "Rootie Tootie," mesmerized by fear and worry.

"Are we done yet, jazz boy?" Sasha Vigo tapped her petite foot petulantly.

"Sasha, you haven't seen Tania today, have you?"

"That bitch better no mess with mi head no more," she spat and grabbed for the phone.

X. Davis failed to appear on national television at six. The reporters gathered around the set in the old kitchen and watched the Hulk wreck buildings instead. There was no explanation of why there was no X. Davis or why the PRO wasn't announcing its results. "The District Computations are proceeding in perfect tranquility." What had happened to Tania?

By dusk, the rain was falling from the crumpled sky, heavy and morose as a grave cloth. Mickey stood in the open courtyard, soaked to the bone and sick with dread. In his inside eye, he saw Tania's sparrow-like body laid out on a shining slab of marble, her little breasts sliced open and her beating red ruby heart being lifted from her broken bosom by the PRO surgeons.

FOR THE FIRST TIME since the crisis had exploded, all five major U.S. networks turned their blinding lights on Tonatiuh Galván. *Smile, you're on Primetime, amigo.* The Doctor looked dubious. He had called lots of press conferences in this long crusade and these bozos had never shown up before.

"Last Sunday, July 2, we won the presidency of our country. Here are the complete printouts for your inspection." He waved at the large boxes of computer paper that Malcreado was now lugging into the room.

"These are the true results, captured from the raw data in

the CAE's mainframe computer before the PRO destroyed them with a computer virus. You will note that we have won the majority vote in 27 out of 31 states and all 30 districts of the capital. In terms of electoral districts, we were victorious in 254 out of a possible 300. Last Sunday, we were elected president by a popular vote of 31 million out of a total of 39 million votes, cast in an election in which just under 74% of the electorate chose to vote. This is not enough.

"Today, one week later, without ever having been inaugurated, we have been stripped of the presidency. Our victory has been stolen from us, first by the PRO computers which we have had to destroy, and now by the government's refusal to open the ballot boxes and recount the paper votes. They seal their refusal with the blood of our people.

"From what we have heard, the situation is grave throughout the country. Nearly 10,000 of our supporters have been taken to concentration camps. Depending on the final count of the dead in the plaza of Gran Huajuco, we are speaking of at least 400 of our people murdered today by the PRO government. Many of our friends are missing.

"Following the massacre of Rambo Fitzgeraldo and a dozen Montec garbage pickers in Tijuana, we are now being told that the Yanqui military has sealed all northern border crossings.

"The Patria is in grave danger tonight, and we would be failing our pledge to our fathers and our grandfathers if we do not commit ourselves to the rescue of the nation. That is why we are summoning every citizen in every town and city and farm and state and street and house and room and bed and hammock who cast a ballot in our behalf to come to the Zócalo beginning at midnight tonight where we will sit in traditional congress for as long we have to, taking council from the people about how we can best remove this cancer called the Party of the Organic Revolution from the breast of the nation.

"I'll take a few questions now."

"Dr. Galván, can you estimate how many people you are inviting to the Zócalo? How long will this congress last?"

"Yes, 31 million citizens voted for us. Yes, we are asking them all to come as personal delegates. Yes, the Congress of the People will last as long as it takes to remove the malignant growth of the PRO from the nation's body. You must remember that I am a medical doctor."

"Señor Galván, by pretending to summon all your supporters to the Zócalo, aren't you inviting complete and total anarchy and revolution? Won't this 'Congress' of yours have devastating repercussions for the nation's economy and foreign trade alliances?"

"Señor Pease, the revolution happened 83 years ago. We're only here to defend it. As for our economy and your NAAFTA, both of them are starving us to death. Yes, what do we lose, Señor Pease, by revolution?"

Killer quote, Raus scribbled. Too bad everyone will have it by tomorrow morning.

"Señor Candidato, do you have any arrangements with the authorities about allowing your people to enter the capital? Do you have the necessary permits for the Zócalo?"

"Yes, we have assurances from the military that the congresistas will be able to enter the city without any problems, Mister Von Voodle. As for the Zócalo, our information is that it has not yet been privatized. Yes, it still belongs to the people."

"But, Don Tonatiuh, will your people be allowed to leave the city once they have encamped here? Could these assurances not be a trap?" The dean of the Latin press corps, Don Andrés Oppenheimer, crippled by a package bomb during the Cuban presidential campaign, leaned forward in his wheelchair.

"The Zócalo is the heart of the nation. It is the seat of our religion and our government. Yes, this is where matters have always been settled, Don Andrés. We would hope the army will remember that there are many more citizens than soldiers in this city but, more importantly, that, yes, it too is composed of citizens and, yes, as citizens, they too share a mutual obligation to save the Patria from the PRO."

"About the army, sir: When you speak of assurances from the army, just what 'assurances' do you mean? From whom do you have these 'assurances'?"

"I'm sorry, compañero, I don't know your face…"

"Chip Chipper Wallace, GE-Disney NBC Nightly News…"

"Yes, Mister Chip, what you must realize is that a long time ago we had a revolution here, and the army that made that revolution is constitutionally committed to defending that revolution. And, yes, in many parts of the country that commitment has held strong. In Malinchico, we understand, the troops have just gone home for the weekend to their communities rather than enforce X. Davis's orders to keep our people from counting the ballots. In fact, wherever troops from Malinchico are stationed, we are informed of, and gratified by, their allegiance. Yes, we invite the rest of the ranks to join arms with the people."

"Doctor, can we get your reaction to the sealing of the border by U.S. President Gingrich?"

"Yes, Jane Ann, but perhaps you can explain it to me better," Tonatiuh smiled, "this sealing of the border. Does it mean that democracy is like some germ that comes from the south and that it must be kept out of your country like a fruit fly or cholera or a so-called illegal alien?"

"A follow-up, Tonatiuh. Can you tell us what contact you've had with the U.S. ambassador?"

"Yes, the North American ambassador claims that he has opened communications with me, but we think he must have called some other Tonatiuh because we have never heard a word from him." The reporters chuckled nervously.

"Compañero Tonatiuh, can Filemón Barcelona govern the nation with so few votes in his favor?" breathed Sasha Vigo. *Where's Tania, bitch?*

"Yes, obviously not, compañera. The PRO candidate is afraid to even appear in public because he knows we know he lost this election. The people are not only asking where is Barcelona, but who is this Barcelona, because they haven't heard from him for so long they've forgotten." The Doctor was turning into a standup comic.

"Tonatiuh?" Raus's hand shot up automatically.

"Compañero Raus has covered our crusade since the very beginning," the Doctor commented, as if to explain why he was calling upon this shabby-looking old gringo when so many media monsters were in the room.

"Tonatiuh?"

"Sí, compañero Raus."

Then something happened that had never happened in all Mickey's life as a reporter. The question simply went out of his head.

Another popped in.

"Tonatiuh, sometime between noon and 1 p.m. this afternoon, my compañera Tania Escobar disappeared in broad daylight in front of the 5th District Computation Center on Holy Ghost Street just three blocks from here. My question is...my question is...where is she? Who has taken her? How can I get her back?"

U.S. SEALS OFF CROSSINGS AS CRISIS DEEPENS SOUTH OF BORDER

PRO ELECTION 'VICTORY' ERADICATED; OPPOSITION TAKES CENTER OF CAPITAL

San Francisco Examiner-Guardian Foreign Bureau
By Miguel Raus

TENOCHTITLAN (July 10)—The ever-deepening political crisis here took a bizarre twist last night following admission by the government that results of disputed presidential vote tallies received from the nation's 300 electoral districts 24 hours earlier had been lost to a computer virus that previously destroyed preliminary results from the July 2 presidential election. Interior Secretary Gonzalo X. Davis indicated that the virus, introduced by supporters of opposition candidate Tonatiuh Galván, had permanently crippled the government's computer capacity.

The now-destroyed tallies allegedly confirmed the victory of former finance minister Filemón Barcelona, candidate of the long-ruling (71 years) Party of the Organic Revolution (PRO), over left challenger Galván by an 8 to 1 margin. The PRO has never lost a presidential election.

Sunday's district computations were marked by nationwide disturbances in which hundreds of Galván supporters were killed and thousands imprisoned, plunging this nation into one of its most violent episodes since its landmark revolution nearly a century ago. The violence moved Washington to seal its southern border late Saturday evening.

Heart of the Nation

Meanwhile, Galván, whose own documentation of the election gives him 28 out of the 32 federal entities and a popular vote of 31 million to Barcelona's 5.5 million, inaugurated last evening a mammoth "congress" of his supporters in the great plaza called the Zócalo, which, since ancient Aztec times, has been described as the "political heart of the nation." The square is flanked by the National Palace, the traditional seat of the PRO-run government, and the presence of hundreds of thousands of galvanistas encamped indefinitely on its doorstep is charged with political significance.

The first days of the huge open-air meeting, which has no fixed agenda or date of conclusion, are being devoted to reports from 102,000 individual polling places around the country. Estimates of the number of Galván supporters encamped in the Zócalo and on the side streets of the city's colonial Centro Histórico (Historic Center) vary between 200,000 and half a million, with thousands more summoned by Galván to "defend" his victory arriving from the provinces every hour.

The general feeling here in this hot, tense capital is that a change of power is imminent but whether by peaceful or violent means remains unclear.

Military Split

The galvanistas' march into the city is being facilitated by a nasty split in the military, with the ousted chief of staff, Brigadier General Gertrudis Niños de Galván (Totonaco) still controlling Military Camp #1 on the western edge of the metropolis. The capital is set in a long, basin-like valley with few natural gateways, all of which are held by Niños de Galván's troops. The General, an adopted brother of the opposition candidate but not thought to be a political ally, is challenged by General of Division Archibaldo A. Ramírez Ramírez, a tough-talking, one-armed "mano dura" (literally, hard hand) appointed as Secretary of Defense by outgoing President Arturo Lomelí to replace Niños de Galván (Totonaco) on the eve of the July 2 presidential vote. Many of the former Chief of Staff's troops voted for his adopted brother.

The two military men appear stalemated over control of the capital, with Niños de Galván having guaranteed safe passage into the capital to the "Congresistas" despite objections by both Lomelí and Ramírez. Some analysts think that the President and his new army chief did not prevent Niños de Galván from permitting galvanistas to congregate in the city because, as one foreign diplomat who preferred anonymity told this reporter, "Now they will be sitting ducks in the Zócalo when the Barcelona government is cohesive enough to act."

Devoured by Worms

Bizarre computer hijinks have thrown the presidential election into persistent turmoil ever since the night of July 2, when X. Davis halted release of preliminary results due to an as yet unexplained "systems crash." It is now thought the PRO destroyed the raw results through the introduction of a computer virus because Galván was handily winning the election. The galvanistas possess the only known backup of the raw results.

In this latest unlikely turn of events, galvanista computer director María Cristina Terrazas Tamal Menchú viuda de Ahumada successfully penetrated the Autonomous Electoral Commission's central data gathering system and introduced an information-devouring worm which eradicated fake results fabricated by the PRO that gave Barcelona an 8 to 1 advantage. This Sunday the galvanista computer queen again invaded the system to consume PRO-generated district results in which the former finance minister held a similar margin over Galván. Tamal Menchú capped her caper by permanently disabling the Autonomous Electoral Commission's computer system. The raw results captured by the agile galvanista hacker July 2 and passed out to the press today give Galván a 6 to 1 lead over Barcelona.

The presumed perpetrator of this extraordinary cybernetic offensive is a 90-year-old former film star and well-known authority on Aztec prophecy, who has authored a series of bestselling books illustrating how ancient Indian writings point to a Galván presidency—a period that, she says, will usher in an Aztec renaissance known as "The Age of the Sixth Sun."

Under the latest electoral reform law passed last spring (the 23rd in the past 10 years), destruction of electoral documentation is a criminal offense punishable by no more than 50 years imprisonment. After declaring that "subversives" had introduced a virus

into government computers last week, X. Davis suggested that ar-
rest warrants were being prepared, and there are reports that Ms.
Tamal Menchú left the country last night for an undisclosed South
American destination.

PRO Paralysis

The destruction of the original electronic results and subsequent
sets of fake numbers made Saturday's tabulation of district tallies
particularly crucial since, other than Tamal Menchú's printouts,
the ballots contained in sealed boxes and bags are now the only
credible proof of who has won this election. Tally sheets read by
electoral technicians and auxiliaries at district computation centers on Sunday differed wildly from copies of these same sheets
held by Galván vote captains. Opposition demands to open each
box and recount the votes were met by government stonewalling,
as well as police and army repression from one end of nation to
the next.

Despite the widespread violence and the disabling of the
government's computer system, X. Davis insists that Barcelona won
30 out of 31 states (Galván was awarded his home state of Malinchico)
and split the federal district. X. Davis also announced that the sealed
ballot boxes will now be escorted up to the capital by General
Ramírez's troops and safeguarded in the National Palace prior to
the forthcoming August 1 convening of the nation's electoral college to finalize Barcelona's victory.

"President-elect" Barcelona has not been seen in public since vot-
ing July 2 and it is not known if he is still in the country. Although
he was expected to speak to the nation following the Interior
Secretary's message last night, Barcelona failed to materialize and
X. Davis was followed instead by a ten-minute highlight film of the
PRO candidate's not very colorful career.

With Barcelona in seclusion and his sponsor, Arturo Lomelí, apparently unable to defuse tensions within his own party, the PRO
has split into increasingly hostile factions labeled "Tecos" (young
technicians) and the old guard "Brontos." The virus scandal was
reportedly manipulated by former PRO co-chairman Bulmaro
Marrano, a hard-line Bronto, in an effort to discredit the PRO's
"modernizing" wing. Marrano was reimprisoned yesterday for
embezzling party funds in a drug scandal several years ago, suggesting a dip in Bronto fortunes. The hard-liners, as represented
by Marrano, PRO Central Committee member Sancho de la Mancha,

and General Ramírez Ramírez, appear to have engineered Sunday's murderous violence against the galvanistas.

Fuel Truck Missile

The toll in the widespread disturbances at the district computation centers now stands at 549 known dead, 1,400 injured, over 8,000 galvanistas imprisoned, and an undetermined number of missing. The most serious incident took place in the southern city of Gran Huajuco, a bustling commercial center on the Huajucan Isthmus, when preventative police fired a mortar into a passing government fuel truck. PRO governor Ignacio Mu has resigned in the wake of the explosion that killed 271 people, including many women and children.

Meanwhile, in neighboring El Horno, the violence took a grisly turn with the discovery of the charred bodies of four members of a group calling itself the "Ismael Caracol Justification Junta." The group had earlier kidnapped the son of Governor Coco Fernández to protest the PRO's attempts to steal the election. The hearts had been removed from all four bodies as well as that of the governor's son, whose nude, mutilated corpse was found stuffed into an air shaft at the luxury GE DisneyMex Pacific Jewel One hotel where the horrific events transpired Sunday afternoon.

Aztec Two Step

The removal of the murdered men's hearts is identical to the mutilations inflicted upon two of Galván's closest aides who were similarly killed on the eve of the July 2 election.

Since the recovery of their bodies one week ago, dozens of copycat murders have been reported in and around the capital, including those of two prominent Indianist spokesmen taken into custody by Investigative Police Chief Florentino Zorrilla in connection with the murder of the two Galván aides. The ritual murders in El Horno were not the first reported from the provinces. At least four states have recorded similar killings.

Removing the heart from a victim's body and offering it to certain sun-oriented deities is an Aztec sacrificial rite designed to placate the gods who kept their empire and universe flourishing. One consequence of this religious system is that the Aztecs had to fight many wars, called "flowery wars," with the sole intent of capturing sacrificial victims. Some observers here worry that a modern comeback of the "flowery war" is being played out against the dramatic political scenario unfolding here. In this respect, Doctor

Ezekial Huipi, an aide and spiritual advisor to Galván, has expressed concern for 5,000 galvanista prisoners being held at the military camp just outside the city. "These illegally detained prisoners are being fattened up for mass sacrifice," Huipi charged, demanding the intervention of international human rights groups.

Border Sealed

The continuing instability of the PRO and the government it runs is increasingly fraying Washington's nerves. The preoccupation was underscored by Sunday night's surprise sealing of the 1,952-mile U.S. southern border by 25,000 Army and Marine troops on maneuvers in the Arizona desert. The unprecedented border closing represents "a U.S. reassessment of its security priorities," according to an unusually tight-lipped embassy here. Ambassador Thaddeus Blackbridge has been called to Washington, where he is expected to huddle with President Gingrich to evaluate the danger of a Galván takeover south of the border.

Despite high tension in Tijuana, where U.S.-born Montec Indian leader Miguel Fitzgeraldo was slain by army troops Sunday, the U.S. border is reported quiet today. Galván is known to have pockets of support all along the dividing line, particularly among Indian garbage pickers and women workers in thousands of U.S. and Japanese-owned "maquiladoras" or assembly plants that produce everything from Dior dresses to nuclear triggers for the North American market.

In announcing the border sealing, Washington described the move as "precautionary." With immigration once again promising to be a hot button issue in upcoming U.S. presidential elections, Gingrich is trying to get out in front of the crisis. Yesterday he told a group of White House reporters that "we will not allow Texas and California to become sanctuaries for refugees from political instability caused by the foolishness of our neighbor's corrupt narco-government."

The ongoing crisis here coincides with the U.S. political convention season. This week, the Republican Party is expected to nominate Newt Gingrich as its official candidate in the November elections. How Gingrich handles the crisis will be crucial to his campaign. As Speaker of the House, the puff-haired Georgia Republican took over the presidency after both Bill Clinton and Al Gore lost their lives in a tragic two-plane accident over the Andes in early 1999.

XII

TONATIUH'S PEOPLE

July 11 – 18, 2000

RAUS COMBED THE THRONG for the glint of her jittery green eyes, a snatch of her voice, the touch of her little lizard hands. He showed the still Bloch had rescued from the footage he shot Sunday on Holy Ghost Street to everyone he met. A merengue man near the Templo Mayor was sure he had seen Tania on Catholic Kings with the sweatshop women, but it wasn't true, it was another woman with the same sort of mop hair and jumpy eyes.

Everyone he showed the photo to wanted to be helpful. Yes, they had seen her with the gomeros of Amapola, or the ski-masked True Zapatistas from the autonomous zones, or the big women from Gran Huajuco, or in the Lesbian tent, or out in the pens at Military Camp #1, but it was always somebody else—darker, fatter, taller, younger. An ambulant oyster salesperson thought he had spotted her hooking in La Bondad. Raus couldn't blame his informants. He was grateful to them. He thought they conjured up their sightings because it would be more hurtful if they said they hadn't seen her at all.

The bottom line was the military camp. If she really wasn't there, she wasn't anywhere.

"Tania? She was right next to us in front of the Computation Center. We were talking with that big black camera guy. Then I went to get a manhole cover." SuperPendejo scratched his bandaged head awkwardly, with his left hand—his right arm had been fractured in the army attack. "Then the bulldozers trapped us. I don't remember seeing her after that. I'm sure she wasn't in the pens with us. We made a list. I never saw her name. Suerte, compa."

Mickey drafted Taxi Andy out of La Putanera and paid him to drive out to Military Camp #1 in the west of the city. "H-how c-c-ome y-y-you al-always h-hire m-me t-t-o dr-drive t-t-to b-b-bad p-places, b-b-b-oss?" Taxi sputtered. Raus told him Tania was missing and he was looking for her.

"I-I'm s-s-orry t-t-o h-hear th-that, b-b-boss." Taxi Andy didn't say another word all the way out to the camp, even when a gray Gran Marquis with tinted windows and no license plates cut right in front of his leaf-colored bug.

The military camp was on alert. Taxi Andy could not get within ten blocks of the perimeter without being turned around by some smudge-eyed soldier. They circled the base for an hour and finally threw in the towel. "I-I'm s-s-sorry, b-b-boss," Taxi repeated.

By the second morning, Raus began to check the hospitals. He presented himself to the Preventative Police and the Investigative Police and the immigration authorities and the secretos, showed the desk sergeant Tania's photo, and meekly asked if maybe they had her. Dewlapped comandantes stared at the likeness of the lean, mop-headed urchin and shook their jowls from side to side soundlessly.

El Machetazo vowed to run her picture every day on the front page until she was returned alive to the paper. *Protesto* commissioned Sasha Vigo to investigate the disappearance of her friend. Raus kept running into Vigo, coming and going from interviews with police officials and morgue attendants. They did not exchange words.

Malcreado accompanied Mickey to the city morgue. He

dreaded finding her there in some stainless steel drawer or laid out on a cold marble slab, her heart ruthlessly ripped from her bird-like chest like the Bishop or Estalin or the two priests of Huitzilopochli or the guerrilleros in El Horno or the King of Cacao in Pantano. How many more hearts were for the taking?

A hunchbacked morgue attendant conducted them through the autopsy room, pulling back the crisp linen sheets with sadistic delight. Raus and Malcreado peaked squeamishly, morbidly mesmerized by the death masks of breastless young women, their chest cavities torn open, their hearts scooped out. None of them was Tania Escobar.

They bumped into Vigo on the ramp outside, Malcreado bussed her on the cheek. Raus didn't. "You're not talking to Sasha?" Malcreado asked later.

"Sasha knows where Tania is. I know it."

"You're still jealous, man," Antonio needled.

"Fuck you, culero." Tonatiuh's press head threw an arm around Mickey's greasy shoulder. "I never figured you as a member of the Coatlicue crew anyway."

"What's that supposed to mean, asshole?"

"Nothing, only Sasha and La India, you know, they were pretty tight."

IT WAS THE THIRD NIGHT of the Congress of the People. The encampment now filled the Zócalo and all the surrounding streets and had begun to spiral out past the Centro Histórico, the borders of the old island of Tenochtitlan. Organizers estimated that a half a million galvanistas were camped out in the center of the city. The police estimated 6,000.

Management of the great encampment was a logistical headache. How to fit more and more of their people into less and less space gave Tonatiuh's braintrust migraines. How to keep the campers fed and clean. How to get more of their bodily wastes out of the city. Sacrilege Alley was filled to the brim.

The organizers formed a thousand committees, but the committees were not enough. The solution came from the people themselves. Sustenance flowed in from the surrounding barrios. The neighbors brought tortas and toilet paper and coffee and greens from their roof gardens, blankets and plastic to keep the rains off and pillows to pad the rough paving stones. Fresh water arrived in tank trucks hijacked mysteriously from the PRO. An anonymous donor contributed 1,000 porta-potties. The gates of La Bondad were thrown open to welcome the congresistas and Doña Metiche's menudo flowed like the mighty Orinoco. In the evenings, after the rain, Tonatiuh's people warmed themselves against the damp around 10,000 campfires fashioned from salvaged newspapers and broken crates, and they talked about what was coming and what they had left behind.

The open mike up on the presidium had citizens lined up all the way to the Pino Suárez metro station, awaiting a turn to put their two cents in and take their three minutes out. Brokers did a brisk business "arranging" special "interventions" by "notables." But at the Congress of the People, sooner or later, everyone would get a chance to speak.

The podium was set up against the far north corner of the great square, adjacent to the partially restored Aztec killing ground known as the Templo Mayor and the dark granite facade of the National Palace. There were soldiers behind all the huge oaken doors of the palace but no tanks or display of weapons or even troops outside. No one knew what game General Gertrudis was playing, what cards he held, or what it was he wanted.

Achilles Plantón had kidnapped the mike, expounding on the parallels between the massacre at Tlatelolco 32 years ago and the massacre of the galvanistas on Bloody Sunday. Plantón was 55, fat, jovially gray-bearded, a chilango knockoff of Abbie Hoffman. Three decades ago he had emerged from a pile of murdered students to place a blood-stained carnation in the still-smoking cannon of an army tank. Now he lived in a campus greenhouse, an apostle of "cellular democratic autonomy," whatever that was. His admirers were few and historic. Those who distrusted him were legion. Plantón, who paid handsomely for his "interventions" on the open mike, always overstayed his three-minute time limit and was—inevitably—tossed from the stage.

THE TRUE ZAPATISTAS had pitched camp under the eaves of the Grand Hotel on the west side of the Zócalo. Curiosity-seekers crowded in around their dark circle—since the agreement in the Basílica, few Zapatistas had ventured up to the capital from the autonomous zones and their sudden appearance here in the concrete jungle had caused an electric stir among the congresistas. It was not known if Marcos was among them.

Mickey searched their serious eyes, framed in the oval of their skimasks, for some flicker of recognition. Marcos was not among them.

Neither was Tania.

Melquíades Chimalpopa, the blind street sweeper, held Tania's picture against his blank eyes. "Sí, señor, now I remember. I saw her just yesterday framed in the doorway of the Cathedral." His friend, the beat cop Abundio Ilhuicamina, promised to keep his antennas peeled for her. The beat cops in the Centro Histórico had all voted for Tonatiuh, he assured Mickey. "Why not? He's our neighbor. We're the good cops, but not all of us are so good. Be careful. Godspeed." He waved Raus off with a friendly white glove.

On the perimeter of the encampment, the secretos prowled in big gray cars, picking off stragglers for "questioning," shoving them into the back seat head down, big guns pressed against their temples, driving them into nowhere. Unlike those taken by the military, these "suspects" didn't show up in the pens. They did not appear in Florentino Zorrilla's torture cells. They could not be found on the hospital wards or in the morgue drawers. Like Tania, they were just gone.

Be careful. Godspeed.

The Tata-mandones from Santa Eulalia Cuacua were huddled by the National Pawnshop. "You must keep the faith, my son," encouraged the archly arthritic Padre Luis, peeking from the tops of his eyeballs. Leaning on a stout cane, the double-bent priest had led the old men in translucent white linens over the moonscaped mountains up to the capital. "I have not walked the roads for a long time, my son. It was good to get away from Cuacua and see what else there is in the world. Maybe I'll never go back."

Raus knelt on the sidewalk so that he might hear the old priest better. "You must remember what we have come here for, m'ijo." Padre Luis slipped a stamped tin image of the Brown Madonna over his ears.

Godspeed. Be careful.

⚔

A TUSSLE WAS IN PROCESS up on the proscenium. Ultras vs. Históricos. Plantón came flying headfirst from the podium. Ultras in ultra-pink mohawks throttled the mike and vomited. "Fuck Nostalgia!" they spewed, demanding that the male congresistas all direct their peckers towards the National Palace and begin pissing. A few men down in front began to unzip their flies.

"¡Provocateurs!" hollered Doña X. "¡Machistas!" The Doñas of Lesbos charged the stage.

"Compañeros and compañeras," a big voice boomed over the loudspeakers strung from all the lampposts in the Centro Histórico. "Let's take time out for a culture break!" Looking frazzled, the Warriors of Huitzilopochli trooped onto the stage.

Raus circled the Zócalo like a seedy buzzard. He had stopped reporting the news. He couldn't search for Tania night and day and cover the story of the century at the same time. He didn't eat and he didn't sleep but he had not sworn off the worm water. Tania's mop head floated up like a balloon before his eyes against the evening sky. He followed her around corners and into cafes and saw her across crowds, but when he got to where he had seen her, she was missing again and no one could remember her ever being there. It was like a game of schoolkid tag, only he was always touching the wrong person.

The fruitless chase wounded Mickey and he tried to nullify

the pain with fermented spirits, just enough to dull the ache but not enough to slow him down—a shot or two at a time whenever he ducked down Holy Ghost Street into Las Ilusiones.

The Tatas and Nanas of Zapicho crouched around a blazing bonfire in the courtyard of the gloomy cathedral and Raus was happy to have found them. Pamfilo took his hand in the limp Indian way and offered Raus a blanket to keep out the cold. Mickey did not remember being cold. He had not shaved or washed for days. People stopped from a sanitary distance to ask him if he had found her yet.

"Nana Cucu must have voted for Tonatiuh, too," Pamfilo giggled as moonshine poked through charged rain clouds. Raus stared at the chipped moon through red-rimmed eyes. The canals up there ran blood-red, as if they were lunar veins.

Who knows if the moon is a balloon? Raus recited to himself. "¿Quién sabe?"

Old Anastacio nodded in the wheelchair the Tatas had rented to roll him down from his mountaintop. Pedro Baltazar snatched the half-empty jug from the deaf man's grasp and passed it to Raus. "Salud…"

Mickey toasted the Tatas: "To Tonatiuh and the Congress of the People! To the Nanas and Tatas of Zapicho!" Then he turned to Tania, toasted his disappeared lover-in-the-moon and gulped the bottle dry as a bone.

THE HUNGER STRIKERS had been translated from the esplanade of the electoral commission. Seventeen thousand starving men and women were hand-carried the 40 city blocks from the CAE in the Reforma skyscraper zone to the Zócalo and laid out in front of the National Palace as a sort of groaning buffer against grouplets of Ultras, inflamed youth gangs, and anarchist blade runners who were continually trying to firebomb the balconies and the doors.

Driven half-mad by the rancid odor of frying grease and bad meat wafting off an acre of taco stands that had welded itself to the encampment, the fasters writhed like eels or lay comatose and drooling in the dark. One had to step gingerly when venturing through their territory.

The starvers were each at distinct stages of starvation ranging from hours to years. Reggio Ahumada Tamal was ten days in, cranky and manic. He was propped up in a customized velvet stretcher to the right of the stage along with the skin and bones saint of the hunger strikers, Padre Pascual Pobrecito, the liberation monk of the Altos and the soup kitchens who had sucked only fresh air and mountain fogs for nearly six years. As they lay side by side, the veteran hunger artist chuckled softly to RAT. The people's sense of absurdity tickled his meatless ribs. "Only a starving nation would think it could change things here by refusing to eat food."

A bony hand grabbed at Raus' shin as he shuffled through the no-man's land by the Supreme Court. He peered down and made out a familiar shape. The Yunqui General lay doubled up on the bare concrete, his military jacket in tatters. He was a long way from the northern desert. Damn, Mickey rued, I never wrote "Yunquis on Crack."

"Do you remember me?" the supine Indian general implored.

"Of course, señor, we met in Desierto de Yunqui…"

"I'm starving myself to death," he gasped.

"I know…"

"Better here where everyone can see us, don't you think?"

"There are many people watching you," Raus assured him.

"That's good to know." The general closed his eyes.

ﷺ

NOW LARGE WOMEN from Gran Huajuco, draped in handsomely embroidered huipiles, had taken over the presidium. Raus saw among them the two women accused of shooting Cantú Cabañas back in July. They were telling how they had been beaten with chairs and the butt handles of bullwhips had been jammed up their vaginas by Preventative Police Chief Edgardo Bobolobo, who then forced them to sign blank confessions.

"The police chief has a bad heart," Olivia Xandani sighed.

"No, compañera, Bobolobo has no heart," giggled Maria Xuhlub. "It was removed by our doctors several nights ago."

Don Cristóbal rocked with laughter on a folding chair behind the big, indignant women—the late police chief had once accused the compañeras of trying to rub out the old orator. Cantú Cabañas's own heart had been recharged by high voltage electrical currents and he was back on his one remaining foot. Mickey was startled to see Ignacio Mu, the resigned governor of Huajuco, seated with the women. Tonatiuh was perched up there too, like a brown stork, his family gathered around him, taking counsel from the People. He had said nothing since inaugurating the congress. He wanted his people to first speak their mind. Perhaps then he would know what to do.

Raus trudged through the encampment. Small children thought he was a ghost and fled his haggard face. A schoolteacher in a flower-print dress threw rose petals on him and smiled sadly. A railroad wife with a vermilion mouth kissed him on the cheek and patted him on the back. He came upon a hobbled man he had seen once before—but could not remember where—who begged Mickey not to tell anyone that he was there. He came upon another man staring into the calluses of his right hand just as when he'd left him in the middle of the street in Ciudad Tacuman. "I hope you find her," the weather-beaten kiwi picker said, never varying his gaze from the center of his palm.

The women from Gran Huajuco had somehow survived the horrific explosion on Sunday with minor burns, but they had lost many loved ones and comadres. The police were drunk, they testified. The PRO had burnt up their children and their sisters and their lovers and it was all just a pinche borrachera. "Death to the PRO!" sobbed Olivia Xandani.

"DEATH TO THE PRO!" The congresistas packing the darkened Zócalo thundered back as if the matter was long decided.

Then Ignacio Mu, the Chinese-Mam Indian former governor of Huajuco arose and slowly began to read the names of those who had been cremated in the gas truck explosion on Sunday.

"Compañera Mirasol Xila Xila…"

Tonatiuh's People responded like one balled fist:
"¡PRESENTAAAAY!"
"Compañera Laura Xila Xila…"
"¡PRESENTAAAAAY!"
"Compañera Adela Xandani Xila…"
"¡PRESENTAAAAAY!"
Raus did not want to hear this litany of the dead anymore. He held his hands to his ears so Mu or the big women could not pronounce her name. He bolted from the Zócalo, breathing with difficulty, and headed for Las Ilusiones. He unstopped his ears. Men in dark raincoats stood under the street lamps on every corner, their teeth tearing on the sinews of her heart.

Halfway down Holy Ghost Street, Raus found the village of Chamul, miraculously resurrected in the cobbled street under a discolored sheet of plastic. "We had a vision," explained Chamul the shaman, who had not been massacred at all. "We left town before the liquidation teams came to kill us for not sleeping. What they killed were the cornstalks twisting in our beds."

Chamul looked deeply into Raus' bloodshot eyes and saw the outline of Tania's face in the photograph there.

"Have you seen her, Chamul?" Raus asked in desperation. They said the shaman could find anything.

Chamul took Mickey's hand and put it to his lips. "You must not look for her anymore. She will come for you when she is ready."

RAUS WAS DRINKING breakfast, lunch, and supper by Thursday. "At least I'm sucking up three squares a day," he argued with Horace Pease, biting off the head of a pickled worm. "Protein," he giggled.

"Not funny, old man, not funny anymore." Pease gurgled down a Bloody Mary. "You're acting irresponsibly. Poncho says you were in here talking to a hallucinatory rooster all night, until he swamped you out this morning."

"I wasn't hallucinating," Raus whined defensively.

"And the little incident yesterday at the Templo Mayor?"

What incident was Pease talking about?

"Jumping off the pedestrian bridge and dashing though the ruins, hollering for Tania to escape from the sacrificial altars? Don't you remember, lad? You nearly were bloody shot by the Anthropology Police."

Mickey signaled Poncho for a refill. The fat man refused to acknowledge the snapping fingers and fixated his gaze on the futbol warm-ups.

"I guess I must be upset," Mickey conceded. How many days had she been gone now? "I don't know what to do next. Look, Horace, I even called Bogotá yesterday. I think it was yesterday. You know the paper she said she was stringing for—*La Fogata*— it doesn't even exist."

Pease had more juice with Poncho at the moment. He coaxed the surly bartender into a fresh round all around. Then he got down to hard tacks. "Listen up, mate, you're walking around in total denial. Just what do you really know about Tania Escobar? The Coatlicue crowd has you by the testicles and they're about to chew them off."

Raus drank down. The mescal rose up. He choked it back and began to sweat profusely. "Tell me, Horace, who are they, the Coatlicue crowd?"

"The Widows of Coatlicue, you naif—La India's lesbian lovers. Sasha Vigo and, by way of carnal association, Vigo's sometime lover, Tania Escobar. There are others—Doña X and her bulldyke clique. Sorry to be the first on the block to tell you all this, old chap."

Mescal-laced tears dribbled from his stinging eyes, and Raus bolted for the urinals. Behind him, President Arturo Lomelí smiled crookedly on Poncho's TV screen.

The outgoing president apologized for interrupting lunch and the futbol warm-ups. He spoke sparingly. *"The election process has concluded. We congratulate the President-elect, Filemón Barcelona, and extend our condolences to those who have lost.*

"On August 1, I will convene the electoral college of the nation to confirm the results of the federal districts. Even as we speak, the sealed

ballot boxes, now held at 300 district computation centers in 31 states and the federal district, are being transported here to the National Palace under the supervision of Secretary of Defense Archibaldo Ramírez to be stored there until the electoral college has terminated its work. Thank you and buen provecho."

"The ruddy bastard's not even speaking from the National Palace. He hasn't been near the place for weeks," Pease belched. Across the table, Raus' pallid ghost was hunting for Tania at the bottom of his glass

"Are you still there, mate? This is bloody serious business." Escorting the ballot boxes to the National Palace gave General Ram Ram presidential fiat to enter the capital and march on the Zócalo. Would Gertrudis, with just a few thousand loyal men at best, be foolhardy enough to try and hold him off at the passes into the valley? "It's bloody civil war, the Revolution! Your nincompoop idol John Reed has come again."

Mickey agreed. It was the story of the century and he had to get himself to a laptop right away but he couldn't even remember where he'd left his lap. Tania's little lizard hands grasped for the stiff worm sinking in the bottle, her tiny voice barely audible even to those who were tuned into her frequency: "Save me...drink me..."

AT 5 p.m., the President-elect made his first official television appearance before both the nation and Las Ilusiones. Pease and Raus were still parked at the zinc counter. The simpering Abraham Mongo introduced young Filemón, a TeleVida exclusive. Barcelona spoke from the main ballroom of Los Primos. The cameras kept bouncing off his very bald little dome. You could see the reflections of the chandeliers there. Raus noted how pronounced his ears were, sticking straight out of his receded sideburns "like Dumbo, the frigging flying elephant." Pease advised the rapidly filling establishment to "watch this guy closely. He's your new chief kleptomaniac!"

Raus shushed the *Times* man. "This place is full of antennas."

"And you're turning into a paranoid schizophrenic. What's come over you, boy?" Horace said loud enough in inglés to turn some heads. Raus was fast drinking himself back to sobriety. Pease would soon pass out.

Despite the lurid rumors of psychosexual regression, Barcelona seemed surprisingly upbeat, coasting along on some smooth-running tranquilizers they had fed him to temper his terror at Tonatiuh's prying eyes. "Compatriotas, I come into your humble homes tonight to offer my apologies for all the confusion of the past days and also to extend my eternal gratitude for your vote. Without it, I never would have been elected our president."

Pease snorted so hard that he had a nosebleed. Or at least the Bloody Mary he had been inhaling erupted from his nostrils.

With an earnest throb in his little throat, Barcelona pleaded for "national unity" and "a plurality of participation." His message was obnoxiously conciliatory. He called his election "the dawn of a new age for our nation and our party." No longer would the PRO be the sole rector of the Organic Revolution. Filemón announced congressional elections in six months "in which all will be welcome to compete in a celebration of the new pluralism." For the time being, it was the hour to damp down the rhetoric and shake hands like gentlemen for the good of the Patria. General Niños de Galván, an honorable and patriotic warrior, should accept the Golden Parachute the military has generously offered in appreciation of his many years of devoted service. Doctor Tonatiuh Galván "should return to his ancestral home in Malinchico—the first state ever to have been won by the left opposition—and avail himself of this opportunity for reflection." The chandelier-domed president-elect invited each and every citizen "regardless of political, religious, or ethical axes to grind" to attend his November 1 "All-Star" inauguration starring Juan Gabriel, Plácido Domingo, Los Lobos, Los Tucanes, Gloria Esteban, and Fidel Castro. "Until then, I bid you adios, amigos and amigas, compatriotas all. Hasta la vista," he chirped with a friendly wave. A bouncy new-age version of the National Hymn, in which the Yanqui Dogs had been transmogrified back to Yanqui Gods blared from the screen.

"What fucking new age is this guy thinking about?" Raus asked out loud.

"It was pre-recorded," burped Pease. "It was in the can. It was all set up so he wouldn't suck his thumb." They both drank to the new age choop-choop-choop of Filemón Barcelona.

"Thank God we're so drunk. They would never even let us in the gate."

⚡

THE INTERIM PRESIDENT of the United States disappeared into the helicopter without even waving behind him to the officials assembled on the White House back lawn. His mind was focused straight ahead on the Miami convention, the next step in this inevitable passage that would finally legitimatize his accidental presidency. *The People's Choice.*

Gingrich puffed up his hair, fastened his seat belt. This thing on the other side of the border was like a bad virus that threatened to infect his bubble. No matter how much Blackbridge tinkered, the situation just kept deteriorating. *Now it seems our new NAAFTA partners are bonafide cannibals.*

The chopper dipped over the capitol and headed southeast for Andrews. *The illegals were the carriers of this virus. It's really a sanitary problem. If they get inside the bubble, I'm contaminated. I would have no one else to blame but a dead Bill Clinton and, like they say in this business, everyone loves a dead man. Hell's bells, I've been president for nine months now. I'm running this circus and the bottom line is that I've decided that it's history, this thing down there. Blackbridge just has to tell whoever is supposed to be running things for us to stop all this nonsense before Uncle has to put his foot down. For chrissakes, hain't we still in charge of our own backyard?*

⚡

THE AMBASSADOR UNDERSTOOD perfectly that no one was in charge anymore, least of all in Washington and in this godforsaken capital. I'm not even in charge of my own shoelaces. He bent down and tied them for the twentieth time today. This Newtie sees only the piece of the picture he wants to see. But he has a good point there—this has to end somewhere and better sooner than later. I mean, Galván has a half million of his people in the Zócalo, killer Aztec gangs are roaming the streets down below, and two generals are about to go for each other's throat at the gates of the city. The new president doesn't even dare appear alive on the television. Blackbridge stashed the syringe and the spoon. He was always quite meticulous about his addiction. "Heigh ho, heigh ho, it's off to work we go," he hummed like the eighth dwarf. "Get me Doctor Galván, Molly. Then X. Davis. Call him on the hotline."

THE CONGRESS OF THE PEOPLE was in its 141st non-stop hour now, with no end in sight. For five days and nights, indefatigable speakers had lined up non-stop behind the microphones to recite their litanies of the dead, or strident stanzas of political poetry, sing revolutionary corridos, bemoan the various plights of the various peoples, argue that Tonatiuh Galván should form a revolutionary socialist party, counter that Tonatiuh should convoke a socialist revolutionary party, insist that the Sixth Sun had come or was coming or had been sabotaged by gavacho technology, swear eternal revenge upon the Gringos and their PRO puppets, and demand—in no uncertain terms—that the ballot boxes should be opened, the bags broken into, and the votes shouted out one by one in the middle of the Zócalo for all to hear!

His brick-red beard frothing at the urgency of the situation, El Compa pushed to the microphones. "Compañeras and compañeros, the army of General Ramírez is marching on the capital under the pretext of concentrating the ballot boxes here in the National Palace. We are many, but we are unarmed and the soldiers of General Niños de Galván cannot be trusted to defend us. We do not have much time, hours perhaps. We must organize ourselves block by block and building by building for our own defense."

"That they should open the packages!" the tunnel-minded hordes on the Zócalo crooned.

"My name is Cabo Felipe Roque Chuspata. I am a soldier in the army of General Gertrudis and I am much in disagreement with what Red Beard has just said. In our division, we are all from Malinchico and we will fight to the ultimate consequences to defend the victory of Doctor Tonatiuh Galván."

"¡Que Se Abren Los Paquetes!"

The pirate eco-saint José María y Cruz Patadas kicked the rabble out of his path and grabbed the microphone: "Live Together or Die Together, Comrades! We cannot allow ourselves to be mired in the unwholesome trenches of fratricidal mayhem. We are more intelligent and more humane than they are, and we must outwit them without resorting to our crude and violent instincts. We must visualize world peace, my brothers and my sisters. Think of the bloodshed that man who is born out of woman is capable of and visualize world peace, my brothers and sisters." Then Patria Verde and the Mothers of Julapa released thousands of sooty pigeons into the shifting night sky.

"Think of our sons, instead! Think of our dead sons and daughters and comadres," wailed a broad woman from Grand Huajuco.

"Think of our trees," sobbed Tata Anastacio when Pamfilo wheeled him up to the microphone.

"Think of us," the True Zapatista Major Moises—the sewed-up Sup's personal mouthpiece—quietly urged the Congress. "Think of how these bourgeois peaceniks have forced us to struggle on without our guns for seven years now."

Nacha Caracol slashed through to the bank of microphones, waving her steel machete menacingly. "They killed my father! They have killed the Bishop and Don Estalin and ripped the beating hearts out of their bodies! This is not the time to use our heads! We ask you to act from your hearts!" The war cry brought the Congress to its feet.

"THAT THEY SHOULD OPEN THE PACKAGES!"

Now the Warriors of Huitzilopochli leapt into the fray, demanding revenge for their murdered tlamatlan, Adolfo Becker

Schultz and Manuel Bravo—El Conchero. "A heart for a heart!" drummed a man with antlers wired to his head.

"A heart for a heart!" wailed a young girl flying a white dove on a golden string.

Listing badly, a starving Reggio Ahumada Tamal sought to impose order upon advancing bedlam. "My fellow citizens, we must discuss politics here and not religious sectarianism. The election has brought us together as the Congress of the People, of his people, Tonatiuh's. What unifies us is the victory of the Aztec Sun." Less weakened hunger strikers propped up the enfeebled RAT. "They offer us Malinchico, and it is an insult because we won it fair and square. They offer us 'a new age of celebratory pluralism' and it is not funny anymore. Whatever they offer us is never enough. It will always be too little and too late. Tonatiuh is our President. We will settle for no less!" The still-portly Ahumada was trundled off by his minions in his customized velvet stretcher.

"JUST OPEN THE PINCHE PACKAGES!"

"Licenciado Ahumada tells us we have won Malinchico and the authorities acknowledge this," sneered the untrustworthy Plantón. "We must be proud of our victories, proud that we have forced the ruling party to call congressional elections in which we will win many seats. Compañeras and compañeros, a new dawn of pluralism is breaking across this land and we are responsible for it. Now, we should consider allowing our worthy opponents the space in which to fulfill their promises. It is time for all of us to pack up and go ho—."

Cavernous boo's swelled out of the night. In front of the National Palace, the hunger strikers, as if they were the conscience of the nation, groaned magnificently: "We will never go home!" A posse of ski-masked Zapatistas swept onto the stage and sat on the paunchy fakir Plantón. Históricos rushed through the aisles in an effort to free their chairman from the hammer locks of the EZLN. A flying squad of masked wrestlers football-tackled them before they could hit pay dirt. Dr. Huipi plunged into the scrum, trying to separate fists from faces, and was soon submerged in a sea of flailing limbs.

In the midst of the melee, Huitzilopochli's Warriors seized the spotlight calling down plagues and flowery death upon the PRO with renewed ferocity. "A Heart for a Heart!"

This is sort of like *Ten Days That Shook the World*, Mickey Raus had to admit, but he was not John Reed tonight. Instead, he had pinpointed Tania's billowing head floating high above the Zócalo again. It looked loony up there, like pale, curdled cheese, not quite full enough to be the moon, but too far away to catch or to touch, a lost balloon pasted against the scalloped night sky.

"¡Ya basta!" Tonatiuh at last broke his silence to reprimand a half million of his people with the True Zapatista's traditional cry of disgust. Enough! "This Congress of the People has become a Tower of Babel, pulling us apart in so many different directions that we are standing still. We should never have asked you to come up here in the first place. Yes, it was a mistake.

"This is supposed to be the Congress of the People, and the People speak with one language. Yes, we have distinct ways of expression but one common history, one story told in one language. And, yes, it is partly a history of resistance and partly one of conquest and slavishness, and you are proving this tonight.

"Yes, tonight we are still a conquered people—the PRO ripping our hearts out and offering them to their new fashioned gods of neo-liberalism and the free market and, yes, 'electoral democracy'—whatever excuse they can invent to force greater and greater sacrifices from the people so that they might remain the rulers of this land for another millennium.

"I have come before you tonight to condemn Gonzalo X. Davis for practicing human sacrifice. Yes, we have the evidence—the execution orders—and we ask that he be condemned by international tribunals.

"Yes, since we began this crusade we have sought change through peaceful mobilization and, yes, we still think this is the path we must take. To those of you who can think no further than revenge, we plead with you not to answer their bloodletting with more bloodletting. We urge you not to yield to the righteous thirst for revenge because we know such a great thirst cannot be slaked with more blood. Yes, we seek another way."

A few desultory "¡Que abren los pinches paquetes, cabrones!" floated in off the Zócalo but Tonatiuh had his people's attention now.

"Compañeras and compañeros, we understand your fury. We have lost many brothers and sisters in these last days. But we must think of our martyrs as the inevitable sacrifices—men and women who were prepared to give their lives and their hearts so that justice and democracy will one day rule our tortured land."

A pin could have dropped somewhere out there on the great plaza and a half million congresistas would have heard it. Tonatiuh had them eating out of his hand.

"There is only one way to honor the noble sacrifice of those who died in Gran Huajuco and El Horno, Ciudad Tacuman, Cocotitlan, Tijuana, and all the rest. To honor all those who have been slaughtered by the PRO since we began this crusade so many months ago now. We think of our companions Ismael Caracol, Don Estalin Lenin, the Bishop, Magnesio Brondo, Rambo Fitzgeraldo, so many more. We have only one way to honor these martyrs and that is now to establish our victory before the world. We must open the ballot boxes and let our votes shout for themselves."

"¡QUE ABREN LOS PAQUETES! ¡LOS PAQUETES! ¡QUE ABREN!"

"Compañeras and compañeros, these ballot boxes are now being brought to the city by a hostile military. In the name of peace and the People, we demand that General Ramírez halt his advance at the city limits and that General Gertrudis Niños de Galván (Totonaco) receive those packets and bring them here to the Zócalo where we will count them ourselves."

🦎

AN HOUR LATER, after an obligatory pit stop at Las Ilusiones, Raus swerved into Sacrilege Alley, pulled apart his fly and sprayed the stinking wall. The warped moon shed little light against the obsidian night.

"Pssst."

Mickey's piss stream froze in mid-arc. He turned full circle. He peered up at the surrounding rooftops but could not roll back the night.

"Pssst."

He reassembled his fly. It would not do to die with his dick falling out of his pants. He was ready to die.

"Pssst. Up here!"

Up where?

"Up here, on the moon, you asshole. Mickey, it's me, Tania."

It was her all right, mophead and all. He marveled at her levity. She had made it all the way to La Luna.

"So that's what you people do when you disappear forever? Sit on the moon and watch us assholes piss and fart?"

"Mickey, be serious. This is a serious situation," Tania-in-the-moon admonished him. "You're drunk again."

"I'm drunk again."

"Mickey, listen. It's all going to get very bad very soon. The técpatls have been unsheathed. Do you understand what this means, Mickey?"

Raus had a glimmer.

The streetlights on Holy Ghost Street blinked twice, then went dark.

"Uh-oh, Mickey. Look, I've got to go. But I'll be up here all night right above you. I can see you even if you can't see me. I will watch your steps and guide you through the bloodletting. Neither Tezcatlipoaca or Huitzilopochli will consume you. The Widows will not find you. You will still be alive in the dawn."

A large scalloped thunderhead blotted out the wan face of the moon.

🙋

TWO SINGULAR EVENTS occurred between Saturday night, July 15, and the Sunday dawn following that left Tonatiuh Galván without the strength or the will to prove his victory to the world and seize the presidency from the PRO.

The first was a phone call from General Gertrudis. There

had been no communication between the doctor-brothers since their meeting at the military camp in early June. Tonatiuh was not home to receive the call. The cellular phone rang and rang in the upstairs bathroom where he'd forgotten it. General Gertrudis was about to hang up when Paloma finally located the machine. "Tell Tonatiuh that I am going. I have held out as long as I can without bloodshed. His people will have safe conduct out of the city. Suerte, hermana, until we meet again." Gertrudis clicked off. They would never meet again.

Paloma rushed to the Zócalo with the troubling message. Even as she communicated Gertrudis's surrender to Tonatiuh, troop transports were rolling into place on the streets behind the National Palace to remove his soldiers from the capital. Under an agreement brokered by Blackbridge, Niños de Galván's army would be stationed in Malinchico. The General himself would accept retirement and appointment as the nation's ambassador to Paraguay.

Corporal Felipe Roque Chuspata publicly denounced Gertrudis's retreat and stripped off his army uniform right there before a million prying eyes. "I will stay here and die with you, defending our victory together," he wept to the congresistas in his jockey shorts.

What General Gertrudis gained from his brief, heroic—if confusing—defiance out at Military Camp #1 never reached the public domain even after he was assassinated 13 months later in an Asunción steak house. Perhaps he had listened more closely than Tonatiuh had figured when the Doctor spoke to his brother of how the PRO was bludgeoning their father's revolution. Perhaps Gertrudis, a poor orphan boy, was just fulfilling an old pledge to the General to protect his kid brother.

Nonetheless, Niños de Galván's decision to stand down left the congresistas inside the city on their own. With General Ramírez just hours away from the capital, the delegates' refusal to leave would inevitably lead to one more blood bath. But this was the Congress of the People and a decision would have to be made by the plenary.

Tonatiuh asked for an hour to consult with his father's ghost.

He hurried off to Carlos Quinto while the rest of the galvanista leadership caucused behind the stage in the shadows of the darkened Templo Mayor. Out in the ruins of the reconstructed temple behind them, obsidian técpatls were being unsheathed.

There was little consensus among Tonatiuh's high command. El Compa, SuperPendejo, Dr. Huipi and Felipe Roque still wanted to organize urban guerrilla units to carry on protracted warfare from the rooftops and the sewers. RAT, Cantú Cabañas, and Antonio Malcreado urged restraint. General Ram Ram would soon be in Satellite City with ten armed-to-the-teeth divisions. He had already issued an ultimatum—the Congress must be dissolved and Tonatiuh's people must be out of town within 24 hours or pay the price of disobedience. The galvanistas argued half-heartedly. The writing was on the wall. On the stage, the Warriors of Huitzilopochtli began one last slow dance of resistance.

Even then, without General Gertrudis to cover for him, Tonatiuh might have risked the confrontation. The street-fighting brigades of the kalpullis could have held out for several months, even against the limited air cover the U.S. would fly for General Ram Ram's invasion.

"This, of course, is all worst case scenario stuff, you do understand that, Doctor?" Blackbridge warned Tonatiuh affably. "But it's perfectly legit. The threatened collapse of a friendly government with which the U.S. shares a 2,000 mile border falls clearly within the protocols of the 'Sphere of Discipline' clause of Article 33 of the 1997 NASTA (North American Security Treaty Agreement) accord. I'm sure you are cognizant that this clause has been recently tested to overthrow Presidente Gonzalo in Perú and was found not to be an unfair trade practice by the World Trade Organization.

"Dr. Galván, the offer of asylum is a standing one from my government. If you don't want to go to L.A.—and I understand your reluctance—New York or Washington would be do-able. You might even consider Paris. We can protect you there."

Blackbridge's extreme unction and the threat of Yanqui intervention only nourished Tonatiuh's resolve to stand and fight. Long months on the struggle line had moved the Doctor much to the left and he listened more to Doctor Huipi and Compa Leñero now than he did Cantú Cabañas and Ahumada Tamal. He thought RAT and his old teacher trusted too much in the PRO's perfidious promises and not enough in the infinite anger of the people. He had learned that much at least.

In the end, then, it was the stunning bloodletting that occurred late on the sixth night of the Congress of the People that sandbagged Tonatiuh's determination to continue to demand his electoral victory and, indeed, brought 10 grueling, miraculous months of a never-ending crusade for a just and democratic Patria shuddering to a stop. At least for now.

THE RITUAL KILLINGS began after midnight and lasted into the dawn. The first group of victims were found on Holy Ghost Street—the entire population of the recently resurrected village of Chamul. The old shaman had run out of visions. Forty-six bodies were spread under the collapsed plastic tarp, 16 of them children, some of them unborn—several pregnant women had the fetuses cut out of their bodies. All of the victims had their throats slit as if they'd been bled, and their hearts surgically extracted from their open breasts, even those of the fetuses.

The next victims were found on the sidewalk outside of the PRO monolith on Avenida: 27 corpses sprawled in clusters on the pavement and in the roadway as if they had been attacked as they left the Party headquarters with their bodyguards. A second mouth had been carved into Victor Manuel Rodriguez Lefkowitz's T-zone. His well-groomed head lolled at right angles in the frothing gutter. The banker's Armani suit coat and Ralph Lauren shirt had been torn open and his heart ripped smoking from his bleeding chest. All around Lefkowitz, as if arranged in a ritual circle, were his five faithful guards and his chauffeur.

The reporters moved to the next cluster, holding back the heaves with cupped hands. Raus was more nauseous than fearful. He knew what would come next and he was not afraid. Tania-in-the-moon was guiding him through the obsidian night.

"It's De la Mancha!" Jane Ann nearly puked on Mickey's shoes. It wasn't just the old hoodlum either. His compadre Warmán Warmán lay heartless in a pool of viscid fluids. Eviscerated henchmen were similarly arranged in a circle around the leaders. The sidewalk was slippery with body parts. The flowery death drew no distinction between the Brontos and the Tecos.

They tracked the trail of blood and mutilated corpses for two city blocks, stumbling from victim to victim, flipping them over to see if they knew their faces. Some were unrecognizable, others familiar. Abraham Mongo's smirk was permanently pasted to his pale lips as the lifeblood leaked out of him on the corner of Calles and Avenida.

The last corpse, when they turned it gently over, was what was left of Horace Pease. A geyser of blood had erupted from his pierced chest and discolored his slashed seersucker suit. A wry smile stained Pease's twisted lips, as if to say "I told you so. These bloody savages are capable of the most despicable acts of cannibalism." Like all the others, the *Times* man's heart had been stolen by his attackers. "A heart for a heart!"

Now it was Raus's turn to get seriously ill, his bilious vomit bubbling into gutters that ran thick with Pease's alcohol-thinned blood. Dried green spittle blemished Arbus's beautifully lip-sticked mouth as she sobbed against Raus's sagging back. Sidney Bloch gagged that he had an open ticket to Tulsa and he was leaving right now.

"You know him? He's your friend, maybe?" barked a dogfaced cop in a black and tan cruiser. The flashing lights illuminated the scene of the butchery. Raus wondered if maybe he hadn't fallen through some open manhole into hell.

"I knew him. He was my friend," Mickey mumbled.

"You tell me his name. I tell you where to get his body, okey-dokey?" The cop licked his fat lips and nonchalantly held out a flabby hand as if he was fixing a traffic violation.

"You see what kind people these Tonatiuh people are, gringo. They kill your friend. They take his heart." The officer frowned at the 100,000 peso note that Raus fished out of his wallet . "You don' have dólares?" he whined but pocketed the bill anyway.

"We send the wagon in a little while. You go here. They give your friend to you." He passed Mickey the receipt and wrung his hand to seal the deal. "Gotta go, amigo, too much bisnis tonight. You be careful. Godspeed." The cop climbed back into his black and tan with a dog laugh, his radio crackling out the locations of many new customers.

Jane Ann hailed a morgue wagon and paid the driver to drop her off at the airport. She wouldn't come back for years. Mickey watched her sad, ragged ass crawl into the ambulance. She didn't even kiss him goodbye.

THE FLOWERY WAR raged full tilt into the darkest hours of the night. Each time the Knights of Tezcatlapoaca struck in the darkened old quarter, the Warriors of Huitzilopochli struck in the swank, security-minded enclaves of El Rolex or Lomas, around the PRO headquarters and outside government ministries.

At 12:25 a.m., four teenagers joy riding in a stolen Chevrolet with Tonatiuh stickers slapped to its bumpers were butchered in the maze of dead-end streets behind La Bondad, their chest cavities vandalized and ransacked for vital organs.

At 12:43 a.m., a pair of telephone receptionists on the graveyard shift hailed a passing cab in front of Investigative Police headquarters. Moments later, all three bodies—the receptionists' and the taxi driver's—were discovered off Reforma behind the bloodstained windshield of the green eco-taxi.

Upstairs in the inner sanctum of the Investigative Police, Florentino Zorrilla, his rib cage splayed open and his bloodhound head dangling by a fragile tendon, grinned like a disemboweled jack-o-lantern.

At 12:56 p.m., His Holiness Santoniño Pigolino stepped from his shower in the elegantly appointed catacombs of the cathedral and right into the razor-sharp blade of a técpatl that deftly dissected the Cardinal's pink flesh like an Eskimo stripping blubber from a right whale. Gloved hands plunked the still-beating prize into a wicker basket.

Some of these ritual killings made no sense—random, opportunistic murders that suggested a third force had a hand in the bloodshed, one whose commitments were to another, more ancient path. They were called the Widows of Coatlicue.

At 1:06 a.m., according to veterinary reports, the throat of a male jaguar at the Chapultepec Park Zoo was sliced from ear to ear, his blood was drunk and his steaming heart eaten on the spot.

At 1:17 a.m., the doorknob twisted soundlessly and Raus's apartment door edged open. The black obsidian blades of the masked intruders flashed in the insipid moonlight. The killers crept across the room and struck again and again at the bedclothes with their técpatls but Mickey was long gone. In fact, he hadn't been home for days.

RAUS PLODDED BACK towards the old section, impervious to the homicidal maniacs who lurked in every dark doorway. She was up there watching over him with her wan light. On every street he could hear the muffled gurglings of throats being ripped; his shoes grew gummy with the life juices pouring from the arteries of fresh kills. Under the blown streetlights, the skull men gnawed on warm, dripping, still-palpitating internal organs. He lived, he figured, because he had no heart of his own. The woman in the moon had flown away with it.

Gran Marquises with tinted windows circled the fringes of the galvanista encampment like gray wolves, sucking up victims into Tezcatlapoaca's kitchen and spewing the bones back out on the blood-spattered pavement. Mickey reached the Zócalo, his hollow gaze fixed on Tania's head, which was now descending into the west above the butchered city.

The debate on the presidium had been reduced to muted sobbing. The dead were stacked up like cordwood on the plaza floor. Dissected corpses were draped like souvenirs from Los Hustlers' little stand. A group of miners had died huddled around their still-smoldering campfire. José Cerro's blood-drained features were lit by the still-crackling embers. Robespierre de las Rosas was crucified on the flagpole. The Caballeros of Tezcatlapoaca had stuffed the gay leader's severed cock and testicles down his gaping throat. Under the portals of the Grand Hotel, the punctured bodies of ski-masked Zapatistas were scattered like smeared petals of a flower. Some embraced their comrades in death. Major Moises held in his arms a spectral figure. Raus bent to touch it. Was this Marcos? His fingers began to glow.

Only when the blue dawn crept into the eastern sky did the flowery war began to dissipate. Exhausted priests, their hair matted with the spurting fluids of so many sacrificial xochiniqui, sheathed their trowel-like técpatls and lay down in the cemeteries to sleep until the next time history would unleash them against the infidels.

The dawn broke and mothers woke to find their sons and daughters slaughtered to satisfy gods they could barely remember. The dead wagons plied the streets of the old quarter, hauling the victims off towards Mictlan, the place of the hopelessly dead, stopping to pick up a chunk of flesh here, a severed limb there. Sirens wailed like hideous roosters against the telltale fingerprints of the new day. Near La Bondad, Raus knelt over the heartless corpse of the Flea, crossed himself, and finally wept.

NO ONE OUTSIDE of Tonatiuh and the General would ever know what had happened behind the locked doors of #2 Carlos Quinto that night. Loud words were heard and objects hurled. General Galván almost certainly argued for revolution, counterattack, and protracted urban guerrilla combat. The capital was a big city with an extensive sewer system from which the strike teams could operate. But the General was only a ghost now. He did not live in the here and now anymore. Even as he tonguelashed Tonatiuh for not marching full speed ahead into battle, the blood of the people was washing down the drains of the Centro Histórico.

By the middle of the sorrowful Sunday morning after the

Night of the Black Blades, the Congress was declared in recess. Antonio Malcreado read a statement from Doctor Galván to the plenary, urging all the congresistas to go home until they were called into session again. No dates were announced. The great encampment dismembered itself methodically for the retreat— tents collapsed, blankets were rolled. The flotsam of a week under the heavens here at the heart of the nation was swept up, bagged and burnt. Villagers gathered their goods up on their backs for the long walk home. Blackbridge had negotiated the safe conduct of the congresistas before the troops of General Ramírez Ramírez entered the capital. Tonatiuh closed himself up behind the big carved doors on Carlos Quinto, and his family would let no one near him.

So the fiesta of the second millennium of death ran its course. By dusk, just about everyone had gone home to mourn their losses. Solitary old women flapped down Holy Ghost Street on their way to evening mass. The echoes of their footfalls could be heard for blocks.

Mickey Raus sat down on the sidewalk in front of #2 Carlos Quinto and waited for a sign. He guzzled a slimjim of mescal down to the worm and smashed the bottle against a stone wall. Then he twisted open another one. "I should go home and write this all down." No matter how drunk he got, he felt obligated to think this way.

Thunder clouds gathered above the stone island of Tenochtitlan, and soon Tlaloc began to pelt him with huge, stinging drops. The rain washed the street clean, washed the blood-clotted stones of this stone city clean of all memory. It felt good. The gods were satiated for once. They picked their teeth and belched in contentment.

The new night domed the dripping sky. The doors in back of him never opened. Raus's conscience twitched. He had drunk himself sober again.

I should go home and write this all down.

"ACCIDENTAL" BALLOT BURNING BRINGS APPARENT END TO ELECTORAL CRISIS SOUTH OF BORDER

San Francisco Examiner-Guardian Foreign Bureau
By Miguel Raus

TENOCHTITLAN (July 18)—A huge fire, attributed to a short circuit in a wiring system, destroyed much of the four-centuries-old National Palace here early this morning, incinerating nearly 40 million ballots that have been at issue since the July 2 presidential election and putting a final ironic touch to a conflict that almost plunged this nation into civil war and brought Washington to the brink of a new invasion of its neighbor to the south.

The fire, which broke out at 2:17 AM in a basement switch box adjacent to the room in which the paper ballots were being protected by the military, could be seen throughout much of the capital and brought thousands of residents of the surrounding old quarter to the great plaza or "Zócalo" that fronts the National Palace, long the seat of government power. Early this morning, army troops under the command of Secretary of Defense Archibaldo Ramírez Ramírez forced the onlookers from the huge square at bayonet point.

The ballots destroyed in the conflagration arrived in the capital only yesterday, hours after the last contingent of supporters of opposition candidate Tonatiuh Galván had abandoned the Zócalo where they had been sitting in congress since July 10. The ballot boxes were being stored at the National Palace pending the ratification of the highly contentious election results by the nation's electoral college, which will be convened August 1. The electoral college is expected to confirm the victory of former finance minister Filemón Barcelona, the candidate of the long-ruling (71 years) Party of the Organic Revolution (PRO), by an 8 to 1 margin over Galván.

A subdued Antonio Malcreado, press spokesman for the secluded opposition candidate, accused the PRO-run government of deliberately setting the blaze "to complete the criminal theft of Tonatiuh Galván's victory."

Triumph to Ashes

The National Palace fire, which caused an estimated $800 million

USD damage to the ancient building, a United Nations World Historical Site, has apparently ended the frustrating final days of Doctor Galván's historic bid for the presidency of his country. Evidence compiled by Galván computer experts substantiate the Doctor's victory by a popular vote of 31 million to Barcelona's 5.5 million in the July 2 balloting—but computer fraud, including the introduction of at least three separate viruses into the ballot tallying system—compromised the credibility of the electronic results.

The computer sabotage left the paper ballots that were destroyed this morning in the Palace blaze as the sole determining evidence of who really won the July 2 election. Ironically, the ballots stored at the National Palace escaped incineration in the wake of the voting when ultimately more than 1,000,000 burnt ballots marked for Galván were discovered in the nation's garbage dumps.

Galván Gives Up

A week following the election, after widespread disturbances outside district vote computation centers in which hundreds of galvanistas lost their lives, the Doctor summoned half a million supporters to the capital to back up his claim to the presidency. Encamped in and around the Zócalo in front of the palace under the rubric of "the Congress of the People," the presence of the galvanistas represented a growing challenge to the PRO's ability to govern the country.

Doctor Galván called off the Congress of the People after support within the military collapsed. A murderous rampage by death squads affiliated with both PRO and galvanista factions during the early hours of July 15 appears to have influenced the opposition candidate's decision to lift what amounted to a siege of the palace and retire from the post-electoral conflict.

Violence Behind Us

Over 300 people are thought to have been murdered during the six hours of ritual killings that began soon after midnight Sunday. Because of the use of obsidian sacrificial knives to extract victims' hearts, the spate of homicidal frenzy has been dubbed the "Night of the Black Blades" by the sensationalist press here. The murderous rampage has stunned the nation and apparently caused Galván to reconsider his efforts to obtain the presidency.

In previous press statements issued in the wake of the ritual killings of two of his closest aides, Galván accused Internal Security

Secretary Gonzalo X. Davis of "practicing human sacrifice" and "cannibalism" and urged action by international human rights groups. A delegation from the London-based Amnesty International arrived here Thursday.

After absenting himself from the public eye for weeks following the July 2 election, President-elect Barcelona has appeared on national television three times since the Sunday morning bloodletting, pleading calm and an end to the killings which took the lives of three sitting PRO Central Committee members. "It is time to put the violence behind us," Barcelona urged again last night prior to the fire at the National Palace.

Warring Gods

The rival death squads thought to be responsible for the murders take the names of two ancient Aztec gods—Tezcatlapoaca or "Smoking Mirror," the god of the underground, and Huitzilopochli, the Aztec god of war. The highly secret Knights of Tezcatlapoaca society is reportedly comprised of government internal security police known as "secretos" and discharged state and federal judicial police agents. An Indian revivalist group, the Warriors of Huitzilopochli, which is closely connected to the galvanistas, is thought to have also participated in the skein of ritual murders. The motives of a third death squad, which communicates on the Internet under the name of "Widows of Coatlicue," are less clear.

Among those killed, almost certainly by the Warriors of Hutzilopochli, were PRO Chairman of the Board Victor Manuel Rodríguez Lefkowitz, the venerable PRO farm leader Bernabé Warmán Warmán, and the notorious popular sector chieftain Sancho de la Mancha, who is himself thought to have been responsible for much electoral violence. Both De la Mancha and Warmán Warmán were charter members of the "Brontos," or old guard of the PRO. Lefkowitz was the acknowledged leader of the "Tecos," or technician wing of the PRO, which appears to have struck a temporary alliance with the incoming Barcelona.

Also murdered was Horace Pease, longtime *New York Times* correspondent in Latin America, whose eviscerated body was found near the PRO headquarters early Sunday morning. A Colombian reporter, Tania Escobar, 40, who was working for the local *El Machetazo*, is listed as missing.

U.S. Spillover

U.S. reaction to Galván's standdown and the probable end to the election crisis has been one of relief. Following the widespread disturbances July 9, President Gingrich ordered the southern border sealed by 25,000 troops as a "precaution" against massive refugee flight. As expected, Gingrich this week was nominated as the Republican standard bearer in the November election, in which illegal immigration is sure to again be an inflammatory issue.

The interim Gingrich administration, alarmed at threats to U.S. national security during an election year, is known to have offered military support to the outgoing president, Arturo Lomeli, to force the end of the galvanista siege of the National Palace.

In Gingrich's Washington, Galván—who strongly opposes the neoliberal model endorsed by the last five presidents of this country— is viewed as the latest Latin ogre to threaten U.S. fortunes in the region. Fidel Castro, Salvador Allende, the Sandanistas, the Salvadoran FMLN, Manuel Antonio Noriega and Peru's President Gonzalo all have topped the list over the past four decades.

Despite Washington's hostility towards Galván, U.S. ambassador Thaddeus Blackbridge reportedly played a role in the deal that allowed the Doctor's supporters to exit the capital before ten divisions, headed by Ramírez Ramírez, entered the city with the ballot boxes that were incinerated in this morning's blaze.

Serpent and Eagle

Galván supporters were still straggling out of the capital early this morning, even as the ballots they had cast and come here to defend were being consumed by flames downtown. Some of the last galvanistas to leave the city were a group of Purépecha Indians from the Doctor's home state of Malinchico.

Most of the men and women who live in Zapicho, a farm town in the Indian sierra of the state, were philosophical about the abrupt end of Doctor Galván's unrequited battle for the presidency. Said Pamfilo Ihautzi, a farmer and forester in that mountain village, "We will aguantar. We still are history happening like the Doctor says. We will never go away." In common usage, the verb "aguantar" roughly translates "to suffer until you get used to the pain."

Ihuatzi and his fellow Zapichans, 104-year-old Tata Anastacio Acuitzi and Pedro Baltazar, all pledged they would soon return to the capital to celebrate Galván's victory. "It is a prophecy," Ihuatzi explained.

"Tonatiuh has called us to meet him at the place where the eagle devours the serpent. We will return to fulfill this prophecy."

President-elect Filemón Barcelona announced this afternoon that he would immediately apply to the World Bank for a $1.3 billion USD loan to restore the damaged National Palace.

(Zam-Guard wire services contributed to this report.)

END OF BOOK ONE

Thus ends the first volume of the Tonatiuh trilogy.
Aficionados of Tonatiuh and his people should look
forward to *Tonatiuh's Revenge*—
to be published sometime in the new millennium.

JOHN ROSS—political activist, poet, investigative journalist and now novelist—was born in New York City in 1938. His father was a Broadway columnist and his mother was a press agent, so his early schooling was on the streets of Greenwich Village where jazz, abstract expressionist painting, radical politics and beat poetry converged in the 1950s. Indeed, Ross first traveled to Mexico in 1958 under the influence of Kerouac and D.H. Lawrence. Since that time he has divided his time between California and Mexico, with sojourns to Spain, Morocco, and most of Latin America.

Ross has served as a Latin American correspondent for the Pacific News Service, the *San Francisco Examiner* and various other newspapers. As a freelance investigative reporter he writes for a string of alternative newspapers, probing environmental carnage, nuclear politics, and judicial and political malfeasance. In the '60s, Ross was active in the civil rights and anti-war efforts, serving a prison term at the Terminal Island federal penitentiary as the first documented resister to the Vietnam War from the Bay Area. He has published seven chapbooks of poetry (the latest is *jazzmexico* from Calaca de Pelon, Mexico, 1997), and is well known in Northern California for his poetry performances.

John's *Rebellion from the Roots: Indian Uprising in Chiapas* (Common Courage Press, 1994) won an American Book Award from the Before Columbus Foundation. It has become a touchstone text for the study of the Zapatistas. His most recent non-fiction book, *The Annexation of Mexico—from the Aztecs to the IMF* (Common Courage, 1998), is the first post-Zapatista history of Mexico. The book traces the invasions, incursions, impositions, amputations, and annexations to which that "distant neighbor" has been subject since pre-Conquest times, and the heroic resistance of the Mexican people to such indignities.

Recent Titles about Mexico and the U.S./Mexico Border from Cinco Puntos Press

THE LATE GREAT MEXICAN BORDER
Reports from a Disappearing Line
edited by Bobby Byrd and Susannah Mississippi Byrd

WOMEN AND OTHER ALIENS
Essays from the U.S./Mexico Border
by Debbie Nathan

DIRTY DEALING
*Drug Smuggling on the Mexican Border and the
Assassination of a Federal Judge—An American Parable*
by Gary Cartwright

MODELO ANTIGUO
A Novel of Mexico City
by Luis Eduardo Reyes

THE MOON WILL FOREVER BE A DISTANT LOVE
a novel by Luis Humberto Crosthwaite

GHOST SICKNESS
A Book of Poems
by Luis Alberto Urrea

For more information or a catalog, contact:
CINCO PUNTOS PRESS
2709 Louisville
El Paso, TX 79930
(800) 566-9072